NATURAL WITCH

Also by K.F. Breene

DDVN WORLD:

FIRE AND ICE TRILOGY
Born in Fire
Raised in Fire
Fused in Fire

MAGICAL MAYHEM SERIES
Natural Witch
Natural Mage
Natural Dual-Mage

FINDING PARADISE SERIES
Fate of Perfection
Fate of Devotion

DARKNESS SERIES
Into the Darkness, Novella 1
Braving the Elements, Novella 2
On a Razor's Edge, Novella 3
Demons, Novella 4
The Council, Novella 5
Shadow Watcher, Novella 6
Jonas, Novella 7
Charles, Novella 8
Jameson, Novella 9
Darkness Series Boxed Set, Books 1-4

WARRIOR CHRONICLES
Chosen, Book 1
Hunted, Book 2
Shadow Lands, Book 3
Invasion, Book 4
Siege, Book 5
Overtaken, Book 6

NATURAL WITCH

K.F. BREENE

Contact info:
www.kfbreene.com
books@kfbreene.com

CHAPTER 1

WHAT WAS I thinking? This was a terrible idea. Probably one of my worst, and given my track record, that was saying something.

Here I was, standing in a field outside of New Orleans, 2505 miles away from home, all because a woman at a crystal shop had suggested I attend a magic retreat. Sure, this particular retreat was heralded as the best in the country, but given that I was a complete novice, did it really matter? I didn't know up from down when it came to the occult. They could teach us how to use a Ouija board and I'd be happy. So why had I thought traveling *so far* from my house, using all my savings, was a rock-solid plan?

Because I was a lunatic with terrible decision-making skills, that was why.

I sighed and scratched my head. Then shook it.

But I didn't turn and leave.

Something was missing from my life. Something that gnawed at my gut and frayed my nerves. I didn't feel complete. For some reason I couldn't understand, this was what kept drawing me in.

Well, not *this*, per se. Not the church I stood awkwardly in front of, strangely removed from civilization. Or the giant price tag on the journey. Or even the lying I'd done to my mother to come this far for something I probably could've found much closer. But witchcraft. Magic. The secrets hidden within the majesty of nature.

My mother thought I was in Eugene, Oregon, looking at haunted houses with my best friend Veronica. She would've lost it if she'd known the truth.

I shouldn't have lied to her. It wasn't that she was unreasonable, after all, it was that—

No, she was unreasonable. I'd already lied to her; I didn't need to lie to myself.

The only way I could've gotten her permission to attend this retreat was if I'd sat her down in her favorite chair, plied her with a plate of brownies and an obscene amount of alcohol, told her what I'd planned while she was roaring drunk, and then snuck out before she regained her senses. In any other scenario, she would've forbidden it. Didn't matter that I was twenty-four years old.

That wasn't why it was a terrible idea.

I surveyed my destination—a large church flanked by weepy trees and surrounded by Louisiana's flatland. Shadows draped across the oddly shaped structure, stones stuck together with mortar and tired souls.

Large, gothic-style windows dotted the front. Gargoyles crouched near the roof, their mouths open and waiting.

There was no way this church had come from this century. Or this continent, for this matter. When it came to an old-world feel, New Orleans couldn't hold a candle to this structure. The church was as out of place here as I was.

I blew out a breath and closed my eyes.

The dark cloud of intent hung heavy over the grounds surrounding the structure. Coated the walls and pooled at the base. Evil purpose existed in that church, I knew it. It lingered and it waited, hoping someone would mold its energy into a useable design bent on destruction. All it needed was the right tweak, and anything alive inside would meet its maker in a horrible, gruesome death.

Wow.

I ran my hand over my face. My imagination was running amok, even by my standards.

I glanced down the lane where brown dust billowed up from behind the retreating cab. My flip phone from yesteryear sat quietly in my clenched fist. Looking back at the church and the animosity hanging invisibly in the air, I thought this all through one more time.

On the one hand, I was going against everything my mother had always said—every rule she'd ever made— and throwing myself into the deep end without much more than internet searches, a wing, and a prayer. I was seeking insight and practical knowledge on something she had expressly forbidden me to pursue. Something she'd tried to guard against with threats and really itchy powders.

Something that had killed my father.

But on the other hand… I *knew* I had a little spark of magic in me. I *knew* it. Despite my mother's favorite saying—*all women have premonitions, intuition, and a natural talent for mischief, and you, Penny Bristol, have the same dose as everyone else*—it certainly didn't seem that way. My best friend Veronica couldn't make a mixing bowl explode by filling it with the right combination of glue, sage, and honey. She'd tried, and nothing had happened besides wasted ingredients. My mother couldn't make the pictures come to life in the untitled red volume stuffed between the dictionary and the book on medicinal uses of herbs in her workroom. She didn't even view the passages the same way, like sleeping wonders waiting to be awoken by the soft whisper of words.

And wasn't Greta the mail lady always eerily surprised when I recited for her what she'd just dropped off into our mailbox without seeing the letters for myself?

Well…she'd accused me of spying on her with hidden cameras, which was nearly the same thing. I felt like they belonged in the same camp.

All of those things hinted at magic flowing through my blood. Didn't they?

You just have a temperamental third eye, dear. You get that from your father, God rest his soul. You'd do best to ignore it, lest you wind up in jail.

I gritted my teeth and shoved my mother's voice away.

I did have a bit of magic. I knew I did. And I was tired of pretending I was normal when I felt anything but. I was tired of being an outcast, however much I tried to fit in. If there was a hope that I belonged here, belonged *anywhere*, I wanted to check it out. Just once.

And really, what harm could any of this do? I'd read reviews and testimonials about this retreat, and they'd all been glowing. It even had a positive Yelp score. The setting—just outside of New Orleans, in a rustic church—only made it more delightful. According to my research, and I'd been fairly thorough, this was an ideal retreat for beginners.

My smile turned into a grimace as I looked at the church.

Rustic wasn't the word I'd use.

Decrepit was a better choice.

"Haunted with the blood of the lost" was a string of words that might also apply.

"Soul eater" and "life stealer" would have also been

accurate choices for the online brochure.

I worried a rock with my toe.

Did I listen to my temperamental third eye, which definitely failed me at least half the time, or my heart, which said I needed to learn this side of myself, if only to see if these feelings were real?

I sighed. This was stupid. I was an idiot, but I hadn't come all this way to balk in the final hour. Sure, there was a Cloud of Doom hanging over the church, and yes, the ancient building was somehow in a place it did not belong. But after twenty-four boring, dutiful years spent living in my mother's shadow, it was time to seize the day. To stretch my comfort zone.

Doing my best to ignore the butterflies filling my stomach, I stepped forward. My feet didn't make a sound on the squishy grass. As I moved closer to the large wooden door, energy prickled across my exposed skin and soaked into my middle. My guts danced with unease.

Summoning my courage and hoping all this was all just a trick of my imagination, I grabbed hold of the large iron handle and pulled the door open.

A musty smell accosted me, like I was unsealing a centuries-old chamber that had been closed up tight. Cold, damp air replaced the warm stickiness from outside. A few wooden benches dotted the mostly empty floor in the spacious room.

A cluster of men looked up in expectation and the room fell silent—their conversation halted, their eyes hard.

"H-hi," I stammered, then cleared my throat and straightened my spine. I knew a thing or two about bullies, thanks to all of stupid Billy Timmons's tormenting, and one thing you couldn't do was look small and weak. I might as well paint a big red target on my forehead. "H-hey."

It would have to do.

The closest man, a burly guy with a permanent sneer, hooked a thumb over his shoulder. "In there. You're late."

"Thanks," I mumbled, and gave them a wide berth.

I paused at the door at the back of the large main room. It wasn't a great idea to wander through this pit of doom blindly. I needed to scout out exit plans in case my temperamental third eye wasn't being temperamental at all.

Turning back, I noticed another man walk in through the main door. Young, gangly, but stiff, he walked into the cursed church like he owned it. He patted the satchel at his side, and I realized all the men had accessorized similarly. Not a lot of originality in man-purses for this crew.

To the right and left there were single doors that presumably led to smaller rooms beyond. Unless flying brooms were real, and these guys lent them out at the retreat, the windows along the front of the building were much too high for a person to break through in a mad dash. Unless there was a back door, there was only one reliable exit.

Letting out a slow exhale to release some of my pent-up anxiety, I quietly opened the door the burly guy had indicated and stepped through, not disturbing the sudden raucous carry-on of the men. The back room spread out before me, and I had to stop and take it all in before I could look for my contact. It wasn't your average setup.

Understatement of the century.

Running the entire width of the church, the space was unexpectedly gigantic—equally as deep as the previous room. The hard, uneven stone floor stretched out in front of me, shinier than the walls. Polished, almost. Ahead, a big fissure cut across it, four feet wide and as long as the room. I inched forward to see if it was a fire pit, or something like that, but as I progressed, the bottom remained elusive. It had to be pretty deep. "Feed the snakes with a virgin" kind of deep.

Beyond the pit was a slightly raised area where a big cauldron sat off to the left, and a podium stood in the center. Maybe that was where they'd lecture? I excelled in school. That method of fact delivery was fine by me. Though...the strange pit separating the professor from the students was jarring. Would we be thrown to our deaths if we didn't pay attention?

A sludgy, get-out-of-there-while-you-still-can feeling rolled over me, prickling my skin, as I caught sight of a group of women chatting in the corner on my side of the pit. They all leaned over a shared sheet of paper. One reached forward and traced a line with her pointer finger.

Nervousness ate through my middle like a cancer. I skulked closer while trying not to fidget, my unease at meeting new people warring with my desire to seem confident. One of the women glanced over, her pale skin framed by a thick mop of black hair. She nudged a portly woman next to her, and her neighbor jerked up her round face to study me.

I smiled, something that probably looked strained. "Is one of you…Tessa?" I asked.

The rest of the women looked up, the expressions ranging from curious to surprised. An older woman with graying hair bobbed around her face took a step away from the others. Her eyes narrowed as they studied me.

"I'm Tessa," she said in a cautious way. "And you would be…?"

"Penny. Penny Bristol. I emailed you. Several times. About the retreat?"

Silence filled the room, only interrupted by one

woman shifting. Her shoe scraped against the stone floor.

"The retreat on…witchcraft?" I said, hoping that might jog someone's memory. This was a little awkward, to say the least. The retreat's Yelp page was going to get a piece of my mind.

"You're so young," Tessa said, stepping closer.

I frowned, swiftly running my gaze over their group. While I was certainly the youngest, I didn't stand out *that* much. The next youngest probably had fifteen years on me. That didn't seem like much of a cause for ageism.

Although perhaps it could be said that Billy Timmons had a point, and my large alien eyes, the clear skin I tried desperately to hide from the sun for fear of sunburn, and the wilting posture I couldn't shake at the moment (if only they'd stop staring!) conspired to make me look much younger than my actual age.

"I'm twenty-four," I said confidently.

"Yes," Tessa said. "And you were able to cross the barrier."

"I…didn't see a barrier. There was just a lane, some strange grass, and this church."

"You passed through the doors of the church."

My smile had probably turned a little toothy at this point. Holding it in place was starting to get difficult, because of course I had passed through the door. I was standing right in front of them. What other way would I have gotten in? With a Batman belt and some climbing gloves?

"Yes," I said.

"Yes," she repeated.

"This *is* the witchcraft retreat, isn't it?" I ventured.

A couple of the women chuckled softly and the group as a whole twisted and turned, looking at one another. A smile slowly crept up Tessa's face.

"No," she said, cool as day. "That was last weekend. We had a shift in plans. I thought we'd contacted everyone."

I could feel the blood drain from my face. Coldness washed through my body, followed by a blast of alarm. I'd paid for the tickets and lodging with my scant savings. I'd lied to my mother, flown halfway across the country, and suffered a constant stomachache from the spices that seemed so prevalent in the French Quarter, all to attend a retreat that I'd missed? Even if they refunded me for the retreat ticket, all that other money was out the window.

"She passed through the barrier, so there must be power in her," the portly woman said, studying me with a narrow-eyed gaze. "Maybe this misunderstanding was fate."

Fate, or my grabby spam folder...

A gleam sparkled in Tessa's eyes. "Yes. Exactly

right, Beatrice. I had not thought of that." The women continued to exchange those quiet, knowing glances before shifting their attention back to Tessa.

"Okay, young Penny." She smiled at me, an inclusive, sweet, witchy sort of expression. This was why I'd signed up in the first place. My sigh coincided with my shoulders relaxing. "Our coven must take responsibility for the confusion. As such, we will invite you into our fold for our activities here today. You may watch and participate as you can, depending on your power and your experience level—" I held my tongue to prevent myself from telling her I had very little of one, and none of the other. "We've been called here for a specific purpose, and you'll get to experience that. Think of this as a rare gift, because it is not often a new witch, such as yourself, would be invited to something like this."

Excitement built within me. It *was* a gift, definitely. I would get a real glimpse of the forbidden world of magic and the sisterhood that went with it. I could scarcely wait. "Thank you," I gushed.

The door to the main body of the church burst open. A few of the men from earlier sauntered in, their man-purses proudly draped at their sides.

"What are you still doing here?" one of the men said to Tessa in annoyance. "They're getting ready to cast the spell outside. Time is running out, and they need to bring in the vamp."

Did he just say vamp? As in...vampire?

I grinned, clearly hearing things, and earned a scowl for it. Or maybe he just had resting snarl face.

"We were just leaving," Tessa said frostily.

"See that you do," he spat back.

"Vile," one of the women murmured as Tessa turned with a straight back and marched for the nearest door. Unless there was some sort of spatial trickery afoot in the church, the door would lead to one of the smaller rooms adjoined to the main room I'd entered. "Just because they're mages, and we're witches, they think they're on a higher level than us."

"They *are* on a higher level than us," someone said as Tessa opened the door. She stepped through and gestured for us to follow her.

"In magic, sure, but not in social status," Beatrice replied.

"They're barely mages, anyway," a gaunt-faced woman said. "They were witches before they were somehow elevated in status. Oh how quickly they forget."

Apparently the term *witch* applied to both women and men. There you were. I'd already learned something.

"They were?" someone asked as we entered a rectangular room with another large black cauldron set up in the middle.

"Yes, didn't you hear?" Gaunt Face said. "They were witches before the high mage approached them. Then, suddenly, they became mages. I find it all rather suspect."

"And *I* think it's a golden opportunity," a woman with a tight bun replied. "I've never heard of that ability, but if it's true, I want in on it."

"It could be illegal!" someone spat out.

"We use magic," Tight Bun said with a scowl. "We have one foot in the human world and one foot in the magical world. What is illegal in one place might not be illegal in another. I vote for leveling up and showing those boys out there what a bunch of determined women can do."

"Yeah!" Beatrice pumped her fist. It didn't take much to rile her up, clearly.

"In the human world, you go to jail," a woman with a large bosom said. Her tone was flat, logical. "But if you break any of the rules set by magical people, there is no telling who you'll have to face. Can you imagine Roger sending his shifters after you? Would you want Vlad as your enemy?"

The group collectively shivered. I widened my eyes, playing those words over in my head again.

"Do you mean shifters like…*shape* shifters?" I asked in a small voice. I felt ridiculous for even voicing the words.

But no one heard me. Or if they did, they weren't

interested in answering.

"Maybe this is a test," Beatrice said with a pinched mouth. "So far, the high mage hasn't asked any women to join his army, but here we are, helping out. Ready to defend the church and battle evil. Maybe this is a trial."

"Sorry, wait…" I blinked too many times in an effort to wrap my brain around this new string of information. "Battle evil?"

"Ladies," Tessa said as she held up the sheet of paper they'd been poring over earlier. She made a circle in the air, indicating they should circle around the cauldron. "Let's get started. We're behind schedule."

"Okay, but—" Beatrice grabbed my upper arm and moved me to a place within the circle they were creating. "We're not here to fight or anything, right?" I asked her.

She smiled and turned her eyes skyward. "Don't be silly. We're on potion duty. The mages will do the fighting. Now…" She resumed analysis of the paper, probably missing the alarm I knew was plastered across my face. Or maybe she just didn't care. "This is very advanced. Lots of steps. We're going to have to be careful or this defensive measure won't materialize." She brought up a pointer finger, and I thought she was going to jab the paper. Instead, she threaded it into the hair at her temple and scratched, the dry sound making me crinkle my nose. "Let me just look over it…"

As I was eyeing everyone to gauge whether they'd

give chase if I ran, a strange sensation crawled up my middle. I gasped as it opened up like a blooming flower, spreading tingles and heat through my body. I noticed the small piles of herbs and other ingredients placed at intervals around the cauldron. My mind sparked with recognition of each item, adding to that strange feeling in my middle.

I knew what all the herbs were from studying my mom's book on medicinal herbs and reading book after endless book on the subject in the library, but I also had a sense for how particular herbs fit together. Like, sometimes when I cooked, I could feel which ingredients would work best with what in order to obtain my desired outcome.

But the feeling had never been this strong. I had *never* been this sure.

I glanced up at the high ceiling. Then shifted my gaze to the stained glass windows at the front of the room. That cloud of evil intent still hung heavily around the church, but the energy within it sang. It called to me. Begging me to use it. To shape it.

I took the sheet of paper from Tessa before even registering I'd moved. Instead of sprinting for the door and calling for a cab, I slipped my phone into my pocket, adjusted the canvas purse draped against my side, and lifted my chin. I was assuming control. I had no idea why, or what would happen next.

CHAPTER 2

"**I** WILL READ this," I said to the circle in a loud, clear voice. To Tessa, I said, "You take one of the stations."

"I understand you want to help, young Penny, but this is much too advanced—"

"I will read this," I repeated in a tone brooking no argument. I'd never used that tone before, and it was as surprising to me as it clearly was to Tessa. But out of the blue, confidence strengthened my resolve, straightening my spine and ringing through my body. I felt perfectly in control, something I'd seldom experienced before.

But the clock was ticking. If there really was some good vs. evil battle coming, as preposterous as it sounded, and if that Cloud of Doom around the church was part of it, I did not want to be here when things got messy. I needed to help them see this potion through, and then get out as fast as possible.

I pulled the sheet closer to my face and looked down the list of ingredients before inspecting the piles assembled near the cauldron. They were organized so each batch could go into the cauldron at the same time.

Thank you, sous chef.

The loopy scrawl, large and evenly spaced, made me immediately think it was a woman's writing. The clusters of directions and scratched-out lines, which were then repeated lower, indicated this was a copied potion.

I want the book this was copied from.

The thought came out of nowhere, and the sense of longing attached to it was so powerful that I startled. Something deep inside of me wanted to see the source. To hold the book and feel the ancient paper beneath my fingers. I somehow knew the true intent of the instructions would be revealed in the artist's renderings, in the crinkle of the pages. The strength of this potion would be embedded there, seeking a master to will it to life.

I was that master.

Confidence flooded me—not just in my ability to read a page and command a group of witches, but to hear the whisper of the original spell. To hear the deeper desire of the creator and turn the words into a physical presence.

Wow, Penny. Just wow.

My imagination had switched from horror-stricken to grandiose. I constantly surprised myself.

"Penny, maybe I should—"

"Here we go," I hastened to say, not giving Tessa a

chance to reclaim leadership. "Now." I scanned the group in front of me as I opened my mind and (it sounds ridiculous, given that they were a group of strangers, but I don't know how else to describe it) my heart. "Ladies, take your positions."

They looked around at each other, none of them appropriately spaced or standing directly in front of their ingredients. It wasn't even a circle. It was an egg.

Having learned from my mother's constant manipulations that it was faster to man-handle everyone into the space I wanted them to occupy than wait for them to fall into line, I briskly visited each person, precious minutes ticking away as I did so.

"I thought you were a beginner," Gaunt Face said as I switched her position with Tight Bun. I had no idea why I did it. Intuition was in the driver's seat at this point.

"I am," I said, moving to the next person. "Don't worry, this transformation is equally shocking to me. Many terrible decisions are being made today. Let's hope I'm done with them by the time I need to *vamoose*. Unless flying brooms are real?" I paused on my way back to my position, my eyebrows raised hopefully.

Judging by the looks, they now realized that I was, indeed, a novice. Oh well. I'd probably lose my balance and fall off a broom anyway.

Back in my place, I held up the paper again. "Here

we go." I read the first line: "Approach the cauldron from the east and take the wooden spoon into your dominant hand."

The ladies all exchanged looks before turning back toward me. I sighed, because that was the simplest of the directions and they were already confused.

"Beatrice, you're the most eastward. Step forward. Grab the spoon with your dominant hand—are you right-handed? Yes, that's it. Dominant hand, there you go."

Who is this woman reading these directions?

I didn't know, but I liked her.

"Now, Gaunt Fa—I mean." I paused, because that would've been a hurtful slip. "You there." I waved my finger at Gaunt Face. "Cup the sage and bay laurel in your hands."

She did so, and I read the next bit of instructions. Namely, how exactly, and where exactly, they should drop the ingredients into the water of the cauldron.

"Focus," I said in a hush, doing as I'd just said. I let out a breath slowly, stilling myself in the moment. Tingles crawled across my skin and the hairs on the back of my neck stood on end. I felt a pull in my middle. Like someone was tugging a string attached to my ribcage. The energy in the room was rising.

I smiled in delight…then my confidence wavered.

"If we're in a circle, all working together, can I say

the words for the spell, or does the person dropping the ingredients into the cauldron need to?" I asked.

"You say the words, and then we repeat them with you. As one," Tessa said, slight irritation in her voice.

"Right. Got it." I bent my face behind the paper to hide the heat in my cheeks.

The words of the spell sounded ancient on my tongue. Dry and crackly. My breath almost wheezed, as though I were being choked by the dust layering the original spell book.

The circle members—memories solid, all—repeated me word for word. As they did, another surge of energy rose between us, connecting us in this large thing we were doing.

I instructed Tight Bun to put in three of her ingredients, then grimaced when she let the steel bar *clop* into the water, splashing Beatrice. "Let's be careful, ladies," I chided them.

The next set of words, simplistic though they were, twisted my tongue in strange ways. "Stir once to the left, and immediately twice to the right. Feel the forces surround you. Feel the call rise within you."

The air crackled. The pull on my ribs increased until it felt like something gushed out of the bottom of my ribcage and filled my center. I continued reciting the instructions, some of the words not making sense, as though a bad translation, some of them increasing the fervor of the room. Static electricity surged, sizzling up my spine. I watched those around me, their focus complete, their eyes sparkling with purpose.

All the while, the tick-tock of a clock sounded in my mind. There was no doubt now. My third eye was telling me to run.

I continued with the spell as fast as I dared, making sure to watch the women to be certain they followed the instructions to the letter. I couldn't leave now, not when it was halfway finished. Something in me needed to see this through to the end. To maybe know for sure if I had what it took to inch my way into this life.

My heart sped up with each passing moment. Nearing the end, I increased the pitch of my voice. The strength of it.

"Drink," I commanded the circle, raising my hands above my head. "Drink!"

The energy pulsed around me; power surged within me. I closed my eyes, getting caught up in the epic feel of it. Pulled and pushed a dozen different ways without physically moving an inch.

I heard slurping, everyone having at it. But while I was tempted to join in, my natural sense of caution invaded the moment. Logic was right on its heels.

"Wait. What is it we're drinking?" I let my eyes drift open, fighting against the power and energy still ripping at me. "The instructions never said what the potion actually did—"

My words caught in my throat. Beatrice held the spoon to Gaunt Face's lips. Another woman in a sack of a dress waited next to them, looking down at the cauldron with a greedy expression. The rest of the coven stood rigid in their places, staring vaguely with placid expressions, their bodies frozen in place.

Something...is...amiss.

That was probably the understatement of the year, made clear after Sack Dress found her place in the circle of Stepfords. As one, the women turned their heads slowly until their glazed-over eyes looked my way. They blinked, perfectly in sync. Waiting.

A translucent weave of colors, textures, and patterns drifted up from the cauldron. Tendrils twisted and bent, spilling over the sides. Whatever it was didn't dampen the lip of the pot. No sheen spoke of wetness. It slid down the black metal like slow-moving water. Above the cauldron, more of it drifted into the air, unfurling like smoke.

Beatrice, as strangely still as a statue, held that spoon out to me.

The potion's colorful textures, a fascinating blend of the ingredients that had gone into the pot, became solider and licked at the edge of the spoon before climbing up the handle like vines. Tendrils latched on to Beatrice's arm, sliding up toward her face.

"You should shake that off, probably," I said in a wispy voice with a heaviness in the pit of my stomach. Whatever spell I'd spoken to life was not the peaceful, fun-loving kind. Its intent was darker. More violent.

I sure wished I'd felt that *before* I'd taken part in all of this.

"No one better ever tell my mother about this. Her *I told you sos* are the absolute worst," I muttered, willing my foot to step backward. To bring me out of the circle.

"You are bound to us," the group said as one, their voices deep and coarse.

Fear flashed through my gut. I heard a tinkling of metal.

The door on the side of the room opened a crack and a face appeared, expression wary. His gaze slid over the group as I struggled to move backward.

"Help," I said through clenched teeth, terror springing up. I could lift my foot, but it would only go forward. It would only carry me toward the potion that I had helped create. "Help," I said again, louder this time.

His bushy eyebrows lowered over his eyes. "Ain't no help for you now. About time, too. The fireworks are supposed to kick off any minute."

"You are bound to us," the group said together, their grating voices sending a shiver through my body.

The man at the door yanked his head back and shut

the door.

He knew what this potion was supposed to do. And he was afraid of it.

"This is bad," I said as a trickle of sweat dribbled down my cheek. Darkness throbbed in my middle. Blackness surrounded us, different than the Cloud of Doom outside the church, but no less potent.

I'd unknowingly added to the problem. And my time was running out.

The women blinked again, the motion even creepier because it was timed so perfectly, and my mouth dropped open. Their eyes were all white. Not rolling-into-the-back-of-their head white, either. Inhumanly white.

The potion was changing them, all right. Morphing them into something evil.

I had to get out of there.

Shouts erupted from the room next door. A loud, clear voice made it through to me. "Feel that, boys? Here she comes!"

I didn't know who *she* was, and I wasn't about to hang around and find out.

"You are bound to—"

"I heard you, I heard you." I folded the paper quickly and stuffed it into my jeans pocket with my phone.

My phone!

The hope was dashed almost immediately. Who

would I call and what would I say? *I'm stuck in an invisible circle at a witchcraft retreat gone wrong, and a magical battle of some sort is about to kick off, so please put on your jetpack and hurry out here since any form of security is miles away?*

Fat chance. They'd tell me to lay off the drugs.

"What do I do, what do I do, what do I do?" I asked as the fear started to rise.

A sizzling sound filtered in from somewhere outside of the church, like an egg frying on hot asphalt. More shouts from the other room. My ears popped with a pressure change. The energy buzzing within the room was supercharged.

A new force had sprung up. Outside somewhere, but aimed at the church. It occurred to me then that the intent of the potion was the opposite of the coven's intent in brewing it.

"I'm cracking up," I muttered, unsure of how I knew these things, or if they were even true.

One thing I did know: if I didn't do something quickly, I'd lose myself to the magic that was taking possession of the others in the circle.

CHAPTER 3

"THE INTENT IS the opposite of what it should be," I murmured to myself, my survival mode kicking in and my brain churning furiously. I was a problem solver. A data head. If I just let my brain toil on the problem for a moment, surely something would come up.

Something had better come up!

I eyed the colorful spectacle creeping across the floor toward my leg. The ladies at large insisted—yet again—that I was bound to them, but I ignored their voices and simultaneously blinking eyes. Instead, I thought over the details. The order in which the ingredients had gone into the cauldron and the group power that had melded them.

That power was still charging the air. Added to that was whatever was happening outside.

More shouts interrupted my thoughts from the main room. The women in the circle twitched. One jolted, her back bending at an odd angle. It didn't break, but it looked like it would hurt someone up there in years. Yet her face was as placid as ever as she straightened up in a jerky sort of way.

No doubt about it—the potion was changing them from the inside out.

The colorful tendrils reached for me. Would they wrap around my legs and drag me toward the cauldron? How long before the coven shook off their paralysis and force-fed me?

That's not helping.

"Think, Penny!" I berated myself while rubbing my temples.

The sizzle from outside grew louder, competing with the murmurs and shouts of males in the main room. I yanked at my foot, lifting it. I pushed back with everything I had. Tried to step backward. An invisible wall kept me put. I shoved it out sideways—or I tried, anyway. Another wall kept me in my spot, only allowing me to move forward.

"What is this?" I yelled at the room, losing any semblance of calm. My terror amping up the closer that colorful arm of death got to my feet. "Let me out!"

Shivers slid over my skin and out through my fingers. A tearing feeling ripped through me, blistering. The air crackled and popped. Something burst within the cauldron, firing liquid out. It sprayed Beatrice in the face, but she didn't even flinch. Her arm was still extended toward me, spoon waiting, perfectly still despite how long it had been in the air.

A thought curled through my memory. *The intent is the opposite of what it should be.*

The words seared my brain. A desperate plea from my subconscious, still active, though fear covered me like a stifling blanket.

Undo the spell.

Use the energy in the room to undo the spell. To reverse it.

I ripped out the sheet of paper. My gaze flew over the instructions.

"Buggity flapjack, give a dog a bone," I muttered, falling into my habit of using nonsense and nursery rhymes to keep from swearing. My mother's influence loomed, even now.

Though for the first time ever, I would not be embarrassed or angry should she barge in and break up the party. For once, her interference to keep me safe would be entirely welcomed. *Entirely* welcomed.

I dashed forward, feeling the invisible barriers directing me toward the potion. Trying to channel a ninja, I leapt over the reaching tendrils on the ground and ducked under others waving in the sky. I snatched the spoon from Beatrice and shoved her away. Strangely stiff, like rigor mortis had set in, she timbered backward. At the last moment, she staggered, catching herself, and crashed into the invisible barrier of the circle. At least I wasn't the only one who was stuck.

I skipped past the "drink" instruction and read the previous one, only to realize I needn't have bothered. It was already stored in my brain, crystal clear. I didn't have a photographic memory, or even an excellent one, but as I started to reverse what I'd had the ladies do earlier, I realized that from start to finish, and backward to boot, this spell was perfectly preserved in my noggin.

"I'll marvel at that later," I muttered, switching sides of the cauldron and stirring. "But how in frick-frack Nickleback am I going to get the ingredients out?"

Tears of frustration pricked my eyes. The colorful tendrils curled out of the sky, drifting toward me.

I squeezed my eyes shut and concentrated on the herbs floating in the gurgling, rolling water. Pulled on my knowledge of their properties. I completed the reversed next step, feeling something dark and evil glance off my hair. A loud *thunk* echoed from the outer chamber.

Ignoring it all, I kept going. Kept working. A blast sounded from beyond the room that startled me out of my fugue. I snapped open my eyes. A wall of colorful texture had manifested in front of my face. Had dropped over my arms. I didn't feel its touch, but there was no denying the throbbing blackness it had set off in my middle.

Reversing the spell wasn't working.

"You have no power over me," I yelled, stealing a line from my favorite children's movie *Labyrinth*. I threw the spoon in defiance. Willing something to happen. Willing my attempt to make a difference, if only a small one.

Another woman jolted. Followed by another. Their shoulders jerked and their heads twisted to the side.

I spun around to face my former position in the circle, gritted my teeth, and prepared for a last-ditch effort. I didn't know how to fight, but I *did* know how to crash through walls. My life's clumsiness had provided good training, and an invisible wall couldn't be too much different from a visible one.

I sprinted forward, dodging an outstretched hand that more resembled a claw, and jumped over the colorful tendrils. I put my forearms in front of my face, led slightly by my hard elbows, and poured everything I had into my intention to bust through the barrier. Sometimes that had worked for me. If I thought of something hard enough, the impossible became reality.

I pulled up the desire to get out from my toes. Felt it throb throughout my body. Used the energy of the room to add to my fervor.

I hit the invisible wall. A bone-deep vibration rocked me to my core. White-hot pain shot up my spine, tearing me in half, but then my limbs slapped against the ground beyond the wall. I rolled to a stop as the pain dissipated.

Another explosion went off in the other room. A surge of light flashed under the door, accompanied by a loud *pop*.

No time to breathe out an incredulous sigh of relief. Within seconds, I was up again, darting for the far chamber. I didn't know where else to go. The outer room sounded like a war zone.

A slice of brown caught my eye to the left. I twisted my head to look, and my toe hit an uneven spot. I sprawled across the ground, still looking.

Another door. Maybe it led outside.

I was up and at the door in a moment, ripping it open. A tiny space filled with brooms and mops greeted me.

"I really wished you things flew."

A glance over my shoulder told me the coven was finishing their transformation. Their bodies jerked and a feeling of decay crowded the air around them.

My guts pinched. I knew I'd had something to do with that, that I might've even made it possible. It was a hard pill to swallow. But swallow it I would, or I'd be joining them soon enough.

"The one time someone does what I say, and look what happens…" I muttered miserably as I darted into the closet and ripped the door closed behind me. I fumbled for a lock, my hands shaking. I couldn't find anything, and my stupid flip phone didn't have a light or glow to it. Great long-term thinking, keeping a flip phone just so my mother couldn't use an app to keep track of me.

Explosions, large and volatile, rumbled the floor. Shouts and yells followed. The coven hadn't been kidding—it was a full-scale battle.

Speaking of the coven…

I tilted my head as women's voices reached me. It sounded like a chorused chant, almost a drumbeat.

I glanced down at the slice of light at the bottom of the closet door. The only thing separating me from danger was the hope that no one wanted to rummage through the closet.

That wasn't good enough.

My brain churned as more explosions shook the foundation. Energy pounded through the air, even in my somewhat removed space. That potion was nothing compared to whatever was going on out there.

I bit my lip, grasping for a solution to this problem. Nothing came to mind. I had nothing with which to brace or tie the door. Not from the inside.

A door slammed somewhere in the building, making me jump. Either the enemy was inside, or the women had left.

I really hoped for the latter, but prepared for the worst and scooted back until I hit the wall. I slid down and burrowed into the rank smell of mopping equipment, pulling buckets and broom handles in front of my body.

A loud gunshot made me jolt.

Were guns allowed at a witching convention? That seemed like cheating, somehow.

A broom handle clattered against the metal bucket. I reached for it in fright, hoping no one had heard. A blast from the room outside shook my closet door and made my teeth chatter.

Clearly, what little noise I was making wouldn't be noticed.

The invisible string started pulling on my ribs again. Another pressure change popped my ears. Something had happened out there, changing the landscape of the energy. It sucked at me, clawing and scraping along my bones.

Screaming erupted. Was that sound the cauldron sliding across the stone floor?

I burrowed a little deeper and squeezed my eyes shut, focusing on my breathing and thinking of being protected. Of locking myself in. Of safety. I used to do this exact thing when I was little: imagining that I was blocking the closet door to keep the monsters at bay. Only this time, the monsters and I had switched places. And the monsters were real.

More blasts shook the closet door, but my deep

breathing and intense focus were calming my quivering muscles. A shout and another gunshot ended the disturbance. Heavy silence fell over the room outside.

Breathe, Penny. Just breathe. They won't look for trouble in a broom closet.

Heavy boots tramped across the floor.

Just go away. Go away. Find trouble elsewhere.

Footsteps drew closer, jogging now. The faint light under the door moved and shifted, something disturbing its flow.

My stomach churned. I should've listened to my temperamental third eye. I wouldn't be in this mess if I'd trusted it.

A rumble from farther away vibrated through the floor. More fighting was going on. Yet the light disturbance lingered.

What were they doing? It was nothing but a nondescript door. Why not just open the thing and be done with it? Or, better yet, move on!

Keeping my breathing rhythmic so I didn't panic and do something stupid (among many stupid decisions today), I straightened up slowly and wrapped my fingers around the nearest wooden handle. I would only have a fraction of a second, but maybe I could jab the attacker and run like the devil was chasing me. I'd be sure to zigzag in case my visitor was the one with the gun.

My heartbeat rang in my ears, fast and heavy. Sweat dampened my face.

Light flared from under the door. Oranges and yellows and reds.

Fire!

Why were they trying to burn me alive in a closet? Didn't witch haters usually prefer something more ceremonious? Capture the witch, tie her to a large post, and *then* light the fire?

I stuck out my free hand, feeling for heat. Looked at the crack of the door for smoke. I didn't feel or smell anything. And yet...the dancing of the light, and the way it glowed, and...

Fear tightened my chest. Pressure made breathing difficult.

I needed to make a move. I needed to run. But how far would I get with someone right in front of the door?

Without warning, that string started tugging on my ribs again right before the door was ripped open.

A flash of white and the roar of fire made me flinch, but when I opened my eyes again, all I saw was a woman dressed in leather from head to toe, staring into the closet with hard, crazy eyes. A gun was strapped to her leg and a sword hilt stuck out from just behind her head. Her confidence could fill an entire room, squeezing everyone else out. It showed in every line of her body, and the subtle way she shifted as she stared down at me, surprise flitting across her very pretty features.

"I will not join you!" I screeched, digging into my canvas purse. Not the greatest buffer against evil, but hey, I was desperate.

"I'm the good guy." She took a step back and wariness crossed her features. Her eyes darted to my fingers curled around the broom handle. "You dodged a zombie-sized bullet, by the way."

This couldn't be a good guy. She was too...lethal.

She paused, and the situation seemed to warrant some kind of response on my part, but the way she looked at me, intelligent and deadly, stuck my tongue to the roof of my mouth and made my brain buzz. She was unlike anyone I had ever met, *ever*. Rules didn't apply to her, I could tell. Laws were things to laugh at.

Something struck me. Well, two things, actually. The first was the memory of what the coven had been discussing prior to the whole potion debacle. Something about a set of rules for the human world and a set for the magical world.

Could this woman be one of the magical defenders they'd mentioned? Did she know the shifters and the scary creature named Vlad?

I had so many questions, but when another explosion went off, they all rattled inside my head and flew away. I was still in a battle zone. I had to get clear. Somehow.

"I thought this was a retreat!" I yelled, grasping for the words to explain how I'd gotten into this mess. "They were going to teach me about magic."

"*They* were going to teach *you*?" The woman laughed, her shift in position revealing a hovering ball of fire behind her. In another moment, it vanished.

I was pretty sure my eyes rounded to the size of my gaping mouth. A potion was one thing, but this woman could do magic. Like…*real* magic!

A zing of excitement ran through me, chasing my fear away.

"They aren't even in your league, sweet cheeks," the woman said as she stalked toward the other door. If she was afraid of what lay beyond, or anything at all, she didn't show it. "Stay alive and I'll introduce you to someone who isn't a moron. I gotta go now, though. I have to save a vampire from eternal death."

Vampire?

But that wasn't even the foremost question on my mind. I wanted to ask how she'd made that fire. Was it another recipe, or something she could just do from birth, like a superpower? But she'd stopped in front of the other door, hesitating, and I could only watch in anticipation.

"Do you know what's through here?" she asked me.

"A big room. In the middle, there's a giant, like, pit thing. Like a long pit from one side to the other."

"How many people?"

"There were only a couple when I was in there. Then I came in here with—" The women from earlier littered the ground, clearly dead. I swallowed. "What happened to the coven?"

"They came down with a case of the stupids." The woman rolled her neck. "Here goes nothin'."

She kicked the door with a burst of intense power I'd never seen a woman wield. Or many men, actually. Wood cracked. The hinges broke. The doorjamb snapped away.

A smile graced her face, and I was thrown for another loop. She was marching into battle, for grievous sake. Surely that would warrant a frown?

A moment later, she was gone, and I was on my own again.

CHAPTER 4

SILENCE DRENCHED MY tiny closet. I continued to breathe evenly, keeping my cool. It wasn't easy, because while the blasts and bangs had stopped, and the floor no longer shuddered with violence, I was hyper-aware of the leftover carnage awaiting me. It would be spilled across the floors and possibly oozing down the walls.

I grimaced at my imagination.

Had the leather-clad woman made it? And what exactly was she fighting?

I still didn't know if she was really the good guy or not. The coven I'd been working with (until the whole thing had gone off the rails) had seemed pretty nice. None of them had toted swords and guns, either.

And now they were…

I rested my chin on my knees and kept myself from thinking the word. A great travesty had happened here today. One that I'd helped cause in my ignorance.

I shouldn't have read that sheet of paper. Or even entered the church in the first place.

The light peeking under the door flickered again. Voices drifted through the closet door.

I grabbed the handle of the broom.

The lights flickered again and a woman's voice drifted under the door. It sounded like she was telling someone to do something, but I couldn't make out what.

Did they know I was here?

The seconds ticked by, turning into stretched-out minutes, each seeming to last longer than the previous. A rumble vibrated through the ground. Muffled shouts and one roar, all distant, made me grit my teeth. And still the presence lingered outside the closet.

Maybe they were waiting for the leather-clad woman to deal with me.

I was no match for Leather Pants. She'd kick me around the room, laughing all the while. Which meant I should run. Right now.

Before I could summon the courage to make a break for it, the light under the door flickered again, and another voice joined the two previous ones, muffled by the door.

Silence descended. My breath caught in my throat, waiting.

A blast shook the closet door, and it ripped open for the second time. Light accosted me and the tug on my ribs was back. By this point I was pretty sure that meant something noteworthy, but my mind was twisted into knots by all the hullabaloo. I could figure it out later…if I made it to later.

"Whoa, whoa, whoa, we're not here to hurt you!" An older woman wearing a purple faux-velvet sweat suit put her hands up. "The show is over. All the bad guys are dead."

"Except the escaped werewolf, but don't worry about her." An older man smiled in a good-natured way, lines creasing his face. "She is terrorizing the closest town. We're but a distant memory."

I stared mutely for a moment, because *what?*

"What are you people?" It was all I could think to say.

"How did you create this spell?" The woman made a circle in the air with her finger.

I frowned at the empty space. Though I had no idea what she was talking about, I could guess from the tone of her demanding voice that I'd probably done something wrong.

"I'm Reagan." Leather Pants stepped into my line of sight and stuck out her hand. "And they are harmless."

"Penny," I said, remembering that fire from before. "Are you a witch?"

"No. I'm an asshole. It's these two you want to talk to." She hooked a thumb over her shoulder.

"She's not an asshole, she's strong-willed," the man

said, stepping closer. He stuck out a soot-stained hand to match his rumpled wardrobe. "I am Desmond, but my friends call me Dizzy. Nice to meet you. We were about to head to our house for some dinner. Would you care to join us?"

"I'm Callie," the woman said. "C'mon, after the night we all had, we need a stiff drink."

"I don't drink," I blurted, not able to get my bearings. A magical battle of some sort had just torn through the church, dead people littered the floor, and I was huddling in a broom closet. They were taking this in stride, but I just couldn't. I probably needed therapy. Lots of therapy. "My mom doesn't think it's ladylike." I rose slowly, focusing hard on my temperamental third eye. It had tried to warn me of danger before, and if it did so again, that was it. I was running.

"Do you know what's not ladylike?" Callie grunted as she bent to get her satchel and then straightened up stiffly. "Hiding in a closet when there is danger near. That's cowardly. *Real* ladies aren't cowards."

"Take it easy," Dizzy said in a low voice.

"Take it easy my left foot." Callie turned and stalked for the door. The word *Savage* cut through the faux-velvet across her butt. "If she wants any hope of controlling her incredible gift, taking it easy is a waste of time."

Reagan jerked her head toward the strangely clothed couple before following after them. I could tell that was my invite.

In a split-second decision, I hastened after them. My internal guidance was giving me the all-clear, and they had defeated whomever had given the coven directions to turn them into…whatever they'd turned into. These three might not be good guys, but for right now, they were the best I had.

They were also headed for the door. If they turned into baddies, I hoped I'd be faster than Reagan. Because running was about the only option I had left at this point.

"They are the best in this area, and they don't usually take on apprentices. If I were you, I'd see what they have to say," Reagan said, sounding tired but completely at ease.

Flutters filled my belly as we walked past the coven. I looked away, not able to bear it. But as we walked into the main room, I staggered with shock. I'd expected chaos, but nothing at this level. Bodies littered the floor, along with great black scorch marks and lingering colored textures and patterns like I'd seen boil out of the cauldron.

"This isn't normal for Dizzy and Callie." Reagan waved her hand through the air, indicating the mayhem, before picking up the pace. "This is my fault, sadly. I get into skirmishes far more than is healthy."

"This is a skirmish?" I asked.

"Well…no. This is a clusterfuck. But you know what I mean." She held the door leading outside open. "So, what do you say? Fancy some dinner? You can ask questions."

I hesitated. I'd ended up in the church because of unanswered questions. I'd ended up helping with that potion for the same reason. The smart thing to do would be to walk away right now. Call a cab, get in, and never disobey my mother again.

But that floating fire from before tugged on my memory. Plus, they'd talked about creatures out of fables as if they were real, and I needed to know if there was anything to it. That wasn't the real reason I followed them, though. I felt the need to figure out the piece of myself that didn't fit in anywhere else. The missing element that had left me feeling hollow my entire life.

I wanted to know if there was a place I truly fit. If I was at all like my father, and a piece of me wasn't meant to be caged in the world of the ordinary.

If anyone could answer that question, it seemed like they could.

CHAPTER 5

E MERY STEPPED THROUGH the tear in the worlds, the gateway invisible to anyone without magic. He blinked at the sudden shift in visuals. Deep blue sky stretched overhead. Lush greenery surrounded him, moving in the light wind, alive and wild.

He sucked in a deep breath and stilled for a moment with his eyes closed. Natural energy buzzed through his body and sizzled along his bones. The slight weariness of crossing from the magical Realm to the Brink, the human world, evaporated. Replaced by the wholeness, and goodness, of the natural magic surrounding him.

Home. He'd missed it.

Solas stepped out a moment later, a scarf covering her fire-red hair. Her intelligent green eyes surveyed their surroundings before going skyward. Her arm brushed his and he stepped away.

"This the place?" she asked, her gaze now sweeping the trees.

He patted his pockets before bringing out a Brink phone, a piece of human technology that didn't work in the Realm. He pushed the button to turn it on, frowning when it wouldn't fire up. He'd have to plug it in. Right after he found a place to stay.

He slipped the phone back into his pocket and took out a map instead. "I think so," he said, starting forward.

She followed him without a word, content to let him take the lead. When this was through, he'd likely never see her again. She was here to repay a favor, nothing more—they weren't friends. He didn't have any of those anymore. Or anyone constant in his life at all. He was a drifter now, or near enough. It was better that way. Safer. There was less to lose.

An hour's walk and they reached a ramshackle office at the end of the sleepy, unimpressive town of Middlebrook. He'd spent a year searching for his former mentor, following vague clues and surmounting near-constant name changes. There was no denying Isaias had a gift for hiding. A gift that he had, in part, taught Emery. But in this, like in all things magical, the pupil had surpassed the teacher. His mentor couldn't hide from him any longer.

"You can stay out here," Emery said, his heart heavy at the thought of the coming confrontation. It was long past due, but that didn't make the prospect any more pleasant.

"What, and miss the show?" Solas chuckled and

stepped to the side, waiting for him to open the door for her like the royalty she someday hoped to be.

"I should go in first," he said by way of apology. He tried the handle and heard a distinct click. A magical warning most people thought was the handle or lock.

It seemed this old dog hadn't learned any new tricks.

"You're tensing," she said. "Will he attack you, then?"

"With certainty. You'll want to stay clear."

Solas slid her hands into her trouser pockets, unmoving and completely unaffected.

A grin threatened his lips. Clearly a worn-out mage being hunted by a Natural wasn't enough to shake her. It was her fire and fearlessness that had intrigued him when they'd first happened on each other in the woods of the Realm a while back. When she got her chance to stand in the coliseum for the Placement Games, a series of bloody and brutal battles magical folk participated in to win a few choice seats within the Realm hierarchy, Emery had no doubt she'd snag one of the top spots. She wasn't favored by the sponsors, and her family did not have a lot of gold, but her people were from a warrior class almost as majestic and ruthless as the fae. From what he'd seen of her practice sessions, her spark and her passion pushed her above anyone else he'd met from the Realm. She was a wild card. An ace in the hole.

"Suit yourself," he mumbled, digging through his pockets for the right elements. He was sure he had a few within easy reach.

"Most mages carry a satchel." She watched him with a steady, assessing gaze.

He stuffed a piece of flint into the door's keyhole before glancing at his feet. After lifting a boot, he scraped off some dirt. He sprinkled it onto the door handle. "Most mages also need to travel with a recipe book and all their ingredients."

"And you are not most mages."

"You knew that." Naturals could draw the materials they needed from their environment—they were not limited to the supplies they could carry on their person.

"I meant, both in and out of bed, you are not most mages."

His face heated. She was trying to bait him with innuendo, but he wouldn't bite. No, he needed to focus on the elements before him. The metal of the door, reacting with the flint. The earth holding them together. The wood pushing against them.

He willed the elements into a tight weave that would form his intended spell.

Black fog clouded his vision. An image took over of the handle exploding off the door and punching a hole through his chest.

He took a step to the right. Problem averted.

Spell finished, he pushed out a small bit of power to finish it off. Immediately, his premonition came true. The handle burst from the door, flying over the small walkway and out into the cracked and crumbling pavement beyond. On the other side of the door, the handle hit the ground with a dull thud.

"Open sesame," Solas said with a smile.

He shoved the door open and stepped through quickly, the wood slamming against the interior wall. A blonde woman stood at a tall desk, dead center in the cramped lobby space, with wide eyes and a gaping mouth. She shrieked and threw up her hands.

Magical components called out to him throughout the room, almost as if they were begging to be used. He'd tried explaining this to a non-natural before, and the best explanation was that he could see the potential elements waving to him from their sources. Almost like they had little translucent tags. He grabbed out five— velvet from a chair, paper from a magazine, plastic from the fake plant, dye from the woman's hair, and the dirt still lingering on his shoes. He willed them together and pushed with his power.

The woman's eyes rolled into the back of her head and she fell behind the counter.

Directly ahead, on the other side of the shabby check-in desk, waited a closed door draped in shadow. Behind that, a dingy hallway led to a bathroom and another office, unoccupied since Isaias, operating under the name Jonas Smith, had taken over the lease.

"That is surprising." Solas wandered in behind Emery and filed off to the side, utterly fearless and unruffled. "I thought you said you didn't kill without reason. Has your sordid life in the Realm changed you?"

Emery kept his voice down. He'd revealed his presence to Isaias, but he didn't want his former mentor to know anything else. "She's not dead. She's knocked out. She'll come to in about an hour." He dug out more flint from his pocket and picked up objects as he worked his way to the visible door, the wood lined and faded.

He summoned up the protective magic that every mage was born with. It required no ingredients outside of the mage's own body. No power or energy other than what was stored. It was the magic of survival, ingrained.

Most mages didn't know how to manipulate the power. It was a blunt tool called up as a last resort, used on instinct. But most mages hadn't spent years running for their lives and hiding in places no sane person would willingly go. A man developed a certain affinity for staying alive when he was forced to struggle for existence every moment of his life.

He dropped the ingredients he'd collected, leaving them in a pile at his feet. Working the elements he needed, he half built the weave before anchoring it to the doorway. The black fog came and went in a flash.

The walls blew out.

Emery smiled to himself. Isaias had been expecting him. He'd built spells into the walls in anticipation.

Did he not remember Emery's natural gift? How had he hoped to hide that particular surprise?

Shaking his head, Emery thought about creating a spell to soak into the wood of the wall, countering Isaias's spell and causing it to disintegrate. But what a waste of time…

He pulled on the magical threads he needed for the protection spell, entwining them with his survival magic for an extra kick, and wove his work along the surface of the wall. The dirty white paint dissolved into blood red. The color stretched to the corner before wrapping around. He'd covered the whole door.

"He was notorious for wasting his resources," Emery muttered, anchoring the spell. "Just around the door would've been fine."

"Maybe he feared you'd bring an army," Solas whispered, thankfully quick at picking up the situation.

"I did." Emery glanced at her. "Oh, you meant more people?"

A pleased smile curled her lips before red crept into her pale cheeks. She looked away in delighted embarrassment.

For all her hardness, the planes and angles of her personality, she wasn't immune to flattery.

"We'll need to get cover just in case he has more power than I expect. The reception desk should be enough." He gestured for Solas to take cover.

"I was content to watch you work, as I find it fascinating, but I am not going to hide behind a dirty desk in a filthy establishment. I may not be from much, but I do have some standards." She flicked her hand. The door handle clicked, but not in the warning way of before. It was the click of the lock.

Emery frowned as anticipation built.

"I didn't know you had control of metal," he said, still for the moment.

"Any Elemental worth their practice grounds has a secret. Some small talent they keep close to the chest. This particular ability can be useful." She paused, her eyes steady on his. "I trust I can count on you to keep this to yourself?"

"Given how tenaciously you'd try to kill me if I passed it on, I'd say so, yes." Emery slowly reached for the handle.

"And given that I know your location...and your enemy."

"That too," he muttered. "It looks like his spells aren't dependent on the lock." He paused before reaching out to touch the metal. "The spells are dependent on that door opening without the correct element to render them dormant. If I just push it open, my protec-

tion spell won't help us. The walls will still blast."
Something occurred to him, and he spun, looking for
the woman he'd put to sleep.

"What element do you need?"

"Not an element in the sense of the ones you wield.
I mean…the properties of natural items. The building
blocks that make up nature. Sometimes it's part of an
object near me, like the cotton in my shirt or rubber on
my shoe, and sometimes it's the object as a whole, like
dirt, flint, or wood. I draw the energy out of the material
and weave it into a spell."

"That is not usual for mages—or anyone. Correct?"

"No, it's not, unless you are a mage with the highest
level of magic. Even if you're a natural, you still have to
learn to harness the ability. You have to practice and
train. That was something my brother and I did together. And we'd still be doing together if this…" He gritted
his teeth to keep from exploding in rage.

Thankfully, Solas let it go.

Pushing the emotion away, he bent to the woman
lying in reception. Elements called to him from each
item making up her wardrobe—all except for one. An
item from her pocket. A plain gem keychain pulsing
with power.

He snatched the keys and headed back to the closed
door, his heart heavy. Once there, he paused, staring at
the handle in trepidation.

"You do not seem like a man who fears battle." Solas's low, feminine hum drifted to him through the heavy silence.

His heart surged in his ears, nearly drowning her out. "It's not the attack that I'm afraid of. It's my past."

He swung the door open before ripping his hand back behind his protective spell. Not a moment later, a stream of spells flew at him—mottled red, brilliant blue, and one orange-yellow. They hit his dual pane of protection and flashed brightly before fizzling into nothing.

Unable to stall any longer, he stepped across the threshold, seeing the undulating strands of magic surrounding him, ready to be used.

Emery's stomach flipped and lead filled his shoes.

There he was, with deeper lines in his face and more gray in his hair.

Isaias.

The man Emery had met as a boy. The man who had recognized potential in his brother, then him. The man who had trained them through the grief of losing their parents, past the rebellion of their teenage years. The man who had shown Emery how to become a dual-mage with his brother, two naturals of the highest caliber entering into one of the most powerful pairings in the world.

The man who had betrayed them. Then disappeared.

One question had been burning in Emery's mind these last few years, begging for an answer.

"Why did you do it?"

Isaias's shoulders straightened for a moment, but then sadness crossed his features and he hunched back down on himself. He didn't bother getting up from the rickety old chair behind his busted and decrepit desk.

"Why did you do it?" Emery repeated, stepping farther into the room. "Conrad trusted you. *I* trusted you."

"It wasn't my fault." Isaias put up his hands. "You have to believe me."

"You sold Conrad out, and then told them how to get past our wards. Then you just left."

"I had to! It was safer for you that way."

Emery gave a humorless laugh. "Safer for me? I'm the Mages' Guild's number one most wanted. You chased me out of my home. You chased me *out* of safety."

The old mage shook his balding head. His jowls jiggled with the movement. "You have to believe me, Emery. It wasn't my fault."

Blackness crept through Emery's mind at the sight of his mentor's guilt-ridden face. "Tell me why," Emery said, his demand sounding more like a plea. "*Tell me why.*"

"They said they wouldn't hurt you boys. They just

wanted you out of the way, that's all. You have to realize, Emery—the Mages' Guild doesn't like anyone they can't control. Conrad was gathering supporters. And he had you, another natural waiting in the wings. He was amassing power, don't you see? Amassing power with the intent of overturning the system. I had to warn them of what Conrad planned. What he wanted to do was madness. Don't you understand how much money we stood to lose if Conrad took over? How much power?"

The world dropped out from under Emery's feet. Weightless, all he could do was stare at his former mentor in confused disbelief for a moment. "How much *we* stood to lose?" he asked incredulously. Painful pressure ripped at his heart. "*We?* As in…you?" He gulped, the action difficult. A humorless smile pulled at his lips and he narrowed his eyes. "You're kidding, right? You just told them what they wanted to know… You weren't actually…one of them, were you?"

Isaias's eyes tightened. His mouth worked for a moment, nothing coming out. Finally, he found his voice. "I should've told you. I should've. That wrong of me. But it wasn't important back then. My job coincided with what you boys needed. We were working together. Why ruin that? Then, when the guild called me in, I had no choice. I thought they'd force you to disappear. Peaceful resolution for everyone. I had no idea they'd kill your brother, Emery. You have to believe me. I thought they'd just scare you boys."

Emery held up his hand to stop the conflicting babble of someone he'd once thought of as a father figure. His limbs slowly numbed, like his mind.

He'd expected a confrontation that would turn his stomach, but he'd thought Isaias would admit to buckling under torture. Or maybe because he'd somehow thought he was helping. Emery had never expected, not once, that Isaias had sold them out because it was his job. That Isaias had befriended them, helped them, trained them…for the guild.

He'd been the enemy from day one.

"Did Conrad know about this?" Emery asked in a wispy voice.

"No." Isaias waved his hands. "But I had intended to tell him. When the time was right, I was going to explain the truth."

"But how…" Memories flashed in bright lights before Emery's eyes. "How could this have escaped him? He had high clearance in the guild."

"He had no reason to go looking." Isaias spread his hands. "And even if he did, his clearance wasn't high enough."

Emery pulled air from his lungs, still unable to get enough. Memories continued to barrel into him. The dark days and sleepless nights after his parents died.

The pain and the fear. Conrad and Emery were given the choice to live with a few distant relations, but no one really wanted them.

Then, out of the blue, they went to the store to pick up some lunch and ran into a man claiming to be a friend of their parents. What a strange and wonderful coincidence. He claimed he'd stopped by the store on his way to the social worker's house to meet them. From the word go, Isaias said all the right things, knew all the right facts, and then he threw the perfect curveball.

They were different, he said.

They were special.

They had magic.

He was a light in their darkness, serving up candied words when everything else tasted like dirt. And what do you know—like the very magic he spoke of, he was approved to take custody of Emery and his brother when they were barely teens, until they could stand on their own. To train them. To shape them.

So the guild could use them.

It had all been a lie. Plotted, planned out. They'd been raised to be instruments.

Looking at it through this lens, the events that had placed Conrad and Emery in Isaias's custody looked a lot less like fate, and lot more like the contrived circumstances of an extremely powerful organization.

Emery let out a shaky breath. "You told them how

to break into Conrad's and my home. The wards you insisted on helping us create, even though we didn't need you at that point."

"You were scrappy. I knew that even if they got in, you'd get away!"

"Just like you probably thought Conrad would get away, too."

A shadow crossed Isaias's visage, and just like that, Emery knew.

Isaias hadn't thought Conrad would get away at all. He'd known what the guild would do to him, and he'd served him up on a platter. Then he'd sent them after Emery, the flunky, next.

Isaias was the reason Conrad was dead. He was the reason Emery had no life. No future.

The kicker was that Emery had had a chance to go with his brother. The invite to see somewhere new—a distant land—had been extended, and it was only because Emery was working on something that he'd declined.

He could've helped his brother. Given him a much-needed ally.

Saved him.

It was hard to breathe. Hard to think.

"And now you're hiding," Emery said in a whisper. "Why is that, I wonder?"

"Because the guild wants him dead," Solas said from

just outside the doorway. "The guild in the Brink are corrupt. Everyone knows that. If you are no longer necessary, you are executed. Although…maybe they left him alive to monitor him in the hopes he'd lure you to him. Like he has done."

"They wouldn't be able to find him." Emery shook his head, his mind racing. "I could barely find him, and I know how his mind works."

"The guild probably didn't predict that," Solas said, crossing her arms. "He is a loose end. One that wronged you horribly. Tie it up. Send him to his maker."

"The new plan is already in place," Isaias said with a manic twinkle in his eyes. All pretense of pleading dropped away. Rage took its place. "With Conrad out of the way, the setup was easy. The rewards plentiful. Dark magic has its benefits. And I could've stayed and reaped those rewards if Conrad had just listened to me. If he had gotten off his high horse and seen what was possible. You should blame your brother, not me. He killed us all." His mouth twisted in distaste and he pinched a casing and threw, still fast despite his age. Or maybe Emery was just horribly slow right then.

A stream of black blistered through the air. Emery lifted his hand to shield himself, but he needn't have bothered.

Hot air rushed in front of his body, filling the space between him and Isaias. It spun like a tornado, sucking up the hex, and then twisted upward, toward the ceiling. Plaster and paint flew from the sides. Wood groaned.

"Shall I end this?" Solas asked with sparkling green eyes. So much electricity filled the air that Emery's hair stood on end. "A lightning bolt would be efficient."

"How did you gain the favor of a weather Elemental?" Isaias asked with widened eyes. He clutched another capsule.

"She is much more than just a weather Elemental," Emery said, siphoning power from the mini-storm. He pulled elements from within the room and bent them to his will. A tight weave wrapped around his old mentor, pinning Isaias's hands to his sides. "And I was in the right place, at the right time. Leave him, Solas. Let the guild deal with him however they will."

"No! Not that. Emery, please. You don't understand—" Isaias pinched the casing in his hand and jerked, trying to throw it. It hit the desk and bounced back, hitting his side instead.

A puff of green was all the warning the spell gave. It ate through Isaias's shirt like acid and into the skin of his stomach, burrowing down.

Isaias started to scream, twisting against the magical binding Emery had just constructed. Emery's heart ached, but not because the spell had been intended for him. In that moment, he didn't care that his mentor had wanted to kill him gruesomely in order to save himself.

This was the man who had pulled him out of the darkness. The man who'd taught Emery and Conrad to use their incredible gifts. Call him sentimental, or a plain fool, but it killed him to see his mentor leave the world like this. Didn't matter what Isaias had done.

"End it," Emery said to Solas as he turned away from the grisly sight. "End his suffering."

A bolt of lightning blasted down from the ceiling. It struck Isaias's head. The screaming cut off suddenly.

The wind died down and silence filled the room.

Heavy-hearted, Emery stripped away his spells from the door.

"You are too soft for this war you fight," Solas said as she stepped aside.

He didn't meet her eyes. "Once upon a time, he was a father figure, of sorts. Regardless of the lies he told, for good or bad, he made me what I am. It's hard to get around that."

"I see. And when you meet the Mages' Guild?"

He led her out of the building and back to the gateway between worlds. This had been a detour. A lingering question. Isaias had nothing to do with the guild members whose names he'd collected thus far. With the war Emery had inherited from Conrad.

The war he intended on fighting with everything he had.

It was time to truly face the guild. He knew the

name of the hired gun that had killed his brother, knew the office that man had worked out of at the time, three years ago. He would visit that office in Seattle to start collecting more information. From then, he had but to follow the trail.

"When I meet the guild," Emery said, "they will rue the day they tore apart my world."

CHAPTER 6

HOLLOW METAL POLES clattered against the dirt walkway. I jumped, flinched, and spun, all at the same time. I'd even managed to grab my sweater and pull it tighter around my chest mid-spin. My reactions were at once fast and useless, something I never would've thought of a month ago.

"You're so jumpy," Geraldine, the stall neighbor on my left, said with a booming laugh. She brushed her short dirty-blonde hair out of her round face as she surveyed me. "You look like a ghost is following you around."

There probably were ghosts following me around. How should I know? There were certain experiences that changed you, plain and simple. Like sitting in an old magical couple's kitchen after a retreat-turned-bloody-battle and learning from them that mythical creatures were real. It was impossible to go through that and then return to reality as you knew it. Because even if everyone I'd talked to in New Orleans had been lying in some elaborate *Penny is so gullible, let's have some*

K . F .   B R E E N E

fun prank, there was still that floating ball of fire behind
Reagan. There was still that inexplicable gothic church
out in the middle of nowhere. And, oh, I don't know,
the cauldron spitting out patterns and colors that
turned people into zombies!

Even my thoughts turned shrill at that last thought.

Because yes, it had been explained to me in calm
tones that I had helped a powerful mage turn a bunch of
unsuspecting women into zombies.

Me. Penny Bristol. The girl who had, until that
point, lived a boring, uneventful, dull life of routine.

Which meant two things. One, I was a fool for randomly trusting a set of instructions without a
description or even a title—lesson learned—and two,
zombies were real. They weren't caused by a super virus
or an experiment gone wrong (yet); they were made by
magic. By a potion that was stored, clear as day, in my
noggin. So I had that riding around with me.

I blew out a breath. The three magical avengers
from New Orleans thought I was a mage.

No, that wasn't true.

Callie, the older, brash one with the inappropriate
sweatpants, said that without training, I was a natural
witch. It was Dizzy, her husband, who said I was a
mage. A very gifted mage who would probably kill a
neighborhood someday soon if I didn't get training. He
liked to deliver horrible news with a smile.

Thankfully, by that point, the third member in the strange magical group, Reagan, had plied me with so much whiskey that I could barely sit on my stool. It made all the news bearable.

Until I woke up, of course, and proceeded to get out of there as fast as I could.

I'd decided to go back to my old life. Ignore the piece of myself that was missing. Because in all honesty, if that aching hole was meant to be filled with murder and mayhem, if magic was dangerous (at least in my hands), I was better off bored but safe. Any idiot could tell you that.

So here I was, in a job my mother found for me, fighting a feeble canvas tent at a medieval-style amusement village outside of Seattle. As soon as the blasted thing would behave and stand up straight, I could set up my usual wares: tarot cards, colorful stones, and fake crystal ball. If people wanted badly told and often wrong fortunetelling, I was open for business on an ever-changing schedule during often weird and annoying mid-day hours.

I ignored Geraldine's second burst of laughter as I clipped the canvas in place. My stall up, I took the flimsy card table off my rickety cart and pulled out the legs.

"Looks like rain," Geraldine said as she went about clicking her poles into each other, making a much sturdier frame than I just had. It was why she got most of the choosey clientele. She didn't look the part of a road-weary and uninterested gypsy out of the medieval times without two cents to rub together. She looked like a modern hobbyist who may or may not have any insight into the occult, but would be an exuberant and fun distraction nonetheless. The fact that her chairs wouldn't buckle under their butts was probably another advantage.

I'd follow that business model if I had the money to spare. As it was, after the New Orleans monetary setback, I'd decided to save every last penny in an attempt to get my own place and escape my mother's ever-watchful gaze.

I draped a tablecloth over the card table, set up a chair, and slowed down. This was the most important part of my setup, and why I showed up earlier than most of the other vendors. What went where on the table mattered…at least for me. If things weren't placed *just so*, I'd draw a blank the moment someone sat across from me. When the setup was right, it was easier for me to pick up on little clues. Tells about what the person might like to hear.

"I doubt we'll make it through the day." Geraldine breathed heavily as she grabbed newish, unstained fabric to drape over her tentlike setup. "Almost summer, though. It'll start drying up soon."

I glanced at the heavy Washington sky, thick and gray. Clouds shifted while drifting, churning up darker patches in the sky. Electric energy gave the soft breeze a positive charge as it rolled by with a slight chill. Green trees and foliage swayed and nodded around the dirt walkway.

I stilled in the moment, taking it all in. The vibrancy and energy of my surroundings invigorated me. I allowed the earthy smell to comfort me, buffering against the supercharged atmosphere that sent shivers of anticipation through my body.

This was one of the reasons I still got mocked. I couldn't help but stand there with my hands splayed out and my face slightly upturned, listening to the nature around me. Feeling it slide across my skin and fill me up with light. In school, I'd been taunted and bullied for being weird. The bullies who bothered me now might limit themselves to strange looks and crooked smiles, but I could always see their eyes calling me crazy.

Before I might've muttered an apology, torn down my arms, and bowed my face in embarrassment. Not anymore. There were worse things a person could do, like turn a bunch of women into zombies.

Coming back to myself, I noticed Geraldine staring at me, like she was waiting for an answer.

"Sorry, what was that?" I asked, figuring she'd asked a question while I was in my mini-trance.

Her eyebrows shot up and she smoothed the fabric along the side pole of her tent. "Not a thing at all. How's your mother?"

"Same as yesterday."

"Surly as ever?"

"Yep." I laughed as I picked up my duffel bag and looked through it. The crystal ball came out first. That thing was a sham if I ever saw one. It went in the same spot it always did—a little off to the side, closer to me than the guest. Same with the tarot cards, though they got to be a little closer to the customer. They were real, even if I couldn't correctly interpret them.

"Eeny, meeny, miny…" Geraldine's voice drifted off as she hefted up her portable table, something too flashy and sturdy to be called a card table.

"The placement of the ancient relics is a serious affair," I said with a lofty voice as I debated what to bring out next.

Her laughter was strained by the wrestling match with the table. I didn't offer to help her. We'd made a deal on my first day out here. She didn't help me, and I didn't help her. If the wind blew my tent to the other side of the medieval village and got stuck in the jousting match while the horses were running, it was my problem.

I would've been offended, thinking she was making that rule after seeing my shoddy setup, but all the other vendors had nodded in unison. Everyone was out for themselves. It was how things were done.

I placed a crystal at the right corner of the table before hesitating. It didn't feel right there, not with the weather the way it was. On the other side, it felt more balanced, so I moved it there. The amethyst was next, placed just off to the side of center, right in the way. That was annoying, but it felt right, so what could I do? I hated fishing for information. The whole outgoing, chatty shtick went against my natural desire to hide in my sweater like a turtle. I'd rather just work around a rock.

All twelve of my stones were placed in this way. It was when I set down the last that I realized I hadn't put down the hippie scarf that seemed to signify my trade.

"Dang it," I muttered, grabbing it out and starting all over. You never knew with the rocks. Sometimes they didn't like to be set in the same place twice.

And that, right there, was another little personality quirk that people made fun of me for. Thinking rocks had personalities. It was no wonder I only had one real friend (who had a very open mind), was still taunted by the school bully (who should've retired when we'd left high school), and an overprotective mother who thought I couldn't tie my own shoes. I was not normal.

Speaking of *not normal...*

I finished setting everything up as my mind strayed

to New Orleans. I'd felt so powerful when reading the zombie-creating spell. So confident. Then, with the mages and Reagan, I'd felt peaceful. Well...bullied, confused, exhausted, stubborn, and eventually drunk, but beyond that, peaceful. They didn't think I was weird, and given the way we'd met, I could see why. My little peccadilloes probably didn't seem like a big deal to them.

"Look alive, here we go," Geraldine said, squeezing her girth between her table and the back of her tent. She'd misjudged the space in there again.

I laughed and stepped over to pull it out a little. "This doesn't count as helping you," I said as a table leg scuffed the ground and the items on her table jiggled. An old-fashioned though cheap-looking candleholder fell over. I smiled at the sound of plastic hitting wood.

"Oh good, then I don't owe you one," she said with a smile.

I straightened up and went to turn, but an interesting blue stone caught my eye. I bent to the area of her table reserved for items for sale. Half the size of my palm, it was translucent, with pinks, blues, and greens inside. Along the bottom, it looked like a brown fog was billowing up inside it.

"Lux Opal," Geraldine said, following my gaze. "With the galaxy inside. Neat, right? My daughter gave it to me as a gift."

"And you're selling it?"

"Do you know how many gems, stones, and every-thing else people give me? They'd fill a truck. Besides, she's in college now. She has other things to worry about than thoughtful gifts to her mother. She probably just grabbed this at a crystal shop."

I frowned at it, feeling the tingle in my fingers to pick it up and add it to my collection. I, too, was given gems and rocks as gifts, and most of them were as useless as the crystal ball. Some of them I'd leave at the playground among the plain pebbles for the kids to find and marvel over. But every once in a while, I came across a rock with a voice. And those needed to be treasured.

I pointed at it as a gangly older man in a rumpled jerkin and obscene doublet walked by with his hands clasped behind his back and a small smile on his face. He came in almost every day, dressed in his Renaissance faire finery, to take in the grounds. He never stopped at the vendors' tables.

"Just Rick," Geraldine said, recognizing him.

"You should keep that," I said. "That's a good one."

Her brow furrowed as she followed my pointing finger. "Really?" She took it up and surveyed it, then glanced at the others on the table. "It's just an opal. They don't have psychic powers."

"Maybe not"—I glanced behind me to make sure no

one could hear, a habit from youth that wouldn't go away—"psychic powers, but there is power in that stone. I'd keep it if I were you."

Her gaze came up and her brows lowered as she surveyed me. I couldn't read her expression. "You take it, then. I have plenty."

"No, really. That's a good one. It was given to you. You should keep it."

She pushed it across the table at me. "Take it. For helping me. And get your clothes on, or no one will want their fortunes read." She tapped the opal. "Hurry. Someone is bound to come through soon."

Normally I'd continue to refuse, because I didn't like taking things like that, but in this instance, the allure of the gem was too much. I thanked her with a heated face and did as she said, hurrying over to my cart and stashing it in the bushes behind my stall. That done, I stood in front of my table one last time, reaching out with the gem to see where it would land.

In the middle, toward the top. It would be a little in the clients' way.

Couldn't be helped. That was where it wanted to be, so that was where it would go.

I really was weird. I'd probably make fun of me too.

My mother's voice drifted into my head. *What doesn't kill you makes you stronger.*

I snickered as I quickly donned a medieval-style

gypsy dress (the costume store said that was a thing, so I'd gone with it), searched for my headscarf and realized I'd forgotten it, and slipped into the rear of the tent. My mother needed to switch out her clichés. That, or I needed to get laughed at a lot more often, because Callie was right about one thing: I was pretty sure tough girls didn't hide in closets at the first sign of danger.

Families and couples came through in a steady stream—not too many people, since it wasn't a holiday, but plenty enough with it being nearly summer and dry (for the moment). A few of them sat at my table, and I was relieved to find that I needed very little fishing to tell them things that awed them. One lady couldn't believe I knew her daughter was about to have a baby. Clearly she'd forgotten that she and her husband had been speaking about it when they wandered by before doubling back and choosing to visit my booth and Geraldine's. Another woman shook her head and stared at me with wide eyes when I revealed her poodle was doing just fine in doggy heaven, and didn't want her to be sorry for its loss (I couldn't tell from the picture keychain dangling off her purse if it was a boy or a girl, but the cross sticker was telling enough).

In the early afternoon, as the sky boiled and rolled above us, turning darker by the minute, the crowd thinned dramatically. It was Duval—residents here knew when it looked like rain.

I peeked out to look at the clouds when a strange knock sounded within my ribcage. A moment later it happened again, as though my heart was swelling to dramatic proportions, rolling over, and slamming against the bars holding it prisoner. The hairs on my arms and the backs of my neck lifted, giving me goosebumps.

I braced my palm to my chest and tilted my gaze skyward again. The intensity of the air jiggled my nerves and quickened my suddenly too-large heart.

"Geraldine," I called. "Geraldine!"

"Get up and go over there if you want to talk to her," my other stall neighbor, Albert, said. "That's just like kids these days. They all think we need to hear their yelling. Lazy as I've ever seen."

A strange blend of excitement and anticipation tingled my scalp before sifting down inside of me. Butterflies filled my belly and my legs turned restless, my heels tapping against the ground.

It was the fight-or-flight reflex. I recognized it from the zombie and closet incident last month, but this time, I couldn't identify the source of the danger.

I also didn't know what I would choose to do.

"Geraldine!"

"What is it, Penny?" she finally called. "Do I have to get up?"

Blue canvas ballooned in places on my tent, catching the increasing breeze. It yanked at the flimsy frame. "Do you feel that?"

A woman passing by with her teenage daughter glanced at me.

"No. What is it?"

"Electric charge." I rubbed my hands against my arms. "Are we going to get hit by lightning?"

CHAPTER 7

THE WOMAN WHO'D been passing by, nearly out of my line of sight, stopped dead and looked upward. Her daughter about-faced without hesitating. In a moment, they were both headed back the way they'd come.

"No," Albert said. "You know when you're going to get hit because your hair stands on end. And it isn't."

"How do you know?" someone called, and I suspected it was Albert's other neighbor, a middle-aged goth woman who played a little too much Dungeons & Dragons. "You don't have any hair."

"I have hair on my arms, don't I?" Albert yelled. He was largely unconcerned with how he appeared to the customers, something not entirely helpful in a sales profession.

"My hair *is* standing up on end," I replied, still feeling the tingles of my scalp.

"All your hair? Even your head hair?"

I ran my hand above my head but didn't feel anything. "No," I said in a smaller voice.

"It's probably a premonition," Geraldine said. "Get out your crystals and reflect on it."

"You should know the difference between getting struck by lightning and intuition, girl," Albert said. "Though I guess now we know why you don't get much business."

"Oh, shut up, Albert," Geraldine hollered. "She doesn't get business because her tent looks like she stole it from a homeless person, her chairs are suspect, and she sinks back into her seat instead of making eye contact and smiling. It has nothing to do with her ability. No offense, Penny."

I frowned at the slight, but she did have a point.

I clasped my hands and rested them on the table as a few more people ambled by. Two, a couple, looked at my setup with interest before glancing in at me. Another, a solitary man behind them, studied Albert's setup. Clearly they'd heard the exchange and wanted to compare for themselves.

"I'll bite," the man from the couple said, directing his lady friend—no ring, so probably his girlfriend— toward me. He wore a good-natured smile, but hers was a tad brittle. Jealousy, or a hatred of divinity-type folk.

I doubted it was the latter, since she hadn't worn that look before coming over, so that meant their relationship was fresh. They were still working on trust and intimacy.

I smiled and straightened into a semblance of professionalism. "Hello."

"Honey?" the man said, stopping in front of the single chair and looking at his girlfriend.

"Sure." She put her hand on the back of the chair. It wobbled a little and she hesitated.

"I can go if you want?" he asked, bending toward her.

"Oh no, it's fine." She gingerly sat in the chair. Her relieved smile when the chair didn't collapse spoke volumes.

Fine. I would get new chairs.

I caught movement behind them, someone veering to the left. The other man had decided he'd try Geraldine's hand at palm reading.

"Would you like a tarot reading?" I asked with my version of a kind smile. My best friend Veronica said it made me look like a cornered animal, but I was pretty sure she was joking.

"Um…" The woman's gaze slid to the crystal ball and my smile tightened.

Please don't pick that. Please don't pick that. Please don't—

"How about the crystal ball?" she said with a sparkle of excitement in her eyes.

I kept my sigh at bay. "Of course."

Careful not to disturb the rocks placed around the

table, I pulled the ball closer and grabbed a cloth from the bag resting on the ground beside me. I slipped the cloth over the ball to cover it, something that seemed very mysterious, but whose only true purpose was to give me time to think.

"Do you have any questions?" I asked her as I laid both palms on the covered ball and made eye contact.

A small knot wormed between her brows and her gaze slipped toward the man before she could drag it back.

Clear as day. People's tells made this job easy.

"No," she said with a forced light tone.

I nodded like I'd known she'd say that, and slowly pulled my hands away from the crystal ball, sliding off the cloth as I did so. I stared at it for a long moment before closing my eyes. Power pulsed in my middle from my rocks and the charged atmosphere. A feeling of inevitability lodged in my chest like a spiked ball.

"Something is coming." The words slipped out of my mouth, unbidden. "Something will happen soon that will change your life forever." The pressure in my chest increased. "But the journey has already begun. You can't hide from it. You won't be able to turn away. A chain of events has started, and at the end will be your destiny." I opened my eyes and she was leaning forward slightly, her eyes riveted to my face.

The ball inside of me loosened a little, and I had a

moment of supreme confusion, like I always did when my intuition forced itself to be heard. Because this reading wasn't meant for her—this was me telling myself what was coming, using extremely vague, general, and unhelpful words.

"Sorry," I said as heat rushed to my face. "That just came to me." I fingered the cloth, half thinking I'd slip it over the ball and start over. I hated doing that. My excuses always sounded lame.

"No." The word sounded more like a release of breath from the woman's mouth, and I belatedly realized I should've asked her name. My bad. "That was dead-on. That sounded right."

"Heavy," the man said, and tried to lean against one of the support poles. It groaned loudly and the whole tent shifted. "Oops." He hopped away.

Fine. Albert and Geraldine were right about my entire setup.

"Wow." The woman smiled and leaned back. The chair shifted and her eyes widened until everything settled again. Clearly she thought she'd be dumped out of it at any second.

I stared into the depths of the twenty-dollar crystal ball, trying to see its middle through the white coloring. Not because any images or messages would await me, but because it made me look like I was concentrating really hard.

I flicked my gaze toward the man, a very quick gesture, before I scrunched my brow and looked at the woman pointedly. The pointed stare was always the way to go in this business. "You will find...what you seek." I let my eyes flicker again, but just in his general direction this time. "The thing you are after...will become permanent down the road. But only if you keep faith. Work on trust."

Red infused her cheeks and a delighted smile pulled at her lips.

"It seems a little general," the man said, crossing his arms.

Please don't make me prove myself. Please don't make—

"No," the woman said, her eyes rooted to mine. She put out her hand to stop him. "No, I know exactly what she means."

I leaned back. Hopefully that would be enough. "I'm glad. When there are two people present, I always worry about being too...descriptive." I gave her a demure smile. "Privacy is important."

"I totally get you." She nodded adamantly. "Sorry, how much—"

"No, let me." The man reached for his wallet, and the woman gave him Bambi eyes as she went to his side.

I collected payment and watched them go. A moment later, Geraldine filled the front of my tent.

"Another happy customer?" she asked.

I frowned at the ball. "Yes. Overly happy. I accidentally blurted out my own premonition, which was as infuriatingly vague as they always are, and she ate it up."

"Ah." Geraldine smiled knowingly, checking out my rock configuration. "Yeah. She was responding to your…" She made a fist and shook it.

"Confidence?"

"Nah…" She pursed her lips. "More like…" She shook her fist again.

I didn't know what that meant, but I went ahead and nodded knowingly anyway. Otherwise these charades might go on all day.

She glanced at the sky and looked down the path. "I just had a stinker. He didn't give me *anything* to go off. And he picked up nearly everything on the table and analyzed it."

"If you weren't such a hack, that wouldn't be a problem," Albert yelled over.

She took a step and angled so she could shoot him a fierce glare. "You sell fake bows and swords. What do you know about it?"

"They aren't fake," he said. "I sell quality items!"

"Quality items my left foot," Geraldine grumbled, stepping back.

Flapping fabric and canvas sounded down the way as the wind picked up. The pressure in the air increased until it felt like we were inside a shaken soda can. A hint of moisture traveled on the salt-encrusted breeze, even though we should've been too far inland to smell the sea.

Geraldine smiled at a teenage couple meandering by. They were never overly worried about the rain. "Anyway, when I tried to fish, real sneaky-like—I disguise my fishing in flattery, you should try it—he smiled like he knew what I was doing." She scowled. "I'll bet he's in the trade. Here to suss out the competition, maybe." She braced her hands on her hips. "I hate looking clueless in front of the handsome ones."

"I'm sure you didn't look clueless. He was probably one of those super-jaded guys. We get them all the time." I put my money away and moved my crystal ball back to its correct position. My tent groaned again, pushed by a particularly strong burst of wind.

Her eyes narrowed as she shook her head. "No, it wasn't that. It was…something else. A certain confidence…" A knot of concentration worked into her forehead. A moment later, her expression cleared and she shrugged, smiling down at me. "Doesn't matter. I got his money in the end, so all is well. I'm going to pack up. I doubt there'll be many more today."

I grimaced and checked the time, then the sky. When the weather turned nasty, the managers of the village would usually stroll through and tell us it was time to leave. Anyone who left before she gave the okay might find themselves out of a space. And while this line of work only made me as much as a low-paying job, it was better than stocking shelves or working in an office. At least until I figured out what I wanted to do with my life.

"I might hang on a little longer," I said, dropping my hands into my lap.

"Little Miss Rule Follower," Geraldine said with a smile, and turned toward her booth.

But a half-hour after Geraldine tugged her wagon past, my resolve had weakened considerably. The patter of the occasional raindrop splatted against my tent. More plunked off the dirt path. Only one or two souls wandered by, and that was to head out. The day was done, regardless of whether anyone had bothered to tell us.

A strange surge of power amped up the energy rolling around my body, the effects of the premonition. I glanced down at my gems and stones, wondering if it was them. It could've been the weather. It was hard to say when the atmosphere was so wound up.

I needed to make a decision.

I glanced back up and started.

His footsteps had been silent, his approach sly. Yet there he stood, a muscular man a few years older than me, looking at me with an impassive face.

"Hello?" I asked, like I'd answered a phone call.

He moved forward with a sure step. The wind worried the dusty blonde hair that fell across his broad forehead. "Are you still open?" he asked, his eyes not leaving mine, even to glance at the table full of objects. It felt like he was assessing me, reaching in through my eyes and down to my soul, finding and reviewing all my secrets along the way.

"Oh." I glanced out through the opening to the angry sky above. "It's probably going to rain soon."

He stood just behind the client chair. Clearly he was waiting for me to give a solid answer, and his patient silence had the odd effect of drawing the words from my mouth.

"Sure," I said, shrugging. I had an umbrella. I'd chance a few drops for another paying customer.

Without a word, he stepped around the chair and sat, not flinching or hesitating when it whimpered in warning. His intense stare never left my eyes, and his face remained perfectly impassive. Like a serial killer's.

I had the sudden thought that there weren't enough closets in the world to save me from him.

"What…would you like?" I asked, running my hand over the table like Vanna White. "Tarot?" I touched the cards before glancing at the crystal ball. I weakly gestured that way instead of actually saying the words.

His gaze followed the movements of my hands, eyeing the tarot deck first and then the crystal ball. Without warning, he palmed the ball with a large, calloused hand and held it up for inspection.

"Ohhh…" I said like a tire losing air. "You're not supposed to touch that."

He squinted into it, as though trying to see the middle.

"I have to…" I made a circle in the air with my pointer finger. "I have to evoke the images, actually. They can't just be gawked at like that. They won't show."

The corner of his mouth stretched into a half-smile before loosening again, back to stoic and serious. He dropped the ball onto the table, next to the stand.

"That just needs—" I flinched as he reached out, fast as lightning. My tarot deck was whisked away. "I'm not sure what experience you've had with these sorts of booths, but this level of manhandling is usually forbidden."

He flicked through the deck, looking at various cards, before dropping them in a mess next to the crystal ball.

"This isn't off to a great start," I mumbled, at a loss. I'd never had someone so confidently wreck my setup before. Clearly this was the same guy that had visited Geraldine. The situation was a little off-putting, yet strangely gratifying.

His gaze landed on my newly acquired opal.

"Nope." I jabbed my hand in front of it before his quick-draw-McGraw snatch could take hold. Instead, his fingers curled around mine.

A bolt of electricity blasted up my arm and into my chest. It stopped my heart and fried my insides as it shot down to my feet. I sucked in a pained breath. Adrenaline rushed into my body. The tug on my ribs that I'd felt in New Orleans was back, only this time it felt like a thick cable attached to my bones was being pulled by a semi.

The turning of the world ground to a halt. The wind died down to nothing and the canvas that had been whipping in the wind fell straight. The murmur of voices deadened.

We were two people moving in a frozen world.

CHAPTER 8

H IS EYES WIDENED as he stared at me, and it felt like that was a big deal. Like he was a man not surprised by much, and this had blindsided him.

I was a woman surprised by a whole lot. But after New Orleans, this didn't seem like much. Just another weird thing following me around like an elephant I pretended not to see.

I drew back my hand. My arm stung from the rush of electricity, and my body trembled from the flash of pain. But I kept my composure and watched the stone, for no other reason than that I didn't want him to take liberties with my gems. That seemed really important for some reason.

"So no on the tarot and crystal ball, then?" I asked lightly.

As suddenly as it had stopped, the turning of the world resumed. The wind rushed back in, pushing at my shabby tent. Birds squawked, probably yelling at each other before finding a place to hunker down for the rain. The chatter of booth workers and the clang of the others putting their things away filled in the background.

His eyebrows dipped low over his expressive eyes and he slowly withdrew his hand.

"Not much of a talker, huh?" I asked.

He leaned back slowly, and the chair leaned back with him. He didn't seem to notice. "Do you know how to read tarot?"

"Yes," I said confidently. "Would you like me to…" My words dried up under the force of his straightforward stare. Silence once again filled the space between us. Just as before, his waiting had the effect of drawing the words out of me. "You caught me. I really don't. I just make things up based on the pictures. When people get the death one, things can get a little dicey on the communication train."

He tilted his head, and it seemed like a nod of approval.

"The ball?" he asked, back to his serial-killer expression.

"I mean, do *any* crystal balls really show images?" I chuckled.

"Yes." His eyes took on a haunted look and his face shut down into a block of granite.

I was out of my league, and I had no idea why, how, or even what league I had wandered into. "Right. Well then, no, that is not a crystal ball. It's a cheap lump of glass."

He nodded again. "So what is it you do…"

"Penny. Penny Bristol."

"What is it you do, Penny Bristol?" He spread his hands, indicating my whole setup.

"Well, I…" I looked at my table. With the tarot and crystal ball cleared off to the side, all that was left was a haphazard layout of gems and stones. My chances for getting paid for this visit were diminishing. "I play poker, really."

"Poker?"

"Yeah." I shrugged. What was the point in lying? He'd seen right through me, I could tell. "I read people and tell them what they want to hear. That's what I do."

"And what do I want to hear?"

"I have absolutely no idea."

A smile slowly worked up his face. "This isn't the right job for you, Penny Bristol."

"Tell me about it."

He leaned forward and put his forearms on the table. The loud creak didn't seem to bother him as he gazed at the various items laid out before him. "May I touch your rocks?"

I narrowed my eyes at him. The way he'd said that sounded dirty.

When his eyes came up, though, they were inquisitive instead of filled with mischief.

"They don't really like to be handled." I clenched my teeth, realizing what I'd said. "I mean, *I* don't like them to be handled. That's what I meant."

"No, it isn't." Another pocket of silence, and I got the distinct impression he wanted me to wave my weird flag.

"Fine, you want the whole shebang?"

"Yes."

"Each of those rocks holds power. They like to be laid out in various ways, which changes nearly every day. If I get it right, this game of poker is much easier. The right words come to me. If I get it wrong, I get very little tips on what my customers want to hear."

"Do you ever get it wrong?"

"In the beginning, I did, yes. They were for decoration, so I just placed them randomly."

"What changed?"

"I spent more time at the library, researching power items. One day I got it right, and it felt…balanced. Peaceful."

"Powerful."

"Yes," I said, shivers coating my body. "Powerful."

"I have some knowledge of power rocks, Penny Bristol, though the ones I use are significantly larger than these." He ran a hand over the table. "You are wrong. They like to be handled. They like to be used, some more than others. But you are right in that they have a will of their own."

The shivers turned into prickles and I straightened up, fear worming into my middle. Flashes of burned bodies and zombie corpses invaded my mind. The feeling of power that had flooded my senses when I was reading that spell…

The memories rattled me, throwing me into a darker place.

Back into that church.

"Do you know of magic?" I asked in a strangled voice.

The glimmer in his eyes dulled. His gaze roamed my face, then my neck and shoulders. He leaned away from the table and dropped his hands into his lap. "I apologize. I think I've overstayed my welcome." He rose and stepped behind the chair. His gaze went back to serious and intense, the brief sparks of humor from moments ago completely gone. "I know your fear. I know it with everything in my person. But remember this. As Nelson Mandela said, courage is not the absence of fear, but the triumph over it. If you hide from that powerful thing inside of you, it will take over in strange ways. It will rule you, and not you it." He turned to go, but stopped mid-turn and swiveled back around. "And remember this also." He touched a scarred finger to the center of his chest. "You don't need fancy words or different languages. You don't need more than what exists in the wild. You just need the strength of your will to make it so. Good luck, Penny Bristol."

And with that, he was gone.

The increasing patter of raindrops sounded overhead, but I couldn't move. My brain whirled with what he'd said, and more, the way he'd said it. Like he knew what I was going through. Like he'd been on the same journey at one point in his life, and he'd overcome the crippling fear.

Like he was encouraging me to overcome it as well.

I took a steadying breath and glanced at my gems and stones, replaying our conversation word for word.

It will rule you, and not you it.

The scenes in the church came back to me again. The decisions I'd made out of ignorance.

I did have some magic. How much or how little was still up for debate, but it was impossible to deny that if I continued to ignore the whole thing, I'd be acting out of fear...just like the stranger had urged me not to do. I'd be hiding from what I was. From finding out exactly what that meant.

Another thing occurred to me.

He hadn't snickered at me once throughout that whole thing. He hadn't made a jest at my expense, or a face that suggested he thought I was loony tunes. He'd been on my same page.

Emotion welled up, shifting things around in my

chest. Excitement and anticipation built, along with anxiety.

Callie had said I could live in her house. That she had too much money for her own good and could cover my expenses. That would loosen the hold my mother had over me. It would erase my monetary obstacles.

Was I really contemplating accepting the dual-mages' offer to train me?

Did I have any choice?

A sour face appeared within the front opening of my tent, followed by a wiry old body with droopy man boobs. I'd never seen a thin man with droopy man boobs until Albert, but there you had it. His white mustache curved down toward his chin, following the contours of his equally downturned mouth.

"Who are you trying to impress?" he asked.

I lifted my eyebrows. "You?"

"Bah!" He batted his hand through the air before pointedly looking at the sky. "Can't you see? It's starting to rain. There'll be a storm tonight, mark my words. Those weather people wouldn't know their business if it was handed to them."

"Well…it is handed to them. Via a teleprompter."

"You know what I mean. They said it'll be light showers. Does that sky look like light showers to you?"

No, it did not. It looked like I needed to start building an ark.

"So what are you waiting for? A second all-clear?"

He frowned at me.

"Did we get a first one?" I asked, standing.

He rolled his eyes and walked away.

That was probably a yes.

I stared at my gems and stones for a long moment before picking them up one at a time.

You just need the strength of your will to make it so.

But what was the "it"?

In a daze, I took my tent and whatnot down and piled it onto my cart. It was annoying to set up and take down every day, but management reserved the right to move us around or cancel us at any time. Clearly they thought keeping us mobile was the easiest way to handle things. For them.

The lane was mostly cleared away as I made my way out, and only one guest of the village was hurrying through the hardening rain. Even in a panic to keep from getting wet, he noticed the strange stain on the side of my umbrella.

I rotated it away from his judgmental eyes. I honestly had no idea what it was from, but it wouldn't let the rain wash it away, and I never remembered to pick up a new umbrella when I was in the store.

At my car, I loaded everything in (the poles were always a problem) and sat in the driver's seat, checking out the mostly empty parking lot. The afternoon sky, dark with clouds, rumbled in the distance. Albert had been exactly right. This wasn't any old rainy day. There was a storm brewing.

Halfway home, after stopping by the store to grab a few things for dinner, I slowed at a barricade blocking off the street. Rain pounded my windshield. The squeak of my wiper blades competed with the radio.

I frowned because this way was never closed. It was a larger street that didn't host any street fairs or races— not that it would be a likely day for such a thing.

I glanced in my rearview mirror, seeing that I'd missed a standing sign that probably read "Detour."

At least they had signs. I'd never strayed from this route, and I'd learned it from MapQuest (flip phones didn't have GPS). I didn't trust my ability to figure out a workaround without guidance. Streets around these parts were windy affairs that messed with my nearly nonexistent directional sense.

A car slowed at the detour sign and turned. Another followed behind.

At least I'd have someone to follow.

As I straightened in my seat and grabbed the gear shift, my gaze caught the barricade again. The image wavered, just for a moment. I turned the wipers on a little faster, trying to see through the driving rain.

My heart quickened.

It wasn't a barrier at all. It was a tightly woven band of multiple colors, patterns, and textures.

It was magic.

CHAPTER 9

ADRENALINE COURSED THROUGH me. Without thinking, because that was clearly my jam, I threw the car into drive and lurched forward.

The hood of the car sliced through the artfully crafted spell. I stopped on the other side and looked back.

The magic was still there, untarnished by my intrusion.

I turned back to drive on, but it occurred to me that an essential part of training was analysis. If I wanted to learn how to work spells, I needed to know how other people put them together. What went into them. I was being presented with that opportunity right now, which clearly meant I should head outside in a storm. Clearly.

Why did I have to think so much?

I pulled over to the side of the road and grabbed my umbrella. The driving rain beat down hard, splashing the concrete around my shoes. I hurried forward, getting hammered in the shins as I did so. They'd be soaked in no time.

The weave was magnificent, like the design of a

master seamstress. The colorful patterns twirled and spun together, exquisite and exciting. I felt the pulse of the spell throbbing in the air before it soaked into my middle, its intent clear.

Keep out. Danger ahead.

I felt goodness within the spell. Light. Good intentions. Whatever was happening, this spell had been crafted by someone with his or her heart in the right place.

I ran back to my car, my shins getting another blast of tumultuous water. A gust of wind layered my side with rain.

What a day to stumble upon magic.

Back in the car, I drove ahead slowly, looking carefully for any sign of additional magic. I felt it before I saw it. Evil intent. A vile undertaking. Something that would cause serious harm. I didn't see any magic, but I could feel it, clear as day. The spell was in the stages of being cast, I'd bet my life on it. Soon, the colorful jet of destruction would bloom over the street toward its intended victim.

I didn't think that was imagination talking, though I couldn't be sure.

I pulled to the side of the street again, watching. If I couldn't see them, they couldn't see me.

I paused.

If magic could make people into zombies, it could

also make people invisible.

Adrenaline mixed with fear had me outside of the car in a flash, umbrella and purse in hand. I thought about grabbing a tent pole, too, just in case I needed to javelin someone or something, but a quick glance at the sky made me think better of the idea. Holding a big lightning rod in a storm wasn't the smartest of moves.

Although my umbrella wasn't far from…

I scurried toward a leafy bush at the side of the road. A streetlight clicked on over me, showering me in its glow.

Great timing.

I tiptoed farther along and crouched beside another bush, looking out at the quiet street. A small, deserted lot sat off to the right, the green grass stretching to the playground beyond. On the other side was a tire business, its windows dark and bays closed. The burger joint was likewise closed, very peculiar for this time of day on a weekday.

"I just want a name," someone shouted, and I recognized the voice immediately. Gravelly and low, it was the stranger from earlier in the day. I couldn't see him, but it sounded like he was on my side of the street.

I patted my pockets, more of a nervous gesture than an attempt to find something. My stones were in my bag in the car. Not that I knew how to do anything more than throw them at someone, but I sure would've been happy to have them with me.

"Let it go," someone else called out from the playground side of the street, the one that emanated evil intent.

"You've lost your mind if you think I'm going to let it go. Just give me a name and you walk away from here."

"There's three of us," Dr. Evil yelled out. I wondered if he had his pinky to his mouth. "We're going to walk away from here regardless."

The stranger's laugh was low and humorless. "My brother and I were dual-mages. Did they tell you that? My power is the same as his. You think you three stand a chance against me?"

"*Were* dual-mages," Dr. Evil said. "How does that feel, when your other half is ripped from you? I've heard it is a wound that doesn't heal. Think you'll find another natural to sew it back up? That's the only way to get peace, isn't it? Join with another mage?"

The sound of rain pounding on cement ate away the silence. The force of the evil intent grew. Dr. Evil and his flunkies were about to throw their spell.

"This is your last chance," the stranger said, warning clear in his voice. I felt absolutely no intent—good, evil, or otherwise—coming from his side. "Who ordered my brother's death?"

Like a rubber band snapping, the evil intent was

released. It rocketed out from the side, a mishmash of murky colors and twisted patterns.

"Watch out!" I yelled, stepping into the street and waving my hands. "Run!"

Three jets shot out from the stranger's location, the weave so fine and intense that it blurred into one color and obscured my ability to judge its purpose. My logic picked it up easily enough, though, and even if it hadn't, I didn't need to wait long to see it in action.

The stranger's magic ate away the evil spell, dissolving it into nothing before blinking out itself.

I had no idea why I hadn't seen the stranger before. He was standing next to the street in front of the tire shop, plain as day. And he could clearly see me. I could tell because his head was turned, his face pointed in my direction.

Fat raindrops pelted my head and face like bullets from a machine gun. Cold water soaked through my sweatshirt. I barely noticed.

Crack.

A shock of death rolled toward me from Dr. Evil. I turned and threw up my hands, fast but useless.

A sheen of bright white arched around me, forming a half bubble to my front. The murky black-brown stream of badness slammed into the sheen of white. It exploded, consuming the incoming magic and then rocketing back out to follow the line of fire.

Someone screamed, a hoarse, terrified sound. It cut out suddenly. Someone else shouted. The stranger stared at me, immobile.

"Run, you blind idiot!" I yelled at him, waving my arm in an arc before turning myself. "They'll only hurl more of them at us." I put on a burst of speed, the same kind that had won me a great many track events.

I was back at my car in a flash. Wet and soggy, I yanked open the door and jumped inside. My seat squelched as I dug through my equally soaked canvas bag for the keys.

Another blast of color tore through the fading light, aimed for the stranger.

"What a blockhead," I muttered, my stomach doing somersaults. They'd lob more at me soon, I had no doubt. I needed to get out of there.

"Should I save him?" I asked the quiet car as I freed my keys from my bag and jammed one into the ignition.

Another jet of magic pierced the sky, followed by two more in quick succession, all coming from the stranger's side. Maybe he could take care of himself. I cranked the ignition as the street fell silent except for the pounding rain. My breath was loud and harried in the purring car. My heart thumped in my ears.

The stranger walked out into the street, his gait powerful and purposeful. He stopped in the very center like it was high noon, then turned toward me slowly, and I read suspicion and vengeance in every line of his tall frame. He looked like he wanted a pistol showdown with *me*.

"Nope!" I slammed my foot on the gas, so far removed from logical thought that my brain could've flopped out onto the center console and I wouldn't have noticed. The engine revved and the car blasted forward, straight for him.

"I should've gone the other way," I yelled at myself. But *I* wasn't driving just then. It was that she-devil who took over covens and spoke zombies to life. The adrenaline junky who loved to push the limits of magic.

Except this wasn't magic. It was a very heavy block of metal, and I was hurtling it at a stranger at hair-raising speeds.

"Get out of the way," I yelled. He'd only take me on if he meant me harm, and that would be strange, since he'd literally just saved my life with the whole white shield thing. But maybe he'd decided he didn't want a witness…

Well, if so, I wouldn't make it easy for him—I'd leave a tire tread up the center of his body and over his face. "Move if you know what's good for you."

He pulled his hands up in front of him. Black fog materialized until it crystalized into a shiny orb, so black it looked like a tear in the universe. Soon it would disappear into the failing light of day.

If I didn't run over him first.

"Last chance," I yelled, even though he couldn't hear me. Not that it mattered. A car headed toward you at high speed, driven by a dishonest fortune-teller, was a pretty good indicator of what was about to come.

My fingers tightened on the steering wheel.

Still he stood.

My knuckles turned white.

He stayed motionless.

My car barreled down on him, closing the distance.

He waited with his chin raised and that ball hovering between his large hands.

I lost the battle of chicken.

I wrenched the wheel. The tires squealed and the car careened, headed now for the park. I jolted in the seat as I popped the curb. Three bodies lay sprawled out on the grass, their limbs splayed at unnatural angles.

I yanked the wheel the other way, my lips forming a curse word. The car responded eagerly, but not in time.

Bump. Bump.

"Oh heavens no," I muttered. Bile rose in my throat.

Although running over a few dead guys wasn't nearly as bad as turning women into zombies. It was all about perspective.

I flopped in the seat as the car rolled off the curb and back into the street. Another wrench of the steering wheel and I was swerving down the middle of the road, headed toward home.

I glanced in the rearview mirror.

The stranger still stood in the middle of the street. Facing me. Watching me go.

And he knew where I worked.

CHAPTER 10

EMERY WATCHED THE car speed away, mouth gaping.

The girl from the medieval village. Penny Bristol. Even from a distance and in the failing, rain-streaked day, he'd recognized her immediately. He would recognize her anywhere. That beautiful face was burned into his brain, with the luminous blue eyes and pixie-like features.

So many questions were running through his mind that all he could do was stand there and stare at the shrinking red taillights.

What had she been doing here?

How had she snuck up on him without tipping off him or the guild mages?

How in hell had she kept what she truly was a secret from him earlier that day?

He'd sat in her rickety chair, leaned against her shaky table, and chatted with her about a fake crystal ball, barely used tarot cards, and tiny power stones. He'd told her about using her magic, and about summoning the will to control it, as if she were a rudimentary witch with a thimbleful of power. All the while, she'd had that *might* trapped within her skin.

Turned out he'd given her terrible advice. Dangerous advice. If that kind of magic turned unruly, or if she started using it without knowing what she was doing, it would take more than will and hope to control the outcome.

He pulled his palms apart, letting the black ball of survival magic dissipate. Rain pelted down around him, sliding off the weather-protectant bubble surrounding his body. Power and energy rolled through the sky.

He turned and stared at the location where she'd stood, remembering the flare of survival magic that had risen around her. The purest of white, directly from the root of her soul. Just like his brother's.

But his brother hadn't been able to control his survival magic like *that*. Penny's magic had tracked the offending spell back to the caster and taken him down. That had been sensational.

The tread of boots shook him out of his thoughts. Solas stopped beside him, her gaze trained in the same direction as his.

"Who was that?" she asked, kept dry in her own rain-free bubble.

He shook his head, thinking back to that flimsy little booth in the medieval village. "The short answer is that

I have no idea. I'd thought she was no one."

"She is certainly more than no one. I felt the sting of her power in my bones. Like I do with you. And she was at a distance."

"I know." He told Solas about meeting Penny earlier in the day, when he'd been killing time. "She acted embarrassed about her tiny power stones."

"Because they were so small?"

"No." He shifted, scratching his head. "Because she knew they had personalities, of a sort. She didn't seem like she knew anything about her craft. Yet…"

"She tried to warn you about the guild's spell," Solas said, shifting her stance. "She charged forward, into view, to warn you."

"Maybe she's working with the guild and knew what they planned."

"I highly doubt she's working with them. Not happily, anyway. She killed one of them, then ran him over with her car out of spite. That is a jilted woman if ever there was one."

"Then how did she know a spell was coming? I hadn't even known exactly what and when—only that they were preparing it."

Solas's brow furrowed. "What do you mean? You can't sense spells and hexes?"

"No. I can see their magical makeup when the weave is formed. Then I can figure out how to counteract it. She knew before it was cast."

"Directly before. There is no way she could've timed that even if she'd known what they planned. She must have sensed it."

"That is not possible."

"Isn't it? This may come as a shock to you, Emery, but just because you can't do something, doesn't mean it cannot be done."

A smile wrestled with Emery's lips. He missed having someone around to banter with. To work out problems with. It reminded him of just how alone he'd been these last few years. "If you're right, that would be an extraordinary gift. Very helpful."

"Another mage with power like yours would be a helpful ally. For either side."

Emery dragged his fingers through his hair. Solas was right. With power that mighty, Penny wouldn't get the chance to choose her fate. Someone of that caliber, once discovered, would be recruited mercilessly by the guild—hunted until they came to their senses and joined, or killed if they didn't.

The question was, had the hunting already started? Maybe Penny was loosely affiliated with the guild already, but she'd taken a liking to him earlier and decided to help him out. It would be easy for her to claim she was never here. The witnesses were gone. She'd made double sure of that when she'd run over them. She had to know he'd destroy the rest of the evidence. He was already the enemy, as everyone knew. No one would suspect the involvement of someone else.

Or did the guild not know about her yet because she hadn't properly entered the magical world? Maybe she was raised as a human, by humans, and no one had yet witnessed her extraordinary capabilities. Kids would've taunted her for being different, but without someone in the know to tell her otherwise, she wouldn't have realized just how valuable her differences were. Emery understood that because he'd lived through it. From what he'd learned, a lot of magical kids did.

He thought back to her little booth, and the way she'd reacted to his questioning. To her beautiful flushes and the fear in her eyes when she'd asked if he was magical.

A heavy weight of certainty filled his stomach.

She didn't know. She had enough power to rival Emery himself, and she didn't know.

He'd found a completely green natural.

But she was on the precipice of learning. Something had already spooked her, and she'd just killed a man. Emery didn't understand why she'd nearly run him down on her way out, only to swerve onto the mages' bodies—possibly she was a bit mad in pressurized situations—but she was standing on the edge of a very high cliff, just about to step off.

Someone would have to be there to catch her. And that someone couldn't be the Mages' Guild. If they added her to their arsenal and trained her up, they'd be unstoppable.

"Damn it," he swore. He started off toward the bodies. "Solas, calm the weather, but leave it lightly raining. This part of the world is always lightly raining."

"Is it? How dreary."

"Then you can go. I won't need an Elemental after this. Thank you for your help."

"You did not need me for this. My debt to you is unresolved."

He shook his head, wanting to be done with her. He wasn't in a position to owe and receive favors—for someone to keep tabs on him out of duty. In truth, he hadn't even needed a storm tonight. He'd done it to satisfy her obligation, to send her on her way. A clean slate.

"That you would even come into the Brink to fulfill an obligation is more than most of your people would agree to," he pushed.

"I am not *most* people—"

"Your obligation is met. We're even."

She stayed silent for a long time, studying him. Finally, she said, "If that is your wish…"

"It is."

"Then so be it." She paused in turning. "What will

you do now?"

He stopped beside the bodies, all dressed in black. "I need to search these guys for clues about the guild hideout in this area, then get rid of the bodies, take down the spell keeping the humans away…"

"What about the pretty mage?"

He bent over the first man, ignoring the squished part from the car tire. "She has been hidden this long. Hopefully she'll keep to herself for another day or two. I'll circle back around to her as soon as I can."

Solas finished her turn and tilted her head up to the sky. The sudden winds brought her words to him, amplified. "You shouldn't assume what the guild knows and what they don't. Never underestimate your enemy."

ELMER CROUCHED A little lower in the bushes, his limbs shaking. The Elemental was staring at the sky. The rain grew noticeably less intense. Not that it mattered for him. Elmer was soaked through, the cold and wet sinking down to his bones.

Fifty yards away, the natural mage dug through Jessiah's pockets before moving on to Claud. They lay there, deathly still.

There was little hope they'd survived the attack. Even if they had withstood the ferocious and incredibly powerful magic from the natural mage and his mysterious ally, they couldn't have withstood the car tires. That female natural was as powerful as she was ruthless. A force to be reckoned with.

Elmer was ever so thankful the mages had told him to stay hidden, to watch the battle and pick up a few pointers instead of getting in the way. They'd thought it a chance to further his training and education, when really, it had saved his life.

Elmer lowered the phone in his hand, gently shaking the bush as he did so.

He froze.

The natural mage straightened up, looking at something he'd pulled out of Claud's pocket. Something damaging, no doubt. Claud had been supremely confident that no one could take him down. He hadn't heeded the others' warnings to be careful. To keep information safely hidden.

The natural mage didn't notice the movement, thank the gods.

Sighing in relief, Elmer glanced at the phone screen. The license plate number had been perfectly captured by his camera. He might not have been able to help his three trainers, but he could help the guild as a whole. He could help them find the girl.

CHAPTER 11

"WHY AREN'T YOU up?"

I jumped at the sound of my mother's voice and curled tighter into a ball underneath the covers.

"Penelope Bristol, I know you're awake. Get up this instant. You're going to be late for work."

"Stop picking my lock," I said with the same petulant tone I'd used since I was a teenager. Some things couldn't be helped.

"Get up. You gave that establishment your word that you would show up five days a week. Come hell or high water, a Bristol keeps her word."

I pushed my sheets down and glared at my mother, who took up a large portion of the doorway. Pink curlers covered her head, and white...stuff covered her mustache line.

"You don't want me to learn anything about witchcraft, but you're totally fine with me being a fortune-teller? Doesn't that strike you as odd, Mother?"

"Don't you give me that sass. Get up. We both know

you're about as gifted in foresight as you are in aquatics. You know enough to keep from drowning, but you better have a floatie handy just in case."

I frowned at her. I wasn't a terrible swimmer. Though she did have a point about fortunetelling. I certainly was terrible at that.

"Still. I basically lie for a living," I said, not moving. "As my mother and the person responsible for teaching me morals, that should give you pause."

"You don't lie. You comfort people. Those are different things. Why they believe you, I have no idea, but they seem to and that's fine. Now get up." She trundled into my room like a Mack truck after a shot of nitrous.

I sat up, immediately thinking back on the night before. The stranger standing in the middle of the street, a black shadow in the low, murky light of a rainy late afternoon. His large stature and powerfully broad shoulders were a threat in themselves, but that inky globe resting between his palms had been the biggest threat of all.

"I think I might just quit that job, actually." I glanced at the window. Water sifted down, a light drizzle—not enough to keep people from visiting the medieval village. The storm had blown out as fast as it had come in. "I can probably find something that pays better. Like an office job. Or, I don't know, maybe traveling. I'd like to travel to New Orleans one day…"

She laid my robe on the bed before opening a drawer and pulling out a pair of sparkly thong panties.

"Mother!" I leapt up. "Get out of there."

"Like I haven't seen this?" She held up the underwear and raised her eyebrows. "You think I was always this old and fat, do you? Well, I wasn't. Your father used to like these little—"

"No, no, no, no, no!" I snatched the thong out of her hand. "I'll get dressed. Fine. You did your job. Get out."

"If you want to quit that job, go ahead. But you'll give your notice like a professional. You will not leave them high and dry."

"They don't even need me. They have me next to a palm reader. We do practically the same thing."

"They must think you're valuable, or you wouldn't have been granted a spot."

"They probably just needed to fill the space and I was the only one who wanted it."

"Don't be ridiculous." She opened another drawer and grabbed out a bra.

"Would you stop?" I snatched it.

She pursed her lips at me before turning for the door. "I'll call you later and check on you. Remember your lunch. You forgot it yesterday. And I'm going to pretend I didn't hear anything about New Orleans," she said as she walked out. "That place is a booze-filled insane asylum. No daughter of mine will be caught dead in a place like that." She shut my door behind her as guilt heated my face.

Miracle of miracles, she hadn't found out about New Orleans. She'd happily accepted my cover story about Oregon and hadn't bothered to look into it. It was the only bit of luck I'd ever been granted.

I sagged against my dresser, replaying the night before for the umpteenth time. And I didn't dwell on the negative parts, either. I mostly slid right past the magical deaths and the whole "running over dead men" thing. Instead, my brain kept turning over the magic I'd seen, trying to parse each spell's intention and the way it was woven together. I compared those various weaves to the one I'd seen crawling out of the cauldron, trying to determine if any of the components matched.

I headed to the shower, going over it all again. And then again, until I had all of the different strands stored in my memory. It wasn't until I was sitting in my car with my still-wet purse and packed lunch that I snapped back to reality.

What the heck was I doing?

There was no way I was going to work. The stranger clearly had no qualms about killing people, and he must've meant the thing in the street as a threat. People didn't play chicken with unhinged ladies and oncoming cars if they didn't mean some sort of harm. Had he managed to lob that spell at me, I probably wouldn't be sitting here right now. Surely he'd show up for round two.

Then again, that street had been completely bare. He'd somehow sectioned it off and cleared it out. He must've wanted to protect innocent bystanders from the magical standoff he knew was coming. Because that barrier had definitely been his magic. It was too finely done to be the others' work.

But even a compassionate outlaw wouldn't want a witness.

By that reasoning, spending all day around people would be my best bet. Certainly the safest. He'd have to go on a huge killing spree to get rid of everyone.

There was also the license plate situation. I'd driven right at him and then away from him. He'd had plenty of opportunity to burn those digits into his head. I didn't know how one went about finding the address of a car's registration, but in today's age of technology, it probably wouldn't be horribly difficult.

Yeah, work might actually be the best bet.

A hard rap sounded on the window.

I jumped and clutched the gear shift. I really needed to work on my reactions. Running someone over with a parked car was not feasible.

My mother leaned down to the window. "Get going, young lady."

"Get out of the road, Ma. You're in your bathrobe, for heaven's sake."

My mother straightened up and jammed her fists onto her hips. "I will walk out into my front yard in whatever I want. If Mr. Timmons wants to complain, he can do so to deaf ears."

Mr. Timmons would complain, all right. To his son. Who would then make sure he told me just how embarrassing my mother was. It was a regular song and dance.

"I'm going, I'm going," I said, starting the car.

"Have a great day." She stood a step farther into the street to see me off.

"Get out of the street," I yelled at her, stepping on the gas.

She stayed right where she was and waved at me, holding up a car coming down the street.

"Is it any wonder I turned out the way I did, with that woman as my genetic dispensary?" I muttered, heading toward the medieval village.

Twenty minutes later, I held my breath as I passed the scene of the magical battle the night before. I needn't have bothered. The street had returned to business as usual. The stores were open, cars were running along, and there was nary a dead body to be seen.

The stranger had done a good job of cleaning everything up. I didn't even see my tire marks burned onto the asphalt.

Then again...I didn't remember slamming on the brakes. In fact, I was pretty certain my foot hadn't left the gas, even after hopping the curb.

My eyes never stopped moving as I made my way to my station along the dirt lane. A couple of others were already setting up in their spots. They spared me a glance and a nod, but no one paid me an unusual amount of attention. Nothing peeked out of the lush foliage along the sides, and no one was lying in wait for me when I reached my destination. I let out a sigh of relief and went about setting up.

The day passed in a slow grind of anxiety and jumpiness. I stared at each new face I saw, expecting the stranger and dreading him at the same time. I looked harder at Geraldine, wanting to ask her if she'd noticed anything special about the stranger. But I didn't do it. I wasn't sure why, just that I didn't want to call attention to the situation. I'd run over someone, for goodness' sake. I didn't want to paint myself into the scene if I didn't have to.

At quitting time, I was shaking from the stress of the day, but he hadn't come. I hadn't so much as felt anyone lurking.

The rain had picked up by the time I got home, going from sifting lazily to falling with purpose. I parked next to the curb and sat for a moment, getting my bearings before going in and facing my mother. The woman was draining, at best, and I was already operating on fumes.

I really needed to move out. I was much too old to be hovered over by my parent. Heck, I'd been too old at sixteen.

Groaning, I grabbed the handle to get out. A large shape loomed in my window.

A shock of fear sizzled through my body. "No!" Reactions still terrible, I slapped the window.

A girlish scream preceded Veronica jumping back from the car. She took off, sprinting for my front door.

It wasn't like her to take off because I'd gotten a fright and slapped the window (usually she'd laugh heartily at my clumsiness), so I immediately went on red alert. I cranked the key in the ignition and clutched my gear shift. I didn't know how to fight, but I clearly knew how to run people over. If that mage had spooked my friend, I was ready with rubber and steel.

The soft patter of raindrops fell against my windshield. A woman with an umbrella passed by on the opposite sidewalk, looking between my car and Veronica on my porch, as she walked her dog. Her little mutt, wearing a bright yellow raincoat, trotted along miserably.

My chest heaved as I waited for something to happen. A zip of a spell or the roar of Death thundering toward me.

Apparently my imagination thought Death rode a Harley.

"What are you doing on my porch like a wet poodle?" I heard, a voice that would have Death turning his hog around and heading back the other way. "Penelope! Get out of that car. Are you trying to cause global warming all by yourself? Get in here. I have a roast in for dinner."

The breath exited my lungs in a whoosh. Just like that, the spell was broken. The sense of caution that had pressed on me lightened, until I was looking out at my peaceful neighborhood, no more dangerous than it had been yesterday.

I climbed from my car and was immediately pelted by cold drops. I ducked back in for my purse before locking up and jogging to the porch. My mother stood there with a scowl and fisted hands jammed into her hips, her default look. Veronica stood next to her with a confused and troubled expression.

"Did you eat your lunch?" my mother asked, not letting me by.

"Yes," I murmured.

A smile worked onto Veronica's face. She thought my mother's antics were hilarious. That was because she had normal, well-adjusted parents who didn't think their daughter should wear bubble wrap.

"Good. Now…" My mother's focus switched to something over my shoulder. Her hand darted out and grabbed me, shoving me behind her. "I'll handle this."

Fear trickled through me again as I looked around wildly. "No, Mother, we should just—" But it wasn't the stranger. It was our across-the-street neighbor, Lewis Timmons, walking out onto his porch and staring out at us. Judging by his posture and the lowering of his hairy unibrow, he was not pleased.

"What's this I hear about you sauntering through the street in your negligee?" Lewis yelled across at us.

"If you think a bathrobe and curlers count as a negligee, then your wife has been bored with you since the beginning," my mother hollered back.

"Leave Peg out of this! Jackie, you can't waltz down the middle of the street in a bathrobe and curlers like the town harlot." Lewis flung his finger through the air to punctuate his words. "There are children on this street, for goodness' sake. Is that the kind of example you want to set for them? One of loose morals and impropriety?"

My mother shifted, and I edged around her bulk just enough to see her sly smile. That meant bad things. "What kind of whorehouses are you visiting that the service providers show up in tatty bathrobes and pink curlers? I always knew you were cheap, but I didn't know you were that cheap. And don't worry about the children. I'm doing a good job teaching them not to be cowed by uptight old farts like you. It's a good lesson to learn, you mark my words."

His answer was sputtering and wild gesturing, which was how these face-offs usually ended. My mother hadn't met an argument that taboo subjects couldn't silence.

She *harrumphed* and turned toward our door. "Get inside, girls. We're letting all the heat out."

"Actually, it's Friday," Veronica said in a meek voice. Her tight curls glimmered with moisture. She held her closed umbrella by her side.

"Oh right. Yes, of course." My mother shoved her way to the door. "Stay out of trouble. And for heaven's sake, Penelope, get an umbrella!"

"Today's not a good day to scout the neighborhood," I whispered as my mother disappeared into the house.

Veronica's expression fell, and the glimmer of analysis sparked in her eyes. "What's the matter? You're jumpier than usual, which is saying something, because since you came back from—"

"What's this about being jumpy?" My mother appeared in the doorway again before thrusting an umbrella at me.

"Nothing. Ronnie just thinks I'm more jumpy than

normal since coming back from Oregon," I said quickly.

"Well, of course she is." My mother narrowed her eyes at Lewis, who was still sulking in his doorway. "Why doesn't he just get lost? I swear that man is intolerable. How a nice lady like Peg deals with him is beyond me." She shook her head and returned her attention to us. "That's why I let you go. I knew a few haunted houses would scare you straight. Ghosts are terrifying. Giving them a wide berth is the right way to play it. You don't want a demon attaching itself to you and following you around the rest of your life. Can you imagine? *Go back in your house, you grumpy old goat!*"

"Oh my God, Mom, stop yelling at the neighbors." I pushed at her. "Get inside."

"Do not take the Lord's name in vain, young lady. I raised you better than that. And don't manhandle your mother. I'm fragile."

"About as fragile as a battle-ax," I muttered.

"But if you didn't want a demon to attach itself to her," Veronica said with a furrowed brow, "why let her go see haunted houses?"

"Bah." My mother waved the thought away. "Tourist houses aren't properly haunted. No. A properly haunted house stays shut up. No one wants to wander through it. You don't make money on terror, just on fear."

Veronica stared at my mother with a tilted head and

open mouth, like she was going to argue, but the statement was too absurd for her to find an angle. "Huh," Veronica finally said.

"Here." My mother handed me a red marker before taking my purse. "Make it right."

"But…" I looked out at the wide-open space, searching for anything that could get me out there.

"Penelope." My mother leveled me with a stare. "It's necessary." She pushed me away from the door, much better at moving me than I was her, and closed it on us a moment later.

It was time for Veronica's version of the neighborhood watch.

CHAPTER 12

VERONICA OPENED HER umbrella before leading me to the sidewalk. She glanced back at the porch before murmuring, "Now can you finally finish telling me what happened in New Orleans? How much does a girl need to beg?"

I scanned the sidewalk and front yards as I opened my umbrella, knowing that with my car parked on the street, its license plate was on full display. Anyone looking for me would know I was home. Which meant it was probably wise to remove myself from the situation. Either my would-be assailant would set up to spy on me, learning my habits, before making a move, or he'd barge right into the house. If he barged into my mother's house before I got back...well, Lord help him. There were worse ways to leave Earth, but I sure couldn't think of any.

"Hello?" Veronica nudged me with her elbow. "I swear you are keeping something from me. What is it?"

I bit my lip. I'd told her about the touristy things I'd done and my chat with the old couple and their younger counterpart, but it hadn't seemed right to share any of the magical stuff. I was still processing it myself. Besides, in light of last night's forays, it was probably better if she could claim ignorance.

"Nothing. That place is creepy and fun…but creepy. It has made me see the world differently, that's all." It wasn't a complete lie. "I'm jumpier because I've been taken out of my mother's carefully constructed bubble of protection. I just have to get used to it. I'll be back to normal in no time."

"You could seriously do with busting out of that bubble, yes. Although, with a woman like your mother, I have no idea how you'll do it. You might have to run away."

Now I wasn't just biting my lip, I was chewing on it. I didn't want to tell Veronica about my tentative relocate-to-New-Orleans plan. Not yet. She'd insist on coming with me, and I couldn't let that happen. Not until I could learn to control my magic and protect myself. The last thing in the world I wanted to do was turn my best friend into a zombie or worse.

Thankfully, Veronica didn't notice my discomfort. "Okay, so what happened since I saw you last? Because a few days ago, you didn't freak out when I showed up by your door, and you certainly didn't make your car buzz with electricity. It sounded like one of those electric fences."

I frowned. "Electric fences don't buzz."

"Oh yes they do. Right before they shock you something fierce."

"Right. Well, yes, they buzz when you are dumb enough to touch them, but if you don't touch them, they don't buzz."

"They do. And your car sounded like one. How'd you do that? Does Toyota have a Batmobile upgrade or something? Because if so, I want it."

"I honestly don't know what you're talking about. I didn't hear any buzzing."

She waggled her finger at me. "You better not be holding out on me. Because that's a feature I could get behind. I wouldn't even have to lock my doors."

I smiled in gratitude. Veronica had always made light of the weird things that went on around me.

She clutched my arm. "There's one. Quick!" She dashed forward to a sagging bright pink sign taped to the light pole.

"I don't know why you hurry. They aren't going anywhere." I followed her, reading the sign. "What's the problem?"

She yanked the cap off her black pen and sliced a small mark after the word *Sunday*. Sighing, she stood back to analyze her handiwork. "It was missing a comma."

Satisfied, she clicked the cap back on and continued

walking.

This was her neighborhood watch. Fixing the grammar and spelling on homemade street signs. Being an editor of fiction, she caught every last mistake, and it annoyed her until she could make it right.

No wonder she was my friend. She was as cracked as I was.

"What was Lewis Timmons talking about?" Veronica asked as we turned the corner. "Another one! Look at that. How people make this mistake is seriously beyond me. It isn't even close! But I see it all the time." She yanked off the cap of her marker. "How do they not notice something like that? It boggles my mind."

She rushed toward the sign saying, "yard sard."

I stood behind her as she made the necessary fix, telling her about my morning. Specifically, my mother's antics—from pulling out my thong to stopping traffic to say goodbye. Veronica was guffawing by the end.

"Your mother is nuts!" She wiped away a tear. "Pure nuts. What is she even doing with herself these days? Wasn't she thinking about getting a job?"

"She has a job. Haunting the house. That's why she wasn't concerned about my bringing a ghost home. Our house is already ruled by a poltergeist. No other entity would dare invade her territory."

Veronica stopped, shaking with laughter. "It's only funny 'cause it's true."

"But anyway, I don't know what she's up to these days. I don't ask, and she doesn't volunteer."

"She's only had...what? A total of five jobs since your dad died, right? Or less?"

I shrugged, a familiar pang tweaking my heart. My father had died when I was eight, an accident at work. The feeling of loss wasn't as strong anymore, but I suspected it would never completely go away.

"About that many. I don't know." We meandered along the street, pausing once for Veronica to read over a sign. No adjustments to be made. "My dad left us plenty of money, supposedly. My mother is great at budgeting, as you've probably noticed. So she doesn't have to work. But she does get bored."

"She's not working now, though?"

"No. Yet she doesn't seem listless, so whatever hobby she's newly developed is keeping her occupied."

"Knitting?"

"She gave up knitting. Couldn't figure it out."

Veronica nodded and smiled. "That's right. She stabbed the couch with a knitting needle in frustration."

"Yes. She has some rage issues."

"We got one. Oh wow, this is a doozy!" Veronica rushed forward to a "missing" sign featuring a black-and-white cat. The woman did not pull any punches when it came to grammar.

"Why are you still living with your parents?" I

asked, digging into my pockets. "Don't you make enough to move on?"

"Yeah. But…" She shrugged as she worked. "I'm in the old part of the house and my parents largely stick to the newer addition. They leave me alone. It's like having roommates while also getting free room and board. I'm fine until you're ready."

"Until I'm ready?"

"Yeah." She straightened up and surveyed her handiwork. "You won't be able to move out of your mom's place on your own. So when you're ready, you and I can get an apartment. Rent is expensive and people are weird. We'd best stick together."

My heart swelled at the same time as a strange itch formed between my shoulder blades. A car passed, kicking up spray that didn't reach the curb. A child looked out, meeting my gaze.

I rolled my shoulders, but while the squishy feeling in my middle from Veronica's offer eased away, that weird itch grew stronger. It felt like…eyes. Like someone watching me.

I turned, surveying the area. A shape in black, like a shoulder and the side of a head, disappeared behind the corner of a house up the way. Bushes swayed from the leg that had passed them. There was no path that way, no easy way of getting around. I doubted the homeowner would've moved around the yard in the same way.

Someone was spying.

"Ronnie," I said, clutching her forearm. "Let's go."

"I just have these last two little slips to do. Honestly, are they too good for spellcheck?"

Shivers of warning replaced the itch. All I could think of was getting home. The safety of my house. But while my mother was a force all her own, I had to own that she was an older woman with nothing but a few knives and decorative swords. If that stranger did barge in, it probably wouldn't go as smoothly as my imagination would like to believe. Spikes wouldn't snap out from the walls and acid wouldn't rain from the ceiling. Even so, everything in me said to get home as quickly as possible.

"We have to go." I took two steps closer to Veronica when that itch came back. The shape hadn't reappeared, but that wasn't the direction of my third eye's warning. It was across the street, down on the left.

I squinted through the falling rain, zeroing in on a messy hedge. The twilight messed with my vision and depth perception. The jagged holes seemed like wells of darkness.

Movement caught my eye, off to the right. I snapped my head that way, but whatever had moved was now out of sight. The street was deserted except for the lurkers I could feel but not see.

"When has this street ever been dead silent?" I

asked Veronica in a weak voice.

She backed away from the sign, checking over her corrections. "It gets quiet. Everything around here gets quiet."

"In the middle of the night, sure. But it's rush hour. People should be on their way home from work."

"Huh. You're right." Veronica put a hand to a hip as she looked up and down the street. Her umbrella swayed as she moved. "That's weird. Maybe the weather is keeping people or something?"

Fear sparked deep in my gut as I remembered the deadened street from last night. The battle just about to kick off.

Again, my mother's house called to me. It might not make sense, and maybe it wasn't the best idea, but it was the only sanctuary I knew. That woman was a pain in my butt, but she always had an answer. Always.

"Let's go." I grabbed Veronica's sleeve. "Let's get out of here."

"What's the matter?" Veronica started moving, hurrying at my side. "Penelope Bristol, something has you spooked. What is it? What's been happening lately?"

"Trust me, I wish I knew." I cut through the grass at the corner, welcoming Old Man Pete to burst out of his house and yell at us to get off his lawn. At least it would be something expected and familiar.

"Speed up," I said.

"Penny, you're starting to scare me." Veronica glanced behind her, making her umbrella war with mine. "Someone is behind us."

I clutched her and spun. I could run fast, and for a long time, but Veronica couldn't. She'd never run track and had hated gym. She'd be dead in the water. I couldn't leave her behind.

I caught sight of the man immediately, a slight figure rolling toward us on a skateboard with a black hood shadowing his face. He stepped down to push his foot off the ground twice before he went back to gliding along, heading straight for us.

"Okay. Okay, think." I racked my brain for anything that might help. Snippets of that zombie spell came to mind, and I searched for a piece that I could take apart and reword. My mother's herb books flashed through my mind, and then the random volume tucked into her forgotten bookshelf. But as the figure bore down on us, nothing magical surfaced. I had no arsenal with which to protect myself.

CHAPTER 13

"WE HAVE TO fight." I grabbed the handle of my umbrella with both hands. "We can gouge him."

"Fight?" Veronica's voice trailed off in fear and confusion, but she followed my lead, clutching her own umbrella. "I should've brought the heavy-duty one," she murmured.

I grinned through the rampaging beat of my heart. Veronica was a trooper.

"Well, well, look what the cat dragged in," we heard, a high-pitched voice dripping with disdain. I recognized it immediately.

"Billy Timmons," I muttered, straightening up. He was the worst, but at least he wasn't smart enough to kill me and hide the body. I had that going for me.

He rolled to a stop and brushed back the dark hood of his jacket. His grin was smeared across his face. "I heard your mother was wandering around the neighborhood in the nude this morning." He *tsk*ed and shook his head. "When are you going to put her in the funny

138

farm? It's a shame that she's not getting the help she so desperately needs."

"She was in a robe, you nitwit," I said, turning and continuing on my way. "Get your story straight."

"Oh yeah, like that's any better. Tell me, are you still living at home because you're broke and desperate, or because your mother is?"

"You're still living at home, too," Veronica said, glancing back at him.

"I'm in school, that's why. What's your excuse?" Billy rolled beside me and shoved me out of his way.

I barreled into Veronica before I could right myself, my fear from earlier quickly turning to rage. "People who are in school for six years are called doctors. What is it you're studying?"

He smirked back at us from his lofty perch. "How to get laid. Maybe you should try it." He pushed the ground and rolled on.

"At least we have actual cars," I yelled after him.

"I hate when he does that. Gives a stupid rebuttal, then takes off so he gets the last word. I mean..." Veronica stared after him. "He's learning how to get laid? Even if that wasn't sleazy and gross, it still wouldn't make him sound cool. In six years, he still can't get a girl? His lack of success speaks for itself. But did I have a chance to sound a logical argument? No, I did not. Because off he went, a twenty-four-year-old on a freaking skateboard. How does he even have the right to taunt us? He's on a skateboard in the rain."

"We're wandering around with markers, fixing signs." I brushed the hair out of my face and glanced around us. The feeling was still there. The watchfulness. The eyes digging into my back.

Billy wasn't the source of that. The lurkers were still out there.

"There is that, yes," Veronica said, oblivious to the danger around us. "But at least we have jobs. We win, whatever way you want to slice it. I wish he'd stay still long enough for me to tell him that."

I saw my car up ahead, waiting out in front of my house, a beacon for anyone who had my license plate number. Down the street, someone was pulling into their garage, the red of their taillights washing across the cement of their driveway.

Amidst the whole sorry scene, my mother's house pulsed with a feeling of safety I'd always taken for granted.

"Come on." I tugged Veronica, getting her to move faster again.

"Penny, you are not telling me something big, and I want to know what it is. Something definitely has you spooked."

"Yes, fine, but not right now." I glanced behind us. A flicker of movement caught my eye, but I couldn't tell if it was a tree waving in the wind, or someone ducking into a yard. "Almost there."

I dragged Veronica across the street by her wrist, sighing in relief as soon as my foot landed on our property. The sense of dread that had been growing in my body muted. I looked out at the quiet neighborhood. Nothing moved.

Had it all been my imagination?

With a last glance down at our property line, I pulled Veronica up the walk and to our porch. "Just come in really quickly, okay? I want to see what my mother has to say."

"Oh, I'm coming in. I don't care if I have to choke down your mother's burned roast—I want to know what's going on."

I turned the handle and pushed, part of me terrified the door would be locked and I'd be trapped outside. After it swung open, thankfully, I dragged Veronica inside and gave her a little shove away from the door so I could shut it and lock it. As soon as it gave a satisfying click, I peered out the window. A car rolled by, the driver looking straight ahead. A light clicked on in the front room window across the street. Lewis Timmons stared over at our house for a moment before raking his gaze along the street. His curtains were pulled shut a moment later.

The breath entering my lungs felt cleansing, and I

realized I'd been holding my breath.

My mother stood over the stove in the kitchen, stirring something in a pot. She glanced up when we walked in before going back to it. "Did you fix everything?"

Veronica looked at me with her eyebrows raised. Apparently I would be spearheading this conversation with my mother. And while that had initially been the plan...now here I was. Theory was much better than reality when it came to this type of thing.

"We probably missed a couple. I thought we'd best head back." I drifted toward the counter, suddenly conscious of my awkward body posture. I had the sinking feeling of a kid who'd broken a window with a baseball.

"Oh?" My mother stirred for all she was worth, clearly making gravy. "I haven't known a little rain to distract you two from grammar-policing the neighborhood."

While my mother was a decent cook, I certainly didn't get my natural affinity for it from her. I grabbed the spoon from her and took over. "It wasn't the rain."

She pulled open the fridge and started digging through. "Do you want a salad tonight? Veronica, are you staying? What about a salad?"

"Yes, I will, and that's fine," Veronica said, her eyes still on me.

"Great. You can make it." My mother deposited a bundle of green items on the counter.

"Awesome," Veronica mumbled dryly.

My mother poured herself a glass of water before leaning against the counter, watching me work. "What happened? Was it that troublemaker Billy Timmons? Because I will march over there right now and drag that little creep out of his house by the ear. I will not abide his taunting you."

"He sucks," Veronica said, clearly still angry she'd been robbed of her comeback. "But he's not worth Lewis calling the cops on you again."

"You think they'll get anything on me? They won't. It'll be their word against ours, and you know Peg never gets involved. The police will have nothing incriminating. In the meantime, he'll get a red ear, and by George, you will get an apology. Have I ever failed to deliver?"

I took a deep breath, glancing out the large window over the sink at the darkening backyard beyond. Shadowy shapes and blotches shook and swung in the wind.

"Have I?" she pushed.

"The time you marched onto the quad at lunchtime was my favorite," Veronica said, chopping lettuce. "He was so shocked when you picked him up by the scruff of his neck and dragged him over to Penny. I died laughing." She stopped what she was doing and chuckled.

"Then you ate his sandwich!"

"Peg makes a mean sandwich." My mother nodded. "As the head of this household, it is my job to protect my daughter. And I will do so, even from little jerks like that Billy Timmons."

I slowed in my stirring, those words slamming into me. I'd heard them all my life. My father had always said he'd protect his family at all costs, and my mother had proudly taken up the mantle. I'd always figured it was just something all parents said, but now, after the last couple of days, they had a different ring to them. They merged with the feeling of safety emanating from the house, countering the threat that I might have imagined outside.

"It's not Billy," I said, lowering the heat on the stove before checking the roast. I immediately pulled it out of the oven. "It's my temperamental third eye. That, or my imagination."

"You do have a pretty extreme imagination," Veronica said, popping a square of cheese into her mouth.

"Your temperamental third eye?" My mother's gaze sharpened. Again, that was something I'd grown up with. The focused gaze she leveled at me when I said certain things. I'd always ignored it, but now...

I set the roast to rest, wondering how much to tell her. Certainly not about the New Orleans trip, but something told me I'd better spill about the stranger. At least parts of it, like his visit to my booth and seeing him standing in the street with a ball of black between his palms.

No need to mention running over the dead people—a girl had to have some secrets, after all.

Veronica would hear everything, too, of course, but I'd promised her the truth anyway. And this wouldn't be the first time she heard me talk about magic.

I opened my mouth and the words just started to spill out. When I finally finished, my mother stood at the sink with her apron stretched over her front and a frown stretched over her face. Silence filled the kitchen, only interrupted by the patter of raindrops outside.

"And you thought you saw someone around this neighborhood?" she finally said, her gaze boring into me.

I shrugged, uncomfortable. I'd hoped she would laugh this off, as she usually did when it came to my temperamental third eye. That was how it had gotten its name, after all. But this time, she was as serious as the grave.

"I thought I saw movement, or someone darting out of sight," I said. "And the street was unnaturally quiet."

"That's true." Veronica nodded as she popped another piece of cheese into her mouth. "The street was quieter than normal. Could've just been the weather."

"Did anyone see you try to gun down the man in

the street?" my mother asked. The rest of her body stayed frozen. Each word dripped with an anxiety I'd never heard from her before.

Fear unfurled in my stomach. The hair stood up along my arms. "I—I don't think so."

Her gaze stayed rooted to mine. "What aren't you telling me, Penelope Bristol?"

Veronica slowed in her chewing and turned toward me, her eyes wide.

Without meaning to, I blurted out the part about getting out of the car and seeing the men fighting each other with what I believed to be magic.

My mother's whole body sagged. Worry clouded her eyes. "Why didn't you tell me last night?"

"I...I sound crazy. It sounds crazy. And some-one...someone died. I think. Maybe a few people." I clamped my mouth shut, determined not to spill anymore.

"You went by there this morning?" she asked.

"Yes. There wasn't even a trace. But this wasn't my imagination. It sounds crazy, but it wasn't—"

Suddenly my mother was striding from the room, her back straight and fire in her eyes. "They will not take my daughter. Not while I walk this earth or beyond. I will be damned if those vultures come for my flesh and blood."

"Did she just swear?" Veronica asked with cheese

still in her mouth, the need to chew apparently forgotten. "What's happening?"

I shook my head lamely, at a complete loss.

A moment later, my mother strode back in with a worn leather book. She set it on the table with a solid thunk. "They won't be able to come in here without studying the ward first. Your father was the best around, and all these years, I've continuously fed his spell. Those goons will head back to their books, you mark my words. We have some time to figure out how to get you out, Penny. A couple days, maybe. But Veronica's house will need some protection, too. They've seen you two together. She's not safe. She could be used as bait." Her brow furrowed as she opened the book. The musty smell of old paper greeted me. The words lining the pages called to me. "I'm not a great mage, but I'm good enough to buy us some time."

CHAPTER 14

H AD SPEECH BEEN possible, I would've broken my mother's rules and let a whole bunch of four-letter words spew from my mouth. As it was, all I could do was stare. The stare of a child who'd believed one thing her whole life, only to discover her parents had believed something entirely different.

My life hadn't been a lie. It had been a series of shadows and secrets that I was only now starting to shed light on.

"I'm a little confused. Did you say mage?" Veronica asked with rapidly blinking eyes. "And why am I in danger? Who is out there, Ms. Bristol?"

"We don't have time for questions, Veronica. Grab some dinner for the road and let's go. I need to head to your house. Your parents will probably think I'm a little eccentric, but that can't be helped right now."

A little eccentric? People had thought she was crazy for years. This would dump her into the "best not to look at her directly" bucket.

"You're a mage?" I finally got out as Veronica

turned up her nose at the overly roasted pork. "Not a witch, but a mage?" I'd learned the distinction from Callie and Dizzy.

"Come on, Veronica, let's get going. We don't have much time." My mother dropped a placeholder in the book and closed it up before motioning for Veronica to get moving. "Come on, come on. Let's go."

"Wait. Mother!" I tried to block them from the doorway, but I was still mostly numb from the shock of my world being flipped upside down. Zombies were bad, but somehow this seemed infinitely worse. "Is that a book of spells? *You can do spells?*"

"Penelope, I do not have time right now to explain your father's and my reasoning for keeping this from you. Or for keeping you from this. You've found out, much later than a curious kid might've, and now we need to move forward. Move *quickly* forward, because we don't have much time. Veronica, would you come on?"

"I still don't know what's happening," Veronica said, allowing herself to be pushed out of the kitchen by my mother. "Penny?"

I didn't have any explanation to offer. I'd fallen into this life and all these terms not much more than a month ago. I'd found magic haphazardly, and gone about it the way I went about everything—crashing and burning. To now hear that all these questions could've been answered by my own mother was beyond my ability to comprehend. It seemed traitorous, somehow. She could've kept me from the zombies. And magical battles. And whatever was happening now.

By the time she returned from Veronica's house (I wasn't allowed to go), anger simmered deep in my gut.

"Why did you keep this from me?" I asked, ignoring her tight eyes and the lines of fatigue on her face. "Why have you kept me from anything—*everything*—concerning witchcraft? Kept me from learning, talking to people..."

"Because you have your daddy's gift," she said, grabbing the book on the table and then disappearing again. I longed to reach for it. To open it up and explore its pages. But the situation in the church stopped me. I didn't want to go blindly into this. I wanted to know what I was getting into. "Maybe more than your daddy's gift." She returned with a bottle of scotch that didn't look as old and dusty as it should've for someone who didn't allow drinking within her house.

She took down two glasses, dropped ice cubes into one of them, and plunked it down in front of me.

"Welcome to womanhood," she said. "We'll start by having a drink."

"I went to New Orleans," I blurted, wanting to surprise her with my own truth.

She sighed as she poured brown liquid into my

glass. "I know. You're horrible at keeping secrets. Clearly you didn't get that from me."

Here came the stare again. My mouth hung open wide enough to catch flies.

"I knew the time was coming, but I'd hoped I had a little longer." She sat down heavily, and suddenly she looked older. Beaten down. "The simple truth is, Penny, that you have a powerful gift. You have a lot of magic. I don't know how much, but more than me. You can do things even your father couldn't do, and you're not trained. But the magical entity in Seattle has grown corrupt. More corrupt than when your father was working there. Much more. His dying wish was to keep you away from them at all costs. *At all costs.*" She wiped her forehead. "I should've moved, probably. The organization isn't as far-reaching as they'd like to be. But I stayed, thinking someone would overthrow them. That they'd crumble and rebuild by the time you were ready. You're past ready, and they are worse than they've ever been. I've even heard they've participated in…" She shook her head as a disgusted look crossed her face. "We've run out of time."

I furrowed my brow, not understanding half of this. "We've run out of time for what?"

"They're lurking around the neighborhood, which means they have an interest in you. It won't take much for them to figure out who you are, who your father was, and what you might've inherited. The fact that I believe you inherited more will… Well. They can be a very charming organization. And when that fails, very hostile." Moisture glossed her eyes. "I'm not powerful enough to keep you safe, Penny. I have to send you away. Which is fine, but I don't know who to send you to. But I have a couple days. I'll find the right fit, don't you worry. Then we'll smuggle you out."

My mind was whirling. Thoughts wouldn't stick. I choked down the scotch and barely tasted the over-cooked roast. After dinner, I trudged up to my room, barely able to keep from crying. I wasn't sad or hurt, just…frustrated. I'd spent my whole life thinking I was supposed to be the same as my peers, that some quirk of fate had made me different. It turned out that I was not supposed to be the same. I was *supposed* to be different. And that difference would've been celebrated by a certain magical group.

I plopped down onto my bed, thinking things through. My mind flitted back to the mages from New Orleans, and how hard they'd tried to get me to train with them. Were they part of this organization that my mother feared? That my father wanted to keep me from?

The scene last night replayed of its own accord. The stranger demanding the name of the person who had killed his brother. No, wait. That was wrong. Who had ordered his brother killed. Those were two very different things.

Organizations ordered people killed. Mobsters and the like. Was that what I was dealing with?

And did that mean the stranger was on the right side of the divide?

But what if there were no lines at all? Just a mess of murkiness I'd never be able to navigate.

I was too gullible. Too easy to prey upon. Just look—my whole life I'd been bullied and badgered by my mother, and I hadn't rebelled or pressed for the truth. The woman swore, drank, and had powerful magical volumes hidden around the house. I'd spent years blindly following rules she didn't follow herself. Living in the dark.

I blew out a breath and pushed myself up off my bed. What better time to morosely stare at the rain? I was approaching the window, planning to stew in my sullenness for a moment, when I caught sight of a person walking down our side of the deserted sidewalk.

I dropped low, all my grievances instantly forgotten.

Peeping out of the corner of the window, a place that would be nearly out of sight from down below, I studied the passerby. The man was lean, wearing a black coat with the collar turned up. He had a bowler hat on his head and his hands in his pockets. No umbrella.

To say he stood out on this drizzly night was to say

a shark stood out in a shallow pool. This man did not belong.

I clutched the window frame. My breath came out fast and shallow.

He turned and stared at the house, his toes only a foot from our grass line. A long moment passed. Silence stretched like taffy.

He tore his hands out of his pockets and threw them forward. A flash of purple sparkled along an invisible wall on the edge of our property. The patterns and colors I'd come to expect from magic flashed into view, the weave artful and delicate, though not nearly as tightly woven as the stranger's.

A boom sounded from somewhere within the house. I jumped. A slice of yellow cut through the front yard.

"You got business with me?" My mother trudged into my line of sight. In her hands, held like she'd been born with it, was a shotgun.

"Holy crap-shack," I said, pushing forward until my forehead was pressed against the glass. "Where did she get a shotgun?"

"I have the right to shoot you. Try me!" she boomed.

The man started and jerked back.

A light clicked on across the street. Lewis must've fallen asleep in his chair. Soon he'd see the spectacle.

Then call the cops.

At least this time it wouldn't be our fault. Kinda.

"That's right. You better run. I know what you're about." My mother stalked out a little farther, staring at the retreating man in the raincoat.

I shrank back from the window so she wouldn't see me. I was supposed to be sleeping, conserving my strength. Though I clearly wasn't the one who needed it. Not that she'd let me tell her that.

Minutes passed, the curtain across the street rustled, and my mother wandered back into the house.

The street fell into an uneasy quiet.

For now.

CHAPTER 15

I BLINKED MY eyes open and slid the back of my hand across the drool lining my chin. With a start, I realized there was soft light shining through the window. I peeled my face off the window frame and adjusted my butt, still asleep, on the chair I'd dragged over to the window.

Some sentinel I was. I hadn't even properly lain down and I'd still fallen asleep.

With the pad of my finger, I wiped away the crust in the corner of my eyes and pushed closer to the window again to make sure all was clear.

A jolt coursed through me. I sucked in a breath.

On the other side of the street was a figure. His broad shoulders strained the T-shirt stretched across his torso. Tall and built, he emanated strength and power in repose as he stared up at my window.

It was him.

The stranger.

I shrank back. Had he seen me? There were no lights on behind me, and the glare of the sky should coat the glass, preventing the ability to see in. But then again, my face had nearly been pressed against it. He might've identified a cheek and some smushed lips.

Leaning closer again, I saw that he was now looking at the corner of the yard. His gaze roamed and his long arms stayed at his sides, thankfully with nothing between them.

A glance at the clock said it was five thirty in the morning. There was no telling how long he'd been standing there.

He stepped forward, into the street. Without looking left or right, he stalked across it with determination. Up on our sidewalk, he stood right in front of the house.

Then glanced up at me again.

Our gazes connected. Something inside of me did a little dance, a remembrance of the time he'd touched me and electricity shocked through my body. That had been fairly awful and painful, but this was more along the lines of pleasure.

Because I was crazy. That was the only explanation.

He spread out his hands in front of him. Rain fell, hitting a bubble around his body like it had the other night. Falling away without soaking him. It had to be some kind of magic, but I didn't see the weave. Just like I couldn't see the weave of the ward.

His fingers waggled slowly. A blast of light materialized on our property line, where I'd seen the purple wall earlier, and slapped into his palms in midair.

He stepped back and dropped his hands a bit as a little grin lit up his face.

His gaze hit mine, and though I couldn't see detail, I knew he thought I'd put up that bit of magic.

After resuming his original place, he lifted his hands once again. A moment later, strings of various colors, textures, and patterns rose from the yards next to mine and the one across the street. They rose from his boots. Twisted out from his clothes. Wafted from the sidewalk. From everywhere. They all met up at his waggling fingers, and were then directed into an extremely intricate weave.

His posture, expression, and the playful drift and dance of the magic made the process look effortless. Beautiful.

The weave plastered itself along the invisible wall my father had created before converging into a diagonal line. Cracks formed along the surface, and then the whole place lit up. What had once been invisible became a gorgeous tapestry of color.

I watched in awe as he called up another weave, this one solely from his pocket. He tapped the wall with his finger. The magic broke like shatter-proof glass, raining down in pieces.

The stranger had cracked the ward. It hadn't taken a

couple days of study. It had taken a couple hours at the most. Ten minutes at the least.

The now-familiar surge of adrenaline ran through me. Fight or flight, and closets wouldn't help me. I had to fight!

I pushed away from the window and grabbed out the scariest thing I could find: a tennis racket. "I need to try harder."

I threw open my bedroom door, going for the biggest, loudest, craziest weapon in the house.

"Mother!" Rounding the corner into the stairwell, I took the steps two at a time, missed one toward the bottom, and tumbled down the rest. After a grunt, I picked myself up off the ground and snatched up the racket again. It might not help, but we were in this together now. "Mother, it's the guy. The stranger. He just got past the first ward. Where's that shotgun?"

I found her on the couch, struggling up to sit and blinking puffy eyes. Her hand slapped down next to her. Onto the gun. "I'm awake."

"I'll get a sword."

"Get King Arthur. It handles the best."

"Who *are* you?"

"A mother that will protect her child at any cost." My mother straightened her top, paused long enough for a scary sort of determined expression to settle on her face, and started forward.

I ducked into her study, grabbed the sword off its decorative holder on the wall, and ran back out. Probably wasn't wise to run with a sword, but desperate times, as they said.

My mother threw open the front door, cocked the shotgun, and lowered the business end, leveling it no more than ten feet from the stranger's large torso. He didn't so much as flinch.

"Mrs. Bristol, right?" the stranger said in his deep, scratchy voice, his gaze roaming the side of the house.

"Mzzzz Bristol. I'm widowed, which means I don't have a man to hide behind. That makes me three times as dangerous. You are on my property. I'd suggest you get off."

His little smile was back. "Yes, ma'am. You are correct, I am on your property. This second ward is expertly done. My compliments to the chef."

"I'll call the cops. Right after I shoot you." My mother moved to get in better position, as though she'd used the gun every day of her life.

Just what hobbies had she been taking up besides knitting?

"You don't want to do that, ma'am. You've had some visitors." He spread out his fingers like he had before. "Thankfully, you had these wards up. But they would've gotten through eventually. I can see you are ready to shoot me. Please don't. My brother worked for the guild. Trusted them. Tried to change them from within. They killed him three years ago." He dropped his hands and looked straight at my mother. "The guild is my enemy. I would sooner tear them down to the ground than help them."

My mother didn't budge an inch. Then again, she didn't pull the trigger, either.

"I didn't think they knew about Penny Bristol yet. But I ran into a member of the guild hiding"—he turned and pointed at Lewis's yard—"just in that yard there. They are watching this house. I don't know how much they know, but knowing even a little is enough. Or it is with your daughter, at any rate. If they saw what I did, more of them will descend on your house. They'll drag her out by her hair if they have to."

"If they saw what you did?" my mother asked.

I grimaced. "I may have left a thing or two out of the story I told you," I murmured.

I could just see my mother thinning her lips.

Magic drifted up from the ground again, thicker streams than before, pulling from at least two dozen places within the yard.

"He's getting ready to break this second ward," I said in a strangely high-pitched squeak. "He's pulling magic from the ground right now."

The stranger's deep blue gaze snapped to mine. His eyes widened. "Even very little would be enough for them to know you're special, Penny Bristol." He sounded impressed. Even proud.

I flushed, then glowered to undermine the effect. This guy killed people. I was not about to develop a soft spot for him because of a few words of praise, however tickled I was to be noticed.

"What do you mean, pulling from the ground?" my mother said, looking at his feet.

I pointed at what I was seeing, which was notably less clear now that I'd vocally made note of it. "He's about to create the weave to break the ward."

My mother glanced back at me, her eyes as wide as the stranger's.

"What?" I asked. "I know a *little* bit of magic. From New Orleans."

"I'd like to come in, Ms. Bristol," the stranger said, his voice solemn. "You can't let them have her. I can help you protect her."

CHAPTER 16

THE BREATH CAUGHT in Emery's chest as he waited for the verdict. He'd meant to tear down both of these wards in order to show his power, then put up better ones to protect Penny and her family, but this second ward must've taken months to put into place. It had been anchored to this spot, maturing, for years. It was expertly crafted, finely woven, and stuffed with fresh power. He could force it to break, but he doubted many others could.

He'd initially thought Penny had placed these wards. They had serious power behind them. But now he was sure she hadn't. Not this one in front of him, at any rate. The magic was too old, too advanced.

He stared through the doorway at the middle-aged woman pointing the shotgun at him. Her eyes held fearlessness and determination. She would kill him without batting an eye. Penny had some solid genetics.

"You're a stranger off the street," Ms. Bristol said. "You look like a stranger that has *lived* on the street. In what world would I trust you?"

"The world in which you have no one else to trust, Ms. Bristol," Emery said. He put up his hands. Sudden movements were probably not wise. "I'm wanted as well. They've been after me since they took down my brother. An enemy of your enemy is a friend."

"They're after you, and you think that makes you a good candidate for keeping my daughter safe?"

"Listen. You know I can break in. And I know you'll kill me. So let's move this inside. Keep the gun on me if you want, but let's get out of the public eye." Emery looked behind him as a car motored by. They glanced over, their brake lights glaring in the low light of the morning, but then they kept going.

"Fine." Ms. Bristol lowered the gun. "I'll need an offering of your blood. Just a moment."

"An offering of blood?" Penny asked, stepping out of the way as her mother turned back into the house.

"This ward is to keep out magical species, except for those who give a blood offering," Emery said, his gaze on the luminous blue eyes of the woman standing across from him. Her tousled brown hair with streaks of reddish-blonde formed a halo around her head. If he hadn't seen her run over dead bodies, one of which she'd killed herself, he would think her too timid to embark on the journey he knew had just started. He'd worry that she wouldn't make it out alive, and his offer to protect would fall through.

But he had seen her in action. He had seen that incredible survival magic track a spell like a dog to a scent, and kill the perpetrator on the other end. Brutal and violent, she had greatness in her, both in battle and in magic. Hell, if she'd inherited even a tenth of her mother's fire, she'd be just fine.

"How did you find me the other night?" he asked, his voice softening, responding to her daintiness without meaning to. She didn't seem like she'd use that sword dangling from her hands. A mistake in his perception that would likely get him killed one day.

She glanced behind her, probably looking for her mother. Her feet edged toward the door. "It was on my way home."

"But the detour signs…"

She shrugged. "I was hesitating because I don't have GPS. Then I saw the magical weave, so I decided to check it out."

"You can see the actual magic in a spell?"

Her eyebrows knitted. "Yes. Why, isn't that normal?"

"For me? Yes. For most everyone else, no."

Her long black lashes fluttered as she looked skyward. "So I'll be an outcast in this too. Great."

A smile worked up his face. "At least you know another outcast, though. So that's something."

Her face flushed, followed by a hard scowl. "I suppose."

He laughed because her expressions were so odd. Her scowl deepened.

"What are you so delighted about?" Ms. Bristol said as she trudged back out with a small plate.

"Wait…is that gold?" Penny asked, inching forward to see. Ms. Bristol held it within the line of the ward, her expression hard and set. "Where have you kept all this stuff?"

Emery pulled a small knife from his back pocket and pricked his finger. He smeared red along the offering plate.

"I take it you've kept some things from your daughter." Emery sucked the rest of the blood off his finger.

"I've kept everything from my daughter for as long as I possibly could. Being that she is the least curious girl in the state of Washington, and I've tried not to leave her home alone, it was surprisingly easy. Until recently." Ms. Bristol dragged the plate through the ward.

A small spark was the only sign he'd been accepted. He put his hand out slowly and his finger passed through the plane.

"Did you put this up?" Emery asked, putting his hands where the ladies could see them and stepping toward the door.

"Her father did, many years ago," Ms. Bristol said.

"He was looking toward the future, though I don't think even he could've known how bad it would get. He moved us here without disclosing the address to the guild. Their recordkeeping was limited to handwritten files at that time. Easy to *misplace*. These days, with computerized recordkeeping, that wouldn't have been possible." Ms. Bristol stepped back and brought up the gun, the black holes in the barrels staring at his chest. "I've kept the ward active. The first ward used to be just a warning, but I amplified it last night as another line of defense. I'm not nearly as good at this type of magic as he was. My gifts lie…elsewhere."

"Wise," Emery said, almost missing Penny's mumbled "Great, more secrets." He grinned. "Direct me where you want me." He walked slowly, keeping his hands up, until he reached a plush recliner in a cozy living room. He glanced around him, taking in the large, decently furnished house. This family had money, though they didn't spend it lavishly. "Was Mr. Bristol employed in a magical field?"

"He was a top-level Sheriff, set to carry out the decree of the Regional, though that title would make a lot more sense if they had expanded like they'd planned." Ms. Bristol sat opposite Emery on the couch, the gun resting on her lap, but at such an angle that she'd still put a hole in him if she pulled the trigger. "Penny, sit farther away."

Penny, who had been lowering herself onto the other end of the couch, straightened and moved to the
recliner next to it.

Emery swallowed, the prolonged focus of the gun
starting to get to him. "He was pretty high up. If I may
ask, how did he die?"

"On the job. That's all they would tell me. I wasn't
in the guild. My craft is too lowly for the likes of them.
They don't release their secrets outside of the organization, not even about a family member's death." Ms.
Bristol's face was so hard it could cut granite. "But he'd
said things before he died. He was uneasy about some of
the laws he was told to uphold. Then he put up these
wards and told me to hide our daughter if he should die.
Hide her away and never let the guild know of her
existence. That was before the accident. He wasn't a
man to get easily riled up. He was mostly calm and
placid, like Penny. The most important thing to him
was his daughter, so I didn't hesitate. I did exactly as he
asked, but I kept an ear out for any whisperings. The
guild grew more corrupt, and I grew more watchful
over Penny."

"My brother was a Regional, trying for a promotion
to Baron," Emery said, the pang of loss cutting him.

Ms. Bristol shifted, and he could see the surprise in
her eyes. "That would've put him just a step down from
the High Chancellor, correct?" He nodded. "He must've

been powerful."

"He was a natural. As am I... As is Penny."

Ms. Bristol sucked a breath through her teeth. It didn't come back out.

"How did your brother die?" Penny asked into the sudden hush, her voice deep and soft, the pain of loss evident. "Do you know the details?"

"No. Just like you, I only know he died on the job. It's the details I intend to find out. That, and who ordered it. I know who killed my brother, and he'll see his judgment, but I want the initiator as well."

"You don't think it was the High Chancellor?" Ms. Bristol asked.

Emery shook his head, rage burning in his gut. "I've ruled him out. He wants to bring me in alive. He wants my power at his disposal, though he'd try to reset my mind through torture or shock therapy. I can only guess he would've wanted the same from my brother. No, he wouldn't have ordered my brother killed."

"So who does that leave with enough clout?" Ms. Bristol asked.

He ran his fingers through his hair. "A Baron or a Regional would've had the power to order it. And only they could've prevented an in-depth investigation afterward."

"My late husband didn't get an investigation at all," Ms. Bristol spat out. A few seconds of concentrated blinking cleared the sudden gloss over her eyes.

Emery nodded solemnly. "He is far from the only one. He had some status, but that only goes so far."

She nodded, blinking quickly again. The sudden emotion didn't show in her voice when she said, "You want to find those responsible. Fine. If I didn't have a daughter, I might've fixated on revenge too. But then what?"

"I kill them."

Her lids drooped and her eyes turned dull, indicating she'd known that, and he was wasting her time. She was a hard woman. "How will that change your future? Anyone you kill will simply be replaced with someone just as corrupt. And it will increase their motivation to bring you in."

"They'll never find me."

"And you'll never have any peace knowing that they won't stop looking."

He stared at her with an open mouth. She was right. He'd been so focused on avenging his brother that he hadn't thought much of the life beyond.

"You are shortsighted and ill-prepared. You plan to march right into the demon's nest, without an exit plan, or even a plan at all, and you think you'll somehow protect my daughter at the same time?"

Each of her words felt like a bludgeon to his head. He had no idea how she did it, but it was extremely effective.

A very hard woman. He felt a little sorry for Penny.

He tried to find a better answer than "Yes?" but failed. He half wished she'd just pull the trigger now and put him out of his misery.

She shook her head and sighed, her body bowing in the process. "I wish you well in your journey, but you're an idiot and no way will I trust you with my daughter."

Black fog drifted through the space between them, showing him what danger was to come: Ms. Bristol would put her gun aside and stand. While she showed him out of the house, Penny would stand behind her mother, her eyes pleading. Her voice mute.

The fog cleared, and the scene was as before.

He couldn't leave Penny behind. It would kill him. Or maybe kill her? He couldn't tell.

"Okay…" Ms. Bristol said, glancing at Penny. Goodbye was in her tone.

The fog rolled through again. The scene played out a second time, just as it had a moment ago. This time, a weight settled in his gut.

They'd both die. He could feel it. Penny had to go with him, or neither of them would see this through.

Ms. Bristol put her gun to the side and stood.

CHAPTER 17

"PLEASE, MS. BRISTOL, she has to go with me," the stranger said, his eyes tight. He clutched the arms of the recliner. "My chief gift is that of *sight* as it pertains to danger. Penny must go with me. It is the safest option."

"For you, or for her?" my mother said, her fists digging stubbornly into her hips.

"For both of us, but I don't know specifics. I just know what situation will cause me damage, and leaving without her will. I mean, in this case, it will cause *us* damage, obviously."

"Yes. Obviously." My mother motioned him up.

He stood and clenched his fists, his arms rippling with muscle. "You would let your daughter die from your own ignorance?"

My mother shifted and a challenge sparkled in her eyes. "*My* ignorance? You are a hotheaded young man with a vendetta against a large, corrupt organization and a half-baked plan to bullheadedly sprint at danger with nothing more than a natural gift you don't have the life experience to truly master. My husband was not as powerful as some, but with his training and experience, he often rose above his more powerful counterparts. Still they took him down. Your brother was a natural, yet they took him down. You've willfully ignored all of that, and yet you wish to challenge *my* ignorance? You would do better not to confuse ego with intelligence."

The stranger's brow furrowed, and he shook his head. "I'm missing something. The scene changes little by little, but it always ends the same. Even if I force her to come, we'll both die. If I stay here, we'll both die. There is something...missing. Something that needs to happen to change our fate..."

"If only I had a real crystal ball, huh?" I asked, the tension so high that I'd fallen out the other side and gone numb. I didn't know what the best solution was; I just wanted to get on with it. Running at danger or hiding from it both sounded just fine, if we could just keep the talk away from dead loved ones and corrupt organizations I alone knew nothing about. "Mother, you could always give tarot a try. You actually know what the cards mean."

A puzzled expression crossed the stranger's face right before his eyes brightened. "A powerful mage in the guild wouldn't normally settle for a lesser-powered mage unless she had extraordinary talents elsewhere. Is that it, then? Tarot focuses your true magic?"

"I'll have you know that I was a knockout back in the day," my mother said, straightening her back in indignation. "I didn't need power. I had sex appeal."

"No." I put up my hand. "No more of that. Move that topic along, please."

"I chose my husband, not the other way around. I could've had—"

"Stop right there," I insisted.

"—my pick. I had plenty of offers, powerful or not. A swing of the hips—"

"You're forgetting the situation."

"—brought the boys to my yard."

"Those aren't even the right lyrics." I groaned. "Ma, you have to stop."

My mother rounded on me, apparently forgetting the stranger in our midst and the fact that there was one less ward protecting us from what waited outside. "Why, because I'm old and fat, I'm not allowed to talk about my past?"

"No. Because you're my mother!"

"You aren't old and fat," the stranger said. "You look great."

My mother put up a finger. "Don't you try to flatter me, boy." She stared at the door, her brow lowered. "It's a waste of time."

"You get set up, and I'll put up another ward," the

stranger said, taking a step toward the door. "I had planned to, anyway. No time will be lost."

"Why are you so interested in hearing my premonition when you have your own?" My mother's fists were back on her hips.

"In this case, I'm open to suggestions." He walked out of the room, his step sure despite the inquisition he'd just endured.

"He believes what he says," I told my mother as she stared after him. "You can see it."

"There are two types of fools. The one who delivers the message, and the one who believes it." She stalked away, muttering to herself. I heard the word "fool" at least two more times.

My feet were carrying me after the stranger before I knew I wanted to follow him. I stopped at the front door, sweeping the street with my gaze.

He turned enough to glance over his shoulder. "I'm Emery, by the way." I nodded, but he'd already turned back and raised his hands, fingers spread. "Can you see the elements in the world around us?"

I frowned and looked at the sky, finally starting to clear after that recent rainstorm. "Like the water, you mean? Rain?"

"No, the…" He pointed at the grass. "Do you see little…tags sticking out of the world around you? The elements making themselves known to you?"

I looked where he pointed, trying to see what he meant. Carefully tended deep green blades stretched toward the well-trimmed hedges along the sides. "No."

"Hmm." Without warning, something tugged on my ribs and streams of magic rose from the ground. "Can you see it now?"

"Yes. Did you check for watchers?"

"Of course. The one I found…is out of commission. They'll think it's heart failure."

The shock that would normally run through me at such a blasé acknowledgement of death was strangely absent. That probably wasn't good.

He wiggled his fingers as the streams reached them, and an expertly woven spell came out the other side. "Do you see how I've formed the elements into a spell? Excuse me—the properties into a spell?"

"Yes," I said.

"What else do you know about what I'm doing?"

I shifted my gaze away from his fingers and let it rest on his broad back. Muscles worked under his thin T-shirt, bunching and rippling. He was thicker than fighters I'd seen on TV or YouTube, a bit bulkier. Yet he wasn't so big as a power lifter. Whatever he did in his off time was strenuous, but it required more movement than simply lifting things. Which would make sense if he was on the run.

I scanned his clothing, which was worn and dirty.

My mother had been right—he did look like he had woken up on the street that day. His blonde-brown hair, a little long and shaggy, probably looked as wild as mine did right now, but somehow it suited him. A pocket flap was upturned on his butt pocket, and a misshapen item rested against his round cheek. Maybe a grouping of items. I wondered if they pertained to magic.

"Penny?" he prompted.

I looked at the weave again, clustering into a ball in front of him. Defense pulsed from it. Protection. I got the impression of impregnable walls and iron studs.

"I know that you are doing as you said—building something that will keep this house safe." I tried to run my fingers through my hair. They tangled immediately. Which was, of course, the exact moment he turned to glance at me.

I ripped my hand away. My head jerked with the effort. A clump of hair separated from my scalp, but the rest held fast, trapping my hand.

"I didn't have time to brush it," I said with a flaming face before ripping my hand again. More hair pulled out, but my fingers came away.

His gaze landed on my hair for a moment, as if he somehow hadn't noticed my wrestling match with it, before he shifted his focus back to the spell. "Do you have any training at all?"

"No. Though…I do know how to make women into

zombies." I settled for patting my hair this time, trying to get it to flatten.

"You know how…to make women…into zombies," he said in bursts, like he was digging into a suitcase and pulling each cluster of words out at a time. "Uh-huh. And where did you learn that?"

"It was a retreat gone bad. In New Orleans. I just read the directions and the coven copied me. I mean, you know, they repeated the directions after me."

"You read…the *directions*…on how to make women…into zombies. Mhm. And the coven was okay with you joining them so that they might turn into flesh-eating creatures?"

The way he said it, blasé and light, had me shaking with silent laughter. "I'm not sure they knew what it did. I took over because it seemed out of their league."

"'They' being the witches, I presume?"

"Yes."

"And you knew what the potion did?"

"No! I would never have participated if I'd known. There wasn't a title or description or anything. But it just…called to me. I took over for the leader of the coven without meaning to. Then I just started to read it, and it felt right."

He pushed his hands out and up, and the ball of magic he'd been knitting into existence drifted into a lumpy, sloppy plane before disappearing from sight.

"How come I can't see it anymore?" I asked, taking a step forward.

He lifted his hands again, and more streams of magic rose from around him, an entirely different set than before. "The power is spread too thin. Wards aren't spells. They are called into reality the same way, but they exist in nature differently. I'll teach you more later. Now, let's get back to your slumber party with a group of zombies. I'm not quite done with my line of questioning."

I bit my lip to keep a smile away. The situation had been dark and horrible, so much more serious than what he was portraying. I felt bad for laughing.

"This coven had a leader?" he asked.

"I don't really know, but she was taking charge."

"Until you, an untrained mage who'd never worked a potion before, relieved her of her duty?"

"Yes."

"Mhm. And how did you come to be at this…retreat, did you say? Magical retreat?"

I told him about the whole sorry situation, which spilled into a story of the potion, and how I'd hidden from the zombies in the closet. By the end, he was laughing helplessly and his magical work was completely stalled. He shook his head when he was through and layered the new spell onto the ward.

"You are something, Penny Bristol. Of all the decisions a person could make in their lifetime, you make the oddest ones, and put them together even more strangely."

"Yeah. Well." I didn't really know what else to say to that. It was true, after all.

"And the other night. Why did you run over those bodies?"

I choked on my spit as he turned and strode back toward me. He stopped in front of me and looked down onto my face. Confusion seeped into his expression.

"No reason," I said, about-facing and marching into the house. "Will we be protected?"

"Your mother will, yes. Hopefully you won't be here."

"She won't let me go if she thinks I'll come to harm."

"I gathered that, yes. So let's hope she convinces herself. I think that is the missing ingredient. I *hope* that is the missing ingredient. I don't have any other ideas."

"For a so-called powerful natural mage, you certainly don't have all the answers," I teased.

"I never claimed to have all the answers. Or a well-thought-out strategy, as your mother has so kindly pointed out."

My humor dried up as I caught sight of my mother, sitting stone-faced at the dining room table, worry in her eyes. Emery's confidence and know-how made it so easy for me to forget the danger I was in. But if he and my mother were to be believed, soon things wouldn't be this quiet. Soon the guild, whoever they were, wouldn't be watching—they'd be attacking.

"Sit," my mother barked.

Both Emery and I took chairs dutifully, and I saw that his humor had dried up as well. He was deadly, knowledgeable, and powerful, but that didn't mean squat when it came to taking orders from my mother.

Her gaze fell on Emery. "I assume you know how tarot works? That you will need to focus?"

He was looking at her worn and beat-up deck, one of her very first, which she only brought out for heavy decision-making. I had seen that deck a few times, including just after my father had died. Unlike when I "read" for paying customers, she did not take these readings lightly.

"I know how it works, and I know what the cards mean," he said in a heavy voice.

"The cards don't always mean what you might imagine," she replied, her attention shifting to her deck.

Her fingers worked in practiced movements, shuffling so fast that I was amazed a card didn't break free from the pack and fly across the room. Her eyes lost focus, staring into nothingness. I'd always thought this was when the real magic started. But now, as I experienced it with new eyes, I *knew* this was when the real magic started.

Energy rose and moved through the room, hovering around us. An electrical current ran along my arms and stood small hairs on end. My stomach dropped, like the first plunge from a high rollercoaster.

A large, rough hand covered mine, and I started with the contact. Emery was staring at me, his eyes slightly rounded and his gaze deep.

"What?" I mouthed, careful not to interrupt my mother.

His little head tilt made it seem like he was asking, "What do you mean, *what?*" But whatever he saw on my face or in my eyes changed his expression to incredulous confusion, and he pulled his hand away from mine.

"The question has been asked," my mother said in a haunting, faraway voice.

She must've asked it internally, which she sometimes did. Just because she said she was going to read for you, didn't mean she planned to do a reading *of* you. I'd learned that the hard way a few times over.

She reached the card deck across the table to Emery before setting it down. Her gaze focused on him. "Cut."

He took half and placed it to the side of the deck. She took the untouched group of cards and placed it on the group Emery had set down. She was about to lay them in a pattern on the table when she paused. Her brow furrowed.

She looked at me for a moment before shifting the deck over to me. "Cut."

I stared at her for a moment. That wasn't right. One person cut.

My mother's glower kept my argument trapped within the cage of my teeth.

I followed Emery's example.

She slapped the cards down in front of her, the configuration not one you'd see in any books, just like the description of what she was looking for wasn't in any how-to blogs. If Emery was taken aback by that, it didn't show.

Silence descended, thick and syrupy. Her eyes darted from one card to the other. Back again. In zigzags and patterns that she probably couldn't have explained if she'd tried. When she was done, she leaned back in her chair, sagging heavily.

The pressure in the room popped, and with it, my ears. Expectation rose.

"You must go, Penelope," she said into the silence. "He was right. To stay would be disastrous. If you go, you at least have a slice of a chance. Any way I read it, that's the result. I would never have believed it. Had I read the cards after he'd left, it would've been too late." Her troubled, sorrowful gaze came up and hit Emery. "If you go, you must use your friends. You will know which ones when the time comes. You won't want to, but you must. It will be the difference between loss and a life fully lived. For both you and my daughter."

He stared at her for a moment, something passing between them. He nodded solemnly. "I won't let you down."

She wiped her face and gathered up her cards. "You need to put a ward on her friend Veronica's house. Mine won't hold up."

"Of course." He shifted, watching the cards go back into their deck. "The ward is still a warning, but I layered it with a spell that will make the eyes slippery. They should glide right past your house. I didn't have time to figure out how to limit that to just a magical person. I'm not even sure it can be done. But you'll have a little more protection, at any rate."

"That's not important," she said, worry etching her face and fear ringing in her tone. She didn't look at me. "My little girl is about to head into battle with no preparation or training. The last thing in the world I care about right now is myself."

CHAPTER 18

"**H**EY!"

I startled out of my light sleep. A shaggy head leaned over me, attached to a hulking body.

Terror flooded me. I flung my hands up to ward off the shape.

"No, no, no, *no*."

I knew that deep, gravelly voice, but it was too late.

A stream of white exploded from my palms. His large hands spread and blackness enveloped the white. The two turned and turned together, the solid colors creating a murky sort of smoke. Magic pulled at my middle and electricity sizzled through my bones.

"It's me, Penny. It's Emery. Pull it back. Imagine sucking in that white. Close your eyes and imagine it."

The tremors from my abrupt awakening faded and I did as he said, feeling that string on my ribs and then consciously reeling it back in.

"That's right. Good," he said, his voice strained.

I opened my eyes with his sigh. The two whirling colors were gone, but electricity still charged the air between our bodies.

"Was that me?" I asked, lowering my hands slowly. "Did I do that?"

"Yes. I'll explain later. Hurry. We're out of time." He reached out a hand to help me up.

I took it without thinking. The electricity pulsing between us soaked into the touch. A blast of fire raced up my arm and boiled through my middle. It traveled the length of my body until it bled out, into the floor. My legs and arms stung in the aftermath and our quickened breaths replaced the silence.

I could just make out his wince in the failing light of the living room. "What makes that happen?" he muttered, sounding mystified.

A charge of electricity using our bodies to find grounding seemed logical to me, whereas a white stream of light shooting out of my palms did not, but since he was supposed to be the expert, I didn't bother answering.

"What's going on?" I let him tug me off the couch and then rolled my stiff neck. "How long was I out?"

"Most of the day. Come on, we're out of time. We have to go."

"But I thought we had a couple of days." I staggered next to him, trying to get my aching body to work. I probably should've lain down on my bed, or spent time packing, or said goodbye to Veronica, but I hadn't thought I'd be out that long. His hand was back, steadying me, but the charge from a moment ago was gone.

"We should've had a couple days. They should've sent minions for at least that long. After the minions couldn't crack the ward, someone else would've come to check it out. That's when you'd get bumped up on the importance scale. At least, that's how it used to work. If anything, their organization should've become less effective, not more. I'm missing something."

We hurried into the dining room, where a cloudy crystal ball sat on the table, the white inside of it rolling lazily. My mother was sitting in the seat next to it, leaning over a metal plate filled with water.

"What the hell?" I said, stopping dead.

"Do not swear in this house, Penelope Bristol," my mother snapped, not looking up from the water-filled plate.

"Don't swear? Really? That's a real crystal ball, isn't it? Because the white part of the twenty-dollar version does not spin and whirl like that."

"Of course it is a real crystal ball. And if you'd had only *Seer* abilities, I might not have hidden all of this from you. But since you got the magical talent from your father, here we are. Don't hate the player. Hate the game."

"You are too old to use that expression, Ma," I

groused.

"I'm not too old for anything."

"Fine. You're too uncool."

She straightened from the plate and looked at Emery. "The problem is something to do with a white stream of magic. I can't tell much more. It is appearing on a small rectangle."

"Shit." Emery crossed his arms and studied the ground between his feet.

"Do not swear in this household, young man," my mother yelled, moving down a chair to sit in front of the crystal ball.

"Someone must've been there the other night." Emery scratched his head. "They must've gotten video. And since you drove through the place"—I got a cockeyed look—"it would've been easy for them to get your license plate. So here they are to investigate."

"Which means they also know you're in town, Emery," my mother said, her hands on either side of the crystal ball, her eyes closed.

"You don't even look at it?" I muttered. "Jeez. You could've given me a pointer or two. I probably looked like a dope."

"Your way sells better," my mother said, touching the sides of the glass.

"They already knew I was in town," Emery said darkly. He studied me for a moment. "They'll send everything they have. They won't take any chances with you."

I opened my mouth to ask why, but he was already striding away.

I glanced at my mother, feeling the energy of her magic once again fill the room.

My answers weren't with her. They would be filtered through Emery. My life was tied with him now. My survival with his.

My premonition from the other day zipped through my mind, and suddenly I knew what everything meant. This was the something that would happen soon and change my life forever. Emery and the guild shoving me onto another course. But the journey had already started in New Orleans, or maybe even before. And no, clearly I couldn't hide from it or turn away. All I could do now was hold on, and do everything in my power to live long enough to claim my destiny, whatever that might be.

Shivers washed over me. I hadn't inherited many *Seer* abilities, maybe, but I sure had ended up with a couple of the most irritating ones.

I rushed after Emery. "Why won't they take any chances with me?" I asked, climbing the stairs after him.

He got to the top landing and turned left, toward my bedroom. He pushed open the door, and shivers of a different nature coated me.

"What are you doing?" Silence met me as he kept moving. "And why won't you answer my damn questions?"

"Don't swear in this household," he said, and I narrowed my eyes at his teasing tone. He glanced at my bed but passed by. He finally slowed near the window. Magic rose from various places in the room. This time, I recognized the elements, as he'd called them. Some were natural things—my plant in the window, a couple of power stones on the dresser, the dirt from my shoes, something from my hamper (which made me frown and want to throw it out of the room in embarrassment). Others were from treated items, like the dresser or my cotton blanket.

I didn't recognize the properties like he seemed to, but I did recognize the patterns. The colors. The way they all wrapped around each other, some braiding, others fusing. It was complex and exciting.

"That's the spell that makes the eye slide by, right?" I asked, chewing on my lip. "Or is it the ward? But why would you do the ward in here? So the eye one is my final answer."

He shook his head. "What would it have been like to learn all this with *your* brain? How much easier would it have been?"

"Just one answer would do. Just one."

"It's the eye-sliding spell, yes. There's a name for it,

but it's Latin, and my Latin sucks."

"You know Latin?"

"A bit. As will you. And you'll probably learn it at three times the speed I did, with a pronunciation that's twice as good. That'll be a fun pill to swallow." He smeared the spell across the window before leaning in and looking down to the front yard.

"Competitive, huh?" I rushed up next to him, accidentally jamming my shoulder into his.

He bumped over. I bounced off, grabbed the chair to steady myself, and brought it crashing to the ground with me.

"At least I'm not clumsy. I have that going for me," he said, not glancing over at me sprawled out on the ground. He also didn't bother helping me up. Somehow, it was less embarrassing that way.

I climbed to my feet and shoved in close, trying not to notice the huge size difference between our arms. I really needed to lay off the TV time.

"Won't they have seen you put that spell up?" I whispered.

"I've only known three naturals. Four, now. Three of those four could see the magic creating a spell with their bare eyes. You are one of those three. As far as I know, no other mages have that ability. Certainly no witches. And you're the first person I've met who can feel the magical intent of a spell. Your parents seem to have created a superhero, then hidden her away from the world. It's a tragedy and a blessing at the same time, given the organization on your doorstep."

"Right," I said. I didn't know what else to say in response to his babbling.

A woman stood on the sidewalk off to the right, at the corner of our house. She had her hands in a satchel resting on her hip. Two men stood across the street, side by side, each with satchels, similar to what I'd seen in the church in New Orleans. The one on the left, a grizzled older guy with straggly white hair and a lean body, had his arms crossed in front of his chest. The stocky middle-aged man next to him was talking and pointing in turns.

Lewis stood at his window behind them, his scowl apparent even from the distance. He'd blame my mother for all this, I had no doubt.

"If you did the eye-sliding spell, why are they still looking at the house?" I asked, watching the woman take out a couple of green items from her satchel. She set them at her feet.

"They have the address, and your neighbors' houses are all numbered. Their eyes might try to find somewhere else to go, but their brains won't be so easily fooled. They'll know what spell has been used."

I nodded, because that made perfect sense. The effect probably annoyed Lewis to no end, since one of his favorite pastimes was glaring at our house.

The woman at the corner took out a few more items. "What is she going to do, create a veggie bomb?" I mumbled. "Look at all the stuff she's piling up."

Chuckles shook Emery's body. "Your naivety is cute."

That was all well and good, but it didn't answer the question.

The woman crushed leaves of some kind before pouring some sort of powder into her palm. She added something green, then straightened.

"That mixture won't tell her squat," Emery mumbled, pushing away from the window. I followed him as he trekked through the house and into my mother's room. He applied the spell from before to the window, letting me memorize a few components of it, before leaning out to look down at the backyard. "There's another one out there. They want this cracked quickly. They know you're trying to hide from them by now. And because of the ward and spell, they know I'm helping."

He turned and looked down at me, and I noticed for the first time the blaze of color within his eyes. They weren't just blue, as I had previously thought. A ring of gold circled his pupils, and from that, light blue streaked and webbed over darker blue, almost like magic itself. The colors deepened to a smoky blue toward the outside.

"You've been dragged into this, Penny Bristol," he said, his voice deep and urgent. "It isn't fair that my fight has suddenly become yours. I realize that. I also realize you know nothing of the magical life. All of this will be new. It's going to be an incredible shock. An incredible, dangerous shock. But neither one of us has a choice. Your magic is both a blessing and a curse, as I said. And you're about to see why, firsthand. But at the end of it all, please know that you can trust me. If everything else falls down around us, you can always trust me. I will never sell you out. I will never turn on you. Never."

Fierce determination rang through his voice. His eyes bored into mine.

"I will tell you as much as I can," he continued, "and explain along the way when I'm able, but when things get hairy, I'll do what needs to be done to protect you. I won't ask. I'll react. That is where the trust will come in. Can you live with that?"

Tingles drifted down over my body. "I have no idea," I blurted. "I'm never really in control during highly pressurized situations. There's no telling what I might do."

A smile tugged at his lips. "Then be smart regarding who you run over with your car."

CHAPTER 19

I TOOK TWO deep breaths and felt Emery's rough hand take mine. He was clearly a hand holder.

We stood facing the front door with my mother and her shotgun at our backs. I'd had enough time for a hasty goodbye before she turned me toward the door. Outside, the two men and the woman were still there, one trying to figure out Emery's ward while the others looked on. The plan was to run out to the car and get out of here without dying.

It was not a very complex plan.

"What do you wash your hands with, sandpaper?" I muttered, my face flaming, though I had no idea why.

"No. Dragon's hide." He put his other palm against the door and lowered his head. I had no idea what he was doing, but I did know my heart was hammering and adrenaline was pumping through my blood. I was a little worried at my unpredictability in stressful situations. We were about to rush out of the door. Anything might happen, and it was likely I'd be the cause.

I tried to ignore him, but the bait was too tempting.

"Do dragons really exist, or are you kidding?"

"I don't know, but someday I'll get down to the underworld to see for myself if the rumors are true."

"Oh super, there's an underworld." I unstuck the hair from my damp face. "That's not terrifying or anything."

"Here we go." Emery ripped open the door and yanked me out behind him.

"I can walk on my own," I muttered, staggering after him.

Magic rose all around us as my heart thundered in my ears. We were still within the protection of the wards, but not for much longer.

"Remember, this is all about your will," Emery yelled, his free hand extended, the fingers moving quickly.

I catalogued all the colors and patterns, the mixtures of them, and compared them with my tiny database of knowledge. I thought about the men on the other side of the street flying away. I *willed* them to roll end over end up the street and give us a second to escape.

They cocked their heads, as if listening for something.

"I think there's more to it than will," I said, yanking my hand out of his iron-clad grip. "Let me go. I'm faster on my own."

We sprinted across the grass and burst through the

ward. Emery swung his hands forward and a concussion of light and sound blasted out, smacking those across the street before they could even raise their hands to defend themselves. They fell backward and tumbled, and I tried to log that into my memory bank, because it was similar to what I'd tried to do with just my mind and naivety.

Magic continued to rise all around us. Emery turned and flung out a hand, sending a streaming jet down the sidewalk. It separated and rounded, turning into a ball and rolling just off the ground.

The woman started and dug in her satchel. She only had time to throw up a handful of orange dust before Emery's magic was upon her.

I tore my gaze away and ran around the car, yanking open the door before sliding into the seat. A shotgun blast made me jump.

"This has nothing to do with you, Lewis, move on!" my mother yelled before opening the back passenger door.

"Did you shoot someone?" I asked, jamming the key into the ignition.

"No. I scared that busybody Lewis back into his house." She shut the door behind her.

"Wait, what are you doing? You're not coming with us!"

Emery flung another hand, directing the magic, before throwing himself into the passenger's seat and slamming the door. "Let's go. Hurry."

"Of course I'm coming with you!" My mother reached up and motioned me on. "Hurry up. There were more out the back."

"But you weren't supposed to come—" Someone ran out from the neighbor's yard, dressed in black. He had something in his hands.

"Go, go, *go*!" Emery pounded on the dash.

I threw the car in gear and slammed on the gas. We shot forward.

The mage's long legs and arms pumped. He raced us to the center of the street.

"You will *lose*, son," I hollered like a madwoman.

"I knew there was some of me in you somewhere," my mother yelled. She leaned forward between the seats.

"Put on your seatbelt, Mother."

"And quite a lot of your father."

Emery grabbed my arm, and a surge of electricity shot up through me and over to him. He reached the other hand out through the window and hit it against the door. My car buzzed, and I remembered what Veronica had said yesterday.

Maybe I had supercharged the car. I just wished I knew how, but this wasn't any time to ask.

The mage in front of us braced. Magic budded in

his hands. A wave of spicy violence rushed toward me.

I cranked the wheel to the right, then zigzagged back to the left. I knew that spell would come right at us, and I didn't want to be an easy target as well as a large one.

We bore down on the mage. He hastened to the right. Suddenly it wasn't enough for us to get away. I didn't want *him* to get away.

I cranked the wheel after him. The violent intent blistered. The spell was about to be released.

My front bumper barely clipped him, but it was enough. A blast of energy flung him back, the sound like a fly hitting a bug zapper. We zoomed down the street, leaving him rolling in our wake. Another mage joined the first on the street, a phone to her ear.

I turned the corner. Tires screeched from behind. I glanced in the rearview mirror to find a black car gaining on us.

"That is probably for us," I said, taking another corner at a breakneck speed.

Emery turned in his seat, looking out the back window. He glanced around him, a knot forming in his brow. "I don't have enough elements in this car to take out an object that large."

"I got this." My mother labored to move her girth over in the seat behind me. She rolled down the window. "Get us to Green Street, then slow down a little. I'll take care of it."

"Mother…" I gritted my teeth. I couldn't very well tell her not to shoot people out of the window. What other option did we have? But I really wanted to, because people her age shouldn't be in car chases and shootouts. It just wasn't normal.

Then again, what in my life was?

"Here—turn right here, Penny!" She stuck her hand up between the seats and jabbed a finger.

"It would be faster if I took the next block," I said.

"Listen to you mother. Turn *here*."

My tires screamed around the next turn. Trees flashed by. Someone honked.

Emery's gaze beat into the side of my head. I made the next turn, his steady focus starting to distract me.

"What?" I asked.

"I'm trying to think of a way to use your power. If we merged our survival magic, we might be able to…do something."

"That kind of merge is only possible if you become dual-mages." My mother rolled down the window. "And there is no way I am letting my daughter tie herself to a scruffy derelict with no future plans and no income. Don't get me wrong, you're a lovely boy, just as long as you marry someone else's daughter. No offense. Penny, in two miles, you can start to slow down."

Emery frowned back at her. "A little late on the no

offense," he muttered.

"Okay, Mother, please don't... I don't know. Just don't..." I couldn't think of a good warning that would in any way matter.

"That's the thing with advanced mages," my mother roared over the rushing wind whipping our hair. "They think with their magic or their genitalia, not with reality. Guns trump magic every time."

I could see her struggling with the gun in the rear-view mirror. She moved it around her bust before shifting. I let off the gas and swerved a little, hopefully giving our pursuers the impression I was afraid of taking the slightly windy road at high speed. The black car shot forward, pulling up beside me in a moment.

I felt a pump of power and intent. *Mine.*

"A spell is coming," I yelled back at my mother. "Hurry."

"Are they trying to kill or capture?" Emery asked over the cacophony of air and cars.

"I'd bet capture. They want us."

"That's someone higher up. Kill them if you can."

"I don't have the right gun for that." My mom pumped the gun and pushed it out of the window. The black car swerved, the reaction of the surprised driver. He didn't get a chance to slow down before the boom of the gun discharging.

I winced at the shock of the noise. A tire popped

and the remaining tires squealed. The car careened and the front corner of the bumper knocked my rear fender.

My back end tried to fishtail. I cranked the wheel and let off the gas, eyeing the approaching curve of the road. The tires caught as the other car broke free and kept turning, the front wheel ruined. Sparks flew up from metal on road. The car hit a small dirt berm, jumped up, and rammed into a tree.

I ripped my eyes back to the road, coaxing my car straight in time to safely make the curve.

"I wish I could take these things off," my mother said, I assumed about her breasts, as she wrestled the gun around her bust again. It wouldn't be the first time she made a comment like that. She bent the gun and pulled out an empty shotgun shell from one of the two barrels. "Ow! Dang it. That was hot." She threaded another shell into its slot.

I ripped my eyes back to the road a second time.

"Two months ago, I was wondering if there was something else out there. Now I'm hoping there isn't." I took a deep breath.

"We don't get to choose what we're given, but we do get to choose what we make of it," my mother said, clicking the gun back into place and looking behind her.

"You got to choose what I was given. Bad choice." I wiped the back of my forearm against my wet forehead. "Very bad choice. Daddy should've made you use your crystal ball."

"I did. If you had learned your trade since childhood, you would've easily broken through all the wards set up around the house, gotten into the secret room, and rooted through your daddy's books. Then you would've created havoc, since you have a gift for creating havoc, and everyone would've known what you were before you hit eighteen. It has been a month since you started researching this side of your life. And look where we are." My mother leaned forward, pushing at my seat. "One month." She leaned back. "At least now you're old enough to run over people. Think about your ability for defense at ten. Or twelve."

"I hate to agree with her, since she doesn't need any help dominating an argument, but I have to," Emery said quietly. "Yours was a precarious situation. My brother and I were trained. We were guided along a certain path. The second we veered from that path, we were targeted. Look at my life now. You're better off, Penny Bristol, trust me."

"There you go. Do you see?" My mother patted Emery on the shoulder. "This is why I told you to stay away from my daughter."

A laugh rode a surprised breath, and Emery turned to glance behind him. When he turned back to me, a full smile took up his face, and all the planes and angles softened. Sometimes his high, sharp cheekbones and narrow nose looked almost too severe to be handsome, but now, with that boyish smile and the delighted sparkle in his eyes, he was breathtaking.

"She is a trip," he said, shifting in his seat to get comfortable.

That was putting it mildly.

"Did the cards say you were supposed to come with us?" I asked my mother, still out of breath. I took my foot off the gas, slowing way down. The last thing I needed was to get pulled over by the cops after hitting someone with my car—for the second time—especially since my mother, who still wasn't wearing a seatbelt, had a loaded shotgun across her lap.

"No. They said we needed to split ways, but they didn't say when. You didn't really think I was going to stay in that house with the guild's higher-ups roaming around, did you?" My mother shook her head. "Madness. You'd better wise up if you hope to stay alive, Penny."

"Okay, but…why did we take my car, then?" I asked, looking at her in the rearview mirror. "Yours is bigger. Not to mention nicer. And it goes faster."

She huffed. "It also costs more to fix."

Emery glanced over at me with a grin before looking out the window. "I have a place we can stay in Seattle. It's small. It'll be tight quarters, but we should be okay for a few days."

"Count me out." My mother put the shotgun at her feet. "Drop me off at Merna's house. I'll stay with her until things cool off."

My stomach clenched with anxiety. Parting with my mother would ease my stress in a million ways. But I couldn't deny her value. She was cunning enough to keep an enormous secret from me for my whole life. Loyal to a fault, handy in a tight spot, and totally fine with shooting people. All those qualities would un-doubtedly be useful in the days, weeks, or months to come.

Then again...she was my mother. What a trial it would be to live in a tight space with her.

WHEN WE ALL stepped out of the car in front of Merna's house, my mother slapped her hands onto Emery's shoulders and gave him a hard stare. "She is my every-thing. I do not want to let her go with you alone, but I have no choice. This is the most logical place for us to split."

His brow furrowed. "I'm not getting a warning. This parting is not a dangerous thing."

The movement was slight, but it was there. The tiny sag of her spine. The increased lines around her eyes. Her jaw tightened, and she nodded. "Please bring her back to me."

"I will, ma'am."

She patted his shoulder. "And clean yourself up. You're a mess."

I got a tight hug, another tight hug, and then she batted her tear away. "Penelope, you are as easygoing as your father, which can be a wonderful thing. But not when you are defending yourself. In those times, you need to be more like me. You need to go at the enemy with everything you have. Fight with tooth and nail. Have no fear of tearing down the world around you so that you can get away. Do you understand me?"

I understood her words just fine, but the crazed light in her eyes was another matter. Caregiver clearly wasn't the role she was born to play. She'd probably come out of the womb with armor and that shotgun. "Yes, Mother," I said dutifully.

She frowned at me. "Stay alive by any means possible, do you understand me?"

"Yes, Mother."

"I'll scribe every night. I'll use my magic every day. I'll try to know when you need help, but use that phone of yours. Call me if something goes wrong and you can't see a way out of it."

"Okay."

After another tight hug, then she was back with Emery. "She is too easygoing for her own good, and you are too wild. Work on the balance between you two. My late husband always said, 'The best magic in the world exists in a perfect balance.'"

"Yes, ma'am. I know something of that."

She narrowed her eyes. "But don't try to merge, mind. Otherwise you'll have me to deal with. And trust me, what you've seen so far is tame compared to what I'm capable of."

"Mother, would you stop?" I tugged at Emery's arm in embarrassment. Without him, we would've been in deep water. He didn't need constant berating about something that surely wouldn't be an issue. I had power, sure, but I didn't have any know-how. Merging with me would just weigh him down.

"Yes, ma'am," he said, his expression solemn.

I rolled my eyes. "If we're going to go, we should go." I tugged at him again. The man was a stack of bricks. He didn't move.

"Wait right there. I'll talk Merna out of her commuter car. That'll give you twenty-four hours."

"Why twenty-four hours?" I asked.

My mother looked at me like I was thick in the head. "We can't wait any longer than that to call it in as stolen or the cops will get suspicious."

Emery nodded like that made sense.

Even with this crew, I was the odd one out, and for once, I was okay with that. Sanity was a good thing.

CHAPTER 20

EMERY TURNED OFF the beat-up old Honda and sat for a moment, staring out at the darkening evening. Parked cars lined the busy Seattle street. People ambled by in light jackets and pulled-up hoods.

I clasped my hands in my lap, giving him a moment to collect his thoughts. His ego had taken a pretty solid beating after a day with my mother. She could bowl over the strongest of people.

"What do you know about the magical world?" he finally asked.

"I know that there are shifters, vampires, witches, mages, and a guy named Vlad. Also that there are two sets of rules: one set for humans, which I know really well, and another set for magical people, which I don't know at all, but it definitely seems killing people doesn't hold the same weight."

"You forgot zombies on your list," he said, his lips curling upward. He wiped his hand over his mouth, as though he hadn't wanted to smile.

"Right. Yes. That probably should've been first on

my list."

His expression returned to stoic and he looked at me, his gaze deep and probing. "In a nutshell, there are a few worlds. The human world, which you know, the underworld, which you'll probably never visit—"

"Even if I die?"

"The underworld isn't hell. Hell is where a person lives when they lose everything. I'm going to make sure you never spend time there. The underworld is full of demons, gargoyles, and trolls, and Lucifer rules them."

"Ah." I nodded like I heard things like that every day.

"Mages primarily live in this world, which magical people call the Brink. I suspect that is because they are humans with magic, instead of magical creatures. They feel the most at home here."

"You live in the Brink, then?"

A troubled look crossed his face. "I have no home. The Brink isn't safe for me for too long, and I'm supposed to be banned from the Realm, which is the magical world that you will probably visit someday. It's run by the elves without a sense of humor, hence my banishment out of a harmless practical joke, and populated with all manner of magical folk, many of which can't live in the Brink because they'd stand out. I'm a gypsy, for the most part, moving from one place to the next."

The loud buzzing in my head from all this new information dimmed and sadness for his situation took root inside of me. Losing his brother must've turned his life upside down. It reminded me of how it had felt to lose my dad. Except my mother, who was as tough and steadfast as a rock, had been there to shield me from the storm. And after the last twenty-four hours, I knew just how dangerous and wild that storm really was. That he had been plunged into it alone broke my heart.

Knowing that he was a hand holder, I reached out, feeling a surge through my middle when he curled his fingers around mine. A thankful smile ghosted his lips.

"Anyway, long story short"—his seriousness came back too quickly—"here's what you need to know. An organized pack of shifters police the Brink on behalf of the Realm. They ensure magical people follow the rules, which are in place so that the humans don't know we exist."

"Because humans are crazy when it comes to anything different than themselves?"

"Yes. Right now, they have each other to bomb. Magical people don't want to help them band together and focus on us."

Something occurred to me. "Didn't you break the rules running out of my house?"

"Yes. I've broken lots of rules lately."

"Are the shifters after you?"

Wariness crossed his face. "The Mages' Guild breaks the rules often, but it's too powerful for the shifters to take down. The shifters don't have much of a choice but to steer clear. There's no lost love there, so they might just ignore me. On the flip side, since the guild is against me, the shifters might take that as a green light to come after me. And you."

The buzzing had taken over again. "Uh-huh," I said, as though I was following along just fine. It would be quicker in the long run.

"Shifters are prevalent in this world. So are their nemeses, vampires."

"Wait." I held up a finger. It didn't help focus my thoughts. "I thought the guild was the shifters' nemesis."

"No. The guild is an entity that has gotten out of hand in this part of the world, and the shifters can't scale it back. That's professional aggravation. When it comes to the vampires, for some reason, it's personal."

"Why?"

"I have no idea," he said, which was not at all helpful. "It might be because vampires turn humans into the undead, thereby increasing their numbers. The shifters have to breed more shifters. That's just a guess. I've never asked—I have my own problems; I don't want to dabble in theirs."

"But...you can magically make shifters. At that retreat—"

"When you turned witches into zombies," he said in a teasing tone.

"Right." I drew the word out. He was getting too much enjoyment out of that. "At that retreat, they also made a werewolf. The mage said the werewolf was out terrorizing a nearby city and it wasn't his problem."

Chuckles shook Emery's body. "That sounds like my kind of mage. But magically made werewolves are not the same as shifters."

I knew I was making a funny face while I tried to process that, but I couldn't help it. Those words made no sense to me. "Uh-huh."

"So it's best not to talk to vampires about shifters, and vice versa," he said, and I hoped that was him finishing his hole-ridden lecture.

"Okay. No problem."

"And don't talk about the Mages' Guild to anyone."

"Got it." I nodded dutifully.

"Oh, and a group of magical people, secretly affiliated with the human authorities, also police the Brink. They tend to take magical crimes the human police stumble upon. But since they're also wary of the guild, I don't suspect we'll need to worry about them."

"But…" I struggled through a sudden bout of information-induced dizziness. "I thought the shifters policed the Earth—I mean, the Brink."

"They do. But they tend to spend their time chasing vampires, and the Magical Law Enforcement Office mostly ignores the vampires and focuses more on human laws broken by magical people. So even though it seems like there is double policing, there's more than enough wrongdoing for both factions."

I stared at him with a frozen smile. My brain had shut off at this point. Learning that the creatures of myth were real and wandering around my world was one thing. Learning there were a couple of entirely different worlds somehow attached to my own was another thing. But then adding bureaucracy and interspecies drama on top of all that?

No.

Just no.

I didn't have the brain capacity for that much *what in the freaking hell*? Not all at once.

"Don't worry," he said softly, his gaze roaming my face. He squeezed my hand. "Since the guild is so heavily involved, no one's likely to touch us with a ten-foot pole. Most likely, we only have one enemy, not three."

I nodded, but the words "most likely" stuck with me.

"Okay." He winked at me, which was incredibly sexy for some reason, before taking back his hand and getting out of the car.

"Okay, pep talk done—on with more scary stuff. Got it," I mumbled as I followed suit. He met me on the sidewalk next to the passenger door. "What's the plan?"

He jerked his head to the right and starting walking. I fell in beside him and startled when he took my hand again.

"You're kind of a touchy-feely guy, huh?" I said quietly, spying a couple ambling toward us down the sidewalk. They were chatting amicably, their focus on each other.

"I've come to realize that your reactions can't be anticipated. If something jumps out at us, I want to keep you by my side. I also want one hand captured so you can't blast me with your survival magic."

I'd misread the touching. That made me feel a little awkward about grabbing his hand in the car. "The white stuff is survival magic? *My* survival magic?"

He choked out a laugh. "I wouldn't go around talking about 'white stuff,' but yes."

"Oh right, because of the rule on not talking about magic." I glanced around to make sure no one had overheard.

He gave me a funny look, then shook his head and looked away.

"I visited the office in Duval where Nicholas once worked before he was promoted," he said, studying the faces of the couple passing us.

"Who is Nicolas?"

"The man who killed my brother."

I swallowed, not knowing what to say.

"I went through the files there. I didn't find much of note, except for one correspondence from the Baron's office to a known assassin." The significance was somewhat lost on me, which he must have noticed, because he added, "There are three Barons, directly under the High Chancellor. The guild operates by the chain of command, so a Baron would give his directives to the Regional, who would give them to the Sheriff to put into place. That a Baron would communicate directly with someone below even the Sheriff's position speaks volumes."

"What did the letter say?"

We slowed as we neared a bar with its door standing open. Noise and music tumbled out and into the street. Laughter preceded a woman exiting, tugging out a man after her. They turned the opposite way, chattering loudly between them.

"I don't know. I don't speak Italian. I need to find someone who does." He glanced behind us before switching the hand holding mine. He dropped the newly freed hand to the swell of my hip, coaxing me forward. "After you."

I wasn't *that* unpredictable.

But then I remembered what he knew of me, which

included my shotgun-wielding mother. I immediately rethought my indignation.

The dimly lit bar looked bare as I walked in. Tables hugged the wall on my right, and there was a small throughway between those and the square bar lined with stools. At the end of the bar, a larger area opened up to the left.

Loud talking and laughter rolled over the counter, and I realized the crowd was in that space near the back, mostly obscured by the bar itself and sheltered from the doorway. My feet stuck to the floor and a pungent aroma of sick wafted toward me.

I wrinkled my nose. "Your Italian-speaking friend hangs out in here?" I asked.

"No." He let go of my hand but not my hip and steered me down the bar, not crossing over to where the crowd roared and gabbed, clearly stuffed full to bursting with alcohol.

A stocky man made of muscle came around the corner. An expression of shock and delight crossed his face before he looked back over his shoulder. He knew Emery, and that over-the-shoulder glance indicated he also knew about his precarious situation. That spoke of friendship.

When the man's gaze drifted to me, his expression turned troubled.

"Joe," Emery said, his eyes sparkling a little, but the

sentiment not enough to bring out a smile. "How goes it?"

"Hey, brother. Long time." Joe reached a hand over the bar and Emery took it, the two men making large hands look totally normal. "What brings you?"

The sparkle left Emery's eyes. "I'm here for a favor. I was wondering if that room over the bar is still free?"

"The stockroom, yeah." Joe glanced at me. "It's the same as it was, except for a few more boxes. There isn't much space."

Emery leaned against the bar and brought me in closer, blocking off my view of the door. "It'll only be for one day, two tops. We need to lie low, and she..." His words faltered and he looked down at me, a mixture of emotion soaking his gaze: pain, embarrassment, and something else I couldn't identify warred with loss.

"And she's not accustomed to sleeping in the park, huh?" A grin spread across Joe's wide face.

Emery looked away. "We'll set it up like last time."

Joe waved the sentiment away, whatever it was. "It's fine. I didn't fix the door after last time. It's still busted. Everyone knows not to mess with my bar." His voice had turned deep and rumbly, almost like an animal growl. Despite my confusion over what they were talking about, my small hairs stood on end and a strange surge of electricity and adrenaline rushed through my body.

Emery's gaze snapped down toward me and he moved his hand from my hip to my wrist. The low hum of electricity vibrated between us.

"Keep the animal at bay around her, bro," Emery said through gritted teeth, his grip tight around my wrist. "Deep breaths, Pe—Little Killer. Try to calm down. Don't think of defending yourself. Think of…unicorns or something."

I spat out a laugh, then wiped my hand across the bar in embarrassment. A sheen of white followed my palm, cracking the wood and infusing me with a lovely, earthy feeling that sang in my bones.

The electricity sizzled between Emery and me before some of it spread across my skin. Small prickles of pain brought a strange awareness. I fluttered my eyes as other feelings bumped against me. The chemicals in the lacquer covering the bar. The leather of the stools. The cotton of my shirt. Most importantly, the thick, heavy feeling of the energy all around us, providing the fuel for me to curl some of those ingredients into a marvelous concoction.

But what would I make?

"Just let it simmer," Emery whispered urgently, his breath against my cheek. "Let that feeling simmer. We're almost out of here, and then we'll deal with it. Can you wait?"

CHAPTER 21

"P ROBABLY," I SAID. "Unless someone comes to rob the bar or something, in which case...there's really no telling what'll happen."

Joe was staring at me with a stone face and hard eyes.

"Sorry about the—" I gestured at the bar. Emery snatched my hand out of the air and pulled it toward the other, which he still held. Magic pulled at my center, the string on my ribs taut and painful. Sparks of colors bloomed where our hands touched.

I stared down at it, transfixed, feeling the surge of my heart. The surge of his. All in tune with the natural elements pulsing around us.

"Like I said, we need to lie low," Emery said in a tight voice. "I can't have anyone knowing I'm here. We're here."

Joe shifted and leaned heavily on the bar, facing the doorway. "The guild knows you're in town. Which means everyone else knows you're in town. They know we're friends from the old days. A few of your old gir—"

He cut off and glanced at me. "A few of your old *friends* told me to tell you to call them if I saw you. I suspect"—I got another glance—"you won't be wanting to."

"That's got nothing to do with me," I said, trying to throw up my hands. How quickly I'd forgotten the reason they were being held in the first place.

Emery tightened his grip as colors, light, patterns, and texture flowered over our touch and drifted up our arms. It was unlike any of the magic I'd seen before. More nuanced even than Emery's. More beautiful.

I watched in fascination, tickled where the wisps and strands touched me. A smile spread over my lips, and this time, when I looked up to Emery, he was staring back at me, a dark shadow across his beautiful blue eyes.

"Talk about buzzkill," I muttered, returning my gaze to the dancing and curling magic.

"I can feel that," Joe said. "You had better do something to hide it, or just walking down the street will get you found out."

"I know," Emery said. "What did you hear?" One by one, the muscles along his sizable frame flexed. In contrast, I was as loose as I'd ever felt, relaxed and open to my surroundings, feeling a strange but delightful magical tune whisper to me, soft and sweet.

"You mean, aside from guild members torturing someone who tried to get out? They're getting bad, man." Joe shook his head and shifted uncomfortably. "But as it pertains to you, that you took out three middle-tier mages that were working together," Joe said. He took a step back and a sheen of moisture covered his eyes, like he was about to start crying. "That your magic is ten times mightier than when you lived in town, which seems about right, judging by the really harsh sting I'm feeling right now. And that something went down at a remote guild office somewhere in the burbs, but the guild is being quiet about it."

"I found the office and broke in. I didn't kill anyone. You know me. I don't want to take down any innocents."

Joe snickered, but there was no humor in it. "Innocence in the Mages' Guild—yeah, sure."

"Are Roger's people looking for me?" Emery asked.

"No. You're clear there." Joe paused, catching the sound of a scuffed shoe near the doorway. I tried to lean back and see, but Emery shifted and blocked my view. A moment later, a burly guy with long arms held a little away from his muscular body, perhaps out of necessity, crossed to the other side of the bar. His gaze was on Joe, his pompous strut ridiculous.

"It's like a muscle convention," I said. "And he thinks he's the big-ticket item."

"Bear shifters." Joe crossed his arms. "They cause the most bar fights out of anyone."

I widened my eyes, straining to look, but the guy was already gone. Then I turned my surprised, bewildered, and possibly a little excited gaze to Joe. "Are you a shifter, too?"

He frowned at me. "Yeah. Why, what'd he tell you?" Joe jerked his head at Emery.

"She was living as a sheltered human until about a month ago," Emery said. "I wouldn't have thought it possible with someone like her, but... Well, you'd have to meet her mother."

"Save yourself the headache." I turned my wrist in Emery's grasp, trying to loosen the hold. "What do you turn into?"

"A wolf." There was that growl again, primal and wild, hinting of lush forest and the scent of a fresh kill.

I smiled, closing my eyes as the air around me sizzled. Spicy green and textured, that was what his magic said to me. In a spell form, I'd read it as protective and loyal, steadfast and trustworthy. Something to help, not hurt. Something to rely on.

I wondered if that changed with his moods, or if his intentions were perhaps different when he was in wolf form.

"Everyone is classifying this as a guild matter," Joe said, and I could feel that he was ignoring Emery's earlier request to keep the wolf at bay. At least the magical part of it. "Roger doesn't have the power to take them down, so he has no choice but to steer clear of anything they're after. Same with the MLE office. It's just you and the guild on this one. But Emery…" Joe scratched his scruffy chin and shifted. Muscle rippled along his robust body. "The guild has gotten stronger since you left. More ruthless. No one engages them, because they rule this town. No one can go up against them. This is a battle you can't win. Even with what's going on, and even if Roger sent some shifters to help, you're no match. I know you want closure for your brother, but it's not worth your life. Or hers. Your brother was a good man. He'd tell you the same thing. You should take your pretty friend and get out of town."

Emery stared down at me, and something I couldn't identify moved in his eyes. "I can't. They would follow."

"You'd be surprised," Joe said. "They haven't had much luck spreading their influence to other towns, and certainly not other states. They rule Seattle, but they don't have a good hold on other places. They'd probably let you go."

Emery's eyes dulled for a moment and his gaze slipped to nothingness. A moment later, he was blinking and back to life. He shook his head. "I appreciate the warning, and that is more tempting than you probably realize, but if I send her away, they'll hunt her down with all their resources and she'll be captured. Not killed, captured. Anyone who helps her will die in the process. I won't leave her to that fate."

Joe nodded. "Stay safe, and let me know if you need anything." He put his hand over the bar for Emery to take. It took him a moment to realize Emery was busy holding my hands.

"Honestly, I'm fine," I said, shaking my arms.

Emery didn't comment, nor did he let go. I was starting to think the time he'd spent with my mother and I had irreversibly scarred him.

Joe dropped his hand and turned to leave, but stopped after a couple steps and turned back. "Just one more thing. I was around when you let loose with Conrad." I could hear the song of the hunt in his tone. I laughed with the exciting and adventurous feel of it. "I've always found it a little jarring to be near naturals, dual-mages or not. The power's almost too harsh. Nearly unbearable. But this…" He made a circle in the air with his finger. "This is more powerful than I remember, but…pleasant. It sings to my primal side. It's almost like it's calling to me, urging me to follow your lead. Is that what you're intending?"

Emery looked down at me, waiting.

"Wait, are you asking me?" I tried to point at myself. Trapped hands were really distracting.

"She hasn't had any training," Emery said, stepping back and dragging me with him. "I don't think she knows what she's doing right now."

I lifted my eyebrows. "You mean the—" I almost said *magic*. "The *stuff* near our hands? Because that isn't me; that's the electricity we keep feeling. Remember earlier today?"

Joe's brow furrowed and he tilted his head at me. "Where did you find her?"

"She tried to run me over with her car." Emery pulled me toward the door.

Booming laughter followed us out. "My kinda girl."

"How'd you know I was trying to run you over?" I asked. Emery wrapped his arm around my shoulders and held my wrists in his other hand. "And what are you assuming I'll do if I have my hands free? I realize the danger is gone. I'm not going to zap anyone."

"You're pulling elements from everything around you right now, whether you can see it or not. You're collecting them together into an extremely organized mass the likes of which I've never seen before. All it would take is a thought for you to cobble them together and create something big. Something lovely, I have no doubt, since Joe was right about how pleasant this magic feels, but something aimed at the shifters in some way. That would affect ninety percent of that bar. You don't need every shifter in town knowing how much power you have. We'll have to find another use for it."

"That was a shifter bar?" I glanced back over my

shoulder. Or tried, anyway. "I'm still in total awe that shifters actually exist! It's nuts. But I heard his wolf. I...felt it. The magic. It was a really awesome feeling."

"What is this strange gift you have? I wonder if it's unique or if others have it in some way." He pushed me down a side street and into an alleyway. A light mist drifted down from the darkened sky, one of the more annoying weather patterns in this area of the world. Sunshine or rain, fine, but don't tease us with this in-between annoyance.

"Couldn't you feel all that? I mean, the power was pumping between us. Right? That's what it felt like."

"Yes, it was," he said roughly, but didn't offer any more. Instead, he veered us to the side and stopped, facing the wall.

"Is this where you kill me?" I asked. "Because that won't go well for you." Unfounded threats—I was great at them.

"If we were in a field with nothing around us, I would simply step away and let you blow. But we're in a city filled with dangerous magical people, and I can't do that. So to control what you have brewing, I'll have to be hands-on."

"Hands on what?"

His smile barely registered in the dim lighting of the alley. "You, unfortunately. I'll be holding your hands...or maybe you'll hold my wrists? It's been a long time since I was trained by a mentor. I forget the guidance portion of it. We'll have to figure out what feels right. So I'm going to step behind you and reach forward for your hands, okay? I'll give you as much space as I can. Only our hands, and maybe arms, need to touch. I'd do it another way, but I don't know how."

"So you're going to expend a lot of effort and probably get the same result?"

His blown-out breath mussed my hair. He pulled my wrists toward his side and shifted, moving behind me. "That's kind of how my life works, so probably."

"Don't worry—that's how my life works, too. Misery loves company."

He did as he said, moving behind me and clasping my wrists in front of my chest. His elbows grazed my upper arms, but his chest did not touch my back. Instead, he strained away, his head back and to the side, as though I had a horrible stink he could barely stand to smell.

I wrinkled my nose and wiggled within his arms. This felt wrong. Uncomfortable and off-putting. The low hum in his hands on mine seemed dangerous and ill at ease. The pulse in the air around us felt sporadic instead of rhythmic. Even the energy I'd grown so comfortable with pushed and pulled aggressively, not finding the peace and natural current I was used to.

It occurred to me that, even before I'd known I had

magic, I'd always been in tune with nature, more so than most people. I knew its currents and could feel them soaking peacefully into my soul. Most importantly, I knew what felt right, and what felt off.

This felt off.

"Okay, so first we're going to—"

"No." I closed my eyes and let my temperamental third eye guide me. Whatever felt wrong needed to be amended, and that didn't require my brain power, it required my intuition.

I just hoped this wasn't one of those times when, instead of helping me, my temperamental third eye created a much bigger problem.

CHAPTER 22

"WHAT'S THE MATTER?" Emery asked with his feet spread apart and his body pulled away to give her as much room as humanly possible. As a kid, when Isaias had done this to help him learn, the size difference between pupil and mentor had been much larger. That, and they'd established trust and a parent-child sort of mentality. As much of a lie as it had been, at the time, proximity hadn't been a problem.

But this was a grown woman. A beautiful, charismatic, witty grown woman with sexiness in spades. The situation was vastly different. Women in general didn't like strange men pressing against them, and this one, with her naivety and overprotective mother, had probably had few encounters up until this point. She might react aggressively to the situation. Not that he would blame her, but with all the magic pumping around her, that would work out badly for him.

"You're not doing this right," she said, annoyance in her voice. She wiggled, and her shapely butt glanced across his groin.

"What—are you doing?" He jerked his lower half away. His jaw hit off her head and she flinched, their hands pushing and pulling at each other.

Magic pulled harder on their surroundings, the tone and mood changing drastically. The pleasant, delicate hum from before turned wild and unruly, the type of magic he'd always struggled with in his dual-mage pairing with Conrad.

"Stop!"

He froze at her whip-crack command.

"Just chill out for a second, would you?" she barked. "You're too wound up. You're messing everything up."

"What are you talking about?" He felt her tug on his hands.

"You're uncomfortable, which is making me un-comfortable, which is affecting everything else. Just...relax. Feel the world around you. It's a pretty gross little alleyway you've pulled us into, but there is still beauty if you look for it. There is still balance."

Her hands spread out within his, her fingers push-ing outward. Following her lead, he threaded his fingers between hers, immediately feeling a soft hum vibrate up his forearms. She tugged again, and he grudgingly stepped forward, his front now glancing against her back.

"Let's pause for a moment and see what we've got," she said, her voice a soft, feminine hum. "Just breathe."

He couldn't help a smile, hearing his words in her firm tone. He breathed. In and out, rhythmically, slowly letting the world drop away. Even though a mistake would mean death or worse, he let his troubles and pain melt until they oozed out of him. He focused on the clean-smelling air, fragrant with her fabric softener and shampoo, filling and exiting his lungs. On the feel of her warm skin against his, so comforting and reassuring, like it had been in the car when she'd taken his hand. On the sparks of fire that ignited in his body each time her back brushed against his front, or her butt or legs slid against him.

He let his eyes droop, then close, listening to her soft breath, the speed and depth matching his own. Feeling the movement of her body. He laid his cheek against her head before pulling her in a little tighter, flush with her now. His hands curled around hers, the grip a little too tight, but the fear of her pulling away took control.

Still he focused, shutting out the world.

Heat unfurled within his body, but not the romantic kind. It wasn't lust or even attraction. It was so much deeper. Raw energy shot up from his core, the source of his survival magic. The hum in his arms intensified until it was traveling his body, a live wire. Energy pulsed around them, comforting, peaceful, pleasurable. Sensual.

Flutters rolled his belly. Tingles rode his skin. A deep, earnest pounding rose within him. A consuming drumbeat.

"Emery, look," Penny said in an awed whisper.

He fluttered his eyes open, but those wonderful feelings stayed with him. His focus didn't fracture. His thoughts didn't scatter.

Holding on to her, he was perfectly grounded. Balanced. The way magic should be, and something he'd never experienced before, not even when he and Conrad had been in the zone.

"What are you, Penny Bristol?" he asked in barely more than a whisper. Bursts of light and color surged through the alleyway, rolling and flowering in the air, the texture highly detailed and intricate. But for all its beauty, it had nothing on her.

"A girl that has had to find peace in the quiet times between getting into trouble and causing havoc." She let her head fall back, hitting his collarbone.

Not able to help it, he turned his head, letting his cheek slide against hers. "That was probably your magical side trying to break free."

"This is beautiful." She dropped her hands until he was holding her tightly around the waist.

"I've never created something like this," he said, watching the magic play and frolic. It seemed like it had a life of its own.

"I haven't either, if it makes you feel any better."

He chuckled. "It does, actually."

He thought she might turn her head a little more. Let her lips glide across his. Instead, she sighed and straightened up. "This is breaking a rule, right? Doing magic in the alleyway?"

Despite her attention shift, the feeling around them didn't wobble. The magic rolling playfully through the air didn't shift or change.

"Your focus is unreal," he said, feeling his eyes go wide. "How can you keep this level of…balance? Does it come naturally to you?"

She shrugged as she glanced around. "Practice, probably. I love this feeling. I mean, it has never been this strong. The zing of electricity, the pulse of the energy, the sheer magnitude of oneness—none of that's normal for me. But the basis of it is. It's something I work toward all the time, like with my stones. It has helped with my temperamental third eye."

"Your what?"

She shrugged again, and now things did falter. The bubble around them cracked, ready to break. Something tugged at his middle, attempting to distract him.

He rubbed his palms up her arms and then back down, refocusing on her. Not letting his attention wander.

Miracle of miracles, the magical pocket they'd created—their bubble of balance and peace in topsy-turvy surroundings—strengthened again.

"What happened just there?" he asked softly, finding her hands again and holding them.

"Nothing. It's fine. Let's—"

"It's not nothing, Penny Bristol. Tell me."

She looked away, and the magic in their surroundings wobbled again. "I have a lot of baggage when it comes to the weird little things I do. I realize that some of those things are magic, but clearly my third eye is just as strange as ever."

"Strange? Somehow I'm helping with this, instead of tearing it down like I used to do when I worked certain spells with Conrad. I'm speaking and moving and having a conversation in the midst of *all this*." He used one of her hands to gesture at the magic. "Because of you. You're stabilizing me, I have no doubt, and the only way you could do that is by hours and hours of focus, trying to find balance your whole life. There is no other explanation. So cherish that third eye of yours, regardless of how temperamental it may be." He laughed and pulled in a set of elements, weaving them through his fingers entwined with hers. Shadows draped over them, obscuring them from anyone passing by. He should've done it immediately, but he'd been too caught up.

"And don't forget," he said, feeling the other elements passing over and around them. "I have a third eye too. It's my *Seer* ability. It has kept me alive more times than I can count."

"My third eye doesn't keep me out of trouble. What was the spell you just did?"

"I didn't say my *Seer* ability kept me out of trouble. I said it's saved my life. Trust me, you have nothing on the amount of havoc I can create." He paused to shift gears. "I created a light-concealing spell. Very little power and energy and focus needed. It's a breeze in this bubble. Here, I'll do it again."

He weaved the spell again, moving slower this time. "This is as slow as I can mix things together without the elements of the spell frazzling."

"Do you use the term 'elements' for everything?"

"Kind of, yes. It's easier." He got to the end and let the identical spell drift into the air around them. "Do you want to try—"

She shrugged off his hand and started weaving immediately. He chanced stepping around the side of her, wondering if the bubble would break. Amazingly, it held, even when his focus switched from the magic at her fingertips to her teeth chewing her plump bottom lip. Her brows dipped in concentration—or maybe frustration—before her eyes squeezed shut.

At once, the wobbly weave drifted into harmony. The spell came together perfectly, the weave not as tight as his, but the elements in all the right places.

She didn't work with magic by seeing, like he did—she worked by *feeling*. Witches did that, for the most part. Was that because they didn't have extensive spell training either? Was this the natural path found by someone who'd been given no map?

She flung her hand and the spell fell against the wall, not doing much to an already shadowed area.

"Did that work?" she asked, opening those large, luminous eyes. She caught him staring and a crease wormed between her brows. Fire sparked in her eyes, and it wasn't the lustful kind. It was the explosive kind that promised pain. Whatever she'd seen on his face, she had not liked it.

"Great job." He took a large step back and barely stopped himself from raising his hands in surrender. Or maybe an apology. "You got it on the first try."

As if pricked by a pin, the bubble between them burst. The sensual throb of energy and electricity, working together, fizzled out. The magic—so playful and pleasant—dissipated into nothing. Cool air rushed in, replacing the heat from a moment before.

He sighed in the aftermath, returned to the dark and wet alleyway with its musty stink. The hollow ache he'd lived with these last three years beat in time with his heart, the small reprieve making the effects so much stronger.

Somehow, she'd sucked him into her balanced bubble. He might've helped keep them on track, but he had to own that she was the anchor. She'd drawn him in, and once there, they'd easily synced up.

When have mages just randomly synced up like this?

He studied her for a moment, remembering the story she'd told about New Orleans. She'd joined a coven, out of the blue, and led them through an advanced potion. She must've synced with them, too. Perfect strangers with no basis of trust, and she'd still turned them to a high-powered circle.

He couldn't help shaking his head in disbelief. He'd never heard of such a thing with mages. In many ways, she seemed more like a witch than a mage. A natural at working with others, with a pulse on the world around her and the emotions of the people around her. Even her intuition was geared toward witchcraft, since mages typically used recipes and remembered spells.

Yet there could be no denying she was a natural of the highest order. In the structure of magic, she was classified a mage.

"Let's get you settled, then I have to get rid of the car," he said, chewing on the differences between the magical hierarchy and nature's way. Maybe the difference was less about power level, and more about corruption of thought.

Maybe being a natural witch would make Penny

stronger than a natural mage in the end. Maybe she was an accidental new breed of power that the world hadn't yet seen. No limits. No rules.

CHAPTER 23

I GRIMACED WHEN I opened the door. Then sneezed.

The tiny stockroom was exactly that. A stockroom. With boxes of glasses, napkins, and a couple of keg shells resting on a bed pushed into the very corner. Across the hall was a restroom with a toilet and a sink, lit by a bare bulb hanging overhead.

I dropped my duffel bag at my feet and moved a few boxes so they were at least properly stacked. Who just opened doors and threw boxes in? Granted, the glassware had its place, but other than that, it was a messy heap of brown squares.

I set about righting everything, trying to reestablish that same calm energy in the air that I'd found in the alleyway. It was there, but watered down. The electrical charge was absent entirely. Something about when I physically touched Emery, or at least stood really close to him, amplified my magical ability.

That was worth exploring.

I thought back to that cursed church. To the spell in the circle of women. I'd felt something similar with them, but not as potent. Certainly not as focused.

I grinned as I made my way into the room, then beamed. Working with magic felt really good. The thrill of it was indescribable. The slide of it against my skin and how it seeped into my middle fired me up. Working with Emery made it that much more awesome. He was all raw power and force, which blasted fire through my usual calm. I liked the change. It was like an upgrade to my programming. Hopefully he wouldn't get annoyed that he had to keep schooling the newbie for fear she'd blow up a neighborhood.

I pulled another box off the floor. Something rushed out, straight at me.

"Turdswallop Donkey Kong!" Energy spiked around me. I plucked out elements from the room by feel and directed them at the thing dodging into a crack in the wall, wanting it fried.

A stream of red blasted from my hand. It hit the box and blew it to the side. The boxes on top fell, tumbling toward me.

"Buttercrack." I threw up my hands to protect myself as something else darted out. "No, no. Holy Hades on a pogo stick." I zapped it. Then zapped it again, pulling harder from the world around me, wanting it dead.

A tower of boxes fell. I jumped out of the way, narrowly missed. Glass shattered.

Oops.

Maybe I should've tried to catch those.

"What's going—"

I blasted the shape in the doorway, surprised. Joe dove to the side, barely missed by my magical zapper, and a shimmer of green surrounded him.

Magic pulled at me. Throbbed in my middle.

The intent of his wolf magic could change, all right.

Attack. Harm. Kill.

"We seem to have come to a slight misunderstanding," I screeched, straightening my arms and feeling electricity crackle all around me.

Huh. When Emery wasn't around, it was necessary to call the magic—it didn't just come to me willy-nilly. I would have to remember that.

"I am simply ridding your establishment of vermin." I pulled out various elements, as Emery called them, naturally categorizing each by what it felt like and whether I had felt it go into a spell before. I knew next to nothing, but I'd managed to create a zapper, so I strongly suspected I'd arrive at something.

A giant gray wolf filled the doorway, and while I'd never seen a wolf in person before, this one had to be larger than the creatures that existed in the wild. Its lip curled, exposing white fangs. A growl rumbled deep in its throat.

"Oh holy shit bombs." My mother would've had to

agree that this situation warranted a genuine swear word. "I can pay for those glasses. Well, my mother can pay. She's good for it, I swear. Oh, I know! How about a stolen car? Can I interest you in selling that to a chop shop? The owner has insurance. It'll be fine." Of course, Emery was currently in the process of getting rid of it, but I would have said pretty much anything to pacify Joe.

The wolf sniffed the air and the growling increased. Hair rose along its spine.

Something zipped by my foot.

"Snicker-frack charms a lot!" I jumped, trying to get off the ground to get away from the thing, but gravity pulled me right back down. "No, no. Dang you to Hades, you horrible little varmint." I zapped without thinking. Then zapped again as more movement brought another box down. "What kind of place are you running here?"

The growling stopped, which was good, but there were boxes all around my feet, and while mice themselves didn't scare me, their unpredictability did. With an imagination like mine, even a tiny thing could turn into a flesh-eating beast.

"Do not scurry around me, you diseased little creatures," I warned, picking up one of the boxes and setting it onto a pile that hadn't been toppled. "Do not jump out at me."

Energy pulsed and electricity sizzled. Emery was back.

I straightened up slowly and pushed hair behind my ears.

Emery stood next to Joe in the doorway, and a crazy grin spread across his face as he looked at me. Joe was back to being Joe, except he was also buck-naked.

"That's"—I averted my gaze—"awkward." I cleared my throat. "Sorry about the mess. I encountered a couple of mice, and things... Things kind of got away from me."

"You should not be left alone," Joe said in a dry voice. I didn't want to chance looking up at his face because I had a feeling my gaze would catch elsewhere, and no one needed that.

"Yes." I nodded. "That has been the general consensus throughout my life. I apologize."

"Sorry, Joe. I didn't realize...the full extent of what she meant when she said she caused havoc." I didn't have to see Emery's face to know he was smiling. "Her mother had a bigger job than I thought."

"Sure, yes. Rub it in." I gingerly righted another box, looking at the ground. Any second, a rabid creature with giant fangs, red eyes, and projectile acidic spit might zip out.

"She doesn't even swear," Joe said, and I heard movement.

K . F . B R E E N E

I glanced up, then tore my gaze away from a less-than-fuzz-free backside. Joe needed a wax.

"I was in the back counting the drawer, and the first thing I heard was 'turdswallop Donkey Kong.' What is that? Teach her to swear first, then work on her magic. Otherwise she'll be a laughingstock." He stalked down the hallway. "I'll tell the staff there's a cat up here in case she goes hopping around," he called back, "but it might be best to muzzle her."

"Well, that is not very nice," I said, piling another box.

"It takes a lot of energy to change to the animal form and back," Emery said, staring instead of helping with the mess. "Doing two changes in such a short time is enough to make a guy like Joe a little cranky."

"Then maybe Joe should've thought about finding a real cat. And a mousetrap or two." I piled another box. Silence dripped between us.

"Turdswallop…Donkey Kong?" Emery still wore that stupid grin. His eyes glittered in the light, and in this moment, I hated how pretty they were.

"You know my mother. I shouldn't have to explain my aversion to swearing. It's been beaten into me."

"I know that your mother hates swearing, yes. I do not know where words like 'turdswallop' come from—"

"England, I think."

"—or what Donkey Kong has to do with it—"

"You'd be surprised what those two get up to to-gether."

"—or why someone would put them together into one swear when freak, or gosh darn, or crap would do."

I straightened up and put my hands on my hips. "You swear how you want to swear, and I'll swear how I want."

Emery took a step forward and shoved a box away with his foot.

"No, no." I pointed at it. "Stack that out of the way. This place is a mess."

His smile burned brighter. "Yes, ma'am." He bent slowly, his sparkling eyes still connected with mine. The first box he picked up jingled with broken glass.

My face burned, the crimson hue probably so deep that I looked like I needed to go to a burn ward. "It'd be best with an aisle so we can easily walk between the bed and the bathroom."

"Yes, it would. You are absolutely right." He picked up another box of broken glass, smiling at me all the while.

I ground my teeth and turned my back on him be-fore gingerly picking up another box. I kept my version of cursing and threatening vermin to myself.

"When I told Joe how I found you earlier…" he said, and another box jingled. He was really concerned about all the ones carrying broken glass. "I was kidding."

I hesitated, the box in my hands hovering over its intended destination. "I know." I shrugged to try and pull it off before gingerly setting the box down.

"Do you? Because your response implies you were actually trying to run me over."

I searched my brain for some way out of this as I resumed my cleanup, but nothing came to mind. I sighed. "I was coming toward you at high speed. Of course I was trying to run you over."

"Then why were you surprised I figured it out?"

"Flinging monkey turds, you are annoying," I yelled. "Fine. Since you never mentioned it, I thought you might not have figured it out. But if you just want to put it all out there—"

"Yes, please."

"When you stalked into the center of the street with that black ball between your hands, I thought you intended to kill the witness to your crimes. Me. So I figured I'd run you over. Only, you didn't move. I was about to run you down, and you just stood there and stared at me with that blasted black ball in your hands. So I lost my nerve, cranked the wheel, and the next thing I knew, I was running over the dead guys and things had gotten out of control. There, happy? You're welcome for not killing you."

His laughter filled the room. He shook with it,

bending over with a box, the fragments inside jingling for all they were worth.

I hit him with a box of napkins. "Shut up. I've never been in that situation before. I panicked."

"What situation? A magic fight or trying to run someone over?"

I rolled my eyes and ignored the questions. "Well, if you didn't want a fight, why did you stalk into the middle of the street with that black ball?" The smile dripped off his face. Then something dawned on me, and my stomach churned. "Oh my God—"

"Don't say the Lord's name in vain," he said, his tone not as teasing as he'd probably intended. His gaze had turned intense. Sorrowful. Something was troubling him.

I couldn't worry about his drama right now. I had my own.

"I killed that one guy, didn't I?" I palmed my chest. "You told me the white magic was mine…"

"Survival magic," he said. "Yours is pure white."

My head spun and my legs weakened as the full extent of what I'd done dawned on me. Running over dead guys killed by someone else was one thing; killing someone with magic was something else entirely. I'd sworn not to use magic until I knew how (I kept breaking that rule), and I'd killed another person because of it.

I stepped back on wobbly knees, reaching behind me for the edge of the bed. My fingers brushed it, but I was already falling, my head light.

"Whoa, whoa. Hey…" The sound of boxes crashing preceded a pair of strong arms wrapping under my legs and around my back. I was rising before I'd hit the ground.

He held me tightly against his body as he stepped closer to the bed, the effort of holding me not causing him any strain. Like always, electricity surged between us. I soaked into it, letting it cocoon me.

"You had no choice." Emery's deep voice rumbled inside his chest. "They would've killed you if you hadn't reacted. That's what our survival magic does. It protects us in the direst situations. Usually our subconscious directs it, like it did with you."

I sighed, burrowing a little deeper into his arms. He paused in putting me down, and I could feel the uncertainty in his hold. I needed him to keep holding me. Needed a couple minutes of his comfort to wash away my growing uncertainty. I was managing as best I could, but it was tough to come to grips with the stark reality of what I'd done with magic—again—not to mention the whole "Joe turning into a wolf" thing. I was living in a daydream half the time, and a nightmare the other half, shifting back and forth by the minute. A little taste of Emery's strength and power was welcomed.

He must've sensed it, because he straightened up and adjusted his hold. My head inched up his shoulder until my face rested against the hollow of his neck.

"I just need a moment," I mumbled into his warm skin.

"Of course. Take as long as you need." He swayed, rocking me. "I mean it, Penny. You honestly didn't have a choice," he cooed, his voice soft. He squeezed me tightly. "Those three men had killed more than their fair share of mages. Innocent people who got in the way of the guild. Your conscience is clear. Should be clear. You were defending yourself."

"I know," I said, and nearly meant it. "It's just a shock, is all. All of this is a shock."

"I can imagine. But you are handling it beautifully. You might be easygoing most of the time, and content to follow directions, but you have a deep fire in you, Penny Bristol. When it is required of you, that fire rages. Don't be ashamed of it. Your father would be happy to know you have some of your mother in you."

The electricity filtered down until it hummed deep and low in my gut, tightening my body. I lifted my head a little as I slid my palm up his chest and then hooked my arm around his shoulder. I wasn't sure where I was going with this, but when he suddenly stilled and the muscles along his arms and chest popped, I blinked out of my reverie.

"Sorry," I said, tearing my hand away. "And thanks. Your words help. Except the bit about my mother, but I guess I should come to grips with that."

His chuckle was soft and his hands felt strong and reassuring against my body. The breath exited my lungs slowly, washing over his neck. I hesitated within the sphere of his heat, knowing exactly what I'd intended when I'd felt him up. But I wouldn't be able to give him what he was expecting, and then it would turn embarrassing for me and frustrating for him. Best not to tease him. Then accidentally kill him with my unconscious power if he got too handsy.

"Anyway." I forced myself to push away. He set me down gently, staying close, and only then did I notice the slow churn of the magic surrounding us. "Am I doing that?"

"We are. We are doing that together. When we create this focused bubble around us, the magic flirts and plays within it."

I stared up into his eyes, like looking at the Milky Way on a clear night. My gaze roamed the angles of his face and his defined jaw before stopping on his lush lips, shapely in a way that softened the severity of his features just enough to make him startlingly attractive.

"We should get the rest of these boxes set to rights." I meant to step away, but my hand ended up on his chest, my palm over his heart.

He covered my hand with his, his gaze open and raw. Inviting and pleading and filled with pain and longing. His whole history was expressed in that look, topped off with the shared need we felt in the moment. "Okay."

Our breath mingled and his head bent a fraction. The air between us heated and I strained upward.

"My bad," Joe said.

I jumped at the sudden intrusion. The magic ballooned around us before morphing into a spear and blasting toward the door. Joe dove out of the way for the second time, his reactions, thankfully, fast.

"Would you stop doing that?" he demanded, not reappearing. "This is my bar, damn it! I shouldn't be shot at with magic in my own bar. Not to mention the door was open."

The electricity around us dissipated, and with it, the magic. I brushed myself off, a random reflex that made no sense in the moment, and looked around at the boxes on the floor. "Sorry about that, Joe. If that was my fault, I mean."

"That was your fault, yes," Emery said, his smile back but his eyes still deep and intense. "I don't make spells that crude. Just jokes."

Joe poked his head into the doorway. "Can I come in, or are you going to shoot at me again?"

CHAPTER 24

I LAY ON my side, my head propped up on my hand, nestled in the small bed beside Emery, who lay on his back next to me, taking up way more room than a normal guy should. I was against the wall, so while I wouldn't fall out, being crushed by muscles was a real possibility.

The pillow had been discarded, since it smelled like a dead person and had suspicious brown stains splotched over the white surface, which made an already uncomfortable situation that much worse. Stacked boxes, some misshapen due to critters darting out for my feet (I couldn't seem to zap the buggers) lined the walls in rows, leaving a small aisle.

Emery had offered to sleep on the floor, but I would not be responsible for vermin eating his face. Besides, there wasn't enough room. I would've fit better, and there was no way I would opt to sleep down there.

A sliver of light cut across the floor from underneath the closed door. Another slice cut through the room from the moonlight peeking in through the single small window. It seemed the sky had finally cleared.

"Why is there a bed in the stockroom?" I asked into the hush. A moment later, the rhythmic pound of bass started up as the jukebox in the bar below began the next song.

Emery drummed his fingers on his stomach. "Whenever Joe and his wife have a big fight, Joe stays here."

"They must be getting along."

"They must. I didn't know about the couch, or I would've thought of somewhere else for us to stay."

"What couch?"

"He used to have a couch, too. I think at one point this was going to be a man cave or something."

"Then where would the supplies go?"

"In the downstairs supply room the employees use. This is overflow, I think. Actually, I'm not really sure. I just know he keeps this bed in it, and he's the only one allowed up here. It's the safest place I could think of. Even though mages do drink at the bar, shifters outnumber them. People don't mess with Joe very often. Not without good cause."

"If they find out we're here, it'll be a good cause."

"Which is why we'll only stay a little while."

My leg was falling asleep. I tried to shift, but his elbow was in the way, sticking out so he could fold his hands across his chest. "Is there anywhere else you can put your hands?"

He straightened the arm on my side. His fingers brushed my upper thigh and rested much too close to my apex. His point made, he pulled his arm back up.

"Ah." I ignored the butterflies and maneuvered enough to curl my arm under my head. My elbow knocked his temple. "Oops, sorry."

He pulled his head away so I could try and figure out my whole arm/pillow situation. Except if I did that, my forearm would smack his face.

"So you thought you'd take the couch, and my mother and I would fit in this bed?" I asked.

A smile spread across his face. "I hadn't remembered how small the bed was."

"Clearly."

"I am a bit large."

"Yes."

"And your mother is larger still. In certain…areas."

I snorted with his attempted delicacy. "At least my mother is squishy. You're all hard planes and dull points." I'd need to grab some clothes from my pack and use them as a pillow, since side-sleeping without one would kill my neck. My only hesitation was that I didn't want my clean clothes to smell like this bed. It was musty and slightly dank. In other words, kind of gross.

At least the room was dry and he was warm. *Silver*

lining.

"Luckily, you are petite," he mumbled.

With a last-ditch effort, I scooched down and curled my arm under me again. My butt hit the wall, my feet dangled over the end, and I rammed my forehead into Emery's elbow.

He jerked his arm away. The bed groaned miserably. "Are you okay?"

I would've rubbed the offending spot, but I was struggling to keep my face from pressing against the blankets.

"Penny?" I felt his hand curl under my upper arm.

"I'm good. I'm fine." I inchwormed back up the bed, my progress eased by his tugging. Oh, who was I kidding? I was dragged up, pulling at the blanket as I went. The guy was strong, even in awkward positions.

"I'm not petite," I said absently as I tried to decide which piece of clothing to sacrifice for my pillow. "I'm a normal-sized woman with a penchant for hunching when I'm embarrassed. Which is often, as you've noticed." I blew out a breath. "The pillow issue is real."

His big arm came away from the bed until it was sliding across my face.

"Put that back." I shoved his arm off my forehead. "There isn't enough room for that thing to go wandering."

"Come in."

"Come in where? We're on top of the covers."

"Use me for a pillow."

I hesitated as a worrying hum sounded in my body again. "No, it's fine. I'll figure it out."

"Suit yourself." He dropped his arm, and his fingers resumed their restless drum on his stomach. I wasn't sure what he was so wound up about. It was good to be the biggest guy in the room. He'd gotten the prime sleeping spot simply because there was a good chance he might shift in his sleep and literally crush me should he have to lie on his side.

"Was your brother as big as you?" I asked, dropping my head to my arm and letting my forearm rest against his face. "Or are you an unfortunate anomaly?"

Emery pulled his head away, apparently under the impression I was shifting again. My hand covered his mouth. He paused for a second, clearly still waiting, until his lips curved into a smile under my fingers. He shifted back and let my arm be, lying across his face.

I laughed and pulled back, but lost my balance and ended up rolling forward and slamming my face against his upper arm. I arched back like a sea creature caught out of water.

"What...are you doing?" he asked, trying to scoot away. There was nowhere to go.

"That settles it. I need to get some clothes for a pillow. This isn't going to work." I let my arm fall across his face again.

"I'm doomed to smell like this bed," he said. "Are you sure you want to suffer the same fate? You have clean clothes; you should keep them that way until you wear them tomorrow."

His chest stilled, and a pregnant pause ballooned between us. He *wanted* me to lean against him.

"Don't try to kill yourself by asphyxiation on my account," I said. His breath blew out, riding a chuckle.

I thought over what he'd said. At the moment, I had his spicy-sweet, masculine smell close at hand to disguise the musk of the unwashed and half-forgotten bed. Even though he was a bit dirty and travel-hardened, I delighted in his natural cologne. There was a strangely comforting quality to it. But tomorrow, wearing those soiled clothes, all I'd have was the bed's musk, accompanied by the memory of mice, dirt, and endless layers of dust.

That wouldn't be pleasant.

I sighed. "Fine, I'll use you as a pillow. Though I doubt it will be any more comfortable."

"Why is that?"

"Why do you think? You're one big rock."

"You get used to sleeping on rocks." That sounded ominous.

I frowned as I scooted closer, ignoring him. Cryptic warnings were another thing I didn't have time for. The more pressing issue was how I was going to sleep wrapped around a near-stranger.

Better than you would've slept curled up beside him.

I ignored myself (my list of things to ignore was drastically increasing) and grabbed his wrist and flung it, expecting him to pick up the slack. Instead, his hand *thwapped* loosely against my face. "Good gravy, Billie Jean, give me a break over here."

His silent laughter shook the bed. He lifted his hand and dropped it near my head, only pulling it around me after I sidled closer to his big frame. "Do you think out your put-downs before you say them?"

I wiggled to get comfortable. "That wasn't a put-down."

"Calling me Billie Jean, which is a woman's name in the song, wasn't a put-down?"

"First of all, being referred to as a woman is a compliment, not a put-down. Women can handle all the banes of existence, including being called the bane of existence, and keep on trucking. *Our* fragile egos don't cause war and famine. You should be so lucky to have me call you a woman's name—"

"There's the fire."

"—and second, I wasn't calling you Billie Jean. It was part of my swear recipe. I used a song. It happens."

"You have a swear recipe?"

"Yes. Don't ask me for it. Get your own."

His silent laughter shook me with the bed this time. I punched his side like I might punch a pillow to fluff it up.

He jerked and laughed harder, moving his arms to protect his (clearly ticklish) side. He squished me between his arm and body while doing so.

"Uncle," I called out, my face smashed and words muffled. "Uncle!"

His laughter only increased as he slowly pulled his hands away, his middle flexing.

"It isn't often the aggressor has to say uncle when they are still under attack," I groused, scooting closer to him again.

He swished the hair away from my face and over my shoulder, sending goosebumps along my skin, before resting his hand on my arm. "Sorry."

"Don't be sorry. That's impressive."

He squeezed my arm. "I'm a little ticklish."

"Clearly."

Silence descended, and we lay quietly, though not restfully. The fingers of his free hand were drumming again, beating a pulse against his body. The music below pounded a deep rhythm, reverberating through the walls.

"Thank you," he said. Each syllable dripped with sincerity.

"For what? And it better not be because I didn't call

you a woman's name. We literally just went over that. Women can—"

"No, I meant thank you for making me laugh. It's been a really long time."

"Oh." I shifted, turning more on my side, then debated what to do with my hand. If I put it out straight, it would be awfully close to his nether region. He was a guy, so he'd probably shift when I wasn't paying attention just so I'd find myself holding his junk. But if I shifted my arm anywhere else, I'd have to rest it on him.

"Do you mind if I just..." I lightly dropped my hand to his pec. It flared, pushing at my palm. "Ah." I jerked my hand away.

He was laughing again, making the bed plead surrender. "You can put your hand wherever you want, Turdswallop."

I hesitated in letting my hand drop again. "You can't call a person turdswallop. That's a word, not a name. And I think it's a bad one, but I can get away with using it because my mother doesn't know what it means."

"Your recipe must involve making up words, because turdswallop is not a word."

"Not even in England?"

Laughter bubbled out of him until he bent from the force of it, his eyes squeezing shut. "No," he wheezed. "Not even in England."

"I think you're wrong. I've definitely heard it before. What is so freaking funny?"

"How can you say all of this with such a serious face?" He started laughing again.

"See? This is why I hunch all the time. I'm the butt of everyone's jokes but usually have no idea why. This is normal life."

He shook his head, wiping an eye. "This is not normal life. This is a blessed life." He calmed. "I mean it. I haven't laughed very much since before my brother died. And yes, he was my size. I'm six-two and he was six-three. Neither of us were this muscular, though. We worked out, but it was different…these last few years on the run have made me tough. Strong and magically powerful. I've worked at it every day. The only way to stay alive is to be at the top of the food chain, no matter how many of them come for you."

"Why since before your brother died? Were you and he fighting?"

He moved his hand until it was sliding under mine where it rested on his chest. He lifted his fingers, and I threaded mine between them. "He was high up in the guild, and like I told you and your mother, he was trying to effect change. Straighten things out. That's why he joined them in the first place. He wanted to help shape the Mages' Guild into an organization our parents would have been proud of. I told him he'd get himself killed, and that it couldn't be done. But he didn't listen. And then it came true. It wasn't even a premonition—just logical thinking. That made it so much worse, because he would've believed my premonition over logic."

"Why didn't you lie and say that it was your premonition?"

"I don't have them about other people. I only have them about myself. He knew that."

"Oh." I thought back to earlier that evening. "So the guild wouldn't really go after me if I left?"

He turned his head until his cheek was against my forehead. "I guess I should've said that I only have them about myself *usually*. Your fate is tied with mine, but I'm honestly not sure why. My fight has nothing to do with you. Nor am I a good teacher to help you with your magic. I'm not even a good guide to the magical world. But for some reason, we're in this together, for good or bad. My danger sensors now encompass you. I don't know much more than that. Maybe I can just tell if you're in danger if I'm in danger too. I'm not sure yet."

Silence descended between us, and the throb of the music downstairs drifted into the background. My eyelids drooped and my body hummed in an aching, unsettled sort of way, but the feeling didn't require action. Despite lying on a near-stranger and admitted criminal who was about to take me into the heart of some serious danger, I was completely content.

"I'm the only mage I know of who has pure black survival magic," Emery said. "I've always assumed it was showing the world what I truly am."

"An egomaniac?"

His huffed laugh made my eyelashes flutter. He squeezed me. "Evil."

I tilted up my head and he glanced down. Our gazes connected in the dim light. His lips twitched, his attempt at a smile he didn't feel, before he rubbed my arm with the hand draped around me and looked back at the ceiling. "I know it's not true."

But I could hear in his voice that he wasn't being honest. He did think it was true. He thought he was evil.

My heart ached for him. What a horrible thing to go through life believing. Especially after losing everyone close to you, and being forced to leave your home and way of life. He was an outcast, more so than anyone I had ever known. He had nothing to his name except his family's legacy and his magic. That he would think he didn't have honor, that he was doomed to darkness, was more than I could bear.

Warmth seeped out from my middle, filling me. I tried to wiggle closer, to paste my body against his, so he had my touch for comfort. It wasn't much, but it was all I knew to do.

"You're not evil, Emery. Far from it. And that's not just an opinion—I can *feel* it. I can feel your goodness."

"I'm not like my brother. His survival magic was pure white. He always saw the good in everything. He wanted to build things. To create things. I was always the kid that knocked over the stack of blocks."

"That makes you a jerk, not evil."

He moved his hand up until he could tuck a strand of hair behind my ear. "Survival magic is a living creature's essence. You felt it in Joe—his survival magic turns him into a wolf. Changes and morphs as he needs it. Non-magical humans have it too, in tiny amounts. That's where intuition and gut feelings come in. If the magic is visible—by someone like you or me—it'll lean toward one color or another. But while a shifter's magic looks like a green haze, if you're close enough, you can see that it is actually an ultra-fine and delicate weave of a great many patterns and textures, like you see in a spell. Mages, witches, vampires—every creature's magic is the same. Except mine. It's jet-black. Like a tear in the universe."

I shrugged, because that didn't mean anything at all. His survival magic was a color just like anyone else's was. But I was sure someone, likely his brother, had explained that before. It hadn't stuck then, so it wouldn't stick now. I decided to go a different direction with my argument.

"Mine is solid too," I said. "Solid white. Devoid of any personality whatsoever. I hate white walls, white cars—I really don't like the color white. My survival magic is taunting me. So you see, you aren't the only one with a grievance."

"White is pure. The color of angels. Of innocence. It is goodness and light."

"It's also the color of the tunnel leading to death." I tilted my face up to his again. This time, though, he didn't look down to meet my eyes. His demons were haunting him. "Look at it this way. White is the absence of color. All the colors bounce off it. Nothing stays. Black absorbs all the colors. It is the culmination of color consumption. So really, I'm a blank canvas, and you are full of it. I think that fits."

He sucked in a breath and choked on it. His body bent, bucking me off, as he coughed, pounding on his chest with his fist. Laughter fought his struggle for air.

I laughed with him, settling again with my head propped up on my hand.

"I think you have it better, quite frankly," I said when he sat up, coughing. "I'd rather be full of color than devoid of it. Besides, black is way cooler. How many goth kids run around in white jumpsuits? None, that's how many. You're the bad boy. Your brother was—Oh." Realization dawned.

I hadn't properly taken in what he'd said moments

before. But now I saw the dilemma. And the connection.

"I have the same unusual color as your brother did," I said softly. "Was that why you stood in the middle of the street that one night? Because it made you think of your brother?"

Emery turned to me and slowly lay back down, but this time, he was on his side facing me. Shadows draped across his face and his expression was lost to the night. "Yes. It was a shock. But you're the real shock, Penny." He took a deep breath and leaned toward me slightly. "I'd thought my brother was the yin to my yang. We had an incredibly tight bond. We usually worked together excellently, and we'd been through hell together. But now I realize that we struggled to maintain our focus together. We fought for leadership. He often won, because he was better at it, and older, but we did fight for it. It made us topsy-turvy at times. Our magic was fire and brimstone, wild and powerful. But it lacked true balance. I see that now. I see that the struggle weakened us. Our bond made being dual-mages possible, but…" His shoulders sagged. When his next words came, they were lined with grief and sorrow. "We weren't a natural dual-mage pair. We were too similar."

"I don't understand."

"Dual-mages are like yin and yang—they work in opposites. When you combine two elements that seemingly contrast, the forces become complementary. When I'm strong, my partner can lean on me. When I'm weak, my partner takes the lead. There is no fighting for control. It's a graceful dance. Rage and turmoil in one partner should be buffered by temperance and steadfastness in the other. The two halves merge to form an interconnected, unshakable, *balanced* bond. My brother and I had an unshakable bond, but not a balanced one."

"But no one is temperate all the time."

"Exactly. When one partner rages, the other must keep their head. And vice versa. The roles shift…"

"In the dance."

"Yes." The word wasn't much more than a breath. "Now I see…"

The words lingered in the air, twisting and turning in the sudden silence between us.

Pressure pushed down on my chest. "What do you see?" I asked, my voice barely making it past my lips.

"I see you, Penny Bristol. With a magic as white as a dove. A soul as pure as my brother's. Full of innocence and wonder and light. I wish I were good enough for you."

Tears filled my eyes, and it wasn't just the beauty of what he'd said—it was the feeling behind it. The aching rawness and absolute conviction that he wasn't good enough. I knew it wasn't *me* he didn't feel good enough for. That line of thought was absurd. It was himself. He didn't feel he warranted his own good opinion. Which was why he thought he was evil.

"Don't be ridiculous," I said, because it was the first thing that came to mind and something my mother would've said. I was freaking turning into my mother. "You have a grasp of magic that I can only wish for. You have friends that let you crash in their failed attempt at a man cave, even though it's dangerous for them, which is loyalty at its finest, and chicks that want you to call them, which I can only assume is for a hookup, even though you're a wanderer. You've had some bumps, some horrible losses, but the color of your magic doesn't decide if you're good or evil. *You* decide that. And an evil guy wouldn't have put up a magical roadblock to keep innocent passersby safe before he killed his enemies. Evil people don't think like that. You're so much better than me. Experience rates ten times as high as innocence ever will. Trust me, I'll be shedding this naivety as soon as possible. So stop with that line of—"

He wrapped his hand around the back of my neck and pulled me toward him. Despite the rush of movement, his touch was gentle. His lips connected with mine.

A shock of electricity ran my length. This time it wasn't painful—it was pure pleasure.

I moaned into the kiss and ran my hand up his

chest. I fell into the feeling of him. The deliciousness of his lips moving against mine. His thumb stroking my jaw.

He pulled back slowly, and my body rolled with his, wanting to linger. Wanting to spend the whole night glued to his kiss.

"I'm sorry," he murmured against my lips. "I didn't mean for that to happen. I'd intended to ask first."

"If you'd asked, I would've made it awkward somehow."

His lips grazed against mine again and his hand swept down over my shoulder. He gently pushed me away. Regret and relief washed through me in equal parts.

"We need to get some rest, Turdswallop, or we'll be a danger to ourselves tomorrow."

I released a breath I hadn't realized I was holding. He really knew how to kill the moment.

He rolled back, and the light slid over his smile. I chuckled and lay back down on his chest.

"Speaking of tomorrow, what's the plan?" I asked, hearing his heart beat quickly against my ear. It matched the pace of mine.

"I need to visit someone that speaks Italian."

"Do you know someone?"

"Yes."

"But what if what's written on that letter isn't Italian? Do you know enough about the language to be sure?" Because I was pretty sure I didn't. Though he did have a phone with internet. He could probably look it up.

I was about to say as much, but he answered.

"I'm going to this...person specifically because he speaks many languages. If it's one of the other Romance languages, it won't be a problem. If there are nuances there, hinted political maneuverings, he'll suss it all out. I'll also be able to trade my work for money and afford a nicer place to stay. I feel like this is the right move because...your mother said to ask for help from a friend I would rather not ask."

"What about the guild? Can you trust him to keep knowledge of your—our—whereabouts safe?"

"There is no fear of him turning us over to the guild. The fear is how he'll try to use the knowledge, and us, to his own ends. You can never trust a vampire."

CHAPTER 25

"LISTEN TO ME carefully," Emery said the next evening as we turned a corner and our destination, an upscale hotel sitting on the water, spanned out to the side and in front of us. Lights twinkled along the sidewalk and the building, showing a red carpet at the front, leading into the hotel. An expensive car pulled up to the front and two people climbed out of the rear doors. Bellboys walked forward to help them. "He'll be charming and captivating. He'll seem civilized and cultivated. All the finery, his dress, his mannerisms—they're intended to seduce you. His very smile will seduce you. But make no mistake, he is a predator. He's above you on the food chain until you learn more of your magic. Keep your wits about you."

I nodded as the energy around us twisted and boiled. It pushed at me in strange ways. Violent ways.

"Is he going to attack us?" I asked, trying to remember how I'd made that magical spear. Or even the lower-powered mouse zappers. Any defense was better than nothing if Emery needed help.

"No. But you should always keep your wits when dealing with a vampire. They're smart and cunning. If a vampire can get one over on you, or use you, or...something else you probably wouldn't even think of, they will. Without hesitation. They have no loyalty."

"Yikes. They sound like a lovely sort of creature."

"They are, in their human form. That's part of the danger."

I frowned, but before I could ask what other form they had, streams of magic—no, Emery would call them elements—drifted up around us.

"If the worst should happen..." Emery wiggled his fingers, and a weave started to form. "Do not try to fight them. Not until you have as thorough a working relationship with magic as I do. They are unbelievably fast and strong. Vicious beyond anything you've experienced thus far. If anything happens, now or down the road, try to find somewhere to hunker down until I can come for you." Magic twisted through Emery's hands, the weave so slow it tried to dissipate at every turn.

"No problem," I said, studying what he was doing. "I excel at fortifying closets."

"That was a spell for corrosive acid. I'll do it again. It's a good spell to throw right before you run." He wiggled his fingers and went through the spell again, walking more slowly as he worked. We were drawing near the entrance now. When he was through, he let the spell dissipate. "Do you have it?"

"The energy around us is...not right. So I'm not sure if the spell will stick in my head. Whatever I put together might have a completely different impact."

His gaze hit mine. "I'm sorry—this is a bad way to train. Balance us out, and I'll do it again."

"It is *a* way to train, and at the moment, that's good news."

A grin tweaked his lips. "You're so positive. Is there any badness in you?"

All the stories I'd told him of my exploits thus far, and he had to ask? His memory wasn't the best.

I focused on the world around me, getting in tune with it—feeling the energy and nature, the chill of the air and smell of the sea. The vibe mellowed out and he went through the spell again, muttering about how much easier it was this time around. By the time he'd gone through it twice, a little too quickly for my taste, we were at the doors.

He dropped my hand and strutted into the hotel like he owned the place, his shoulders back and his head held high. I slouched in next to him, not great at making entrances. I found it better not to be noticed at all.

Hard plastic antlers reached from the walls all around the lobby, held in place by bold metal brackets.

Two ladies stood behind a smallish check-in counter to the left, and a few guests converged toward the large sitting area at the back of the room. The lobby was tastefully furnished with a few groupings of chairs and couches. A large stone fireplace adorned the wall to the right, and floor-to-ceiling windows showed the blackness beyond. In the day, that window would be filled with the crystal-blue waters of Elliot Bay.

Vampires clearly liked luxury.

Emery stood straight and tall at the check-in desk, holding his frame with power and confidence. Despite his stained shirt and messy hair, he looked like he belonged—like he was born to the right of finery.

"I'd like to speak with Mr. Regent, please." Emery's hard words of command seemed to fill the room.

Eyes drifted our way. The check-in ladies both looked startled.

"Tone it down, there, chief," I muttered, resting a hand on his arm.

"Do you have an appointment?" the blonde check-in lady asked, her smile frozen, uncertain. The other woman motioned to the couple standing behind us and started to check them in.

Emery lowered his voice. "I have a standing appointment. Tell him the natural has resurfaced. That's all he need know."

My phone buzzed in my pocket. I fished it out, not

catching the check-in lady's words but understanding their tone just fine. She intended to brush him off.

I flipped the phone open and clicked the button to read the text message. The letters came up on the antiquated screen. *You need the boss of the boss. He'll connect you to the highest level of power in the underworld.*

I stared at my mom's message, tremors racking my body. This was evidence that my mother had *seen* something. I could scarcely believe in my own ability to work magic, let alone hers. But there was no way she could fabricate this message.

I tugged on Emery's sleeve and put the phone in front of him. He cut off whatever he was saying and glanced down, his brow furrowing as he read the message.

"Are you looking for the boss of this establishment?" I asked quietly.

His gaze hit mine, and I could see the affirmation in it…and the wheels that had started turning.

I pushed him to the side, purpose sizzling inside of me. It was time to own a little of my mother's side, God help me.

The check-in woman's stubborn blue gaze slid from Emery to me, and her chin lifted a fraction. I could tell by the set of her jaw and the height of her shoulders that she didn't intend to budge.

"Hello." I gave her a pleasant smile. "We seem to

have some confusion here."

"Mr. Regent does not take unsolicited—"

"Yes, that is the confusion." I leaned over the counter, my smile turning fierce. This was happening, and it was going to happen now. "He is waiting for us, not the other way around. He is hoping for our call. Now, you will let him know we are here so that you don't get fired. Not only that, but you will tell him we need a meeting with his boss." Fire licked at my insides, and I felt the familiar yank I now recognized as magic. "Get him on the phone as soon as possible. We'll be sitting by the fireplace. You can see in my eyes that, should you ignore me, I will do something you will regret. Is that reading clearly?"

Her widened eyes were glued to mine. She nodded mutely. No one around us seemed to notice the exchange.

This was why skulking worked so incredibly well for me.

I straightened up, releasing the fire I'd been holding inside of me. Sparkles danced before my eyes for just a moment before settling and winking out. She blinked twice, and immediately reached for the phone.

"This way." I grabbed Emery's forearm and steered him around the couple still checking in. Near the fireplace, I chose a seat in which I was facing one direction, and gestured to the seat opposite me so he was facing the other. If someone came at us, we'd see them coming.

Then it occurred to me. I'd forgotten to look for a single closet on the way over.

I mouthed a swear, which didn't really count as swearing, and glanced behind me in case one was hidden in the wall. Nothing. There was the luggage holding area that bellboys used, and the hallway disappearing behind me led to rooms, it looked like, so there were bound to be closets that way. Should the world fall down around me, I had options.

Satisfied, I turned back to Emery, only then noticing his steady, blank-faced stare.

"What? Is he coming?" I glanced around, looking at people this time. Well-dressed hotel guests roamed around the lobby, or headed to the bar and disappeared down one of the hallways. No one seemed unnaturally pretty or alluring, and no one noticed us, except for a teenage girl who wouldn't stop staring at Emery.

"I have no idea what spell you did back there." His tone was flat, giving nothing away.

"Oh." I frowned as I thought back. A part of me had realized I was using magic, but it hadn't occurred to me that I was doing anything constructive with it. "Did you see the weave?"

"Yes. It was extremely intricate, which comes with experience." His eyes glittered and a smile broke

K . F . B R E E N E

through his stoic expression. "You are very tricky, Turdswallop. I am rather impressed. Have you ever used that with your mother?"

I waved the comment away, trying to ignore the horrible pet name he insisted on using. "I've tried to sweet-talk her. It never goes well."

"Your mother isn't strong in spell-casting magic, but she has hidden depths. Her strength of will is incredible. It has to be, to get out from under the kind of spell you just blindsided that poor woman with. No wonder your mother was able to match with someone like your father. And keep you in line. Fate has plans for you, Penny Bristol. I wish I could watch them unfold."

"I have news for you—you're going to get a front-row seat. Just as soon as danger comes our way, we'll experience my reactions together, equally as clueless as to what I'll do next."

His smile slid away, slowly replaced by sadness. He averted his gaze.

That was when I noticed the handsome man gliding through the room in black slacks and a white button-down shirt, the top two buttons opened.

I didn't need anyone to tell me. The vampire was on the scene.

CHAPTER 26

"EMERY, HELLO," THE insanely handsome man said as he stopped near our seats. His expressive, deep brown eyes shone as he stuck out his hand. His smile curved perfectly shaped lips into a mouth-watering smile. "So good of you to visit."

Emery stood, his face stoic but not any more so than usual. He almost seemed bored, which went against the warnings he'd given me earlier.

Then it occurred to me about his power and strife in what I assumed was the wilds—he strove to be the top of the food chain. In this room, he clearly thought he was.

"Hi, Clyde," Emery said, shaking hands.

Clyde? What kind of a vampire name was Clyde?

"And who is your beautiful friend?" Clyde turned to me, his gorgeous features made even more attractive by a wide smile. But his eyes weren't shining with delight. That sheen was something else. Something lurking. Predatory. Watchful.

I closed my eyes, unable to help it. My sleeping-while-standing-up look wasn't exactly appropriate mid-greeting, but the vampire's energy had changed the tune of my surroundings. I needed to know if my imagination was running amok, or if the magic within him was speaking to me.

I sucked in a breath. Though I could hear Emery's deep bass mingling with the enchanting, alluring song of Clyde, the words eluded me. Spicy, silky, and masterful, the vampire's magic caressed my skin and flirted with my senses. It soaked into my being and settled into my core, tightening my body pleasantly. But unlike with Emery, this wasn't a natural feeling. It was magical in nature, and its intent was my ultimate submission.

Electricity rolled over my skin, spicy and hot. I opened my eyes and met the keen gaze of the ultimate predator.

Emery hadn't needed to tell me what vampires were capable of. I could see it plain as day—and, for better or worse, feel it in every fiber of my being.

It would be so good.

I knifed the thought curling out of my consciousness.

Yes, they were the ultimate predators—turning their prey against themselves.

But I was not prey. And he'd die before I submitted.

Emery took two quick steps to my side and grabbed my wrists, holding them low. Our electricity merged, as it always did, amplifying the power and energy dancing around us. Within us. He took my wrists in one hand and wrapped his other arm around me, holding me tightly to his body.

It was his *Penny is not stable* positioning. And he was exactly right: I was far from stable. I felt threatened to my very being, and every fiber in my body wanted to meet that challenge. Wanted to show this vampire that I would end him if he tried to move in and take what was mine: my body, my choice, my freedom.

"Take us to somewhere private, Clyde. *Now*." Emery turned me away from the people passing us. "Deep breaths, Penny. Deep breaths. Try to calm it."

The energy changed again, now supercharged. The vampire's magic screamed *destruction*. Clyde's demeanor had changed, as well, the cultivated grace from a moment before turning fluid and deadly. Fangs dropped down from blackening gums and his pupils enlarged until they filled the whites of his eyes. A strange, gristly hue coated his once-flawless skin.

"Wow. He turns really ugly when he's amped up." I hadn't meant to say that. I'd meant to breathe. But the vampire's magic licked at me, knives slicing down my skin. The fire inside me raged. Streams of magic started to weave around the vampire.

"I'm not doing this," Emery said urgently, looking down at my hands. Then back up at me. His eyes widened, and his head snapped toward Clyde. "And she is untrained. She's reacting to your magic in ways I wasn't taught. You're out of control, Clyde, and so is she. *Fix this!*"

The vampire blinked twice, his brow furrowing and that ghastly hue diminishing slightly.

Emery bent down to me, his lips by my ear. "Breathe, Penny. Just breathe. Focus on my touch. On my voice. He won't hurt us here. But you can't release that spell."

"I don't know how to keep from releasing that spell," I said through clenched teeth. "I don't know how I'm making it. I'm just reacting to what I feel."

"I know. But remember, if a spell is woven too slowly, it'll dissipate. Just slow it down. Slow everything down."

I closed my eyes, focusing on his hands holding my wrists. On his arm tightly around me. His comforting feeling and smell.

I remembered how soundly I'd slept the night before, wrapped in a near-stranger's arms. When I'd finally roused in the morning, Emery's eyes were already open and staring at the ceiling. He'd lain still for who knew how long because he hadn't wanted to wake me up.

My mind shifted to his admissions of not feeling good enough. His belief that he was evil. He'd trusted me enough to tell me all of that. I realized that the trust was mutual. So if he said I could relax and still be safe, I believed him.

As though a valve had been turned, pressure whooshed out of the situation. The spell fizzled and the energy slowed, no longer boiling around us. The spicy danger was still there, the vampire's magic, but I ignored it, instead focusing on the positive feeling of Emery's touch.

I opened my eyes, taking in the scene—people moving around within the hotel. When Emery shifted a little, I once again caught sight of the vampire, his eyes and skin back to normal, his fangs pulling up into his gums.

His hard brown eyes studied me before he adopted a disarming smile. "And here we are. Back to normal."

I leveled him with a glare. "Don't try to charm me, bub. I've seen you without your makeup. It's not pretty."

To my surprise, his smile spread. "And I have seen you without yours, so to speak. I will take the opposite assertion. You are breathtaking. Please, come with me." He spared a glance for Emery, a sparkling, excited sort of thing, before leading us toward the bar area. Once there, we continued down the hall, past the dining area, and descended the stairs. "Are you hungry? I can have something brought to us now, or you can order room service later."

"We won't be staying." Emery released my wrists but not my shoulders.

My stomach growled and I put a hand over it. "Will he try to drug us? Because I'm starving."

"I will not try to drug you... I did not catch your name." Clyde turned at a crossroads in the hall and bent slightly, as though readying for a bow.

"Penny." I gingerly put out my hand. "Penny Bristol."

He completed the bow, but didn't take my hand. "I think we can both agree that holding off on touching is probably the best course of action for us right now."

"Thank you," I said, pulling my hand back. "We also need to speak with your boss."

"Yes." Clyde's gaze flicked to Emery and back to me. "My lobby administrator said something to that effect. I was surprised. She is new. She did not know to contact me immediately with your message. Nor, it seems, did she know your name. I was intrigued by how a trick such as that was pulled off. I expected one of the Mages' Guild. Follow me." He led us to the right and then to a large office at the end of the hall. He flicked a switch, and subdued light rained down on a large wooden desk facing two leather chairs. A bookcase stood against the wall behind the desk, stuffed full. Wooden filing cabinets adorned another wall and a coat rack waited by the door. Watching it all was a lone plant in the corner, scared for its life among all the dead wood.

"Please, have a seat." Clyde paused. "This is the most sterile private place available to us on such short notice. As soon as everyone is comfortable, we can move up to my quarters."

A smile tickled Emery's lips. "It's not often a vampire of your age is this cautious."

Clyde stopped next to the chair behind the desk, his hand resting on the back. "Not often, no." He waited for us to sit before taking his own seat. "I need a little more information before I call Mr. Durant. He doesn't like surprises. I'm sure you understand."

Emery leaned back in his chair and clasped his hands in front of him. "In all honesty, I hadn't expected to ask for Darius. I thought this would be one of our more typical interactions, with the exception of me asking you about translating a letter. But…"

I raised my hand, realizing Emery was at a loss for words. He probably worried about how much of my situation to give away. "Going above your head is my doing. I had a premonition to ask for the boss's boss. Since Emery was coming here to see you, I need your boss. I have no idea why."

Clyde steepled his fingers. "I see."

"Well, then at least someone does. But your boss

needs to come. That is non-negotiable."

"You are lying, Miss Bristol." Clyde's cunning gaze made my scalp tingle. Fire crept up my middle again. I was having an awful time keeping my cool around this vampire. The guy was mighty dangerous, that was clear. "But I can't tell about which part."

"Then how could you possibly tell I'm lying?"

"Certain things. Little things. When studied, there are little tells that—"

"Yeah, I don't care." I waved his words away, suddenly impatient. My phone vibrated in my pocket. Urgency overcame me, and I knew what the message would say before I even opened it.

Time is running out.

I passed the phone to Emery, my mother's message pulled up. The phone rang a moment later. It had been agreed upon that she would text us the messages she'd received through her magic, but no one had discussed the best way for her to badger us afterward. She'd want to know what our plans were—basically why our time was running out.

She would not be pleased that we had no idea. Maybe this Darius person could shed light on something. Or the letter could.

"Give him the letter," I told Emery.

Emery handed the phone back. "Don't answer it."

What did he think I was, insane?

I silenced the phone and put it in my pocket.

"Why don't you start at the beginning?" Clyde said, spreading his hands and smiling patiently.

Emery pushed the letter across the desk. "I'll start from what I'm okay with you knowing. I'm in town to hunt down the men responsible for my brother's death. I wish to claim vengeance, and find the place where my brother died. He needs a proper burial. I will give it to him."

Clyde took the letter and dropped it in front of him, not looking at the words.

Emery pointed at it. "I recovered that letter from the office of my brother's killer. I'm wondering if the man who sent him that was the one that ordered his death. I need to know what it says."

Clyde glanced down. It was unclear if he'd be able to read the letter or not. The man didn't give much away. "And if this letter is nothing?"

"I break into the Mages' Guild and look around." Emery's lips turned into a thin line, and shivers rolled over my body, making my small hairs stand on end.

"You and Penny will break in?" Clyde asked.

Emery's expression turned uncomfortable. He didn't answer.

"And what is your part in all of this?" Clyde asked me, entirely too patient.

I took a deep breath, because I didn't know how I'd

go about hanging him up by his toes and demanding action. "No one knows, least of all Emery and me. I don't fit into Emery's plans at all. I don't have a squabble with the guild—"

"You are a terrible liar, Miss Bristol. What is your squabble with the guild?"

I felt my eyebrows slip low. That was an annoying trait he had.

"It's best to be relaxed, and just let the lies come," Emery said nonchalantly.

"But she hasn't had practice." Clyde smiled, oozing charm. "How fortunate for me."

"I've had practice—it just never goes very well." I swatted the hair out of my eyes.

"Honesty. How refreshing." Clyde's smile grew.

"Her squabble," Emery said, taking over, thankfully, "should be fairly obvious. The guild found out about her when I did. I got past her mother first."

Clyde sat back in his chair. His gaze went back and forth between Emery and me. He glanced at the letter in front of him before reaching for the phone on the corner of his desk.

He was going to call his boss.

CHAPTER 27

A COUPLE OF hours later, Emery looked at the closed door of his adjoining suite with Penny. Clyde had given them one of the vampire suites at the bottom of the hotel to freshen up while he looked at Emery's letter and pulled any information that might be relevant. On his orders, clothes were brought to them, a hairdresser was sent down to Emery, and they were also encouraged to order whatever they wanted from room service. Everything would be paid for.

There was nothing to worry about. Penny was undoubtedly alone, and perfectly safe, on the other side of that door. Emery bent forward on the expensive couch and clasped his fingers together, struggling against the urge to knock on the door and ask if she was okay. He'd know if she was in danger. Everyone in the hotel would know. She'd probably blow the place sky high.

Darius had agreed to head out as soon as could be arranged. The guy had his own jet. That meant he'd be on site in no time, which was probably best. No one would know how to protect Penny better than Darius.

The problem was that no one would know how to better use her, either. They were putting another layer between themselves and the guild, yes, but they were also delivering themselves into the hands of uncertainty. Emery knew how to fight the guild. He didn't know how to fight the vampires. And likely wouldn't know until it was too late and he was outsmarted.

Now Penny was on her own, completely at the mercy of the one species that could wring every ounce of worth from her person. And sure, she could take care of herself in most situations...but what if she seized up and her magic wouldn't come? Sometimes that happened to people when they panicked. They turned into a deer in the headlights, freezing until run over.

He pushed off the couch and stalked over to the door adjoining their rooms. Emery braced his hands on the door frame and bent toward it, not sure what to do. This had to be right. Penny's mom had directed them on this path, and she was the genuine article. A powerful *Seer* the likes of which Emery had only met once or twice on his journey.

So why did it feel like they were wrapping themselves in Death's cloak?

A knock sounded at the main door. With a hard stare at the white wood in front of him, Emery pushed off and moved to answer it.

"Mr. Westbrook." Clyde stood at the door with papers and a knowing smile. "You are looking worlds better. You're almost another person. Isn't it a wonder what a haircut and a little water can do?"

Emery turned back into the room, sparing a glance for the closed door, and another for the clock. The middle of the night. They'd need to wrap this up and get some sleep so tomorrow wouldn't be a wasted day. He wanted to check out some of the guild's compounds and see how things had changed.

The door closed as he settled on the couch.

"Miss Bristol has been seen to and food delivered," Clyde said, taking the chair opposite Emery. His back was to the adjoining door. The vampire's positioning probably meant something, or was being used to convey a message in some way, but Emery had no idea what. For vampires, subtlety was an art form. "I thought you might want to know."

The tight bands around Emery's chest relaxed a little. What else would Clyde say? That they'd delivered her drink laced with drugs and scurried her away while he was getting his haircut? Emery had left her completely alone in a predator's nest—he should've been by her side, protecting her.

He was overreacting. He knew he was.

The vampires would want to keep their business relationship with Emery in good standing, and harming or harassing Penny in any way would severely jeopardize it. Because of Emery, Darius had access to some of the most potent, unique spells in the world. No way would an elder vampire throw that away for an untrained natural.

No, elders were interested in the long game. Darius would set this up to pay off in the years to come, not right now. Hopefully by then, Penny would be a rockstar mage. She'd be able to look out for herself.

Emery took a deep breath. His head and his gut were at war with each other.

"I've looked over the letter," Clyde said, "and checked with as many sources as I could reach."

He'd probably also made a copy and kept it for his records.

Clyde reached forward and placed the paper on the glass table between them. "It is not signed, as you know, but of the three Barons, only two speak Italian. That helps narrow things down. Of course, of the two that speak Italian, only one is proficient." He paused for dramatic effect. Emery waited. No point playing into the vampire's sense of theatrics. "This was written by the lesser of the proficient speakers, I am sure of it. But it has been polished up. He must've employed a proofreader or cheap translator to catch the larger issues. To an untrained eye, it would pass muster. Given that Nicholas is likely rusty with the language, he wouldn't notice."

"Who is the lesser of the proficient speakers?" Emery asked.

"Grimshaw."

"And the more fluent one?"

"Happerhust."

"Right." Emery rubbed his chin. "If what you say is true, it sounds like Grimshaw was trying to get Nicholas, a known killer within the guild, to believe Happerhust sent that note. And there are only a couple reasons why that would be. Either Nicholas was already assassinating people for Happerhust and Grimshaw wanted in on it without going through the proper channels, or Grimshaw wanted the finger pointed at Happerhust."

Clyde nodded.

Emery narrowed his eyes at Clyde, who was a vampire and therefore couldn't be trusted. Hence his issue with leaving Penny alone.

"From what I know, those two don't feud or disagree all that often," Emery said.

"They certainly do not, but you can never know what is brewing outside of the public eye."

Clyde would know that all too well. Vampires were notorious for their secrets.

"What did the letter say?" Emery asked.

"It is a vague message with a few lines of code to which I have no cipher. In time, I might be able to turn up something, but it was written four years ago. If they are not currently using this same code, I doubt we'll find much. As it is, what I can gather is that the creator of the letter was checking up on his instructions. He wants to know if all has been tucked away accordingly."

"What are your thoughts on that?"

"I can't be sure, of course, but the letter was dated, and it was written at about that time when three high-powered magical members of the guild disappeared. They were never found. A lackluster search and a watered-down investigation was the only effort the guild put into finding out what happened."

"You're sure of that?"

"Yes. I've been keeping track of disappearances and higher-level maneuverings within the guild for some time. Often I am able to get extensive details. If someone outside of the guild commits a crime against a guild member, the killer is usually discovered and punished. Other crimes go unsolved for no notable reason. This was of the latter variety. As was your brother's death."

"Which reeks of an inside job."

"Of course. The mages that disappeared around the date of the letter belonged to the field office fifty miles from the office you ransacked."

"You checked up on me."

"I should've known you were in the area the second you stepped onto our soil. That I didn't is...troublesome." A wrinkle formed in Clyde's forehead. Someone would be punished, Emery had no doubt. A vampire's whole existence was based on knowledge. They couldn't play political games without it.

"Given the unusual jump in the chain of command, the time frame, the deaths, and the fact that Nicholas is a known killer, I have no doubt all of this is connected to my brother's death." Emery scratched his temple. The *who* didn't really add up. From what he remembered, those two mages generally got along. They were on each other's sides and didn't go behind each other's backs to this degree. Of course, the guild operated on secrets and lies. There was no telling what was going on behind the scenes. And besides, this one instance didn't give Emery direct proof regarding his brother's case. He was a tiny bit closer to getting answers, but his next steps hadn't changed.

"What about someone that could get access to a Baron's office?" Emery asked, trying to consider all the possibilities.

"That is a possibility, though remote. Getting into those offices is not easy. I have tried to infiltrate them in a great many ways. It would have to be someone with a direct relationship to the Baron and a lot of magic. Mages as a whole are solitary and territorial, guarding their power with traps and fail-safes. The guild amplifies those traits in its members."

Emery had always thought that too, but Penny had changed his mind. She wasn't territorial. She worked with others as well as she breathed.

Maybe mages would be more powerful if they worked more like witches.

He ran his fingers through his hair, forgetting halfway through that the hairdresser had put a styling serum in it. He untangled his fingers and patted things back into place. He hadn't cared much about his appearance since he'd left town after his brother had died, but a big part of him wanted Penny to see the man he once was. It would make him feel normal for once.

"It must have been a Baron," Emery said, sighing and leaning back. "Besides the High Chancellor, there's no one else powerful enough to water down an investigation. The only way someone could use a Baron's office without his knowledge, then get an investigation evaporated, is if someone in a lower position ordered the killing, and the Baron went along with it after the fact."

"Doubtful."

Emery had to agree. Those in the guild liked to hold on to power with everything they had.

"I have to break into the guild compound." He felt resignation bleed through him. "I have to check out their main offices. It's the only way to know for sure."

"If you want to confirm the particular circumstances of your brother's death, then yes. Or you could just kill them all. I would help you, of course. I know where they live and their daily routines. Though I couldn't let my assistance to you be known, you understand. Even with the top tier taken out, they will still be able to function. They would have their whole faction hunting my vampires. My businesses would be in jeopardy."

The thought struck home. Emery's gaze slid over to the adjoining door.

What would happen to Penny when this was all over? Her house was in this area. Her family and her life. She couldn't leave with him and traipse across the worlds—it was no way for a girl like her to live. She deserved so much more.

But where would she go if the guild continued tracking her?

"They don't know that she is a natural," Clyde said. He'd clearly seen Emery's worry roll across his features. He was agitated enough that he wasn't doing much to disguise his thoughts right now. "Not yet. Right now, they are just curious about her. They are still working on your first ward, which they know is yours. We have time."

"After they break mine, they'll find the one her father put up a long time ago. That one will throw them for a loop. It's old and put together well. It's held up all these years. It'll help."

"We can distract them with something else, and burn down the house so they can't get any information on her."

Emery sat forward. "Burn down the house? That's her family's house. You can't burn it down."

Clyde put his hands up. "That is not for me to decide. I apologize; I spoke out of turn. This matter has been handed over to Darius. He'll take over the logistics."

Emery tapped his phone in his pocket, just making sure it was still there. He had exactly one number stored in it. Hers. He'd exchanged digits with her before closing that adjoining door, with a command to text him if she didn't feel like knocking. He'd figured texting would be easier if she felt shy. It had been a shot in the dark. One that had clearly failed. She should've checked in by now.

Had he remembered to tell her that vampires could magically open locks? She could be operating under a false sense of security.

"Speaking of Darius." Clyde held up the second sheet of paper before laying it onto the table. "These are the spells he is requesting. We'll supply all the necessary ingredients, as usual. They are being assembled now, and will be in the warehouse as early as tomorrow morning. Some are from a newly procured volume. The pages have been copied and will be given to you when Darius gets here, but the book itself will not be supplied. I apologize for the inconvenience." They didn't want Emery to steal the book. Wise. He would've tried, just like the last time. "Payment will be in cash or gold, as usual. For the usual spells, the price will be as previously established, and they're to be color-coded as specified on the paper. You can negotiate your fee for the new spells with Darius when he arrives."

"Fine."

The knock on the inner door had Emery's heart speeding up. Holding his breath, he crossed the distance and pulled open the door.

His breath caught in his throat. Her brown hair tumbled down over her shoulders, the reddish streaks like flames in the low light. A large T-shirt draped over her frame, hinting at breasts and ignoring curves altogether. It ended mid-thigh, showing shapely legs below. Fluffy white slippers supplied by the hotel covered her feet.

It took her a moment to focus on him, her eyes tired and vague, but when she did, it was the best feeling in the world. Surprise rolled over her features and her gaze dropped down his body before climbing back up to his face. There they roamed, growing increasingly more intense until her face flushed. She didn't look away. Instead, her gaze held his, and lust kindled in her eyes.

CHAPTER 28

I STOOD THERE like a dope with my mouth hanging open. Emery's hair had been cut and styled in what I called a *whoosh* number, very trendy, and for good reason. His scruff had been cut off completely, but the clean-shaven look didn't erase the tough, masculine quality that he so effortlessly exuded. His button-up shirt hugged his broad shoulders and kissed his pecs before falling down his flat stomach. His light-colored slacks showed off his powerful legs, and I couldn't stop staring.

I just couldn't stop.

Looking like this, with the dirt and crust stripped away (that sounded gross, but I honestly hadn't noticed it until now), he was easily on par with the vampire. Sleek and sexy.

His smile reached his glittering eyes. He'd noticed his effect on me, but I wasn't embarrassed. He'd earned it. He could just add this to his ego bucket.

"You're ready for bed," he said, stepping back into his room.

I'd meant to say goodnight and turn in, but I found myself walking after him like a lost lamb.

Get a hold of yourself!

"As I said—"

"Ah!" A jet of red zipped from my hand at the unexpected voice.

The shape moved so fast that I barely saw it, but not fast enough. My stream of magic raked across a limb, searing away shirt fabric and blistering the flesh underneath.

Clyde stopped near the door, his eyes tight and his burned arm hanging at his side.

"Oh God, I hope you heal quickly." I bit my lip.

"Don't take the Lord's name in vain." Emery laughed and crossed to the couch.

"Sorry. I didn't know Emery had company." I grimaced. "I probably should've started with sorry, shouldn't I have? Double sorry, then."

"I thought you weren't trained." Clyde glanced at his arm, already a bit less black.

"Oh. There you go. You do heal. That's great." I tucked a strand of hair behind my ear. "And no, I'm not trained. I randomly came up with that red zapping spell last night when mice ran out at me."

"Then you are a better mouser than a cat. How wonderful." His tone was so dry that he could light it on fire.

"No, actually. I didn't get any of the mice. They're faster—" His face hardened. "Never mind. It doesn't matter."

Emery laughed harder.

"I'll just…" I backed toward the door to my room.

"No, no, please." Clyde held up his arm, probably to show that he wasn't hurt. He wasn't fooling anyone. His ruined shirt sleeve dangled down his side and the blackened skin oozed pus. "I was just telling Emery that a haircut and a little bit of soap and water can do wonders."

"And first aid. First aid also does wonders." I pointed at his arm, glinting in the soft light of the room. "And bandages. A word to the wise. Don't walk by the dining room until you've got bandages. Otherwise you'll sell far less desserts."

Emery doubled over, holding his stomach, guffawing.

"Yes. Cute." Clyde's lips twisted, and I was pretty sure that was meant to be a smile. My unplanned attack had tarnished his good mood, though I couldn't exactly blame him for that. "I will check in with you tomorrow evening. During the day, a car will be made available, should you need it. If you do attempt to infiltrate the guild compound, I would caution you—"

"You're going to drip on the floor." I pointed at the oozing drop crawling down his forearm. He gave me a dead stare. As in, soon I'd be dead if I kept talking. "Sorry. It's just that the rug is white. But it's fine. Your house, your rules."

Emery's laughter was making this worse.

Well, technically, my continued babbling was making this worse, but he wasn't helping.

"As I was saying—"

"Sorry." I curled my lips inward.

"—their compound is a complex system. It would be wise to thoroughly study it before attempting entry, and even then, consulting with me will yield you the best results. I have a semblance of a map, which I'll leave at the front desk. It's not detailed, but it's something. Also, and I'm sure you've thought of this, three-year-old files from the Baron's office would've surely been purged to their recordkeeping facility. It might not be as easy to break into that facility magically, but there will certainly be less people. But on all of this, I'd advise you to wait until Darius arrives."

"Thank you, Clyde, I'll take that under advisement." Emery wiped his eyes.

"I'll take my leave. Miss Bristol, a pleasure." Clyde nodded stiffly and made for the door.

After he left, Emery braced his forearms on his knees. "Very little rattles that vampire. I've known him for years, and he's always in good spirits and teasing. Yet in less than twelve hours, you've made him lose control over and over. He's wary of you, and I think you've ruined his mood altogether." He shook his head and straightened back up, his eyes shining with unshed tears of laughter. "You are an absolute gem."

I stared at the door and picked at a fingernail. "He was pissed. I really didn't mean to rattle him."

"It's fine. Come here. Sit down. Do you need anything?"

I trudged toward Emery, the fatigue of uncertainty dragging at me. I plopped down next to him on the couch, careful of what I was doing with my legs because I didn't have pants on. "I need sleep. You?"

"Same. What... Uhm." He rubbed his nose. "Did you have an okay evening? Oh, did I tell you that vampires can magically open locks?"

I frowned, thinking back. "No, don't think so. Huh. Well, there goes my sense of security."

He straightened up, looking at me intensely. "This place isn't ideal, but they won't try to hurt us. At least not until Darius gets here. We'll be safe enough tonight, I'm almost positive."

"It's not ideal, sure, but there are no mice that I've seen, and it is absolute luxury. I'll take this and the predator lock-pickers over a musty bed above a noisy bar any day."

He smiled and bumped me gently with his shoulder. "You might not always say that, but for now, I'd have to agree." His eyes clouded over and the smile dripped off his face. He glanced at my open door. "Would you..." Butterflies filled my stomach. "It's no big deal if not, but would you mind... Uhm."

I shrugged, playing it cool. "Yeah, sure. The bed is big enough. We'll have plenty of room, so I won't have to lie on you."

He hesitated. "What?"

"What?"

His brow furrowed. "Oh, I just..." He pointed at the door to my room.

"Wanted to sleep in the same room, right? Because that would be safer, just in case?"

His stare intensified and a queasy feeling replaced the butterflies. "Oh. Yeah, we could do that," he said. "If you wanted."

My stomach clenched and heat rushed to my face. "What were you going to say?"

"Oh, nothing. Yeah, sleeping in the same bed would be fine, if that would make you feel safer. I sleep the same wherever. On my back." He cleared his throat. "I can just..." He waved his finger in the air, trying for some sort of communication that didn't communicate anything. "I'll just get something... I'll just change." Emery got up stiffly. Uncomfortably.

Crap on a cracker.

He hadn't meant for us to sleep in the same bed.

And now he probably thought I was throwing myself at him because of his new look.

"I didn't mean sex," I blurted, immediately making the situation more awkward. I wanted to go stick my head in a toilet and flush. "I mean—ha ha. That came out too blunt. But I just thought you'd meant we'd sleep, you know…like last night. I mean, but with more space. Because of the lock issue. The locks here, not last night—"

His constipated expression dropped away until his eyes were laughing again. His shoulders relaxed. "I knew what you meant, Turdswallop. I just didn't know you'd be up for it. Or even leaving the door open. But this is better. If anything should happen, we won't have to waste precious seconds running to each other."

He'd just wanted to sleep with the door open. Our own beds, with an open door between them. But here I was, trying to take a running leap and dive into his bed. "Oh. The door. Ha ha. Right. That's cool—"

"Let's use this room. It's the vampire room. It'll have better fortifications."

"This is the vampire room?" I asked, looking around as he slipped into the bathroom. It was bigger than mine, but not by much, and the setup looked just as luxurious—plush bed, check; fireplace, check; and stylishly decorated dressers, check. "Why is my room adjoined? Is it for a lesser vampire or something?"

I pulled back the duvet on the bed. Down, and delightful. I loved snuggling into a bed, and this setup would absolutely provide.

"Your room is for the blood source." Emery emerged from the bathroom in a pair of boxer briefs and a white T-shirt. I averted my eyes in case I embarrassed myself further.

"I spoke to my mother." I climbed into the bed and sighed as I sank into the plush mattress. "Oh, this is good. Vampires sure know how to live."

"They have a lot of practice." Emery pushed the door to my room wide open and glanced in. "If they come in on your side, we'll have more time to hear them."

"My mother says that as soon as they confront my father's ward, they'll know exactly who I am. They'll know my lineage, that he had been lying when he said I got my mother's magic and not his, though I have no idea how, and the race will be on."

"The race is already on." He hesitated at his side of the bed, looking at the duvet.

"What?" I asked, already making a pillow fort for my head.

A troubled expression crossed his face before he gingerly pulled back the covers and slid into the depths. His sigh matched mine from a moment before.

"Nice, right?" I punched my pillows so they were

the optimum level of fluffy.

He grabbed a pillow, and I could see he planned to put them all away so he could sleep as he always slept in the many places he substituted for a real bed.

"No." I put my hand on his arm to stop the lunacy. "No, you need to remember what a bed should feel like. This no-pillow ballyhoo is doing yourself a disservice. Get out. I'll deal with this."

"What?"

"Get out." I shoved him with all I had, getting one of his butt cheeks off the mattress. As expected, he got the message. "There is an art to cloudlike sleeping. Just like a spell, there are lots of ingredients."

"You've been making spells your whole life," Emery said, watching my face. He really should've been watching my hands so he could remember how to re-create this setup. Once he tried it, it would change his life, I was certain. "Your organization, your ingredients, your way of doing things...the motions of magic have been expressing themselves, even if your actual magic has not."

I gave my creation a test lie. "Oh yeah. This is the stuff." I rolled out and readjusted it before gesturing for him to take my place. "Hurry up, I'm tired." I shoved him down. His eyes were glued to mine and a little smile played across his lips.

For a guy who hadn't laughed much in the last few

years, he sure seemed to find a lot funny.

"So even though I couldn't express my real magic, I found ways to express the nature of it." I tucked him in until the covers were snuggled up to his face and his body was cocooned. "There. What says you?"

His stare still held mine. "It's hot."

"Tough. You'll learn to love it." I peeled away with a laugh and made my own cocoon. "So anyway, no, the race isn't on yet. They aren't actively looking for me or you; they are looking *out* for you. They aren't hunting— they are preparing. My mother says that's a big difference."

Emery's head moved against the pillows. "Yes, it is. We don't have much time, but we do have some. I don't want to wait for Darius to do recon, but we'll get a few hours of sleep first. Then we'll check out the compound. I want to see what spells I'm working against. Clyde was right. I need the record room. Everything I need is sure to be there."

"And then?"

"And then I'll make a store of spells, using your increased power to help, and go back and peel that room open like a can of sardines. They have a natural working for them, but she has no imagination. No drive. I don't need to overpower her spells; I need to outthink them. Given my training over the last three years, that won't be a problem."

"Maybe it's not that she doesn't have drive or imagination—it's that she doesn't want to be there in the first place. Maybe she doesn't have any other options."

I heard movement before Emery's fingers wrapped around my wrist and pulled.

"Don't disturb the cocoon!" But it was no use—he was sliding me toward him while scooting toward me. We met in the middle and he pulled me to his chest.

"That will not be your life. You *will* get to choose your own future, do you hear me? I made a promise and I will see it through." His breath rustled my hair. "Somehow," he whispered.

I truly hadn't been thinking of myself. The life of that other natural would never be mine. Could never. I'd lived in someone else's shadow all my life. My mother had been looking out for me, and I was grateful for her protection, but those days were done. I'd never again be someone's captive. I was ready to stand in the sun and make my own shadow.

Let the guild come. They'd rue the day they'd tried to rule me.

CHAPTER 29

"YOU READY—" EMERY cut off as he stood in the doorway to my room.

I buckled my utility belt around my waist, then pulled at the leather vest covering my long-sleeved shirt. My leather pants hugged my legs in claustrophobic ways, but in addition to looking badass, they'd protect me against spells and other nasty things. If the guild only attacked me with half of the artillery I was imagining, I'd be just fine.

"I'm good." I rolled my shoulders before flicking my braid to my back.

Emery nodded, his gaze intense, before turning away.

He wore similar leather apparel, and I had no idea where Clyde had gotten it on such short notice, but it couldn't have been easy. The stuff fit like a glove, and Emery's size and build weren't exactly common.

"I have a bunch of herbs and stuff in this belt." I tapped my belt as I sauntered into his room. "And my power stones. One didn't want to come along for the ride, though."

He glanced at my belt. "Open the flaps."

I did as he said, unbuttoning each compartment and pulling the leather away. His eyes moved from one compartment to the other before he pulled away and nodded. "You have different elements—ingredients—than I do. When we're there, leave those compartments open. I'll need them. As I go through the various spells, feel them out as best you can. Learn what the different herbs and stones can do. Also, leave those power stones behind for now. Otherwise I'll rob them of their strength."

I frowned, bracing my hands over the stones. I thought about taking them out, but a strange vibration crawled across my palms. "Nope, they stay. They don't want to go."

A line formed in his brow and he tilted his head.

I held up a finger. "Remember you told me it wasn't weird that they have personalities? You said that, so you can't make fun of me."

A smile twisted his lips. "I'm not making fun of you. I'm...perplexed. You have a different type of magic than I do, I'm sure of it. Before I met you, I thought all naturals were the same."

"Still the outcast. Awesome." I trudged toward the door.

His strong hand wrapped around my wrist and

swung me toward him. I hit his chest and lost my breath as his gaze rooted to mine. It sank in deep, all the way down to my core.

"I love that you are different, Penny Bristol. I love that you challenge my way of thinking. You are opening my mind, making me more adaptable. Able to yield. And that will make me stronger. Celebrate your differences. It is remarkable to be unique in a world of the mundane. You are one in a million."

Something moved, shifting inside of me. Fitting into place.

I encircled his neck with my arms and pulled him toward me. His lips were soft yet firm, insistent yet gentle. His hands splayed against my back, pulling me tightly against his body, before his arms wrapped me up in a strong embrace.

I moaned against his lips, heat boiling my blood and electricity surging within my core. Magic danced and played around us, light and free. I deepened the kiss, an unsettling ache coming over me. A deep longing that I knew only he could fill.

All too soon, he was pulling back, his beautiful eyes on fire, matching the feeling he'd stirred inside of me. "We have to go, Turdswallop."

I smiled at his attempt to tone down the moment.

"Okay." I stood on my tiptoes for one last kiss before pulling my hands away from around his neck. I slid them down his torso because...well, I was a warm-blooded female and he had an awesome body. After a deep breath, I turned and headed for the door.

The car had been waiting, just as Clyde had prom-ised, along with the map and a reminder about using caution and not engaging. "He wants you to survive this," I'd mumbled.

"Yes, but for the benefit of the vampires."

Before I knew it, Emery and I were on foot on a small, forested hillside, looking out at a sprawling complex of buildings, connected with tree-lined walk-ways and nestled together with large, geometric patches of grass. Shimmering magic emanated from it, blending into a series of color. My eyes kept trying to get lost, to convince my brain nothing was there. But if I focused hard enough, I could pick out more and more details.

The driver had dropped us off on a small access road, advising us to text when finished. He had been as quiet, hard-faced, and stoic as Clyde. He clearly worked for the vampire and not for the hotel. It was a distinc-tion that was now burned into my brain.

"I thought the buildings would be nicer," I mur-mured, looking over the one- and two-story buildings with cracked paint and dirty walls. The architecture was right out of the seventies, pointed and flat, and didn't appear to have been updated or upgraded since.

"They are less worried about appearances than they

are the money in their pockets. Spending money on trivial things like paint and polish is not in their way of thinking."

"Clearly." I closed my eyes and tried to feel the spells surrounding the campus. We were too far away.

"Let's get closer and have a look." He took my hand and crawled out of the trees.

"It's probably better if you don't waste a hand on helping me walk," I whispered, following him down the hillside.

"It's not for you. It's for me. To balance me out."

I felt the surge of aggression and wildness pump through the energy around us. The effect of soothing it made my brow crinkle. "I think you have anger issues."

"A few, yes."

"A relaxing bath would do wonders. Maybe some meditation."

"Your ability to focus even when talking nonsense is extraordinary."

"Because of baths. Trust me, you'll see." I let his surprised snort fan a smile on my face as I checked in with my surroundings.

I loved being in the trees and feeling the roots sink deeply into the earth. Feeling the air caress my skin before shaking the branches around me. Birds lent us their shrieks of warning and chatter, which sounded like soft chirps and happy songs.

Peace. That was what being immersed in all this nature made me feel.

Emery staggered to a stop as the playful magic curled around us. He spared me a glance before continuing on, the change in our magical environment clearly throwing him for a loop.

"I cannot control it, so don't bitch." I felt a strange pulsing from somewhere in front of us, high above and pressing down. The pressure was light right now, but it was getting stronger the closer we got.

"'Bitch' counts as swearing, I'm pretty sure. I'm going to tell your mother."

"I dare you."

"Yeah, I was bluffing."

He slowed as we neared the bottom of the hillside. The trees thinned until they cleared out altogether, the last yards barren until the shielding spell touched ground.

Now I could see the weave, tight and organized—it was solid and well put together, a real thing standing in our way.

"There are a few spells mixed in there," Emery said, squinting as he looked. "The ward is a classic blood offering, like your father's. Another spell to make the place invisible, and the third…"

I closed my eyes, letting the vibrations and intents push at me. Secrecy, mystery, and a warning. A sharp feeling, like an iron gate coming down at our necks, stabbed into my middle.

"An attack of some sort." I shook my head, frustrated. The feelings I was getting were all connected somehow, but I couldn't see the bridge. "Obviously the secrecy is the ward. Maybe the feeling of mystery. They are similar. Then the warning. The iron gate. Like it's spring-loaded, ready to pounce."

"Stupid." Emery made an exasperated sound. "Of course. If you don't pass the ward, you suffer the price."

"Death, or..."

"Doubtful. Pain, I would imagine. Unconsciousness, probably. Imagine a hiker wandered down here. You wouldn't want to kill them or the human cops would be all over it. You'd want to remove them without anyone being the wiser."

As I studied the weave, I felt magic rise all around us, not from our pouches, but from the ground, the trees, and the breeze rustling our hair. Emery's fingers waggled, and I watched what he made. Felt it.

A key.

"Are you countering the ward?"

"Yes, but just enough to offer up our blood. Put your hand up under my vest and touch my skin. I need my other hand, but I don't want to lose skin contact. I'm not sure if I can hold my focus without your touch."

I did as he said, quickly, forcing my hand between

the tight leather and onto his smooth skin. He walked forward, his other hand now weaving in a different way. Creating a shadow to drape over us.

I tried to follow both of his castings, but the work was too advanced for me. He was going too fast. So instead, I let my awareness spread out around us, feeling the various throbs of energy and trying to pair them with the spells. One persisted, not at all dispersed by his work. It was the one I'd noticed earlier, high overhead. It bore down on us, benign but insistent. Magical pressure that didn't seem to take a shape or cause a reaction from me.

"Give me your hand."

I pushed my free hand in front of Emery, looking out to the side where the collection of spells curved around, following the detour of the compound. He sliced my finger, quick and shallow, but the pressure from above continued to pulse.

"Something is…" I squinted up at the sky. I found a brief shimmer, but when I tried to focus on it, nothing but clear skies stretched overhead.

"Ready?" Emery's eyebrows pinched together before he followed my gaze. "What's up?"

"I don't know. I feel something, but I don't see any-thing. I'm not sure if it's magic or not. It has no intent, but…it watches, I think."

"It watches…" He glanced from one side to the other, a contemplative expression on his face. He shook his head and looked upward again. "Should we keep going?"

Another kind of pressure settled over me, and I realized that I had been blindly following Emery's lead. I was acting like a passenger and not a participant.

And that might get us killed.

Everything changed with that shift in perception. The spell in front of us mixed together and simmered like soup. The strange pressing sensation from above.

I dug out a power stone, then another, allowing my temperamental third eye to lead. Immediately my stomach curdled, and I realized danger was coming. Not right away, but my third eye was saying, *Go,* and my gut was saying, *Run away right now, you stupid idiot.* That always meant trouble.

One day I would take heed.

"Speed is key," I said, the words drifting from my mouth unbidden. "Things are going to get a little hairy later on."

I crouched, and he bent down beside me, watching my hands as I pressed them to the ground. Closing my eyes, I let my other senses soak in the world around us. Something was pressed deeply into the ground. Natural, but not alive. Not in the traditional sense. It pulsed with power, connecting with the sky in an elaborate construct I didn't understand.

"Watching, yes," I said, opening my eyes and looking at Emery. "It's watching. It's intelligent but has no brain." I crinkled my nose, frustrated with myself. "This isn't making sense. But it's not an immediate danger."

"I'm not getting a premonition."

He stared at me, inquiring. I stared back, debating.

A surge of excitement licked my middle and brought a grin to my face.

His lips twisted up at the corners. "Here comes the girl that runs over dead people."

"Yup. Let's go. In and out before that spying thing makes its decision about whether we're friends or foes."

CHAPTER 30

MY PHONE VIBRATED in one of my belt compartments. I fished it out as we jogged past the
perimeter magic and into the compound, prepared to
ignore anyone in the world except for my mother, and
only then if it was a text.

The spongy grass, wet from morning sprinklers, left
moisture on the sides of my boots. The first building
loomed large in front of us, and we crouched near the
corner of a hedge. Emery's fingers waved, and a spell
emerged. I got a *who's there?* vibe from it. He was going
to let magic be our eyes. Clever.

I flipped the phone open and read the text.

Plant seeds for future harvest.

I touched Emery's back as he pushed the spell into
existence, then stuck the phone in front of him. He
looked back, his gaze inquiring. I shrugged. I didn't
know what it meant, either.

How? I texted back. *And don't call. Need silenct.* I
didn't correct my typo. That would drive her nuts. Talk
about planting seeds.

Emery sat at the corner, watching ahead, intent. Silence descended around us, no birdsong drifting through the still and stagnant air. I tuned in as I waited for my mother's response, and Emery waited for his results.

As we crouched in silence, it struck me that this place felt…dead. A world devoid. No electricity surged outside of our sphere, and the usual sweet, sour, or heavy sensations were absent from the air. The life in this place was pushed off to the sides, contained and stifled.

They'd largely cut nature out of their compound. They'd cut themselves off from the source of all life, and they'd done it on purpose.

"They are rotting," I murmured, pulling at Emery. "They are rotting from within. They are skeletons propped up, waiting for the tide to wash them away."

He studied my face. "How do we wash them away?"

I shook my head. "I don't know. I'm new at this."

His hand came up so quickly that I flinched. When I stilled, he rested it on my chin and stroked the bottom of my lip, back and forth. "Steadfast," he said.

It felt like an odd sentiment right then, because I was just relaying what I knew, not giving up. "Okay."

He nodded, like he'd imparted wisdom, and turned back.

Another text came in. *Long game.*

"What in hell's lemonade are you talking about, Mother?" I muttered at the phone, shoving it in front of Emery's face. "That doesn't tell me about the seeds, you blasted woman."

He studied it for a second, turned that imploring gaze at me, and startled when I stood and shoved the phone into its compartment. Urgency had overcome me. The third eye said, *Move*, and the logical part of me said, *Run away quickly*. Yes, they were pointing me in different directions, but the idea was the same. No good would come of sitting here.

Emery's head jerked around and he burst up from his crouch. He grabbed my wrist and pulled me back behind the suffering hedges, green with brown patches, and around another corner. He released me and then started jogging in front of me. I kept up easily, right at his side but a little behind. He seemed to know where he was going.

A moment later, he sped up, and so did I. Faster still. He'd been intentionally taking a slower speed because I ran like a girl.

If only he would, too, we could speed up and finally get somewhere.

He rounded another corner and then paused. Something moved out of the corner of my eye. I reached for him, but he was already flattening against the wall, snatching at my leather. I crashed against the stucco, my own momentum and his anxious intervention making my speed too fast to stop. My face bounced off and my body followed.

His hand curled around my mouth, muffling the *oomph*. He ducked down as I fell, not helping me stay on my feet, but quieting me until I hit the ground. He held a finger to his lips.

He'd finally had a premonition. How lucky for me, who hadn't needed it, and would now have a bruise where the wall had sucker-punched me.

I climbed to my feet, and he rose with me, his hand hovering near my mouth. I slapped it away.

Footsteps stilled me. Emery gracefully plastered himself against the wall, between me and whoever was coming our way. His fingers worked quickly, creating the shadow spell. He stilled for long enough that the spell disintegrated. His head came around and he stared at me, his mouth closed but his eyes trying to impart a message.

I shook my head. *Not computing.*

He glanced down at his fingers. Then back to me. His eyes flicked down and to his left. Footsteps pressed against the concrete. The sole of a boot scuffed against a rock. They were close.

I couldn't help closing my eyes, feeling the deadened life around us crying for help. Feeling the fresh and vibrant items in my compartments. The opal stone that begged to be held.

Acting without thinking, I dug it out quickly and pulled on the other ingredients, willing them to cover us and hide us from view. But we needed more than shadows. We needed a walking cloak, a soundless bubble that would merge seamlessly with the walls and cling to whatever natural things were willing to help us.

The opal warmed in my hand. The magic flew around Emery and me, outlining our sphere of energy, protecting it. It felt like the stone was holding my hand as I worked with it, not doing my bidding so much as rushing to my aid. A tear leaked out of my eye, the emotion part of the recipe, and the spell drifted into the world.

I blinked my eyes open, my lashes wet, and looked around wildly.

Wrinkles lined Emery's forehead as he glanced at the bubble I'd made, a slight shimmer the only visible indication it was there. He didn't have time to spare me a *what kind of a weird magical worker cries when making spells* glance, because at that moment, two forms wearing purple robes sauntered along the cracked concrete, their backs straight, their shoulders squared, and their chins held a fraction too high. They thought the world of themselves, walking around in this stripped and deadened compound.

Fire rose within me and my power stones pulsed.

What little nature I could feel whispered to me, and I closed my eyes to listen to its calls. Emery's fingers curled around my wrist, amping my power with his electric touch. The energy swirled around and between us, frenzied.

Listening to impulse, I slapped my hands against the wall, cupping the opal, and sank down until my fingertips could feel the dirt at its base. This was what my mother had meant. Plant seeds. Seeds of destruction, to be harvested later, once I knew how to sow them.

Emery wasn't the only one who had yet to claim vengeance. I wanted to punish them for what they'd done to my father. And for what they'd done to everything and everyone inside of this compound. I wasn't a hero, but I was done hiding in closets, pretending it wasn't my business. They'd made it my business.

This time, there were no tears. Rage boiled up and slithered along my skin before meeting the threads of magic at my fingertips. It sank down into the ground before spreading out. I wanted to push. To pump in more magic. But Emery's hand pulled, tearing me away.

I sucked in a breath. My heart hammered and sweat beaded on my forehead. I felt like I'd run two marathons back to back.

Emery's lips met my ear. "Pull it back. You can't expend all your energy in one place."

The mages passed within five feet of us, their eyes

scanning. Their hubris obvious.

The one closest to us pulled a fistful of powder from his pocket. He threw it, murmuring something with barely moving lips. The powder burst into color and texture. The murmured words kept coming, and the elements spun, weaving into a haphazard sort of spell. Still, it must've worked as intended, because it spread out and coated the wall.

Emery leaned back, as though about to be seen. I leaned forward, wishing I'd brought a knife.

The mage's badly realized spell splattered against mine, then slipped off and pooled into a ball of colorful muck. The magic on the walls stuck, and I held my breath, wondering if the mages would notice part of their spell had failed. Surely they could feel it, even if they couldn't see it.

The mage walked on, strutting like a peacock with burned tail feathers.

"You are magnificent when you're riled up. We go this way." Emery pointed across the way and started forward.

I followed without hesitation, the rage from a moment ago draining away, leaving me shaky and confused. I wasn't sure where that had come from. Or what had come over me. Yet the throb around us was still present, and the bubble I'd created moved with us.

A grin spread across Emery's face as we reached the

next building and he paused, analyzing. "Very clever. Darius would pay you handsomely for that spell. I need to make friends with some stones. Maybe you can introduce me around."

I couldn't tell if he was making fun of me or not.

He peeked around the corner before taking me by the wrist and pulling. Clearly it was easier than words. I had to agree.

The pressure above intensified and a warning crackled against my skin. Emery must've felt it, because he glanced back at me in confusion.

I pointed upward. He followed my finger with his eyes, his brow furrowing as he pulled us down to a crouch beneath a suffocated and dying tree hugging the wall of another building.

A young man in a green robe hurried along the path, holding a satchel at his side. He hunched like he didn't want to be seen, something I understood pretty well. A woman dressed in red approached from the right, her straightforward stare denoting confidence. The air around her shimmered, wafting importance and authority.

"Sheriff," Emery whispered, watching her. He held his hands out toward them, both sets of fingers moving, spinning magic between them. I'd never seen this method before, but it looked more intense than doing two spells at the same time.

"Where are you going, boy?" the Sheriff called out, stopping the young man in his tracks.

His back bowed deeply. "I am late for my meeting, Sheriff."

"I see. How late?"

"I will make it if I run."

"But then you won't learn." She pulled a couple of things from the satchel at her side, raised them to her mouth, and murmured words to form the weave.

"I need to learn that," I muttered, watching the waves awkwardly twist together.

"You don't have to speak magic, because you can will it," he whispered, glancing around us, probably wondering if the spell would deaden our wards. "She aspires to do what you do, but doesn't have the ability or discipline. Probably both. The power has gone to her head, like the rest of them." Emery glanced down at his hands, but didn't stop working, creating the most complex weave I'd ever seen. He was a loom of magic, and it was extraordinary.

"There." The woman threw the power in the young man's face. He flinched as the magic wrapped around him. "That'll wear off in three minutes, give or take. Maybe next time you'll watch the clock a little closer."

"Yes, Sheriff," the man said miserably.

Emery lowered his hands to the ground and then swooped them back up to the wall. The spell attached to both before soaking in and disappearing.

I gave him a questioning gaze, earning a grin. "I can't let you plant *all* the seeds, now can I? I, too, like to create havoc." He winked, and we were up again, running across the complex.

Vicious intent pulsed from the records facility, a medium-sized building on the back corner of the compound. We'd skirted by three more fools, strutting around, throwing dust and whispering words. I couldn't tell if they were security, or if someone had assigned a few flunkies a made-up job to keep them out of sight.

Emery knew his stuff, though. He'd said most of the guild didn't really get going until about noon or thereafter, their workdays, so to speak, reaching into the night—when the other magical creatures in the Brink were most active. Judging by the overall lack of activity, the place did seem like it was in its off hours, similar to an office facility at night.

Unlike the other buildings, the records building had a protective spell stretching over it like a spider web. It pulsed with power, and the various weaves intermingled expertly. A lot of time and effort had been expended on this spell.

Emery crouched at one end of the wall, staring down at the door, which was covered with both another pulsing spell and a camera. They weren't just trusting magic with their secrets—they were using technology as well.

A grouping of benches formed a circle a ways in front of the door. Two other buildings helped surround them, making this area a little nook away from the rest of the compound.

"What do you feel?" Emery asked quietly, sparing a glance for a woman in an orange robe meandering through. She stopped near one of the benches and hesitated before sitting and bending to her phone.

"Spikes. Painful. This is an attack spell. A very good one."

"Very good, yes. The natural helped. The power rivals mine." He frowned as he looked it over, splaying his hand and waving it in front of the building as if feeling the various textures of the spell.

The woman straightened up and stretched, looking around. She wiggled her shoulders, as though something bothered the upper middle of her back.

"Crap-filled cupcakes..." I put my hand on Emery's shoulder. "Work fast. We got us a woman."

"What does that mean?" he asked, following my gaze.

I slapped his shoulder. "Don't look! She already feels our presence. She's in tune with her magically enhanced intuition. Looking will just bring her around faster."

"She's only middle tier. She stands no chance."

"Of fighting us? No. Of blowing our cover? She certainly does. Half a brain and she'll know someone is crouching here."

"How do you know all this?"

"Because I have half a brain. Haven't you ever just *felt* someone lurking? Someone watching you? Someone keeping close?"

"Yes, but that's because I've lived in the wild. She's in relative safety here."

"Women are never in relative safety, you moron. We train to watch out for danger from girlhood. Spoiler alert: the danger is menfolk. Dark streets and parking lots to us are like the wilds for you. Trust me, she knows when hidden eyes are on her. Look at her. She keeps looking around. I bet there are some power-tripping creeps with wandering hands in the Mages' Guild."

Emery spared one moment to meet my gaze, his way of gauging my severity, before nodding and turning back to the spell.

The woman in orange bent to her phone before lowering it again and tilting her head. Her shoulders tensed, and she looked back at the records facility pointedly, scanning the front door before looking up at the camera. She scanned the front again, her expression uneasy, before pausing, probably opening herself up to her surroundings.

Emery had been wrong. I wasn't one in a million. I

just knew better than to shrug off the first magic I'd ever learned for recipes and ingredients. I kept my temperamental third eye firmly in the mix, and so did this girl.

Her eyes flicked our way.

"Hurry, hurry, hurry." I bounced where I crouched. We had a long way to run back to the pickup point.

CHAPTER 31

"HELP ME." HE held out his hand. "And add more power to your cloak and dagger spell."

I entwined my fingers within his, feeling the sizzle roll up my skin and soak down into my middle. This time, it kept going, blistering through my legs and all the way to my feet. It bled into the ground.

Magic rolled and boiled within our circle as I poured energy into whatever Emery had been doing.

He shot me a wide-eyed, fearful glance. It lasted only a moment before he shifted his attention back to the spell, and I was left wondering what had happened.

I focused on his splayed hand, and for the first time, I saw the small tendrils connecting his palm to the spell coating the building. More, I felt them, each individual little strand like a tiny shock to the skin.

I put my hand up with his, trying not to notice the girl on the bench, who was still looking in our direction with a pronounced frown.

"We'll need to counteract this, or maybe burn a hole through it." He moved his palm, covering more ground.

I felt the evil and corruption of the spell sink into my palm. Emery used his other hand to create a weave similar to that of the poisoned protection spell. He was trying to duplicate it so he could work out how to reverse it.

Logic. It didn't always rush to my aid.

The girl lifted her phone and pointed it in our direction. She was taking a picture.

"Can photos see magic?" I asked.

"A picture will help the eye focus on a spell designed to confuse it. This isn't that type of spell. It is more advanced than that. That picture won't help her."

I closed my eyes again, feeling the pulse from above us. It bore down, pressing. I still had no idea what it was supposed to do. The general idea—to spot intruders—was clear, but the detail was so beyond my experience that I couldn't go much further.

"What is the problem, Jessica?" A large woman in a purple robe stalked toward the benches. Beside her, a tall, spindly man kept pace, his eyes scanning.

"Let's get to the front door." Emery stood and pulled me with him. If not for that, I would've spooked in the other direction.

"There isn't any upkeep planned for the records room, is there?" Jessica asked, her head tilting as she stared at our former position.

"No. Last month, you're thinking," the woman said.

"You called us all the way down here for a memory lapse?" The man scoffed.

"I beg forgiveness, sir, but I simply asked—"

"I know what you asked." The man looked around. "No, there are no scheduled drills, and no, there is nothing scheduled for the records room. It is business as usual. What's prompted this?"

"Here." Emery pulled me down beside him. "Hurry."

Oh sure, now he was a believer.

I turned toward the door, feeling the spell as I heard, "I feel...something...here." Feet scraped against concrete. The woman was turning. She sensed us, and she was really good at doing so.

"Where, Jessica?" the other woman asked.

"Just..."

Another scoff, from someone who thought Jessica's intuition was ridiculous, but who clearly knew better than to ignore it. That guy was a turd.

Footsteps sounded, and I had no doubt they were coming in our direction.

"Focus," Emery whispered, squeezing my hand. "Focus on me, Penny."

I did, and the feelings from the spell came through more strongly. The prickles on my palm helped me pick out the elements in the weave. He used his eyes. I used my feelers. He seemed to think it was two halves of the same coin. We could sense what the other was doing through the energy flowing between us.

Canvas scraped canvas and something rattled.

Emery shook my hand, bringing me back. The clink of rocks interrupted my thoughts.

The mages were close. They would cast that spell and find us. I knew that as sure as I was sitting there.

We needed a distraction.

I tore my hand out of Emery's and stood. He'd have to figure out the weave while I covered us. We'd have to come back another time to break through, but at least I could buy him as much time as possible to come up with a solution for when we returned.

The two mages in purple faced us, pushed up close, equipped with rocks, sticks, and basil. Their mouths were moving and magic curled into the air around them like smoke. A weak discovery feeling came to me, and I knew they still had a ways to go. Ish.

I racked my brain and closed my eyes, trying to think of something to do. Throwing a ball of fire might work. If only I knew how to make fire. Lighting them on fire would help. Still needed fire for that, though.

I let magic sizzle through me, wishing them away. Wishing for them to get bored and wander off. Another option would be to create a spell that crawled across the ground and then sprang up ten feet away. That would give us the ability to run.

Magic coursed through me. It turned and spun, pulling out determination from my middle. I shook with it, wanting so badly for them to leave.

I gritted my teeth and my heart sped up. My nails dug into my palms. The string in my middle yanked on my ribs. I let go of the spell and opened my eyes in anticipation.

The purple mages had their discovery spell hovering in the air. Ready to go.

My spell wrapped around me, swirling with purpose…and then bled into the ground. Gone.

"Uppity, gerbil-loving—" I clenched my teeth to cut off the words.

The mages bent to blow the spell at us.

Desperate, I punched the older woman in the face.

"We gotta go!" I grabbed Emery by the hair and yanked him up.

"What happened?" the man yelled.

"I saw a fist. Someone is there!" the younger woman hollered.

"My nose! My nose!"

"Run, run, run!" With a fistful of Emery's hair, I took off.

"Let go," he yelled, staggering after me. "What happened?"

"I created a diversion." I let go of his head and put on the jets. "Keep up or this spell protecting us will pop."

"I don't think it works like that."

"Who's to say? Just keep up." I turned a corner and hopped to the side at the last moment, nearly running full sprint into a guy with a huge belly. I would not have won that battle.

Emery tore around the corner right after me, not nearly as nimble. He bowled into the guy, the weight of his muscle no match for the other man's fat.

The guy let out an "*Arrrrgh*," which made me giggle manically, before falling backward and rolling twice. I grabbed Emery's arm as he staggered back. I held on, staying with him as he caught himself and straightened. We picked up speed as the man yelled out obscenities behind us. Together we ran, Emery's long legs the only thing keeping him in pace with me. We reached for each other at the same time, clasping hands right before we turned the corner, keeping close to stay in the bubble.

The pressure from above bore down harder and small points of pain tickled my awareness. The intent became clear. The blood we'd given was a guest pass, allotting us a certain amount of time.

Time had run out.

"Hurry, hurry, hurry," I yelled, putting on a burst of fear-inspired speed. I yanked Emery to keep up even though I was pretty sure the guys in the movies didn't do that to the girls. Call me a butthead, but I didn't want to die.

"What is that?" Emery asked. We turned a corner, almost there. Two people in red robes stood in the way, magic stretched out in front of them. "Nope."

Emery tugged me the other way. Sight was helpful, because I hadn't been able to feel the spell. Had I been relying on feel alone, I would've sprinted right through, Red Rover style.

An invisible hand slashed my arm. The pressure from above throbbed in my chest, squeezing my lungs. Invisible teeth bit at my back thigh.

"Where is this coming from?" Emery asked, and then grunted in pain.

I cried out, magic stabbing down through my shoulder.

"Faster, Emery. Everything you have."

He staggered. I grabbed his wrist with both hands, keeping us together (and yanking—once a butthead, always a butthead).

"Right." His yank was much more effective. "We have to go right. Then left. Pain is better than death."

Not always, but it wasn't the moment to split hairs.

I followed his lead. Pain stabbed my leg. I wobbled, pulled upright by Emery. He staggered, but kept going. My breath wheezed out of my chest, my lungs closing down. His breathing was labored as well. My stomach clenched and sight left my right eye. Razors clawed down my arms.

"There. Just there." The ward draped down in front of us, twenty feet away.

The air dried up in my lungs. I'd run out of time.

CHAPTER 32

I PUSHED ON with everything I had. Black spots danced in my vision. Agony welled up through my body.

Emery grabbed me by the back of my vest and flung me, trying to sacrifice himself to get me clear.

Over my dead body! Probably literally.

I twisted and reached back, catching hold of his wrist and refusing to release it. I did get a good yank in that time, ripping at my shoulder. He used the momentum, took a leap, and we rolled beyond the line.

Sweet air rushed into my lungs. The bone-crunching pain drifted away, leaving only an unpleasant memory in its wake. Gasping, Emery army-crawled toward me. He half lay on me, his hands on my face, looking worried.

"Are you okay?" He peered in my eyes before looking down over my body, touching gently. Back up at my face, he ran a thumb over my chin. "Penny, are you hurt?"

I breathed deeply, staring into those Milky Way

eyes. "I'm okay. But that was a close one."

His relieved exhale fell across my face. "Yes, it was. I couldn't see any magic drifting down. I have no idea what kind of a spell that was."

"It connected with something in the ground, I think. I can't be sure, but in the beginning, that's what it felt like."

A small line appeared between his eyebrows and he shook his head. "I've never heard of something like that. But the guild has access to a lot of resources. With all their manpower, they could afford to keep a huge spell running."

"Whatever this spell was, it must've created the dead feeling there. The lack of anything natural. Which will stifle their magic in the end, mark my words."

His thumb still stroked a burning line along my jaw. His eyes roamed my face slowly, landing on my lips. "We should get going. We don't want to be caught. Right now, they don't know who was lurking around."

I nodded, but my hand had its own ideas. I felt up his arms to his shoulders, the warmth in my chest intensifying.

His head bowed a fraction, his eyes glued to my lips. Someone shouted behind us. He jerked away and looked over his shoulder.

"We have to go." He got to his feet and pulled me up with him. "Can you walk?"

"Of course I can walk." Limping counted.

"Come on, Turdswallop." He swooped me up, and for a second I thought he would carry me romantically in his arms. Instead, he flung me over his shoulder and hastened toward the tree line. "Let's get you in that bath you were talking about."

"Will you join me?" I hadn't meant to say it. It just sorta fell out of my mouth.

I held my breath in the silence that followed, knowing I should retract the question…but I didn't want to. The guy was *way* more experienced than I was. I'd probably make a fool of myself with whatever followed the bath. But for once, I was sure the result would be worth the embarrassment.

Finally, he answered, his voice thick. "I don't think your mother would approve." He pulled his phone out of his back pocket. I saw the crack in the screen from my dangling position. He'd obviously fallen on it.

I opened my mouth to argue, because really, what parent *would* approve of their unwed child's naked activities, but I let it go. My mother had given him an awful lot of harassing about his life. He was probably still working through the sting. Eventually he'd get his confidence back, and I would awkwardly pedal myself out when the time came. No sweat.

The driver met us at the pickup point, and we gratefully fell into the plush leather seats.

"That ward's going to be a problem," Emery said softly, looking out his window. "It doesn't give us much time, even if it would let us in a second time after overstaying our welcome this time."

"If we think on it, maybe we can counteract it, like with the invisible bubble I created."

"If that bubble fails, though, we won't have time to get out."

"Okay, well, then we'll need to get in another way. Clearly the Looming Press of Death knew we were up to no good." I saw his cheek lift in a smile, but he didn't turn back my way. "Just look at where we entered the compound. If I were them, I'd leave all the non-access areas booby-trapped. So then, we get in through a normal access way. That should help us get around the problem."

"Pardon me for interrupting," the driver said. His eyes studied me in the rearview mirror. "But Mr. Regent has access to that facility during non-peak hours. He can get you into the compound, and into a couple of the buildings, too."

This time, Emery did look away from the window. His expression said he was not amused, but he didn't comment.

So I did it for him.

"And you only thought to mention this now, *after* we risked our lives to break in?"

The driver's eyes flashed to me again, but they held no apology. "Mr. Regent's orders."

"They want control over the situation." Emery looked back out the window. "And they want their magic."

"What magic?"

"The magic you're going to help me make."

AFTER WE'D HAD showers and an impromptu nap, the driver brought us to a spacious, mostly empty warehouse near a shipping yard. The daylight hours were waning and I was exhausted, but we couldn't stop now. If we wanted the vampires' help, we had to play their game.

Or so Emery had said.

"Wow." I widened my eyes as we approached the ingredient station. Every type of herb imaginable rested on the long table. Various stones, gems, and even sticks dominated the other end.

"Check out those power stones." Emery picked up a stack of papers and started leafing through.

Large and small, the stones and gems were an array of beautiful colors and textures, each prettier than the last. Power pulsed within them, the feelings warring or working with one another. Two of them needed to be separated immediately. They absolutely hated each other.

It was times like this that I was reminded why people thought I was so weird.

"What do you want to know about them?" I asked, zeroing in on one in particular. It was shaped almost like a diamond, and the inside looked like fire. Streaks of red were enhanced with dark red and black, giving a blazing sort of appearance and vibe. I placed it in my palm and let my eyes drift shut, feeling the pleasant pulse match the beating of my heart.

Electricity sizzled across my skin, and I felt Emery silently draw near. For a large man, he could walk softly. "A red beryl, as rare and beautiful as you are."

Butterflies filled my stomach, and I smiled, opening my eyes to find him staring at me. "This one has a lot of power even though it's not very big."

He stepped up to the table and put out his hand. "Let me know which ones want to be my friend."

I laughed and moved closer until my side was touching his, watching as his hand moved over the stones. He looked my way. "Well?"

"Oh. You were serious?"

"Of course. Some girls have dolls. Apparently you have rocks. I can work with that."

I crinkled my nose. That wasn't the best analogy…

"Haven't you been working with power stones for a long time?" I ran my hand down his arm and then grasped his hand, homing in on the rocks again as I concentrated on the pulse of his power and energy.

"Yes," I said. "I can use any power stone, but some are easier to work with than others. I'm wondering if that's because of something you can feel but I can't."

"Ah." Our hands moved over the various rocks and gems. A nondescript brown one, as dull and plain as they came, surged when our joined touch floated over it. I took my hand away, and it settled back down, the power simmering. "That one should be used if we're working together." I pointed. "Keep moving your hand over them." I closed my eyes, paying attention to the surges and grumpiness. Because some of the stones were not pleased with Emery's energy. Too wild and crazy. That made me smile.

"What?" Emery asked.

I opened my eyes and pointed at the various stones that would work best for him. "The reactions between your and their energy are funny. I've never experienced a grouchy stone before, but you set it off in them."

A funny look crossed his face and he started laughing. "You're a trip, Penny Bristol."

"That's one way to put it." I grabbed a few more stones for myself and tucked them into my utility belt, which Emery had insisted I wear over my jeans.

He handed me a sheet of paper. "I heard somewhere that you can do a spell if you have directions. Here are some directions. Can you handle it?"

"Oh no." I waved my hands and backed away. "No way. I'm not falling for that again."

A grin tickled his lips. "This isn't going to turn you into a zombie, Turdswallop."

"There are plenty of awful things out there, and this could be any one of those things. No. I'd rather watch from a safe distance."

"It says what it does. Right on the top." He pointed. "This one is titled and everything."

"Anyone could write a fake title and vague description on a piece of paper." I shook my head.

"Trust me, the vampires don't want to kill us."

It was the *trust me* that had me reaching forward like a fool. "I will never forgive you if this kills me."

He laughed and separated two sheets of paper before dropping the stack to the table. "Let me know if you need any help. It has the elements—sorry, ingredients—listed, so you should be able to match up the feeling with the item."

I nodded, glancing over the sheet of paper. As with last time, power and energy surged around me. A force I couldn't explain came over me, and the words and characters jumped on the page. It was calling out to me, willing me to bring the spell to life.

"You're a natural." Emery was studying me. "If I'd had any doubt before, this would prove it. You were born to this, Penny Bristol. You'll be one of the greatest mages the world has ever seen." He paused. "But first you'll need to properly learn to swear."

I released the breath I'd been holding. "Jerk."

He laughed, and it began. I went through the spell exactly like he'd said—like I was born to it. Ingredients came to life, and the magic weaved together so tightly and perfectly that it was a miracle to look at. With each spell, different emotions throbbed in my middle, pouring into my work as surely as the leaf of basil or pinch of dirt. It was my emotion that glued it all together and made it sing.

After each, I tucked the spell into a color-coded casing like Emery had showed me, and moved on to the next. As the day waned and my exhaustion rose, I reached the end of the list Emery had given me. He was back to staring at me, his pile of spells only a fraction larger than my own.

"Ready for the last one?" He held up three sheets of paper. "I can't do this alone."

"Why not?" I wiped the hair away from my wet forehead and headed over, taking the pages and looking over them.

He moved until he stood at my back, then reached his arms around me and slid them along mine. "Because it requires multiple mages working in tandem. It's a beast of a spell that will require extreme focus. Focus I only have with you."

"You need to work on that." My words were wispy, and I leaned against his body. The hum deep in my core rose to a fever pitch. This time, I didn't want to ignore it. I wanted to soak in it and let it overcome me. Emery was the first man I'd ever wanted to give myself to completely. In some ways, it felt like I already had. I'd given my magical self to him in its entirety, and now I wanted to follow up with the rest of me.

I tabled that for now, since I didn't think a warehouse was the optimum place to express my growing need, and read over the spell. Some parts required the mages to work together, and others—the hardest bits—were divided between the two.

"Ready?" His hands tracked back up my arms and then down my sides until they rested low on my hips.

Maybe this warehouse was exactly where I should express myself. Judging by my body's sudden fever pitch, it certainly seemed so.

"Yes." I nestled against his collarbone, and when I tilted my face up, his lips immediately settled on mine. The energy and power I'd come to expect didn't disappoint as it rolled over and through us. I deepened the kiss, turning and looping my arm around his neck.

As though a floodgate had burst open, passion overcame us. I slid my hands under his shirt, feeling the sculpted muscle there. He cupped my butt and pulled me tighter against him.

I moaned against his lips and worked my hands between us, ripping at his belt and reaching in. He groaned and followed suit, tracing his fingers along my panty line before dipping in and making my mind buzz.

An unsettling ache vibrated through me, a need that defied thought but required action.

But there was one thing that he had to know before this went where I finally wanted it to.

CHAPTER 33

"YOU'LL BE MY first, Emery," I said without preamble, expecting to be extremely embarrassed by my lack of experience. Surprisingly, I wasn't. Not at all. My lack of follow-through in the past had not been because of my mother's overprotectiveness. I'd had the opportunity a few times; I'd just never taken it. I'd gotten really close, but never jumped the hurdle. It just hadn't felt right. I'd felt my way through my sensual side in the same way I felt out spells and the power stones, and no one had properly fit.

Until Emery.

He fit perfectly, and it felt like I'd been waiting for him all this time.

He slowed his ministrations as a soft moan escaped his lips. A moment later, his fingers started up again, winding me up and making me gasp for breath.

"And you would choose me?" he asked, emotion soaking his words.

"Yes."

His kiss expressed his reaction, raw and consuming.

His touch spiraled me higher until my whole body tightened and I clung to him helplessly. I blasted apart, shuddering against him.

He slowed then and backed off. Before I could completely get my breath back, he was holding me tightly, crushing me to his chest.

"I can't let you give me something so precious, Penny. I can't let you do it. You deserve a man that can offer you the world. One that has both legs under him and pureness and light to match your own. Someone that can take care of you. I'm not any of that. I can barely take care of myself."

"Is this because of what my mother said, because—"

"No, this has nothing to do with your mother. It has to do with what's right. I am extremely honored. You have no idea how much I want you, Penny. Beyond thinking. It goes all the way down to my bones. But…" His voice broke. "I'm no good for you. In time you'll see that, and you'll thank me for this moment."

My heart swelled and ached over his mini-speech, but it didn't break. We fit together, him and I. Call me stubborn, but I wouldn't be the one who came around in the end; it'd be him. But I had turned violent in the past when someone had tried to rush me, so out of courtesy, I wouldn't rush him. He wasn't ready. He had too many hang-ups and self-loathing issues. Fine. I'd waited this long for him; I could wait a little longer.

"Okay," I said, resting my face in the hollow of his neck. I breathed in his smell, soap, cotton, and his own blend of *masculine*.

"It's not that—"

"Shhh." I leaned back and put a finger to his lips. His eyes held torment and sorrow. "It's okay. I respect your decision. But there are a great many things two people can do to pass the time that don't cross any lines."

He blinked a couple times, and a small smile ghosted across his lips. He shook his head and pulled me closer. "You're...dangerous, Penny Bristol."

"Takes one to know one, am I right? Now let's get this last spell done. I need food and I'm going to order the whole menu. Clyde owes us, the secret-keeping jerk. We could've been killed."

"He did warn us subtly. It's just too bad I don't do subtlety that well."

"You and me both."

I turned in his arms, keeping my body flush with his, and thought about the spell and the necessary steps and the vibrating power stone in my belt that was begging to help with this. It was getting bored, and I was holding it up.

"The red beryl is a little pushy," I muttered, dragging it out as Emery held up the sheet of paper in front of us.

"God, you're weird."

"Don't use the Lord's name in vain, or I'll tell my mother."

"Please don't." I could hear the smile in his voice and see the sudden lift of magic in the air.

Twenty minutes later, I was sweating and shaking. A complex weave draped in front of Emery and me, intricate and intense. I added to it from one side, and Emery added from the other. We melded them into one in various places, keeping them apart in others. When the shadows crawling across the floor blended into the darkness, we finally forced the spell into two separate capsules, since one would never hold all of that power.

I sagged into Emery. "I hope you are getting paid a lot of money for this."

"That is on—"

"Ah!" I sprayed out a series of red bursts of magic toward the deep and velvety voice in the corner of the warehouse.

The shape of a man moved forward so fast it blurred, my surprise zaps narrowly missing him.

A sheet of magic dropped down in front of us, a re-taining wall of sorts, meant to keep us at bay. Working together, Emery and I counteracted it easily, ripping through it. A well of power rose between us, ready for us to form it.

"Calm yourselves," the man said, standing in front

of the door of the warehouse with his hands up. One hand flicked, and bright light showered down on us.

I jerked back and blinked. Fire licked up my middle at the surprise.

"No, no, no, no." Emery snatched my hands and held them low. "That's Darius. Don't release that survival magic. You need to work on controlling it."

My heart battered my ribs. Calming, I resumed my sag. "Well, they need to work on announcing their presence, the sneaky buggers."

"Miss Bristol, I am happy to make your acquaintance." Darius swaggered toward us, confidence and arrogance plain in his movements. With close-cropped black hair and hazel eyes, he was every bit as much of a heartthrob as the other vampire. And he probably turned every bit as ugly when he got riled up. A perfectly tailored suit outlined his powerful body, but despite his size and strength, he moved with the lithe grace of a dancer.

He was more lethal than Clyde—I could see it in his movements and the intelligent cunning of his eyes.

A shiver rolled through my body, and I desperately shoved down my welling magic, which was eager to strike out at something so obviously dangerous as this vampire.

"Hi," I said evenly. "How long were you creeping around in that corner?

"Just the last five minutes or so. I didn't want to break your concentration." Darius switched his gaze to Emery. "Mr. Westbrook. So good to see you again. I hear you're in town on business?"

"Yes," Emery replied.

"Fantastic. I'm glad you could stop in and visit us." Darius made his way to the table, pausing to glance at the two round rubber casings on the ground that contained the beast of a spell. When he reached the table, he bent to survey the other spells we'd completed. "I see two distinct groups."

"Penny did the ones on the right. They'll be just as strong as mine, but more"—Emery scratched his nose—"more effective, I think. She adds something to her spells that speaks more closely to nature. It...fuses her spells with their surroundings, somehow. I haven't figured out how to duplicate it."

"Just tune in to the world around you." I shrugged. "That middle-tiered mage in the guild did it. There's no reason you can't."

"Penny hasn't been trained in the traditional ways," Emery told Darius. "It shows. In a good way. Those spells are powerful."

"I have no doubt." Darius turned to survey me, his eyes holding the experience of a few lifetimes. "I have heard a lot about you, Miss Bristol. We have...friends in common."

"Clyde is calling himself my friend after last night? That's forgiveness for you. I might like him a little better for it."

Darius clasped his hands behind his back. "Mr. Regent has a grudging respect for you, though I don't think he's eager to be in your company."

"Ah. Yes, that sounds a bit more like it." I pulled up some concrete and had a seat. I was tired.

"No, I was referring to Reagan Somerset and Callie and Desmond Banks. You and I were in that church together in Louisiana. Sadly, I didn't get the opportunity to meet you. I was otherwise engaged."

Emery's eyes widened and he shifted, looking down at me.

"I have a special relationship with Reagan…and the Bankses," Darius said, also looking down at me. "It seems you do, too. The Bankses wish to train you, is that correct?"

"Yes. And I was going to agree, but something came up."

"The guild, yes. You're a natural. It seems everyone agrees. So. What's next, Miss Bristol? Mr. Westbrook? How can I help?"

Emery put a hand in his pocket. "Easy. You can help us break into the records room in the guild."

CHAPTER 34

THE LONG GAME.

Penny's mom had said it, and the vampires lived by it. Emery needed to get on board. He couldn't just live for the moment anymore. He had to think ahead.

Just after midnight, Emery stood with the rest of their thrown-together team, nestled in a patch of trees near the guild entrance. The area was completely covered by cameras. Fencing stretched away on both sides, leaving a space for entering and exiting cars, separated by a guard station in the middle. To the casual, non-magical observer, it would seem like any large business, not horribly worried about someone sneaking over the fence, but concerned with security all the same.

To the magical eye, however, the place looked like Fort Knox, with a couple of different spells protecting the entrance, and the ward and various other spells stretching out to the sides. It was set up to keep people out, and as he and Penny had discovered earlier, there was an even better setup to keep guests from overstaying their welcome.

"Here we are." Darius, smooth and self-assured as only an elder vampire could be, squeezed a casing. The magic wafted out and draped around Penny, shimmering as it settled onto her skin.

Emery pulled the elements needed and re-created the spell easily, protecting himself. It was a badge, of sorts, and it would apparently get them into the front entrance.

"How did you get that spell?" Emery asked, draping the spell over the half-dozen mid-level vampires standing around them. Darius had called in a crew to help.

Emery was either aligning himself with a powerful ally or a formidable enemy. He hoped their relationship didn't go sour.

At least he was in the same boat as Penny, who had already unknowingly aligned herself with Darius. That had come as a shock. But Emery was happy to know she had a powerful dual-mage team interested in training her. He'd looked them up in the hours before this heist kicked off, in the time they'd been allotted for rest. The pair was powerful and influential in New Orleans. They had no interest in the guild. And since Darius wanted to keep Penny under his wing, she would be protected and well looked after—better than Emery could manage, at any rate. Darius had extremely deep pockets—he could move Penny and her mother anywhere in the world without a problem. He'd keep her safe from the guild.

"Mr. Regent tortured it out of a guild member who had affected his business," Darius said. "It is useful information."

Emery finally draped the protection spell over Darius. "All good."

The vampire nodded and looked around at the well-dressed and hard-faced crew. Penny started and glanced down at her utility belt. She tugged out her phone and her face crumpled. Darius's phone chimed a moment later.

He took it out and flicked the screen. "Yes?" His eyes darted to Penny.

Emery's heart sank when he saw the look in her eyes. "They know who I am. They want me in their control."

"They'll be passing this up the chain of command," Darius said, lowering his phone. "They'll organize and actively pursue her. Let's get this done and get her out of town."

"I'm staying with Emery," Penny said defiantly. Her eyes flashed fire. "Wherever he goes, I go. My life is tied with his."

Emery's heart ached. He wished that could be true. Wished his life was what it had once been. But there was no point in telling her that her naive, misguided feelings for him were just a result of the danger bringing them together. She wouldn't believe him. Hell, *he* didn't believe him. But he couldn't let her give him something she couldn't give to anyone else, not when he knew he'd have to walk away from her—for her own good.

"They'll be in early today. Someone might even be on their way here now." Emery stalked forward. "Let's get this done. Are you sure this spell will keep us protected within the compound for an extended period of time?"

"The longest tested is twelve hours." Darius glanced at a female vampire on his left. She nodded and took off, running at an inhuman speed. "That will be more than enough time for us to figure out if we have a shot—or if we need to reconvene and come up with different spells."

"We don't need different spells. I have what I need." Emery watched the woman reach the guard station, rip the door open, and duck inside. He'd worked out the counter-spell in the hotel room after Penny had fallen asleep. She'd offered to help, but needed the rest. He was used to doing without.

The vamp stepped out of the station, glanced their way, and continued on, running into the compound.

Emery started to jog. Penny easily met his pace, unbelievably fast and agile. The vampires sped up, too,

though they still looked like they were out for a Sunday stroll.

Passing the guard station, Penny gasped. "Did she kill them?"

A vampire peeled off from the group. A glance back said he was hiding the bodies.

"Yes." Darius didn't spare the scene a glance. "The guild is a cesspit of corruption. Judgment is on their doorstep."

"Good grief, you don't pull any punches, do you?" she muttered, flinching when they passed through the ward. "What were you doing in that church in New Orleans, anyway? I didn't see you. Where were you?"

"I was tied up in the back." His voice held a roughness that made Emery glance his way. There was a story behind that statement.

Penny must've also picked up on it. "Doing what?"

"Fighting magical werewolves. Why do you keep looking up?"

"Dizzy said one of those werewolves got loose."

"So I heard. What is so interesting about the sky?"

Penny looked down at her feet as they jogged through a spacious area between the buildings. They passed a small shack with a large, steaming cup of coffee painted on the front. The windows were all dark and a padlock secured the doors.

"Do you feel the larger ward from before?" Emery

asked, jogging by her side. "The one connected with the ground?"

A man in an orange robe lay facedown on the grass. Darius's female vampire helper was fast and brutal, not to mention excellent at her task. Clearly she'd had a lot of practice.

The vampire on body duty peeled off to take care of it.

"Not like before," Penny said. "It's there, but it isn't pressing. It isn't watching."

"What is this we are speaking of?" Darius asked.

Emery quickly filled him in as they all turned, heading to the back corner of the compound. Another two bodies lay off to the side, one with the head facing the wrong way. Another vampire darted out to help the first remove the bodies.

"Throwing up is probably bad form, right?" Penny's eyes widened at the sight of the body. She wiped her face, not getting an answer.

"I want to know what spell they are using for that ward," Emery said. "It is enormous if it covers the whole compound like a dome, and extremely effective."

Turning another corner, they found the ruthless female vampire standing in the path, her hip cocked and face placid. Darius slowed as they reached her.

"They have a small crew guarding the destination while two high-tier mages set up what looks like a spell," she said. "Two Sheriffs, the high-tier mages, and three middle-tiered mages as backup. Their eyes are alert and hands full."

Darius turned to Emery, the question silent: *What's the best course of action?*

Either that, or *Can you give us enough magical cover to defeat them?*

He wasn't great at reading "vampire."

Emery thought for a moment. "This place isn't on high alert, so they either don't know it's me, or they're overconfident in their abilities. Putting up another couple of spells is just a precaution, probably an attempt to derail any trespassers until they can meet with the Regionals and figure out if they need to overhaul the spells."

"Will you be derailed?" Darius asked.

"No." Emery took Penny's hand. "Especially not when working with Penny. Let me go first. I can distract them with a couple of spells. Then unleash the vampires."

Darius nodded and shifted, opening the way for Emery to pass.

"Love the new look." The female vampire gave him a feral grin, her eyes sparkling with lust. "It suits you."

"Good gracious," Penny muttered, staring at the woman. "There would be worse ways to go than with her hanging off your neck."

He stifled a bark of laughter. "Her kind aren't my type."

"Well, no, not if you want to keep your life, but still."

They paused at the corner. "Dig out that rock, Turdswallop," he whispered, then couldn't help but grin when she narrowed her eyes at the name. She was so easy to tease. He loved it. "Do you remember any attack spells from the lists earlier?"

"I remember all of them. For some reason, when it comes to magic, I have a photographic memory."

He'd said it before, but he'd say it again. "How much easier would life be if I had your brain?" He took a breath, readying for the charge. "Hit them with everything you've got. I'll take the ones on the right. You take the ones on the left. Keep them busy so the vampires can do the dirty work."

"What if I kill them?"

"Then you can pretend it was the vampires, and your conscience will be clear."

"Good call. Yes, I'll go with that. Because I think those spells are going to be nasty."

Emery agreed. He wanted the book from which Darius had gotten them.

"Here we go." He sprinted around the corner. She was at his side a second later.

They ran straight down the path, through the middle of the circular benches. The group at the front of the records building tensed. They all started talking together, their hands out and up, ready to loose their spells. The high-tiered mages in purple straightened from where they'd been crouched and then turned, their hands going to their satchels, full of raw ingredients.

Why they didn't use casings with spells for quick release, Emery didn't know. Arrogance, probably. That would cost them their lives.

Magic rose from Emery's belt. Penny was already weaving, fast, efficient, and perfect, like she'd been doing it all her life. He finished his own weave a moment later, still charging toward the clustered group of mages.

"It's the natural and the girl," someone shouted.

Their movements grew more harried, their fear evident.

Penny's weave darted out in front of her. His loosed a moment later. Invisible knives slashed at the two mages in front of Emery, lines of red opening up on their robes. The people on Penny's side shrieked and grabbed at their heads. Their screams turned piercing as they writhed in agony.

Someone got a spell off. It flashed out toward Penny.

Emery called up a defense spell, but he didn't have the time to lash out. A pure shield of white rose in front of Penny before blasting out, eating through the coming spell and then continuing on to the attacker. Just like he'd witnessed that first night, it acted as a homing device, locating the caster and contorting her body until a loud crack cut off her scream.

"Gross," he heard. Then, "Darius's fault."

Shapes darted in from the sides, lightning fast and incredibly lethal. Vampires snatched up anyone left standing and broke them in some way, their strength unparalleled. The mages' bodies were tossed away, and the predators drifted to the sides, giving Emery and Penny room.

Silence descended over the scene like a smothering blanket.

"I do not want a vampire for an enemy," Penny whispered out of the side of her mouth.

Not any of the vampires under Darius's leadership, at any rate. They were organized and exceptional, just like their maker.

Emery looked at the spell covering the door. "Okay, let's break this spell open and get what we need before the cavalry shows up."

CHAPTER 35

E MERY STARED AT the front of the door before wrapping his fingers around my wrist. The harried energy around us slowly smoothed out. We both took a deep breath at the same time, analyzing the spells draping the entrance.

"Help where you can," he said, before removing his hand and starting his weave, a complex spell spinning into existence between his hands.

I closed my eyes and lowered my head, feeling the intent of the spell he was creating, then that of the spell standing in our way. A key and a barrier.

Those two didn't fit together.

I held out my hand, eyes still closed, letting it drift until I could feel Emery's creation right beneath my fingertips. Peeling open a lid, I glanced at him. He looked confused, but he didn't stop, and he didn't tell me to move away. He trusted what an untrained mage with more power than sense planned to do. It was a miracle he was still alive.

Ignoring my inner naysayer, I closed my eye again,

feeling the energy in the bubble around us pulse and play. I imagined the barrier in front of us, and immediately thought of a great oak, with its strong roots and sturdy branches. Such a tree could bust the barrier down, but it would take too long.

Tilting my head, I envisioned a jackhammer to go with the tree. After fusing the two, nature and steel, together in my mind, I connected them with the key Emery was building. Heat warmed the air between us. Fire burned my palm, followed by an icy sensation, mixing and meshing with the spell below. Changing it.

The new energy sang in my blood. Whispered to me of freshly plowed fields and lightning storms. Magic flowed through me, the tug on my ribs resulting in heat dripping down my middle. That meant I was onto something.

I sincerely hoped that something didn't go *boom*.

"Enough."

I yanked my hand away at Emery's command and opened my eyes. He spread his hands, revealing a thick weave made up of many smaller weaves, all twisting and interconnecting at irregular intervals. But while it looked like a hot mess at first glance, upon closer inspection, it held a chaotic beauty, the patterns and shapes organized even if the layout was not.

"Incredible," Emery said in not much more than a whisper. "I wish we could train together. You'd teach me as much as I would teach you."

I ignored the twist in my gut at his comment about not training together. "I don't even know what I'm doing most of the time. How could I teach it?"

"By doing, and letting me be a part of it." He pushed his hands away.

The spell released and spread out in front of us before sending tendrils down into the ground—the roots I had imagined.

"Simply incredible," Emery said, watching. "I have so many ideas."

"And I have all the resources you'll need to create them," Darius said, standing directly behind us with his hands behind his back.

Emery's brow furrowed and his gaze returned to the front door. Light flashed in the lines that now ran the length of the building. It flared in front of us.

I grabbed Emery's arm. "How do we know it won't explode?"

"It won't."

"Right." I stared at the changing colors, the spell growing more furious as it ate through the ward. "And how do you know?"

"By the look of it."

"Uh-huh." He'd just acted as though he'd never seen anything like it, so I found his confidence a little tough to believe.

A large black line opened up in the spell, right over the doorway. Like an egg breaking, it ran down to the ground. The lines along the sides became wider. Red flashed.

I took a step back, ready to hide behind the vampires. They could heal. I could not.

One final soundless flash, and the spell protecting the building disappeared into nothing, sending me a laughing farewell as it did so.

"Uh-oh," I said, realizing what that meant. "It's going to tell on us."

"Yeah. I just saw that."

"What is this?" Darius asked.

"There was a spell hidden in the depths of the ward. One I didn't know was there." Emery rushed toward the door.

"A tattletale spell." I followed quickly.

"It will alert the spell casters of a breach." Emery yanked at the locked door. "We don't have much time." He turned, moving me to the side.

Darius flicked his fingers. The click of a lock sounded.

"Giving their species that power is just plain cruel," I said.

The spacious interior of the records building spread out before us, an extremely organized collection of boxes and containers housed in rows upon rows of numbered and labeled shelves. Magic hugged the walls, and I realized it was to keep the atmosphere climate-controlled in order to preserve the various documents stored inside.

"This is helpful," Darius said, strolling in. He looked behind him, and vampires filed in faster than thought.

Emery was off like a shot, looking at the white labels on the front of each row. Darius came to a stop beside me, his gaze constantly moving before turning back toward the door.

"You might join Miss Beauchene outside," he said. "She'll show you what to do."

"You mean, kill anyone close enough to see what's going on?" I asked.

"Fabulous. You already know what's needed." He nodded at the doorway and then took off, heading toward Emery. Even in a highly pressurized situation, he was as cultivated and smooth as silk.

I about-faced and hurried outside, not loving the detail I'd been given, but knowing it would help Emery. He needed closure, and hopefully this would do it for him.

Miss Beauchene, the ferocious killer with a face that would make angels sing, stood at the front door with a relaxed posture. She looked out at the dark and quiet grounds, the calm before the storm.

I stood on the other side of the door, feeling my surroundings. The moon sprinkled light onto the ground, creating shadows by the walls and under the bushes. I analyzed those, growing familiar with their shapes in case someone tried to use them for cover.

"You are new to this life?" Miss Beauchene asked. Her lovely voice, heavily accented, barely reached my ears.

"Yes."

"You do not have to speak so loud. I have excellent hearing."

I nodded—couldn't get much quieter than that.

"You seem to be adjusting well." Her head snapped to the left. Her whole body stilled and she shifted silently, facing that direction. "Your name is Penelope, is that correct?"

"Technically, but I go by Penny."

"A poor choice. Penelope is fitting." A tad opinionated, this vampire. "I am Marie. Now stay here." And with that, she was off, zooming away.

A rustle and a grunt broke the silence. Something slid across the cement, ending in a heavy object slapping the ground. In rushed the dense, murky silence.

Marie strode around the corner, her eyes back to scanning.

I gulped and tried desperately to stuff all of this on the "ignore list." That became increasingly more difficult when she said, "I left a line of blood on the footpath. Sloppy."

Shifting my weight from one foot to the other, I glanced behind me through the door. A sheet of paper fluttered to the ground. Two more followed it before an open box was placed near the entrance. A vampire zipped by, carrying another box.

"You guys had your own agenda," I murmured, remembering what Clyde had said.

"Of course." She looked straight ahead, and her body went on point again.

That was when it hit me. Like the undertow before a tsunami, the magic sucked at me. Dark, thick, and evil, something was in the works, and it would not be pretty.

"Skin peeling…" Eyes closed, I leaned away from it, focusing on the prickles rolling across my skin. My stomach churned. "Pulling our insides out." The darkness rose in the distance, a growing balloon intent on our bodily destruction.

"What do I do?" Marie asked, at my side.

My power stones, all six of them, begged me to take them out, to spread them out in front of me. I complied quickly, pausing twice when one groused about the location. Once those were arrayed on the ground, I stripped off my utility belt and sprinkled the contents on the ground around the stones, creating a circle around me. A slight breeze stirred my hair and dusted my face. A sweet fragrance filled my senses and calmed my nerves.

My phone buzzed, clattering against the ground where I'd dropped it. Marie was there in an instant, quieting it. My mother had been pulling double duty lately, always awake, always sending new readings. She had to be exhausted. That, or she had friends she never told me about, and they were taking shifts.

Probably the latter.

"What does it say, Marie? Quickly."

"'Use the vampire.'"

"Okay, well, you heard her. Get in here." I stepped closer to the power stones, allowing room for Marie at my back.

Without question, Marie stepped into the circle, more courageous than I would've been in her situation. And less curious. Did she not wonder who was giving me orders via text?

Ignore list.

I centered myself in my self-made haven of natural magic, focusing on the feeling of what was looming out there in the darkness. Nature guided me in the weave, as it so often did, attaching to what I now knew was my will. Marie's magic drifted into the mix, predatory and sharp, a lethal killer who hunted in the shadows. Finally, a complex mix of emotions that could best be compared with PMS rose through my middle, confused and sad and annoyed and ragey all at the same time.

Power pulsed around me. The sky crackled.

"They are getting closer," Marie whispered. "Muttering. I can't hear what they are saying."

"I know. I can feel it."

The huge wave was loosed, rolling toward us quickly.

My hands spread out like claws, my teeth gritted, and my eyes closed. I had one moment to issue a plea that this would work as intended and save everyone in the records room, before I shoved my arms forward, and with them, my spell.

A complex wave, glimmering white, stretched out in front of us. It drifted toward the oncoming spell, slow and steady. Thick and violent.

A cloud of deep green slammed into my wall. Pops and sparks flew out, cracking and banging. The green mass tried to burrow through my weave. Eat it away. Punch holes into it.

My magic held fast, retreating with the onslaught.

My power stones burst with power, feeding the spell I'd already sent into the world. I had no idea how or why.

The colors changed. The weaves continued to do war. My spell held fast, wearing the other down. Corroding it.

"I'll get the casters," Marie said.

I snatched her arm and got a nasty scratch from a

claw for my efforts. "No! My spell is just getting going. This is the defensive part. Your magic will be kicking off in just a moment."

"My magic?" Marie said, stilling.

Electricity rolled across my skin, and then Emery was behind us. "What's happening? Do you need help?"

"No," I whispered, keeping a tight grip on Marie's hand. This was about to be the worst thing I'd ever created. I could feel it. I needed to hold a hand—or in this case, a vicious-looking set of claws—to keep my courage. "This is the vampires' fault, by the way. Let's all acknowledge that up front."

"I see them," Marie said. "Walking forward slowly. Six of them. Arrogance at work."

A bright flare of light lit everyone up, and suddenly I could see them too. Six, as Marie had said, three in red robes, two in purple, and one in orange. They had more ingredients in their hands, but no one's lips were moving. They wanted to see how their first spell did before moving on to another.

How dumb could this organization possibly be? Emery and I didn't need to memorize words or separate our ingredients out beforehand, so time would always be on our side.

As the full weight of what I was, and how lucky I was, hit me, my spell morphed into a strange, grisly-looking thing, replete with magical spikes and gaping black holes.

"What the hell did you create?" Emery asked, stepping closer.

"Something a vampire would be proud of," I muttered, feeling a little sick to my stomach.

"We shall see." Marie laid a hand on my shoulder, thankfully without claws. I wasn't sure being her buddy was a good thing.

The spell flew forward as fast as Darius could run, drifting over the ground silently. It crashed into the mages, piercing them in a hundred places each, the spikes digging into their flesh. Now attached, it began eating away at its new hosts, a magical parasite.

Screams rent the night sky. Emery acted quickly, pulling from the ingredients scattering the ground and dropping a magical noise cap onto the scene.

He turned to me, his eyes intense, before a little smile curved his lips. A moment later, he was sprinting back into the building.

"He is proud of you." Marie's grip tightened on my shoulder. One by one, the bodies fell into a heap. "And I would be honored to take responsibility for the effects of that spell. It was magnificent. I hope to be in battle with you someday."

I grimaced. Definitely not a personal goal to be her friend.

She stiffened, and I felt the coming spell. I turned to throw my hands up, not sure what I would do, but I went airborne. I hit the side of the building and tumbled to the ground. The spell harmlessly zipped past.

"My apologies. I didn't know if you'd react in time." Marie was zooming away.

Climbing to my feet, I felt another spell coming. These weren't being created; they were already made. From casings, I'd bet. Weaker, but harder to sense until they were on top of me.

"We're under siege," I yelled over my shoulder. "We gotta go."

I called up another shield and ran forward. A blast of light hit my magic, fizzing and popping. I shot out, my red jet of electricity enhanced with a few tricks I'd learned recently. A scream rose. A man in orange crumpled to the ground. Another turned and ran toward the building on my right.

I patched together a rolling ball of heat and really, *really* wished I knew how to make fire. The fire Reagan had summoned in that church had been way cooler than my efforts, not to mention more effective. I needed that kind of firepower. Literally.

It rolled over him, and his robes burst into flames. With the door open, the ball continued inside, searing the frame as it boiled through.

Good enough.

Smoke puffed out of the building. Light glowed and flickered from within.

"Oooooh…" I grimaced. If all the screaming and

blasts of light didn't get us noticed, a burning building would surely do the trick. "We gotta go!"

I turned and started running. Marie was beside me in a moment.

"We gotta go," I yelled again, bursting into the records room.

Paper and overturned boxes littered the entire right side of the building. Gaping holes announced missing boxes from shelves. In front of me, three vampires waited, six boxes strapped to each of their backs with thick netting. The others were getting loaded up. Darius clearly planned to take as much of the record room with him as possible, but he didn't think he was above hard labor. It looked like he'd be carrying out boxes too.

"Clearly we're even in this endeavor," I said, indignant for reasons I couldn't name. "Just in case you try to call in a favor for helping us get into the compound"—I waggled my finger at Darius—"this is that favor. You're welcome for our role in getting you in here."

Emery smiled in approval and gave me a small nod. He only had one file, I noticed.

"You are not so naive as you seem," Darius said, adjusting the straps of the netting over his shoulders. "How unfortunate."

"Oh no, I'm horribly naive. It's annoying and I hate it. But I'm not stupid. Now let's go. I may or may not have set a building on fire."

CHAPTER 36

WE SPRINTED OUT of the records building. Smoke coughed out of the opened door a ways up. Flames flickered in the windows. No denying *that*. I'd definitely set fire to it.

A jet of magic came at us. Emery shot something back before I could even blink.

I collected up my power stones and whatever handfuls I could of the natural items. I stuffed them into my belt and strapped it on as the vampires converged around us.

"Stay near me," Emery said, grabbing my arm and pulling me close. Our bubble flared to life almost immediately, our power instantly amping up.

We jogged out the way we'd come. Movement caught my eye from the right, a pulsing beacon of death flaring to life in front of us.

"They're creating a nasty spell that way." I pointed in front of us.

"Exit strategy. Go left," Darius commanded.

Like a flock of birds, everyone turned, the vampires

gliding along effortlessly, seemingly untroubled by the weight and bulk strapped to their backs. Emery dropped a hazy shield around us, similar to the spell I'd used against the mage attack on our first visit. He could say what he wanted, but his brain was clearly just fine at quickly picking up and remembering spells.

We picked up the speed until Emery and I were flat-out running. The boxes bounced on the backs of the vampires. Evil sparked behind us.

"Incoming," I hollered, whirling another heat ball into existence, then bowling it behind us.

"You have a very creative imagination." Emery created a weave above us, perfectly done regardless of how fast we were running. "And a very scary one."

"You literally have no idea." Movement caught my eye to the right and I sent a red zapper that way. Someone shrieked. Marie sprinted away and the sound cut off.

"Left," Darius said.

Emery and I turned together, moving into a part of the compound we hadn't seen earlier. We passed between shabby buildings with black windows and sickly trees with bare branches. Marie caught up to us before stalling and drifting behind. I felt a surge of aggression, spiky and hot, ready to be realized.

"Oh no." I jumped to the side so the vampires could pass me and sprinted back toward her, my heart in my throat. She was terrifying, but she had helped me. I didn't want to see her die.

"Penny," Emery called out, chasing after me.

The spell loosed, hurtling in roughly our direction. Marie ran in front of us, right at it. It would slice her in pieces. Even superior healing would not help her.

White-hot fire rose through me. I clapped my hand on Emery's wrist, closed my eyes, and opened up to my intention. *Blast away that spell.*

My center exploded out, my power acidic. I staggered, clutching at my chest. Emery wrapped his arm around my shoulders, supporting me as my spell sailed right above Marie's head. It hit the spell five feet before it reached her. An explosion of heat and light blasted Marie off her feet. She flew backward at us, her hair burned away and her clothes smoking.

Her body hit mine, throwing me back. My head smacked against the ground and my vision swam.

"Get Penny," Emery yelled, his voice hard. Hexes exploded through the air, firing out from Emery faster than I could think. Energy boiled and frayed around us.

Screams pierced the darkness. Agonized groans filled in the gaps. Movement came from the right. Emery gracefully turned his upper body to shift his aim, his file at his feet and his magic rising around him like he was some sort of God. He flung the spells every which way, aggressive and powerful, cutting out the enemy with cool efficiency.

A hairless, gristly-green monster yanked me up off the ground and threw me over its shoulder. Black filled its eyes, fangs dropped down from black gums surrounded by black lips, and jutting cheekbones with hollowed cheeks made me cringe.

"Am I hallucinating?" I tried to hold my hands away from touching its half-scorched, half-swampy back. My head pounded and simultaneously felt like it had been stuffed with feathers, but I could still make out the greenish-white skin dipping between the creature's ribs, the bony butt, and stringy, bowed legs.

And we were running. So fast I couldn't focus. Legs churning and air whipping my face. I squeezed my eyes shut, then opened them again, thinking of Emery. He had been left behind to deal with the mages. Alone.

"Let me down. I can help," I said. "I'm fine."

"He comes," the horrifying monster said through a mouthful of fangs.

I arched, looking back. Sure enough, Emery was sprinting, his file safely in hand. We turned a corner and the sight of him cut out. I was about to roll off the bony, extremely uncomfortable shoulder of the swamp thing, when Emery came around after us.

"He and I leave together," I said, pounding a fist on the back of the monster. "Did you hear that? I don't leave this compound unless it is with him."

Miracle of miracles, the swamp thing listened, slowing as we ran up to the ward leading out of this hellhole. Emery caught up with us, his eyes anxious, glimmering in the moonlight. As a unit, we ran out together, our magical key from previously entering enough to get us back out again.

Thoughts dizzied after that. We ran up a small hillside and to a small road where a line of cars and trucks awaited us. The others.

"Dawn is fast approaching. Let's get to the safe house," Darius said, thrusting a finger in the air.

I ended up in an SUV on Emery's lap, my head still pounding and a huge lump on it to show why.

"Did you get it?" I asked.

"I think so. I need Darius or Clyde to read over a couple pages to be sure, but I really think so." His eyes held relief and sadness. "I never would've guessed. It wasn't the person I'd suspected. But one document in particular..." He shook his head and grazed my forehead with his lips. "It just goes to show how conniving that bunch really is. They're almost a match for the vampires."

"So you can get closure."

He gave me a squeeze. "After trading with the vampires for information, yes. Clyde has all the details I need to end it. Finally." He looked down on me, his eyes deep and soft. "I couldn't have done it without you. You have more courage than combat-trained men. You went in there knowing next to nothing, but you never once balked. I am in awe of you, Penny Bristol."

"It's easier to have courage when you don't know what's coming. You're the courageous one, not me."

His lips were firm and insistent on mine, fluttering my heart. "Thank you for helping me," he said. "I will never forget it."

His heavy tone sent a tendril of fear worming through my heart. "Is that an invitation to constantly remind you of my heroics?" I asked, keeping it light.

A flash of sadness and regret rolled across his expression, there one moment and gone the next, so fast I wondered if I'd imagined it. Before I could press the point, because if he thought he was walking away after all this, he was sorely mistaken, the procession of vehicles slowed.

"Wait...where are we?" I asked, straightening up and looking out the window. Lush greenery lined both sides of the narrow road. Ahead of us loomed a large house nestled into the trees, mostly obscured by the natural surroundings. "We got him what he wanted, so now the vampire is going to kill us, is that it?"

The light came on as we stopped beside the road. "Do not be absurd." The dark gaze of the driver flashed into the rearview mirror. "You are much too valuable to kill."

"Well there you go. See?" Emery opened the door. "And you were worried."

"Okay, but where are we?"

The driver was next to the door in a flash, his hand outstretched to help me. Judging by the grumpy expression on his face, this was the last thing in the world he wanted to be doing. "We are at a friend's estate. The guild does not know of it. You'll be safe here."

"Thank you, Mr. LaRay, I'll take it from here." The driver peeled away to reveal Darius, just as immaculate and freshly pressed as when he'd shown up earlier at the warehouse. How was beyond me. I was pretty sure I looked like a dead rat that had been dragged by the tail through the apocalypse.

Darius held out his hand, and I took it, because it seemed rude not to. The man had some serious manners.

"I didn't want this venture to be associated with Mr. Regent in any way," Darius said, steadying me until Emery had climbed from the car and slipped an arm around my shoulders.

"I'm good, you guys," I said. "Aside from the headache, I'm fine."

"We merely encountered a small, on-hand staff tonight," Darius continued as though not hearing me. Clearly he had his own ignore list.

He directed us up the driveway to the house and continued. "The Mages' Guild will be out for blood. I do not want them knowing who exactly the perpetrators were."

"But they had cameras." I watched the vampires zip by, carrying their boxes.

"Vampires don't show up in cameras or video equipment," Emery mumbled. "They'll only see you and me."

"Yes," Darius said. "They will know you were working with vampires, but they will not know which vampires. Mr. Regent has been with guests and in the public eye all night, along with his prized children—"

"Wait, vampires can have kids?" I asked.

"That's what they call the new vampires they make," Emery whispered.

"When they inevitably go looking for him," Darius continued, "he'll have an alibi. As for you two...well, you are already at the top of their list. Now they know to fear you."

Dread pounded in my middle. "People kill what they fear."

"Not in your case." Darius nodded to a woman holding the door open. Not a woman, judging by the predatory stare—another vampire. "They will see you—both of you—as the greatest prizes available to them. You blew through their facility as though peasants had created the spells guarding it. You are firmly at the top of the power pyramid."

"Being the top of the pyramid didn't help my brother," Emery said darkly.

Darius held out his hand at the bottom of a wide set of stairs, the house large, spacious, and fashionably rustic. It was gorgeous. "Please. I'll show you to your room. I'll have dinner and drinks brought up, if you're hungry?"

My stomach growled in answer.

"Yes, I thought so." He followed us up. "Your brother, Mr. Westbrook, was in an entirely different situation than are you. He thought he could change the guild from the inside. You, wisely, realize that to do any benefit, the guild must be torn down and rebuilt. Which you have the power to do. With my help."

"I'm not saying I don't agree, but it's going to take a lot more magical might than someone like me to change the guild." Emery stopped at the top of the long hall. Darius gestured us to the right. "Even with Penny, we can't do much more than make a dent. Not if they organize. Which, after tonight, you can bet they will. I'll never be able to set foot in this town again."

My heart squeezed and I grabbed hold of his shirt. Though what was I responding to? I wouldn't be able to stay in this town either. Not after tonight. My home wouldn't be my home anymore. I needed to come to grips with that.

"There are…others that can help in the struggle, I think," Darius said, his voice far away. He was strategizing, probably. "The guild won't be taken down immediately, but all good things come to those who wait."

We stopped at a closed door that looked the same as the closed doors to the right and left. Darius opened it and pushed it wide.

"I wasn't sure if you wanted two rooms or one. This—"

"One," Emery said. He squeezed me, and butterflies filled my stomach.

Darius offered a slight bow and stepped back. "I'll have clothes brought up to you. After you're rested, we'll create a plan for what is next."

"I need someone to look at a couple letters," Emery said.

"Of course. And you'll want to know what we dig up from the records we've collected, I trust?"

"I would, thanks." Without a goodbye, Emery walked us into the room and closed the door after us. He conjured up a spell and smeared it against the door. "It's unusual for a vampire to offer to share information." He unzipped his vest and shrugged out of it. His white shirt underneath was plastered to his body with sweat. "I'm not sure what that's about."

"Seems like he wants the guild brought to the ground for his own reasons, and realizes you have to help. You need to know your enemy."

Uneasiness wrestled with his expression, but he didn't comment. Instead, his gaze connected with mine, raw, deep, and bare. "How about that bath?"

CHAPTER 37

SOMETHING CLATTERED AGAINST the nightstand. Before I could open my eyes, it clattered again. And one more time. The accompanying buzzing finally registered.

My phone was ringing. Probably my mother. If she'd sent another text, she'd now be calling to chat about it.

I willed myself to roll away from Emery's heat and grab the phone, but I couldn't find the strength to peel my eyes open, let alone move my body. I hadn't stayed awake long enough for dinner the night before. I'd let Emery slowly strip me of my clothes, kissing every cut and scratch along the way, plus a little extra kissing on certain areas of my body that had made me curl my toes and arch in pleasure. We'd sunk into the hot waters of the bath, the tub large and easily able to accommodate us. But while my body was gloriously wound up, and my ache for him had only grown stronger, I'd fallen asleep nearly immediately. The next thing I'd known, he was carrying me to bed and settling in beside me, comfort, trust, and magic making the air buzz around us. I'd never felt so safe in all my life, and given the circumstances, that was saying something.

The clattering sounded again. I moaned and Emery stirred under my cheek. His arms, wrapped around me, squeezed before he tilted his head on the pillow and his breath, heavy and content, drifted over me.

Sure, I *felt* safe, but we were in a house with a bunch of night dwellers, and it was most certainly daytime. Anyone could crash through the place, and it would come down to Emery and I to fight them off. If my mother could help with that, it was worth it to roll out of Emery's arms and answer the phone.

Just barely.

I slapped my hand on the nightstand, capturing the jumping flip phone that had endured these last few days better than Emery's smart phone. Take that, modern technology!

I pulled it over and forced a groggy, puffy eye open. Two in the afternoon and fatigue still pulled on my every limb.

Was it too late for an office job?

Two missed calls from Veronica, which was strange, since my mother had called her and told her some of what was going on. She'd been told to wait for me to contact her—which I planned to do once this was all over. Then two calls from my mother, which were the last two, plus three texts. I was usually a light sleeper, but it looked like my body had pulled me way under.

I rubbed my eyes as I pulled up the texts. The first was from the early morning, probably when we were still in the thick of it. *Not all monsters are bad.*

Monsters. A vampire's other form, like when shifters changed into animals. That was what Marie had turned into last night in order to heal quicker. They were faster and stronger that way, but so, *so* much uglier.

"A little too late on that one, Mother," I muttered into the quiet room.

They won't go to you. You will go to them.

I nodded, because clearly she meant the Mages' Guild, and I had gone to them, all right. Right into the heart of their whole operation.

I frowned, because that text had been sent at nine in the morning. Until now, my mother's premonitions had always arrived before the event or, at the latest, during. It was strange this one would come so late.

In a moment, I saw why.

They've got Veronica. Call me ASAP.

I clicked into my voice messages. The first one was from Veronica. "Penny...I'm sorry. They—" A man's voice sounded in the background. Veronica sobbed into the phone. "I'm sorry, but they want you to come here. They say that they'll"—more sobbing—"k-kill me and my family if you don't."

My eyes snapped open fully. Adrenaline rushed in to replace the fatigue from a moment before. I hopped off the bed, seeing two trays of food waiting by the door and a couple of sets of clothes beside it. Emery must've lifted the spell he'd used to keep people out the night before, probably for just that reason. Pulling on the new leathers, I spared a hand to call my mother, then trapped the phone between my ear and my shoulder.

"It's about time you called," my mother said by way of answering the phone. "I was worried sick. What have you been doing?"

"I was storming the guild with a bunch of vampires last night." I couldn't help the sullen teenager approach, even now. Some things were hard-wired. "But I'm up. I'm getting ready."

"They are not to be trusted, Penny, no matter what pretty lies they might tell you."

"Yes, I've been told—"

"But they do have their uses. Where are you?"

"I'm at one of their houses. Have you talked to Veronica?"

"Yes. Briefly. She snuck a phone call to me when they weren't paying attention. They have her phone now, though. She's cut off."

"What is it?" Emery asked, sitting up with bleary eyes.

My mother's tone took on a hard edge. "Is that boy sleeping in the same room—Never mind. It doesn't matter right now. We can deal with that later." She took a deep breath, and I knew she was pinching the bridge of her nose like she did when she was trying not to get worked up about something. "From what I understand, there is a group of them working on our house, trying to get in, and another group guarding Veronica and her family. Since the houses are so close, they essentially have a large host waiting for us."

"Waiting for *us*, Mother? No. You don't know what they can do."

Emery swung his feet out of the sheets and dropped them to the floor. He stood stiffly, his body clearly as tired and sore as mine. "What's the matter?" he asked.

"You had better believe that I know *exactly* what that crooked institution is capable of," my mother said. "I will enjoy getting a little revenge. I'm sitting down the street right now, watching their movements. The arrogance is staggering. They puff out their chests like a bunch of turkeys when they walk down the street. And that's exactly what they are. Turkeys."

"It's Veronica," I said to Emery. "They have her." Worry choked me, threatening to derail the anger and determination. "They made her leave a message on my phone saying that if I don't come, they'll kill her. I haven't called her back yet."

Emery's movements sped up and he hurried for his leathers. "Has your mother foretold anything?"

I put the phone on speaker and repeated the question to my mother.

"I've got nothing," she said. "All is appearing blank. I have a feeling it's because of you. The images will come in a flurry once you choose a path. That's what's happened in the past, based on the things I was seeing."

Emery nodded, pulling on his pants. "Call them back. Let's see how long we have."

"Call me right after," my mother said. "Did you hear what I said? Right. After."

I hesitated. "Right now, they're on the defensive, trying to regain the upper hand." I thought it through. "They will know what we did to the guild, they'll know we're together, and they'll know we're working with vampires. They fear us, Darius said."

"Darius Durant? The elder vampire?" my mother said breathlessly. "He's extremely high up in their hierarchy, not to mention powerful. He's the one helping you?"

"Yes," I answered distractedly. "The people that have Veronica will know what to expect. They'll be able to prepare. If I call them, they'll demand that I come alone."

"What are you thinking?" Emery asked.

I met his steady gaze. He was game for anything. He

would put off his vengeance and help me save my friend without batting an eye.

"By now, they'll guess we have vampires working with us," I said slowly, thinking it out. "A large host means they're worried about a fight. They'll look for us as the sun sets."

"Yes," Emery said softly. "And by then, they'll be dead."

"Wait a minute," my mother said. "They have a lot of power waiting here. A Sheriff, some high-level mages—even with Emery, they'll easily out-power us."

"What about all those spells we made?" I asked Emery. "Is it too much to hope they're still in the warehouse?"

His eyes sparkled. "Darius and I didn't get a chance to barter about the price. Since money hasn't exchanged hands, those spells are still ours. They'll be in that warehouse, along with the ingredients. Maybe with the addition of a guard."

"A human guard." I nodded, hopeful. "That won't be a problem for you. What about the locked door?"

"That also won't be a problem for me." He smiled ruefully. "It seems a misspent couple of years will come in handy this once."

"It has come in handy repeatedly." I stepped forward and put my hand in his.

"Don't encourage him," my mother said.

She could sure spoil a moment.

"Mother, hang tight. We'll be there as soon as we can, and we'll have a world of firepower with us."

CHAPTER 38

W E GOT OUT of the black SUV at the end of the block, back far enough that we were hidden behind the corner of the last house. My utility belt was stuffed with herbs, power stones, and powerful spells contained in color-coded casings. Various spells rolled through my head, some that I'd learned the day before, and some my imagination was cooking up.

A cloud of evil intent thrummed, even from this distance, and I knew they were working up some nastiness, preparing for the battle they were sure was coming. I only hoped they expected it a bit later.

Emery looked at the darkening blue sky.

"What?" I asked, shaking out my hands. My body trembled with adrenaline, fear, and anxiety. I needed to get going, or I might not go at all.

"A nasty storm would be better so everyone would go inside. I don't like fighting where innocent people might get hit in the crossfire."

"Says the evilest man in the whole world." I sniffed at him. "See? I hadn't even thought of that. I was too busy wondering if I could do that vampire spell without the vampire. But don't worry. The neighbors across the street are the worst. That jerk Billy Timmons deserves whatever he gets. Although watch. He'll be the only one left unscathed."

Emery took my hand and started forward, the flaps up on his utility belt. We crossed the street like a couple walking to the store, strolling along casually. I glanced down the street, seeing someone on the sidewalk outside my house, looking the other way. A moment later, his gaze switched direction, and he took notice of us.

"Look away and keep walking forward," Emery murmured, and I recognized the spell he was using with his other hand—my concealment spell from the previous day.

"All those spells in your head, and you use the one I made up." I smiled to mask the tremor in my voice, but he looked at me, his eyes filled with regret.

"We'll make it out of this," he said, continuing down the street. "We can handle this."

My phone buzzed and I took it out. *I saw you cross at the other end of the street. You'll need a better disguise than hand holding.*

"What'd she say?" Emery asked.

I sighed and shook my head. "Nothing relevant." We hurried along the block and turned at the next corner. "Are we going to go in the back way?" I asked.

"Hopefully. Point out the house that is behind yours."

A couple of minutes later, after checking to make sure the coast was clear, we crossed to the side of the house behind mine and let ourselves through the gate of the fence. A small dog rushed forward, able to sense us even though we were covered by the invisibility spell. It stopped ten feet away, not at all pleased.

I draped a sound-deadening spell over it.

"All those spells in your head, and you use the one I stole from my brother." He clucked his tongue. "Shoddy."

The teasing lightened the heaviness on my limbs, but didn't relieve the shaking. I didn't know if I could duplicate everything I'd done last night. Half the things I did were spur of the moment. What if nothing came to me this time around? What if I let Emery down? Lives would be lost. The people I loved would be hurt.

"Easy does it, Turdswallop," Emery whispered as we slowed by the back fence on the other side of my yard. "This is the worst part. It's understandable that you're anxious."

I gulped and nodded as he stepped up onto the bottom board running parallel, clung to the top one, and slowly lifted his head over. He dropped back down quickly, before pushing back up a moment later. Then farther up still. The spell clearly worked, and also, there was someone in my backyard.

He lowered back down as I palmed my chest. This slow approach might kill me.

"Three of them in the backyard. They have a table of casings." His brow furrowed and he looked down. "I really wish I'd called in my favor for this instead of when I first got here."

"What?" I asked.

He shook his head and looked into the yard. "I can…" Streams of magic spewed from our belts, then all around us. "I can create a type of tornado. It'll be powerful. It should scatter their casings." He paused. "Hopefully."

"They can't see us." I hopped from one foot to the other. My breath came in pants. "Let's just sneak up, zap them, take their stuff, and bust into my house." I swatted my braid from over my shoulder. "Let's do it fast."

His spell ground to a halt and a smile graced his face. "Why didn't I think of that?"

"Because you are the world's worst planner, obviously. Come on."

His body shook with chuckles, and he bent with his fingers entwined and palms up, ready to give me a boost.

"I'm good," I said, gesturing to the fence beside me.

"You'll probably slip and scrape your face. Take a

hand." He shook his hands at me.

"You better not start on the overbearing train. I've got one mother. I don't need two."

Despite my talk, I took the boost, not wanting to admit he was probably right. It had happened a few times before.

I climbed up to the top and threw a leg over. When he was in the same position, I nodded and threw the other leg over after it. He dropped down right beside me.

A mage in a purple robe drew her penciled-on eyebrows together and looked right at me. Her gaze slid away and she eyed the top of the fence.

"It seems suspicious that she hasn't called," an orange-robed mage said from beside her. "She and that other natural are planning something, mark my words. And do you know which way they'll come through? The back."

The female mage shifted her weight and rolled the casings between her fingertips, one in each hand. "Which is why we're here. The Baron doesn't think they'll be here until dark. They hit the guild last night really late with a bunch of vampires. Seems likely the vampires helped them, at any rate. They think she'll do the same thing tonight. The Baron is bringing in more people."

"I heard the Chancellor's anxious to capture them.

He wants all that power at his disposal."

"It depends on how much the girl cares about her friend. She doesn't have a smart phone—"

My foot crunched in the grass. I froze. Streams of magic drew up from around us, and Emery's energy wobbled. He was planning something nasty.

"What?" the male mage said, bracing.

"Nothing. Thought I heard something." The woman scanned the backyard, not seeing us even though we were fifteen feet away. Thank God most mages couldn't see magic. "The Baron was going to cut off the friend's finger and send the video, but the girl has one of those old-school flip phones. She can't get video."

"Oh, so that's why they can't find her. She can't access Facebook or apps or anything."

"Yeah, she can't check in anywhere. They're still planning to do it when the reinforcements arrive. They'll just record the whole thing on her answering machine. Should be any time."

My fear for Veronica turned to rage. The energy brewing between Emery and I changed again, pulsing and swirling, ready for action.

Emery let loose his spell. I ran forward, my own spell surging up and out. Two blasts of magic hit the mages, our spells combining at the last moment and piercing their chests. I was grabbing bland beige casings off the table before their bodies hit the ground, stuffing the spells wherever they would fit.

Thank you, Darius, for insisting on the color coding.

Emery plucked at my sleeve, running for the back door of my house. I sprinted ahead and got there first, throwing my shoulder into it with everything I had. I smashed into the door...and bounced off. I staggered, and my butt hit the ground as Emery barreled into it next. Wood splintered and a crack resounded through the door. Emery crashed through.

"I need to start working out," I muttered, grabbing his proffered hand and following him inside. "We have to hurry. We can't let them cut off her finger." I sprinted to the front of the house as my phone buzzed.

Dread choked me as I dug it out, worried I was too late.

CHAPTER 39

A CALL FROM my mother.

I let out a shaky sigh as Emery looked out the front window and swore.

"Where are you?" my mother demanded as soon as I said hello.

"We're in the house. We just got in."

"Okay. Get ready. I'll meet you there."

"No. Wait! Mother—" But the line went dead.

"What?" Emery asked, stepping away from the window.

"She said she's going to meet us here."

Shouting filtered in from the way we'd come. The crash must've brought someone around. But it didn't matter. The ward didn't require a door. It would still protect the house and us inside of it.

"They've almost cracked the ward," Emery said. "I can see the exact place where they need to unravel it. As soon as they get out of their own way and discover it, we're wide open."

The sound of a car drew closer. Shouts erupted

from the front of the house this time. Emery got to the window first, swore again, and started back-pedaling.

"Your mother is nuts. Watch out!" He swung me up over his shoulder and ran as an earsplitting crash shook the house. The roof groaned and the walls trembled. Cracks ran down the cream-colored walls.

Emery stopped at the foot of the stairs, breathing hard.

"Barbra Streisand's hand-me-downs, what in the holy hanging dong was that?" I wiggled out of his grip as more shouting drifted into the house.

"Joe was right—we need to work on your swearing." Emery grabbed me with one hand, catching a handful of leather, and took out a casing with the other. "Your mother just rammed the house with her car."

A door banged somewhere. I stood paralyzed, trying to process the situation, when my mother came barreling in, her shotgun over her shoulder and a mad-dog look on her face.

"What are you standing around for?" she barked. "They're about to come in after me."

"How did you..." I followed behind her like a puppy dog. Emery did the same. Some things couldn't be helped when it came to my mother. "Did you ram the house with your car?"

"No. I rammed the house with *your* car. Well, actually, I just parked it in the garage. We'll need a new garage door. And a new ping-pong table. It didn't fare so well. But thank goodness for two-car garages, right? Now." She set the gun down and trudged into her office. In the corner, she moved the potted plant out of the way, bent down, and pulled up a doorstop that didn't have a door to stop. A click sounded behind me. I turned and my mouth fell open as my mother wrestled the desk out of the way, pushed aside the tapestry, and shoved a hidden door inward.

"Your father said I should let you in here when you were ready. I don't think you're ready, but we've run out of time." She stepped out of the way and held up her hand to stop me. "Not you. You won't know what you're looking at. Emery?" She jerked her thumb into the opening. "That is all Penny's, so if you steal anything, I'll hunt you down and cut off your arm. See if I'm joking."

"Yes, ma'am. I know you're not joking, ma'am." Emery gave me a hard look, clearly a little too worried about my mother's threat, before disappearing into the hole in the wall.

"Okay." My mother grabbed my shoulder and strong-armed me out of the room. "Unless they are the stupidest beings alive, which is not impossible, they know you're here. So we need to hurry. Soon they'll drag Veronica out and do a demonstration, demanding you trade yourself for her."

"They are going to cut off her finger."

"I wouldn't put it past them, the filthy vagrants. But now they'll do it on our lawn. So let's get cracking."

My mother grabbed her shotgun on her way past it and once again took up residence near the door. The shouting had died down, and I looked out the window. Two cars stopped in the middle of the street, and a full load of mages hopped out of each. Just beyond them, I saw Lewis at his window.

"Why doesn't Lewis call the police?" I asked.

"He probably has. But the guild has the Magical Law Enforcement office in this town in their pocket, so they can detour the human police. We aren't going to get any help. The guild owns this town."

"For now," I said, because this had gotten personal, and the guild would not retain its hold over Seattle forever. Not if I had anything to say about it.

The ward winked into view—one minute, a fascinating weave, and the next, invisible again. I told my mother what I had seen.

"They've taken down one of the roots," Emery said, strolling into the room with two books and a small sack. He put the sack on the ground. "I have no idea how old these spells are, but I wouldn't want to chance using them."

"Probably wise." My mother pointed at the books he still held. "I know you can use those. But I don't think Penny is ready."

Emery laughed in that humorless way of his. "Don't you?"

"Don't sass me, boy."

Emery's face straightened again. "Sorry, ma'am."

"I can read directions," I said, taking one of the books.

"Then you'll need a stand," my mother said. "Your father always used stands. Very practical, your father. It drove me batty." She stalked farther into the house.

"There isn't a lot that terrifies me, but that woman is certainly on the list," Emery mumbled, looking out the window. "We have ten minutes, tops. That ward is coming down."

"Here we go." My mother was back in a moment, setting up a handy little stand that held the book and even had a shelf for the necessary ingredients. "There is only one, though."

"Take it, Penny." Emery flipped through the pages of the one he held.

My phone vibrated and my heart crawled up into my throat. I took it out and opened it with a shaking hand. After pressing speaker, I answered. "Hello?"

"Penny Bristol, I presume?" The voice was dry and scratchy, as though its owner had sucked on the end of a great many cigarettes in his life.

"Yes. Who is speaking?"

"This is Baron Kempworth, and I am here to collect you."

"Over my dead body you'll be collecting her, you stupidly dressed piece of trash. Now come out and fight like a man." My mother grabbed the phone out of my hand, closed it, and threw it behind us. "Don't answer that anymore. You don't want to hear him give you an ultimatum. Come on. Time's up. It's time to save Veronica's family." She marched to the door, tore it open, cocked her gun, and aimed.

The blast made me jump.

"Got one," my mother yelled.

"High on the list," Emery muttered, a manic smile spreading across his face. "Come on, Penny. Let's get some space."

He ran me through the house and to the door leading to the garage. He slapped the button to open the left garage door, still intact, and it rattled upward. The door next to it was lying on the hood of my badly dented car.

Outside, in the driveway, sat my mom's car, unblemished. Behind it, spread across the lawn and into the street, many of them running for cover from my mother, lurked a dozen mages.

CHAPTER 40

"TURN IT INTO rage, Penny," Emery yelled as he stopped at the edge of the garage, still within the ward's protection. "Turn the pain into anger, and let it fly."

Loud crying preceded my first glimpse of Veronica. Her face bloody and one eye swollen, she was being dragged down the street by a man in a blood-red robe.

"Kempworth," Emery said with a release of breath.

I cracked a casing and threw. The spell burst out and sliced through the air, a magical machete. A slash of red appeared on the mage closest me, and then the two next to her suffered the same fate. They all looked down in surprise as their top halves slid off their bottom halves.

The mage in the blood-red robe stopped suddenly. He stepped behind Veronica and started to back-pedal, dragging her with him.

"Nope." I ran, no longer thinking logically. He had Veronica. He planned to hurt her. Emery called my name, and then he was beside me, leaving the safety of the ward and venturing into the fray.

A shotgun blast tore through the late afternoon. A man screamed and staggered, gingerly touching his bloody side. I cracked another casing, pushing the spell forward. Razor blades and acid rained down on the mages in front of me, ripping and burning and tearing. Darius had asked for some really foul spells.

Emery threw up a shield and captured a spell zipping at us. Then another. He broke them apart before releasing a spell of his own.

"I'm going for more firepower," my mother yelled.

I let the rage continue to course through me, but I let the pain from the knowledge that they were tormenting my friends come, too. I pulled on the energy and electricity and created my own spell, throwing it to the right. Immediately after, I grabbed two of the guild casings and threw them at the cluster of mages walking toward us, their mouths moving.

"I need to start thinking before I act," I said. "We shouldn't have left the ward."

"The best offense is unpredictability. You're doing great." Emery threw spells so fast that I was in awe. They flew out, one after the other, in a steady stream of color. He pulled magic from all around us, forming spells seemingly without thought. I tried to keep up but failed, filling in with casings.

Out of the corner of my eye, I saw cars slowly pull

up at the end of the street. My heart pounded. *So many.*

"This way," Emery said, pulling me toward Veronica's house. "You face front. I'll face the back."

Clouds drifted in from all sides above us, dark gray and forbidding. A spell flashed at me and I caught it with my white survival magic. I opened a casing from the guild and threw it in front of me. It skittered along the ground before wrapping itself around a green-robed mage running at us. The younger man screamed and writhed, sinking to the ground.

The guild had intended to play nasty too. At least we were all on the same page.

Emery bumped back into me. I turned around, seeing that he'd barely kept a spell from hitting him. "We need to speed this up and take cover, Turdswallop. I'm under heavy fire here."

Another shotgun blast.

"Let's go," I shouted over the noise as clouds blanketed the sky. Wind picked up, rushing through the street. Tree branches swung wildly.

We ran toward Veronica's house, where half a dozen mages stood out front next to a table stacked with casings. Emery expertly wove the various elements together and then set his tornado loose. It rose into the sky and churned the air. A spell zipped our way and I slashed it with my own spell, catching it midair and fizzling it out. Sirens sounded in the distance, this level

BREENE

of disturbance clearly too much for the guild to keep quiet.

Emery fired off more spells. I opened a guild casing, but nothing came out. With the clouds and waning light, my eyes started to play tricks on me, so it took me a moment to realize nothing had happened.

"Some you have to speak to life," Emery yelled over the noise. Men and women in robes ran at us, fleeing my mother. "Try another."

I cracked one of Darius's casings and sent the spell flying at the mages coming up behind us. A fog emerged and spread. It would peel people like potatoes. Really nasty stuff. This battle would give me nightmares.

I cracked another, this one a spell for magical laughing gas, as Emery threw more spells at the mages boiling from Veronica's house. The garage doors opened, and more poured out from there. Someone broke a window on the top floor and a surge of putrid evil came shooting toward us.

"Move!" I yelled, yanking Emery with me as I dove to the side.

He hit the ground and rolled, then jumped up like an action hero. I slid on my face and groaned before I climbed to my feet.

Mages surrounded us now, too many to fight. My mother couldn't help, not if she wanted to keep from shooting us.

"We have to make a run for it," I said, holding Emery's arm.

"No. If we don't stay here, you'll die. I can see when you're in danger, Penny." He held a ball of black survival magic cupped between his hands. "I saw it last night, too. That was why I told Marie to carry you off. If she didn't, you would've died. If we leave this circle, despite the horrible odds, you will die."

"What about you?"

"I would die right along with you, but not physically."

"That makes no sense."

"Please trust me. Stop your magic, and let them advance."

Shaking, desperate to make one last stand, I held it back. I held it all in. I took Emery's hand and stilled, my back pressed to his.

"There, now." The man in the blood-red robe stepped out, Veronica not with him this time. She must've been left behind in the house. A smile of triumph twisted his thin lips. "You see? Even naturals can be outdone. Emery, how nice to see you again. I heard you were back to get vengeance for your brother. Too bad you won't get to see that day."

"I will. Before I say goodbye to this world, I will see that day," Emery said through clenched teeth. The clouds rolled and boiled above us. A streak of lightning cut through the sky.

The man spread his arms. "I am right here. So close. But alas, you'll die just like your brother did."

"He was going to take your job," Emery said. "The Chancellor had all but signed the papers. I have copies to prove it."

I sucked in a breath. Emery clearly had found his proof.

"Yes. But then he went on that fateful trip into dangerous lands. So sad." The man, who could only be the Baron, put on a frowny face.

"You almost had me," Emery said, his hand holding mine shaking. "I thought it was Grimshaw. But no, it was you all along. Trying to use Happerhust's man. Trying to hide behind the other Barons."

"Trying?" The Baron laughed. "Succeeding, you mean. The old fools have no ambition. If it were up to them, the guild would languish. We'd be no better than a social club. It's *me* that has steered the ship. That has done away with all the bleeding-heart do-gooders and put this organization on the right track. Power, plenty, rewards—*I* have made all that possible."

"Through torture, murder, and corruption," Emery spat.

"You think power comes easy?" The Baron gave a rueful smile. "Such a dreamer, like your brother. Useless." His gaze traveled the circle surrounding us.

Another streak of lightning lit the quickly darkening sky, the day losing the battle to night unnaturally early. "But that's enough chatter. You are sentenced to death, Emery Westbrook, for taking a guild member's life. Several lives, actually."

Emery stilled and his gaze drifted. He was having a premonition. "Do not avenge me," he said to me in a deathly quiet tone. "Promise me."

"No sweat, because you're not going to die."

"Penny, please. You need to stay alive. You'll have a wonderful future. Live it. Find someone worthy of you."

"I did. I found you. I will not let him kill you."

Emery spun and grabbed my face in his hands. He crushed his lips to mine.

He was going to do something crazy.

But that was my role.

I pushed him back, dug into my belt, and grabbed a casing I'd prepared yesterday. His eyes widened and he grabbed my hand, stopping me from cracking it. "Not yet."

"Ah look, so sweet," the Baron said. "And if I could control you, Emery, I'd let you keep her in the hopes you'd become a dual-mage pair. But sadly, you're as headstrong as your brother. Rest assured, though, I have high hopes for her. She'll do just fine. Maybe I'll even keep her for my own."

Emery's jaw clenched and his eyes lit on fire, but he

didn't turn away from me. He stared down into my eyes, like he was saying goodbye. Like the fool thought I would let that happen.

"Kill him and capture the girl," the Baron ordered.

I ripped my hand out of Emery's grasp and applied pressure to crack the casing.

"No—"

A bolt of lightning stabbed down from the nearly black sky. It hit the corner of the property, blasting us all with an electric shock wave. I felt my eyes widen as the natural urge to flee took hold of me.

Another cracked down, closer this time, right next to the porch on which the Baron stood. The circle of mages around us shifted and danced, looking at the sky with pale faces and eyes probably as wide as mine.

"How did—" Emery cut off. His eyes weren't heavenward like everyone else's—they were roaming the road.

A small tornado spun down the street, traveling a seemingly controlled path. It dipped in as it neared the front of the house, tearing up the grass and heading our way.

"What…is…happening?" I said in a series of terrified bleats, backing away with everyone else.

The circle of mages turned into an egg and then a haphazard cluster. The Baron yelled for them to follow his orders, but the wind ripped his words away, then shoved at us and pushed us toward the property line.

Another crack of lightning smacked down to my right, fifteen feet away. It fried the man standing there and blasted Emery and me into jogging away.

Panic choked me. Man-made horrors I could handle, but something about natural disasters of any kind had me ready to retreat like my butt was on fire. "We have to get to cover—"

Grisly shapes sped toward us, startling me into a frozen stupor for a moment. The monsters resembled Marie's shifted form from last night, their swampy skin rendered even more frightful by the light burns marring it. They rushed forward in the near-darkness, wicked claws flashing through the air, cutting through mages. One picked a mage up, lifted him into the air, and then cracked him over a knee.

"Now you can fight," Emery yelled over the din, launching forward toward the Baron. "Don't worry about the weather. She has excellent control."

A shock of evil stilled my heart, erasing my supreme confusion and terror. The Baron had a spell ready, and it was aimed for Emery.

"Watch out!" A jet of white burst from me as a stream of black tore from his fingers. Our magic slid against each other and twirled in the air, keeping its perfect colors, before merging into a plate in front of Emery. Unlike with other magic, my survival magic didn't retaliate with Emery's. It formed this perfect picture. The sizzle of the Baron's aggressive magic drowned out the screams of the mages under attack by the vampires.

Emery dodged the warring spells, punched a mage, and raced to the porch of Veronica's house. Another bolt of lightning cracked down, perfectly illuminating the fear crossing the Baron's face. Emery reached him a moment later, smashing a fist into his face. The Baron was flung backward before being caught by Emery again. This time, Emery's hands went to the Baron's head. He twisted.

I grimaced and looked away as the Baron's lifeless body slid to the ground.

The small twister picked up two mages and flung them before angling back, clearing the way for the vampires, who continued to crowd into the yard, fangs and claws working. The twister dissipated as it left the front yard.

"Is it magic—" More lightning, two bolts at the same time, hit behind the house. Then four more. A woman walked down the middle of the street, her arms raised and fire-red hair whipping around her. A mage, previously running in her direction, away from the vampire-created carnage, came to a sudden stop and held out a casing.

The woman's hands barely moved, her fingers flicking. Lightning shot down in front of her, piercing the top of the mage's head. His casing fell safely to the ground.

"What the—"

The scene slowed around us. Monsters stilled. Bodies lay strewn across the carefully manicured lawn.

Emery heaved, staring down at the Baron. A tear leaked out of his eye, and he wiped it away. "That was for Conrad," he said in a hoarse voice.

I ran to him, not knowing what the heck was going on with the red-haired woman, but thankful to her, since she seemed to be on our side, and thankful to the vampires.

I slid my hand down his arm and fit my palm into his. He took his hand back before pulling me into his body.

"I knew the pain wouldn't go away," he said, resting his cheek on my head. "But I didn't expect it to get worse." He crushed me to his chest.

"You've reopened the wound," came Darius's eloquent voice. He moved up beside me in human form, and I got an eyeful. He hadn't a stitch of clothing on him. "And you can finally let it heal. Now, why don't you introduce me to your Elemental friend." It was worded like a question but not stated as one.

"Elemental?" I said softly, trying to remember if I'd ever heard of that. It sounded vaguely familiar.

"They control the elements," Darius said, walking beside us. "They range in power, like mages, and usually specialize in one main element, and possibly a few sub-elements. They can be quite useful, as we've seen."

The woman shifted and stuck out her hip when we neared, a hard gaze directed at Darius.

"Since when are you in league with vampires?" she said with heat to her voice.

"That's the way it had to go." Emery stopped in front of her. "Solas, this is Darius. He's helped us survive the last couple of nights. Darius, Solas is an acolyte. She hopes to rank in the next Placement Games."

"Is that right?" Darius studied her face. "I am heavily active in the sponsorship of those games. I thought I knew all the big players."

Solas lifted her chin and a fierce expression crossed her face. "Outside *gamblers*"—she spat the word—"know only what they are told. It has no bearing on actual talent."

I grinned despite my fatigue. I liked her fire.

"Clearly." Darius glanced around the yard, his gaze flicking to the blackened spots and the uprooted areas. "Well, Solas." He offered her a bow. "It was a pleasure." He turned to Emery and me. "I will let you chat for a moment, but as the human police will soon arrive, we don't have much time. I'll see to Penny's mother."

And with that, he was gone, striding away.

"You're going to have a vampire meddling in your affairs," Emery told Solas, and from the ease with which he spoke to her, I could tell they knew each other well.

She shrugged. "If he wants to sponsor me, he can be my guest. There is paperwork for a reason. He won't own me."

"Keep your wits." Emery grinned, but the sentiment didn't reach his eyes.

Solas's eyes widened. "What's this? A smile?" She turned her crystal-clear green eyes on me, and I got the feeling I was being measured somehow.

"How did you know to come?" Emery asked, glancing behind him at the others preparing to leave. The sirens blared in the distance.

"You move through the world like a minotaur through a crowd of fairies," Solas said. "I stayed in the area and listened. Traveling into the guild compound was too dangerous, but a sleepy neighborhood in this rainy town? Perfect."

"But why? We were even."

She shook her head and took a step back. "We weren't even. You were trying to brush me off, and I had too much honor to let you. *Now* we are even." Her eyes flicked to me again. "Aren't you going to introduce me to the one who has cleared away the clouds of your disposition?"

Emery squeezed me again. "This is Penelope Bristol. She has recently learned she's a natural."

Solas turned to me and offered a deep bow. "A pleasure. You are a lucky woman, Penelope Bristol. Because now you know me." Her smile made her eyes sparkle. She turned to Emery. "What? Did you think I meant that she was lucky for landing you?" She laughed and playfully pushed him. "My, no. You are the lucky one, clearly." Solas smiled at me again and stepped back. "If either of you want to swap favors, please remember me. I'd love to have a natural in my pocket."

"I am aware," Emery muttered.

"There it is." She pointed at his surly expression. "There's the frown I remember. Now *that* is the Emery I know." Her laughter followed her down the street.

"She's lovely…while also being nuts," I said, letting Emery turn us in the opposite direction.

"Yeah. It's what will make her sensational in the Placement Games. She'll charm the crowd and then destroy her opponents. She just needs to get there. Hopefully Darius will take an interest and make it happen."

"Huh." I was too tired to ask more about it.

Up ahead I saw Veronica huddled, wrapped in a blanket. I was running before I knew it, pushing through vampires trying to make her comfortable and wrapping my arms around her.

"Are you okay, are you hurt?" I asked, rifling through her blanket to get at her fingers. Eight, with two thumbs. "Oh good, they didn't chop anything off."

"I'm okay. I'm fine. My family is really shaken up, but we're okay."

I hugged her again before I heard the wail of the sirens getting louder. It was almost time to leave.

CHAPTER 41

I HAD TO release my death grip on Veronica so they could hasten her toward her family, who were being hastened away by the vampires. Her mother needed her more than I did, and since I was responsible for all this, I wasn't welcome at the moment.

"How did Darius find us?" I asked as we made our way toward my house. "I mean, remind me to thank him for saving the day and everything, but we snuck out the window in that house for a reason."

"I left a note. I knew he'd want to protect his interests." Emery started to jog, my hand clasped in his. My mother was on her lawn, gun in hand, more bodies on the grass. Beautiful naked people lingered in the street, waiting for Darius. The wail of the sirens rode the breeze.

"You see? I knew you were crazy. Well, you've gone too far this time," Lewis shouted across the street. "I've called the cops. And tell your naked friends to put some clothes on, for God's sake."

"Do not take the Lord's name in vain, Lewis," my

mother shouted back.

"Mother, come on, we have to go!" I patted her arm as I passed her before running inside and grabbing her car keys. "The cops are coming."

"I did not want that old goat to get the last word, that's all." My mother gave Lewis a hard stare.

"What sort of person yells at their neighbors about naked people when there was a magic fight outside of his house half an hour before?" Emery asked, staring in that direction.

"Don't try to wrap your head around it," I said. "He and my mother make no sense."

After I hugged Veronica within an inch of her life, then pushed her and her family toward their vampire handlers, who would take them to safety, we loaded into the car. Darius and the rest of the vampires were running toward their hearses at the end of the street. I'd thought those vehicles were full of mages when they'd pulled up, but it had been the vampires the whole time, waiting for enough darkness to go outside. Clearly he had human workers to help him. Darius had certainly wanted to protect his interests, and while I was pretty sure that would be a very bad thing down the road, it was totally welcome in the moment. If it hadn't been for him and Solas, Emery and I would probably be dead. There had been too many mages, and my hail Mary spell at the end wouldn't have saved the day. I owed

Darius one, and he surely knew it.

Back at the house we'd slept in the night before, I sagged in weariness. We drifted into the living room and fell onto the couches. Veronica and her family had been relocated somewhere else, safely behind a wall of fangs.

"Well that was some adventure, right there," my mother said, way more upbeat than she should've been, considering the nearly fatal battle we'd just endured. "All the training I've done has finally paid off. At the shooting range, the younger guys always snicker at the older woman shooting the heavy artillery, but today I would've wiped the smiles off their faces. If only I could have used the semiautomatic. I didn't, of course, because stray bullets would've gunned down the neighbors, but I could've..." She sighed. "Next time."

"We were lucky to have you, Ms. Bristol," Emery said, sitting a little too straight.

"I hate to say it, but we were lucky to have those vampires." My mother stretched and kneaded her shoulders. "I wasn't sure how I was going to help. I couldn't very well shoot in your direction. My next option was to run a car through them and hope you guys jumped out of the way."

Emery looked at me, a sparkle of humor in his eyes. "Now I see where you get it."

I frowned, because so did I.

"But you best be careful where those vampires are concerned, young lady." My mother lifted her eyebrows at me. "They are not the sort you want to get mixed up with. One second, you think you're ahead. The next second, they own you. Best to steer clear if you can."

"That might be a little harder after today," I murmured, leaning against Emery. He didn't lift his arm to invite me to lean against his chest. I had the feeling it was because of my mother. "So you knew it was Kempworth going in?" I asked him.

Sadness dragged on his features and he leaned harder into the couch, a little at an angle, subtly inviting me to keep leaning against him. "I was almost positive. I just needed Clyde or Darius to read a couple of letters to verify."

"And it wasn't who you thought?"

"Not at first, no, but I suspected something was amiss. What Clyde told me about the letter I brought him made sense, but the people in question didn't. The two Barons he implicated used to agree on most things. I didn't think they'd stab each other in the back. Since Kempworth was always at odds with them back in the day, I figured it was still the case.

"On a hunch, I riffled through his file first. It was ballsy, given the time constraints, but I figured something would jump out at me. And it did. There was a magically sealed box in the file. I broke in easily, and in it, I found Italian letters like the one I found in Nicholas's office. Same style, not signed, everything. One was dated two weeks before my brother was scheduled to leave on his trip. I checked the other barons' files, and while they also had secret letters in their possession, they didn't have the same style. Not quite."

"But why didn't Nicholas—the guy who actually carried out the orders—notice the style was different?" I asked.

"I'm not a genius, but I do have some intelligence. Nicholas does not. He's a hired gun, nothing more. He does what he's told, completely controlled, and they love him for it. There are a couple like him. Still, I wasn't positive. The letters are in Italian, after all. Then I found a correspondence between the two other barons about the possibility of Conrad replacing Kempworth. Another nail in the coffin. And now there's a hole in their organization."

"Now there are a *lot* of holes," my mother said. "It'll take them a while to recoup. It gives us some time."

"But not much—"

"Ah!" I jumped and moved to fling out my hands, but Emery caught them, keeping the spell contained.

Darius stood in the archway to the living room, wearing slacks and a pressed shirt, his hair perfectly in place. He looked like he'd just walked off a runway. How did the guy do it? Also, why hadn't he learned to make more noise when creeping into a room with me in it?

He sauntered in, all confidence, with a manila envelope. "You don't have much time. A couple of months for them to regroup, but they'll be back. We'll need to think about changing locations."

"*We*"—my mother gestured between the two of us—"will need to think about changing locations. *You*"—she jabbed a finger at Darius—"will get some spells and a thank you and asked to be on your merry way."

"Mother," I said, trying to shush her.

"Don't worry, Miss Bristol," Darius said, handing the envelope to my mother. "Lately, I've grown used to that kind of talk from the magically inclined." Darius turned to me as my mother gingerly opened the envelope, her eyes narrowing. It looked like she expected a snake to jump out. "You know, of course, that you have a standing invitation for training from the dual-mages in New Orleans. As I've mentioned, I know them personally, buy spells from them consistently, and can attest to their excellent standing and knowledge within the magical community. You couldn't ask for better training, or pushier people."

"I'm liking the sound of these people already," my mother mumbled, pulling out a few sheets of paper.

"Yes. Given your excitement level when heavily

armed, I'd say you'd get along with them just fine," Darius said dryly. His gaze flicked to Emery. "If you can't get training elsewhere, then they are always an option."

Emery stiffened, and pain I didn't want to acknowledge squeezed my heart.

"Thank you," I said to Darius, hooking a hand around Emery's forearm. "You saved the day. And it looked like you got a little burned doing it."

"Some of the younger vampires, yes. It couldn't be helped. I'm sure you likely know I wasn't solely concerned with your interests."

"Wow. That's not something I thought you would admit," I murmured. Emery chuckled.

Darius didn't seem to hear me, which was impossible, given his preternatural hearing ability. "Naturals are so very rare, and a pair with gifts such as yours is rarer still. The magical community would be loath to lose you, not to mention there was a debt that my child needed to settle. I didn't wish to lose either of you."

"What now?" my mother asked, lowering the papers so she could look over them.

As if on cue, Marie sauntered into the room, all hips and breasts and super-fancy clothes. Just like Darius, she looked like a million dollars, freshly minted.

Her smoky gaze hit me. "You saved me from eternal death within the guild compound. I had not expected that from a pixie-like creature such as yourself. You intrigue me, Penelope." Lust sparked in her eyes. Her gaze flicked to Emery, like Darius's had earlier. "I would not keep you all to myself, Penelope. I am willing to share."

"What the... That was *not* where I thought this was going." I grabbed Emery's arm with my other hand.

"This just got weird," my mother said, shaking her head as she bent over the papers. Emery was shaking with chuckles now. I had no idea what he thought was so funny.

"That'll be all, Miss Beauchene," Darius said, his eyes now on Emery. Marie made a soft sound, almost like a purr, before turning with so much hip she looked double-jointed and stalking out. "Mr. Westbrook, we need to discuss finances."

Emery sobered. "We do. The inventory is significantly decreased. We had to use some of the spells."

"That is no harm. They can be redone."

Emery's jaw tightened, but he nodded.

"Well, then." Darius looked us over before glancing at my mother and turning. "I have business to attend to. Rooms have been made up for all of you. My assistant, Mr. LaRay, will make sure you're comfortable. Please feel free to stay as long as you would like. Should you be willing to allow me to assist you in a future move, I hope you'll let me know."

"We'll manage," my mother said.

"Mother!" I said through my teeth. I'd never heard her be so rude to a host. It was embarrassing.

With a nod, he strode away, leaving us to ourselves.

My mother shook the pages she'd been reading, and I realized her eyes were glistening. "He was shot in the back by another Sheriff," she said in a rough voice. "The other Sheriff tried to make it look like an accident. I remember him. Meuler. Your dad and Meuler hated each other. They were always at odds." She shook her head, looking at the pages again. "I'd thought it was a larger conspiracy, like with Emery's brother, but no, it was blind hatred. Meuler probably thought he could get away with it, so he went for it."

"So they did investigate," Emery said.

"Yes." She shook the pages again, indicating that she was reading the file itself. "And they executed Meuler. Why didn't they tell me?"

"The guild would keep something like that under wraps. They wouldn't want it to give them a bad name." Emery sighed. "It's terrible, what happened."

My mother nodded, flipping to the last page. "If I had known...I'm not sure I would've kept my daughter under lock and key. The guild did the right thing, in the end."

"Then it's a good thing you never found out," Emery said.

My mother looked at him for a moment before nodding. "Yes. It certainly seems so. The guild was going in the same direction then as it is now. My husband saw it, even if his death didn't prove it."

"It did prove it, in a subtler way. There's plenty of poison in the guild. Has been for a while."

She took a big, shuddering breath. "I suppose you're right." She lowered the pages to her lap, looking at nothing for a second. "It feels good to know."

"Closure," Emery said. "I have yet to completely get mine."

"Will you go after Nicholas now?" I asked quietly, my heart aching for my father. It didn't feel like closure to me. The loss still felt raw, like a hole in my life, and knowing more about his death didn't change that.

"No," Emery said. "I want him to live for a while longer, knowing I'll come for him eventually. I want him jumping at shadows. Seeing my face in passing strangers. Haunting his dreams. He deserves that, after all the people he's hunted down in cold blood."

I turned my lips downward, because that was intense, and let it go. Nicholas probably did deserve such a fate...and Emery probably wanted a break, knowing he'd finally gotten to the root of the problem.

"I need a bath, then sleep," I said, struggling to get up. Emery stood quickly and helped me.

"Do not think, for one second, you will be sleeping

in the same room, young lady. Not under my borrowed roof." There were tears in her eyes from reading about my father, and still my mother was a ball buster.

I rolled my eyes and pulled Emery with me. I wasn't too old to sneak around like a coward, and neither was Emery. Not when it concerned a woman who happily fired rounds into a group of evil mages.

"My life has taken a very strange turn," I said as we walked down the hall.

He slipped his arm around my waist. "Can I speak to you for a second, Penny?"

Shivers washed over me. His tone was regretful and contained not one ounce of teasing.

"What's up?" I asked, sitting on the bed.

He sat down next to me. "I was stalling earlier, when I asked you to stay alive. To not avenge my death. If we'd acted, either one of us, one or both of us would've died. I needed to give the vampires a chance to get in position. But your answer..." His thumb moved along the line of my lips, slowly back and forth. Pain blossomed in his eyes. "I just... You shouldn't—" Frustration warred with sorrow in his expression. "I'm sorry. But I'm not the man for you. Not for you. You need someone with the world at his fingertips. Someone who's not broken."

"Emery, you don't get to tell me what I need. I have my mother for that." I smiled, reaching out to rest my palm on his chest. "I know that you are hurting, and you need to punish yourself for your brother a little more. So that's fine. Do what you need to do. Then come back."

The pain in his eyes increased. They dripped with it. That and regret. He shook his head slowly. "I have to leave. I don't know if I'll ever be back. Find someone else. Please."

Tears welled up in my eyes, and I nodded for his benefit.

He kissed me, hard at first, his lips smashed into mine, but then pulling away slightly until the contact was soft and lingering. My heart ached. I knew he was saying goodbye. Knew that I had to let him. He was a man of the wind. A gypsy. I couldn't make him stay if he didn't want to. I just had to hope what I knew he felt in his heart ate away at him until he decided to end his suffering.

"Will you lie down with me until I fall asleep?" I asked.

"I am so glad I can see when death is coming," he murmured, glancing at the closed door.

CHAPTER 42

WHEN HER BREATHING slowed to deep and even, Emery slid out from under her and cocooned her body in the covers the way she liked. He stared down at her for a long while, memorizing her beautiful face, playing through all her hilarious anecdotes and funny musings. Remembering the way she'd looked at him as she stood within that press of enemies and vowed not to let him die.

She was so much woman. Brave, strong, yet sweet. A breath of life. The very essence of nature.

He blew out a breath and turned, but it was impossible to walk away like this. He couldn't do that to her.

Faltering, he found a piece of paper and scratched out a quick goodbye note. He wished he could do more.

He closed the door softly and turned, hiding his surprise when he saw Darius waiting down the hall. The vampire's face was impassive, but his eyes were knowing.

"The most powerful of the spells that Penny and I did are still in our utility belts. They didn't fit the situation."

"Lucky for me." Darius walked closer. "I assume you are headed out."

"Yes. We'll have to settle up for what we have. Or what I have. I'm not sure what she wants to do with hers."

"She'll give them to me and insist you get paid for it. Her mother will agree, because she doesn't trust my kind. Would you like to go through the spells now, or…"

"No." Emery looked in the direction of the door. "It's best that I leave now."

"You don't have to. I can easily hide you, if that is your fear. You can help with Penny's training, if you want. The dual-mages would take you in, or you could stay at any number of my properties. Your life a month ago doesn't have to be your life tomorrow."

Emery shook his head, the desire to give in and stay almost buckling him. But he had an obligation to his brother to fulfill, and he meant what he'd said to Penny. She was an angel. She deserved the absolute best, and in his absence, hopefully she'd find it.

The memory of her body pressed against his as she asked him to be her first burned through his brain. He bowed with regret, stabilizing himself with a hand on the wall. Refusing her had taken more strength than he'd known he possessed.

"I have the location of my brother's death," Emery said. "I need to visit the site and say goodbye properly. I need to apologize in person. Then I need to disappear."

"Well." Darius walked Emery toward the door. "Whenever you need money, you know where to come. I am most often in New Orleans of late. I have an interest there. Should you want to speak with me directly, that is the best place to find me. That is, of course, assuming you lose your phone."

Not this time. Emery wouldn't be losing this phone like he had lost all the others. He had Penny's number stored in it. One day, if he could ever figure out how to change his stars, he'd contact her again. Just to see how her life was turning out. Just to hear her voice.

"Do me a favor," Emery said, knowing he was putting himself at the debt of a vampire, a very bad place to be. For her, though, it was worth it. "Watch out for Penny. Keep an eye on her. Make sure she stays safe. I will exclusively sell magic to you if you agree."

Darius nodded. "Done. As I said, my interest in her has many facets. As does my interest in you."

"I know. But you'd be surprised at how much harder she's going to be to manage."

"Oh, I doubt it. Not compared to..." He paused, and his face softened before a confused scowl crossed his visage.

Emery didn't want to know. Whatever gave a vampire pause was not something he wanted any part of.

"Anyway." Emery stepped away. "I'll be off. I'll stay with a friend tonight and meet you tomorrow night for the handoff. You have my number?"

"I do." Darius looked at him for a long moment before shifting. "Keep your head down."

"Don't I always?" Emery smirked and turned, then strode for the door.

He didn't get very far when someone much scarier than a vampire could ever be stepped into his path.

He threw up his hands. "I'm leaving. I told her goodbye. I told you I'd leave, and I am. Penny is safe from me. She's free to find someone with some worth, like you said."

Penny's mom, whose first name she still hadn't divulged, stared him down with all the fire he occasionally saw spark in Penny's eyes right before she did something crazy. "She found someone with worth. She just needs that someone to express it."

Emery stared at her stupidly, gobsmacked. That had not been what he'd expected.

"Listen." Ms. Bristol shifted and gingerly switched the hand still holding the envelope from earlier. "My daughter is a lot like her father was. She always sees the best in people. She can be timid, and she can wreak havoc, but she is true to herself. When it comes to her principles, or matters of the heart, she is immovable.

Stubborn as all get out. She believes in you. She trusts you. And I would have to agree with her sentiments. Now it's just *you* who has to believe in yourself. *You* who has to trust yourself. If you could do that, then you would be deserving of her, and her of you. It all comes down to you."

All he could do was stare and blink. Of all the unexpected things these last few days, this was probably the most surreal.

"Now that that's out of the way." She glanced around him and lowered her voice. "Where did the vampire get this?" She indicated the envelope.

"Stole it, and a lot of other records, out of the guild's records room. They are surely sorting through everything and scanning like mad."

Her eyes narrowed. "Can't be a coincidence that they picked out a random Sheriff's file."

"I suspect not. He wants to know more about Penny."

Her lips tightened. "Well, if he thinks getting one over on her is going to be easy, he doesn't know very much about me."

He couldn't help a wry grin. "I suspect not."

She *harrumphed*. "Well, then." She patted his shoulder. "Take care, Emery. Don't forget about us."

"Yes, ma'am."

He waited for her to disappear into the hallway before he headed for the door.

CHAPTER 43

"READY TO POLICE the neighborhood?" Veronica asked, standing on my porch with a red pen in hand.

"Go get 'em all, ladies." My mother handed me a black pen and nodded seriously. "There's a lot of work to be done." Her pat was more like a shove.

With an annoyed scowl, since my mother was still very much herself, I followed Veronica down the walk of my new neighborhood. Two weeks after the magical battle involving guns, hostages, colorful robes, and naked people (which somehow didn't appear in any newspapers or result in an extended police investigation), we were squared away in a temporary home near Duval. It was a pretty small rental, but thanks to the new identities that Darius had arranged for us, no one knew who we were. The guild wasn't actively looking for me yet (more like licking their wounds and rebuilding their compound), so for the moment, we could just breathe.

The lull also gave me time to work up the courage to

tell my mother I'd be leaving for New Orleans as soon as she was safely settled somewhere.

"Here's one already!" Veronica jogged toward a missing cat sign featuring a shocking lack of commas. "Oh, I keep forgetting to tell you. My dad says you're banned from our new home."

Veronica's family had also needed to move. They were in the witness protection program, vampire-style. Which meant they thought they were dealing with the cops, but were actually dealing with walking corpses.

"I can't really blame the guy. You and your parents went through hell on my behalf." I walked beside her as we moved on.

She shrugged. "Yeah, I guess. That didn't stop me from telling him I was moving out soon, though."

"Oh? Where are you going?"

She gave me a funny look. "With you, dummy. To New Orleans when you finally get up the courage to tell your mom. I told you. I can edit anywhere."

"Oh." I frowned at her. "I might be staying with someone, though. I'm going to learn…how to better…tell fortunes."

"To do magic. Don't act like I didn't see you doing magic, Penelope Bristol. I saw freaking monsters running around! I told you, I was just inside the doorway. My hands were tied, but I could see everything."

"Oh. Right."

"Stop saying 'oh.' I'm coming. Face it."

"Oh…kay."

She nudged me, laughing. "Anyway, has Emery contacted you?"

I'd told her all about the sexy, handsome, supremely hot-bodied man who'd fought by my side—her words. She'd become fascinated by him and his quest for vengeance (though, thankfully, she contained her swoon out of respect for me).

My hand drifted to my jeans pocket. The letter I'd found on my nightstand crinkled as my fingers pressed against it. I carried it everywhere.

I'll think of you always.—Emery

My heart swelled. Then I thought about what my mother had said the next morning. "If you love him, set him free. If his heart is truly yours, it won't stay gone for too long before it finds its way back to you." She'd paused, letting that sink in, before ruining the moment. "Just don't wait too long. You're not getting any young-er."

Heat prickled my eyes and I shrugged with one shoulder. "No. I don't expect him to. He's fighting some demons right now. He needs to sort himself out."

"A troubled hero. God, that's hot." She threw a finger up at me. "Do not tell me not to—"

"Don't say the Lord's name in vain."

"Gah!" Veronica put her hands up into claws. "You

hate being like your mother. Why do you say it?"

I laughed, but my laughter was cut short by the sight of someone skateboarding down the center of the sidewalk, right for us. "I can't help it. Oh my gosh, it can't be... It *can't* be, can it?"

"I do not believe it. That is Billy freaking Timmons! What the heck is he doing *here*?"

"I thought my dad said you moved to these parts," he said when he got closer. His stupid face wore a big sneer. "You should be in jail, whack job."

"Why are you here?" Veronica demanded.

"I work downtown. I figured you'd keep up with your nerd-fest. Look at you. You're such losers."

Veronica pointed at his skateboard. "You took the bus in order to stalk us and call us losers *on a skateboard*? How can you possibly have all this confidence?"

"Whatever, jailbirds." He flipped us off and pushed off on his skateboard.

"That is such bull." I stared after him, in complete disbelief. Magic tingled my fingers, begging for release. No one was around.

In a blast of frustration, I sent a magical lasso—one of my own creations—after him, catching his legs and yanking. His legs flew out from under him and he fell forward, hitting the ground face-first and skidding.

"Oh sh—" Veronica covered her smile with her hand, her eyes wide.

I looked around worriedly, not able to help laughing. "Hurry, let's get out of here. I don't want to get in trouble."

"Serves you right, you turd," Veronica yelled at him. We turned and ran, his yelling about witches and cops following us up the street.

"Magic has its uses," Veronica said.

I had to agree. It was a crazy new life in which I'd found myself, but I already loved it. And soon, I'd really learn what I could do when I tried to control it. My time of hiding in closets was finished.

Made in the USA
Coppell, TX
26 February 2024